for Love and Ransom

D. A. Walters

for Love and Ransom is a work of fiction. Names, characters, and incidents are the products of the authors' imaginations, or are used fictitiously. Any resemblance to actual events, locales, or persons, living or dead, is entirely coincidental.

Copyright©2010 by Deborah Walters
Library of Congress Control Number TX0007484469
All rights reserved.

Without limiting the rights under copyright reserved above, no part of this publication may be reproduced, stored in, or introduced into a retrieval system, or transmitted, in any form or by any means (electronic, mechanical, photocopy, recording, or otherwise) without the prior written permission of the copyright owner and publisher of this book.

Book Design by Alex Riley

For my children
Brian, James, Jeffrey, Lindsay, and Auriel

for Love and Ransom

Prologue

The door to the room creaked as it opened and seven men in long black robes and black hoods covering their faces walked in. Matthew Corban looked up. His hair was long and disheveled and his once clean shaven face covered. He doubted anyone he knew would recognize the thin gaunt man with dark sunken eyes that sat on the dirt floor.

The leader gestured and two men walked over to Matthew, grabbed him by the arms, and dragged him to his feet.

"Kneel," commanded the leader.

The guard brought the gun butt down on Matthew's shoulder and he fell to the floor. He gasped. The guard grabbed him by the hair and pulled him up on his knees. He stuck his knee in Matthew's back so he'd kneel up straight.

"Mr. Corban, do you know what day it is?" asked the leader.

Matthew remained silent.

"It's judgment day, Mr. Corban. Today, we send you to your maker."

The leader stood towering over Matthew.

"Mr. Corban, it seems no one really even cares about you. Your country has said repeatedly that they won't deal with us. Pity," said the leader shaking his head. "Time and again we've shown them exactly what we'll do. We've given them time. Their refusal to deal with us is unacceptable. It is an insult!" he said outraged. "We will not tolerate such insolence! We'll bring the great country of the United States to its knees, if we have to do it one person at a time! Soon they'll know how deadly we can be...soon, Mr. Corban, very soon." The leader paused and changed the tone of his voice. "Ah, but you won't be able to watch our triumph, will you, Mr. Corban? No...because you're merely one more step along the way to our ultimate triumph."

The leader stopped to revel in the very thought of such a victory.

"And now, Mr. Corban, I suggest, if you have a God, you begin praying. You're going to see him very soon."

Matthew Corban bowed his head and the guard yanked his hair back. Never in a million years could he ever have conceived of being in this situation. He knew today he would die. There was no doubt in his mind. Only a miracle would save him and he knew there'd be none. He hoped his wife and children weren't watching. He knew these men loved sensationalism. What they did, they did to strike terror in the hearts of compassionate people, in the hearts of the American public. He had seen it many times before with others who found themselves in this situation. He had always felt so sorry for the victim, but more for the family. Now he worried about his.

"What're you thinking about, Mr. Corban? Your wife, perhaps, your children? Such a shame isn't it. You know who's to blame for all of this, don't you, Mr. Corban?" the leader asked slapping his sword against his other hand. "Your government is to blame. Yes, Mr. Corban, they're to blame. Do you think if you were the father or the son of the President of your great country, they would've allowed you to rot like this? In your country, as in all countries, all are not equal are they? What really matters is who you are and how much money you have. Common people, like you, are expendable. If we kill you one by one, who will they have to rule? No one. Then where will the great United States be? Sooner or later, they'll start to care. It's too bad, Mr. Corban, it's not now."

"Where is your great constitution? Where is your Bill of Rights now, Mr. Corban?" he said coming within inches of Matthew's face. "Where is your right to life? They took it away from you, didn't they? Where is your right to liberty? They'd rather liberate people in foreign countries than one of their own citizens. You're not a crazy man, are you, Mr. Corban? You don't consider this happiness, do you? Your government violated your constitutional rights. I haven't. And everyone who's watching this right now will know just what the government of the great United States is like. Yes, Mr. Corban, some of those will think about today and then start looking back on their lives. They'll soon realize they have no rights, Mr. Corban, because your government can take them away anytime they want for whatever reason they want."

The leader straightened up and stepped back. "With me, Mr. Corban, you have no rights. They're not men of their word. We are. We gave them a time limit to get you back and that time is up."

The leader turned his back to Matthew and walked a few feet away. He stood there in silence for several minutes before speaking.

"You may say good-bye to your wife and your children if you choose."

"Janie, I love you," said Matthew in the strongest voice he could summon. "Matt, Sarah, I'll be watching over you."

With that, the leader raised his hands. The guard pulled Matthew's head up by his hair and yanked it until it was in position. The other guards severed Matthew Corban's head from the rest of his body and held up his head for the entire world to see.

D. A. Walters

Chapter One

Laura Darmer opened the glass door of Global Connections Consulting Firm and walked into the lobby. A crystal chandelier hung in the center of the room offsetting the olive green, cream, and gold leaf stepped ceiling. The room had several seating sections with upholstered chairs, coffee tables, and end tables with lamps that carried through the crystal motif.

Laura walked to the desk just to the far end of center. Her shiny dark brown hair hung almost shoulder length. Although she had been shopping, Laura was dressed in a light pink suit and white pumps, just perfect for the type of day and season.

"Good morning Maggie," she said to the woman seated at the desk. "How are you this morning?"

"Good morning, Laura," said Maggie smiling. "I'm fine. How are you?"

"I'm doing very well."

"So, what brings you out here?"

"I was restless and had to get out of the house."

"Did you see the news this morning?" asked Maggie leaning forward.

"About the hostage?"

"Yes."

"That's why I had to get out of the house," said Laura shaking her head. "Things like that really bother me."

"I can't imagine how his family's feeling."

"It amazes me how anyone could be that cold and callous," said Laura putting her purse down on the ledge.

"They have no regard for life," said Maggie disapprovingly.

"They have no regard for the lives of Americans," said Laura, "and that leader made sure everyone knew how wrong the 'great United States' was."

"Sometimes I wonder what I'd do if it was someone I knew," said Maggie as though she was thinking of something else at the same time.

"Oh, God, Maggie," said Laura aghast, "don't even think it."

"I can't help it. It's something I think about."

"Well, let's hope we never find out," said Laura shuddering. "I get so nauseated every time the media announces someone else has been taken."

"I know what you mean. You know what the outcome's going to be," said Maggie dramatically, "torture and death."

"Enough, Maggie," said Laura putting her hands up. "I can't bear to think about it anymore. Is Michael busy?" she asked changing the subject.

"Let me check for you."

Maggie got up and walked down the hall to Michael Braedon's office. She had been with the company since it started and was barely twenty at the time. She and the partners grew with the business and she took her job very seriously. Her taffy brown hair was pulled back and rested just below the collar of her smart looking black and grey pinstriped tailored suit.

Laura walked around the lobby looking at the pictures hanging on the walls. Some had been taken a long time ago and the partners looked so young then. She especially liked the one taken the day the Pittsburgh office opened. She knew it was the day Michael's dreams about his business came true.

"Laura," said Maggie, "Michael will see you now."

"Thanks, Maggie."

Laura walked down the hallway, stopped in front of Michael's door, and knocked. He walked to the door buttoning his suit jacket. He had dark brown hair and his brown eyes lit up as soon as he saw her.

"Come in," he said holding the door open.

"Hi," she said walking past him.

"This is a pleasant surprise," said Michael closing the door. He put his arms around her and gave her a hug and a kiss. "You're just what I need."

"Really."

"What brings you here?" he asked.

"I thought if you weren't doing anything, maybe we could have lunch."

"I'd like that. I'm free until one-thirty."

"Great. It'll give us time to talk."

"Sounds like you have something in mind," said Michael looking at her with a twinkle in his eyes.

"I always have something in mind," she said reaching up and giving him a kiss.

Michael reached past her and opened the door. She paused outside the door for him and they walked to the desk.

"Maggie," he said stopping at her desk, "We're going to lunch. I'll be back before the meeting this afternoon. If anyone calls, tell them I'll get back to them as soon as I return."

The bells in the steeple tolled the age of the man carried into the church. The mourning family and friends walked silently along up the stone steps of the old church behind the casket. Nothing moved, even in the gardens. Every flower and blade of grass seemed to stand still out of respect.

Off to the right, along a path in the garden, stood a man dressed in a black suit. In his left hand he carried a briefcase and he reached in his pocket for his phone to check the time. The light flashed and he turned and moved further away from the funeral procession to answer it.

"Yes," he said quietly.

"Has it arrived?" asked the voice.

"Not yet. There are still several minutes left."

"It is imperative that it gets to me today," said the voice impatiently.

"I understand. Everything is under control. I assure you."

"It better be. I cannot afford any mistakes. Have I made myself clear enough?"

"Yes, very clear."

"Do not fail me."

"I will not."

The voice was gone and the man put the phone into his pocket. He turned around and walked to his original spot. From the end of the procession, a man dressed in a black suit walked over to him carrying a briefcase. He placed it on the ground and the man waiting in the garden followed suit.

"I apologize if I gave you cause for worry," said the man as soon as he arrived.

"You made good time. There were still two minutes to spare."

"I do not like to be late for these meetings. I know he times everything down to the second."

"Yes. He has called. Is everything there?"

"As much as we have. Hopefully it will help."

"I am sure he will tell us."

The man picked up the briefcase and went to the church. The other man took out his phone, turned, and walked away.

"It has been delivered. I am on my way."

Michael and Laura walked into their favorite restaurant and were seated at a table on the arched portico. They started with the wedding soup made "the real way," according to the owner and then had the eggplant delicately seasoned and complimented, not drowned in that light sauce with the special blend of spices and cheese.

"What were you doing this morning?" asked Michael sipping his wine.

"Looking at some wedding gowns."

"Did you find any you liked?"

"A few, but they weren't exactly what I wanted," she said, "and I want everything to be perfect."

"What was wrong with them?" asked Michael.

"I liked the bodice of one, the train of another, and the color and texture of the third," she said picturing the three in her mind as she spoke. "There wasn't one that had everything."

"I see," he said smiling at her.

"Michael, I've been thinking," she said.

"About what?"

"I think I'd like to get married in Paris," she said quickly and exhaled a big sigh. "There, I've said it."

"Paris?" Michael asked somewhat surprised. "Why Paris?"

"It's so special to us and has so many memories. After all, it's where you proposed and we first made love there," she said smiling at him and drawing a heart on the back of his hand with her index finger.

Michael smiled at her and kissed her hand.

"What about the guests?" he asked. "Do you think they'd come to Paris?"

"If they have enough time, they'll be able to plan for it. A lot of people we're inviting are already in Paris and Europe. If we get married here, they'll have to travel. Besides, this may be the only time some of our friends and relatives will get to go to Europe."

"There are a lot of other things to consider, too. We need to find a place for the ceremony and for the reception," said Michael. "I wouldn't know where to begin to find those."

"I know, but our friends will. You know they're going to love helping," she said. She knew he was going to have reservations and she felt she came up with the perfect answers to his arguments. "Most importantly, Michael, I love Paris."

"So do I," he said smiling. "Tell you what. Maybe we can go to Paris just for pleasure."

Laura laughed. "That'll never happen. Even if we don't tell anyone we're coming, somehow they'll know you're there the minute you land."

"We can dream, can't we?"

"Yes, Michael, we can dream."

Michael returned to the office and walked up to Maggie's desk. Aside from the meeting at one-thirty, nothing else was on his agenda. He wanted to leave a little earlier to discuss the idea of getting married in Paris with Laura in greater detail. He hoped to have a minute to jot down his ideas before his meeting.

"How was lunch?" asked Maggie smiling up at him.

"Great. What do you think of Paris?" asked Michael nonchalantly.

"Paris is nice. I enjoy it when I have the chance to go, you know when my boss is being nice and asks me to go there on business," said Maggie with a questioning look. "Why?"

"Oh, just wondering," said Michael and he paused for a moment. "Would you go to a wedding in Paris if you were invited?"

"It would depend upon whose wedding and whether my boss would let me have the time off."

"Your boss sounds like an ogre."

"Really, he can be nice," said Maggie smiling. "Whose wedding are we talking about?"

Michael gave her a look.

"Oh, your wedding! Well, if my boss gives me the time off, I'd love to go."

"Maybe I can talk to him for you," he said winking at her. "Did I have any calls?"

"Pierre called from Paris. He wants you to call him immediately."

"Put in a call to him, please."

"Sure. Here's the mail."

Michael sorted through the mail as he walked down the hall. He put the stack on his desk, took off his jacket, hung it up and sat in his chair. No sooner had he done so than Maggie appeared at the door.

"Pierre's on line one."

"Thanks,"

Michael picked up the phone, leaned back in his chair, and swiveled around.

"Pierre, how are you?"

"Fine, Michael. How are you?"

"Couldn't be better. What's going on in Paris?"

"I just met with Edgar Reinholdt, the Owner and CEO of Reinholdt International."

"Now, why would Edgar Reinholdt, the national security genius for all those countries, want to meet with us?"

"His company is contemplating an expansion into the public sector, but before it does, he wants studies done to show the feasibility of such a move."

"In other words, he doesn't want to piss off any of the countries he deals with."

"Exactly. How soon can you come to Paris? We're going to need everyone's input on this one."

Michael swiveled the chair around to face his desk, leaned forward and looked at his planner.

"I can clear my calendar here and be there day after tomorrow. Is that soon enough?"

"That's good."

"You know Mark and Gwen won't be able to be there this soon. They're really busy with things in Sydney."

"I already talked to them. They'll be available for a conference call if we need them."

"Sounds good. See you day after tomorrow."

"Oh, Michael, one other thing…if I don't ask this, my wife will never let me hear the end of it."

"What's that?"

"Can you bring Laura with you?"

"I don't know," said Michael sarcastically. "You know how she feels about Paris."

"I know," said Pierre laughing. "I'll tell Margo she'll be here."

When he hung up, Michael shook his head and laughed. "You're right, Laura," he said looking at her picture, "somehow they knew."

He walked out to Maggie's desk.

"Maggie, I have to go to Paris tomorrow. Could you please check my calendar for the next two weeks and tell Jared, Kelly, and Vince I'd like to meet with them tomorrow morning at nine."

"Sure."

"See if you can book two tickets on the late afternoon flight."

"I can do that," she said making notes on a slip of paper. "Just a reminder, Mr. Crenshaw is due to arrive in about ten minutes."

"Thanks. Let me know when he gets here."

Michael looked at his watch as he walked to his office. He still had a few minutes.

Laura answered her phone. "That was fast. Finished already?" she asked.

"No, I'm waiting for Mr. Crenshaw. Pierre called. I have to go to Paris tomorrow. Would you like to come?"

"Oh, Michael, I'd love to go."
"Maybe we can look at places for the wedding."
"Michael, I love you."
"I love you, too. Gotta go. See you later."

She put her phone back in her purse and walked back into the boutique.

Laura arrived home shortly after Michael. She parked and carefully gathered her shopping bags. She was determined to take them in all at once. Putting the bags down from one hand, she unlocked the door and pushed it open. She grabbed the rest of the bags turned sideways and squeezed through the doorway.

"Something smells wonderful," she said walking into the kitchen.

Michael turned and gave her a kiss. He looked down at the bags in her hands.

"Find anything at the store?" he asked smiling and gesturing to the bags.

"Not much," she said casually. "I bought a few things to take with me."

"A few?"

"You're going to like them," she said winking. "Trust me. How soon will dinner be ready? I'm starving."

"Ten minutes."

"Great, I'll get changed," she said slipping off her heels as soon as she was on the carpet. "I have some ideas about the wedding."

"I have some, too."

"I'll bring my planner with me," she said struggling with the bags.

Michael smiled and shook his head.

"Why don't you just drop those packages in the living room? I'll bring the suitcase downstairs later and you can pack."

"Good idea," said Laura dropping the packages.

Chapter Two

The airport was unusually noisy and the man in the dark suit walked through the corridor looking for signs pointing to the restrooms. Although this wasn't his first time here, something about it seemed to cancel his sense of direction. He got to a crossroads of corridors and looked to the left and right. A woman ushered three children towards him and as he looked beyond her he saw the sign.

Standing about six-feet away from the doorway stood a man he recognized. He walked up to him and put his briefcase next to the one already on the floor.

"He sends his greetings," said the man who had been waiting.

"Thank him for me," he said.

"Hopefully all went well."

"Everything went smoothly.

"He will be pleased to know."

"Tell him that I am looking forward to serving him again."

"I will make certain to tell him," said the man as the flight to Jordan was announced.

"I must be going. They have announced my flight," he said picking up a briefcase from the floor.

"May you have a safe journey."

"Thank you," he said and walked away.

The man watched him leave and others come and go several minutes before picking up the remaining briefcase and walking out of the airport. He stood at the curb and a black limousine pulled up. He opened the back door and got in.

"Was he on time?" asked the older gentleman.

"Yes, sir."

"Did you ask him if all went well?"

"He said it went smoothly."

"When is he leaving?"

"Immediately. His flight was called as we made the exchange."

"Where is he going?"

"Jordan."

"Excellent."

Michael buttoned his suit jacket as he headed for the building. It was always good to come to Paris. This was where most of the action was and he loved being in the thick of things. As soon as he walked through the door, Lizbeth got a big smile on her face. Her long red hair was pulled back and like her counterpart in Pittsburgh, Lizbeth had been with the company since the beginning. She was twenty-one when she started with Global and she learned the business quickly. Like Maggie, Lizbeth dressed impeccably and when she was talking to one of the partners in a hallway or an office, one who didn't know who was who would be hard pressed to choose which one was not a partner.

"Hi, Lizbeth," said Michael smiling.

"Hi, Michael, it's so nice to see you. Did you have a good flight?"

"Yes, thank you."

"Did Laura come with you?" she asked almost looking around him.

"Yes, she did." He paused and turned to look. Not seeing anyone, he turned back. "She's at the house. I'm sure she'll come to the office while we're here."

"Great," said Lizbeth bringing her attention back to him. "They're all working in the conference room."

"Thanks."

Michael walked into the room where the partners were working. Each was in their special place. It was something that could be expected. Pierre, who unofficially headed the Paris office, had been Michael's best friend throughout college. His striking blue eyes almost mesmerized people when he talked. It was during college that he met his wife Margo. She captured his heart the first time he laid eyes on her. She was a beautiful blonde with green eyes and a petite figure. She had a flare for fashion and commanded attention when she walked into a room. They sat beside one another.

To the left of Margo sat Jean who was deep in conversation with his wife Angelique. To look at him, with his blonde hair and blue eyes, one would expect to find a very carefree spirit. While he knew how to have a good time, he was very serious about anything that dealt with the business and would be the one to bring everyone back to task when things bordered on the brink of the ridiculous. His wife tempered him well. Her taffy colored hair hung slightly below shoulder length. She could bring him out of his serious moods and was the half of the relationship that enjoyed surprises, especially surprising him.

"Michael, it's good to see you," said Gina smiling at him as she walked back to her seat with a bottle of water in hand. She was a beautiful quiet spoken redhead married to Paul who was seated next to her. Her green eyes sparkled as she spoke. "Is Laura with you?"

"She's at the house," he said as he made his way to his chair, "and before I forget, she's cooking and wants all of you to come to dinner. She said to make sure you know it's nothing fancy."

"I'll take nothing fancy from Laura anytime," said Henri raising his eyebrows. He was the only one of the partners that sported a mustache. He always thought it made him look intriguing. "I think I gained ten pounds the last time she was here."

"Don't blame Laura for those extra pounds," said his wife, Brigit, poking him lovingly in the stomach. She pushed her blonde hair behind her ear. "You didn't have to have two pieces of pie or cake."

"It would be impolite to say no when she was so sweet to offer," he said looking at his wife and giving her a kiss on the cheek.

"Not to change the subject, I read everything I could find on Reinholdt International," said Michael. "How extensive is this expansion Mr. Reinholdt's contemplating."

Pierre quickly briefed Michael on the Reinholdt project. He outlined the desire Edgar Reinholdt had to enter the more commercial aspect of the communications business, something Edgar personally thought could be done with a minimum of fuss. What he really wanted was for Global Connections to substantiate his thoughts.

"He needs to be careful with whatever he does," said Paul in his usual blunt manner. "He can't afford to alienate his present clients."

George leaned back in his chair and put his hands together before he spoke. "The only people who can tell Edgar if this is going to work or not are his current clients. If they feel the least bit threatened, it's not worth pursuing."

"Are we getting this down?" asked Pierre.

"Way ahead of you," said Jacques holding up the paper that looked more like a detailed organizational chart than a collection of random notes. "This is just a sketchy list and it's going to take more time later."

"Let's do a little now," said Michael. "Then we'll do more after dinner."

When Michael walked into the house, the aroma of Laura's cooking drew him into the kitchen. She was panning dinner rolls to set off to the side to rise. There were sacks of groceries that needed put away and she worked on those little by little.

"Hey, Honey, something smells wonderful," he said putting his arms around her and kissing her.

"Thank you."

"The others will be here shortly. We have work to do on this Reinholdt account." He opened the oven to look and then lifted the lid of a pot on the stove. "I didn't realize how hungry I was until now." He looked in the bags. "Need help putting this away?"

"If you don't mind," said Laura. "I didn't get that far."

Michael put everything away and then took a spoon out of the drawer, lifted the lid of the pot again, and took a taste.

"This is so good," he said.

"Dinner will be ready in a little while. Why don't you get changed before they get here?"

"Good idea," he said as he reached for something off a tray in the refrigerator.

Michael walked out of the kitchen to the bedroom. It only took him a few minutes to change and as he came out the doorbell rang.

"I'll get it," he yelled to Laura.

Laura took trays out of the refrigerator. She heard voices as they came into the living room. She turned and saw Brigit coming into the kitchen.

"Laura," said Brigit giving her a hug. "I'm so glad you're here."

"I couldn't wait to get here," said Laura.

"Dinner smells wonderful."

"It'll be done in a little bit. I hope you like it," she said picking up a tray. "Help me take these in the room, please."

"Sure," said Brigit.

The rest of the ladies arrived and came directly to the kitchen. They got something to drink and sat down.

"Any more about the wedding?" asked Nicole sitting down beside Margo.

"As a matter of fact, yes," said Laura looking around smiling. "Michael and I have been talking about getting married in Paris."

"Paris?" asked Monique taking a piece of broccoli from the tray.

"I think it's perfect," said Angelique. "Not just because I live here, but you and Michael have a history here."

"If we get married here, we need to find places to have the ceremony and the reception. I was hoping you could all help."

"We need paper and pens," said Nicole getting up from the table. Planning parties was one of her favorite things to do. "We have a lot to do," she said as she naturally took over.

Michael looked around the room. Paris was quite a distance from where he grew up just outside of Pittsburgh with his brother, Mark. He found himself thinking about the day that changed his life. He could hear the phone ring as though it was yesterday.

"Hello."

"May I speak to Michael Braedon, please?"

"This is Michael."

"Michael, this is Pierre Lemont."

"Pierre, how the hell are you?" asked Michael getting up from the couch and running his fingers through his hair.

"Fine, how are you?"

"Great," said Michael pacing the floor. "Where are you?"

"Pittsburgh."

"Pittsburgh!" said Michael stopping dead in his tracks. "What the hell are you doing here?"

"We're all here. We came for a conference."

"Why would you ever come to Pittsburgh, of all places?"

"We're looking for a new direction and we thought we might be able to find you," said Pierre. "How long's it been, Michael?"

"Too long. So what kind of conference?"

"Business," said Pierre, "and this was a perfect excuse to come to the States."

"Really. You needed an excuse to come to the States?"

"Yah, you know how it is. Anyway, we wanted to know if you wanted to go to dinner tonight."

"Love to"

He hadn't wanted to tell Pierre how he really was doing. Somehow he couldn't bring himself to tell him about getting fired from the best job he ever had or having to quit another dream job because of his parents' illness. It hadn't been a really good time for Michael. Within a year he had lost virtually everything; his job, his parents, and his house. Nothing seemed to be going right and no matter how hard he tried, he just couldn't seem to get the train of his life back on track. For the first time in months, his spirits were lifted. He looked in the mirror and there was actually a smile on his face.

When he walked into the restaurant that night, it didn't take him long to find his party. Pierre stood up and greeted him with a hug.

"Michael, it's so good to see you."

"It's great to see you, too," said Michael. Then he looked at the others, "all of you."

They took time to catch up on what had been going on since they last saw each other. This had been the first time since graduation that they'd all been together.

"What kind of business were you thinking about?" asked Michael.

D. A. Walters

Each of them told him in some detail just what they wanted to do. The entire time they were talking Michael's mind was working. He knew exactly what they should be doing.

"So, you're really talking about starting multiple businesses," said Michael.

"Yes," said Jean.

"I've been thinking ever since I got your call," said Michael.

"Thinking, Michael?" teased Henri smoothing his moustache. "You were thinking?"

"Yes, Henri, I was really thinking."

"About what?" said Brigit giving her husband a gentle poke. Henri winced as though she actually hurt him.

"I suggest we leave this restaurant and go back to my apartment or to your hotel. It may be in our best interest to create a business together."

Michael had such a smile on his face. He couldn't believe how providence had stepped in when he was at his lowest to bring him out of those depths.

Jean tapped Michael on the shoulder.

"Michael, you were a million miles away, my friend," he said.

"Just thinking about our first meeting back in Pittsburgh," said Michael smiling.

"Look how far we've come," said Jean gesturing around the room. "Who would've ever thought this would've developed out of that meeting."

Over the years, the group became extremely close as friends in addition to being business partners. Yet, even with the excitement that the business continually brought, there was always something missing in Michael's life. He was close to his brother Mark, his wife Gwen and their two children; simply speaking, they were all the family he had in the world. Then one day, when he least expected it, Laura came into his life and changed his world forever. She gave him something to look forward to at the end of the day and even though they weren't married yet, Laura made her home with him.

She was the person in his life he'd do anything for and he knew she'd do anything for him. When they were apart, he always knew when she was thinking about him. He could feel it. Most of the time, he'd just start smiling, yet there were times when he'd just have to pick up the phone and call her.

Now as he looked around the room, he realized Laura's idea of getting married in Paris was the right decision to make. He wanted everything to be perfect. With his friends and Mark and Gwen, it would be.

"Excuse me, for a moment," he said putting his drink down on the end table and heading for the kitchen.

He walked over to Laura, took her by the hand. "Excuse us," he said.

He led her outside to the patio, put his arms around her, and she looked into his eyes.

"Michael, what is it?"

"I needed to hold you," he said. "I want to marry you. I want to marry you here, in this city."

"Oh Michael," she said smiling at him, "kiss me."

Chapter Three

"Mr. Reinholdt, thank you for coming back," said Pierre when Edgar Reinholdt came into the reception area. "Let me introduce one of our other partners, Michael Braedon."

"Mr. Reinholdt, it's a pleasure," said Michael shaking his hand.

"It's a pleasure meeting you, too, Mr. Braedon," said Edgar. His dark hair was kept short and his blue eyes sparkled behind his glasses.

"This is a very interesting proposition you're making for the future of your company," said Michael.

"Right now, I'm contemplating it."

The three men walked down the hall and into the room where the rest had already gathered discussing various other accounts. On the table in front of them were folders of information for the Reinholdt project. The first part of the meeting dealt with laying out what Edgar envisioned. Even though they had heard most of it before, hearing it again more than reinforced the ideas they were presenting. Once Edgar finished, the team gave their ideas and as time went on, they got into the areas that weren't as cut and dry.

"Mr. Reinholdt, the issue of conflict of interest arises with this new direction," said Jean. "I'm concerned your current clients may perceive this as a blending of the two divisions."

"I thought the two divisions could be kept quite separate," said Edgar.

"This move could cause some damaging repercussions," said Michael, "especially if your current clients feel that what they pay for exclusively may be duplicated and sold to the public."

"That was one of my chief concerns," said Edgar, "and I want to make absolutely certain my present clients are comfortable in the fact that these two operations will be absolutely different in scope."

"To some people, communications are all the same," said Monique. "They'll assume that what's being developed for the governments is also being made available to the general public."

"That can't be further from the truth," said Edgar emphatically. "I would never!"

"I understand, Mr. Reinholdt," said Michael. "I know you'd never do anything unethical. You would've never survived in your business this long if you had."

"Mr. Braedon, I pride myself on my ethics," said Edgar. "I always have and always will run my business in that manner."

"Mr. Reinholdt," said George, "in order for us to get a real idea about what you have in place right now that can be used to move you safely into this new division and what you can do in the future to keep the new entity separate from your current dealings, we need to visit your facilities."

"That shouldn't be a problem," said Edgar. "I'll tell you right up front that there'll be areas I cannot permit you to access because of security reasons."

"We understand," said Jean. "What we want to see is the current layout and what can be done, if anything, to physically separate this new project from your existing endeavors."

"This way, hopefully, we'll be able to get on the same page with you and make this move the best it can be," said Pierre, "if it proves to be feasible."

Laura clicked through all the documents she had worked on. It had been a very productive morning. After she emailed the last of the articles, she took a sip of the coffee that had been sitting there since early that morning.

"That's awful," she said getting up to throw the remaining coffee away. She refilled her cup, sat back down, and took a sip. "Much better."

A fifteen minute break was called for and she sat back, watched, and listened to what was going on around her. She found people fascinating and had a special notebook to log interesting people and pieces of conversations. She jotted down notes as quickly as possible. Today, even the conversations were cryptic.

She closed her notebook and opened the laptop. Out of the corner of her eye, she noticed two men. She looked up in time to watch the two exchange large white envelopes. One man walked out of the café. The second man watched him leave and took out his phone.

"The sixth part has been delivered," he said. "I'm on the move."

The sound of the phone interrupted her observations.

"Hello," she said.

"Hey sweetheart, what're you doing?" asked Michael.

"Working on those projects."

"I asked Edgar Reinholdt to come to dinner tonight."

"That's fine. I'm just about done and can finish at the house after I start dinner."

"He'll be there a little after six."

"That's perfect. Everyone coming?"

"Of course."

"Okay, I'll see you when you get home. I love you."

"I love you, too."

Laura put her phone in her purse and started packing up her work. When she picked up the notebook, she remembered the exchange between the men, quickly jotted it down, and left.

Edgar Reinholdt arrived at Michael's home shortly after six o'clock. It was the first time they saw him dressed casually. Most of the others had arrived and were having drinks in the living room.

"Mr. Reinholdt, I'd like you to meet my fiancée, Laura Darmer," said Michael.

"Mr. Reinholdt, it's very nice to meet you," said Laura.

"Miss Darmer, the pleasure is mine."

"Did your wife come with you?" she asked.

"No she didn't. She's in the midst of preparing for the yearly charity gala her group has."

"A gala?"

"Yes, she instituted a gala that benefits the Children's Hospital in Frankfurt. It's the main fundraiser for their free care fund."

"That's wonderful. How long has she been doing this?"

"She began twenty years ago. Our son was very ill as an infant and in desperate need of care. We had to borrow money for his hospital stay from whomever we could because there were only very limited funds then for free care. My wife vowed that no other mother or father would ever have to choose between putting food on the table and the health of their child. For her, this is a full-time job which she takes very seriously."

"How much does she raise?"

"The first year, she and her little committee raised in excess of $50,000."

"That was quite an accomplishment," said Laura.

"Now, with each passing year, Gabrielle challenges herself to continually beat the previous year's total and right now is the most intense preparation time."

"Hopefully the next time you come to Paris, she'll be able to come with you," said Laura.

"I hope so, too."

"I'd love to talk to her about this."

"And she'd love to tell you," said Edgar smiling.

By this time, the rest of the group arrived. Laura excused herself and when everything was ready, she invited them to join her in the dining room. The pleasant conversation over dinner turned once again to business almost as soon as they were finished.

"Mr. Reinholdt, Michael will be going back to Frankfurt with you," said Pierre.

"That's fine," he said. "Please, call me Edgar. Michael, it'll be best if we both stay at a hotel in the city. That way we'll be able to meet and discuss anything you need me to clarify. I already called my wife and told her as well as Erika, my secretary."

"You're going to stay downtown, also?" asked Michael, "I thought you lived just outside the city."

"I do, but we'll not have a moment's peace with all of the preparation for the gala. Gabrielle and her committee are almost inseparable as the time for the gala approaches."

Laura curled up on the love seat in their room. She took the book off the lamp table and opened to the marked page. She always liked to take a few minutes before bed every night to read. Tonight, she had trouble concentrating. Her mind went back to the conversation she had with Michael about coming to Paris just for fun. Somehow she knew work would be involved. She smiled when she thought about it. Michael was so at home here. He loved his business and never considered it work. It was always a challenge, a game, or a puzzle to be solved. She loved watching his eyes light up when they were able to figure out the answer.

She looked around the room and thought about the first time she was in it. She remembered how nervous she was, how much she loved him, and how wonderful being with him for the first time was. That excitement never seemed to fade. Even now, her heart was racing at the thought of making love with him. She put the book back on the lamp table, got up from the love seat and walked into the bathroom, dropped her clothes on the floor, and stepped into the shower with Michael. She looked at him and smiled.

"I couldn't wait."

Chapter Four

The older gentleman sat at his desk finishing the last note. Once more he read the communication. All that remained was waiting for confirmation. He knew it would come soon and they had to be ready to move.

The mission was critical and the stakes were high. Success would put the world at his feet; make it all worthwhile.

He picked up the stack of envelopes and looked at the name on each one. Every one was needed without a doubt. He took a deep breath, put them down on the desk, and leaned back in his chair.

There was a knock on the door.

"Come in," he said.

"You sent for me?"

"Yes, I need you to deliver these immediately," he said picking up the envelopes and handing them over. "We must be ready to leave as soon as word comes."

"Yes, sir," he said taking the envelopes. He turned and left, closing the door behind him.

Michael and Edgar walked into the hotel in the center of Frankfurt. The intricate carvings of the woodwork told the story of its age. It was evident the owner kept the furnishings in line with the architecture.

There were only two guests sitting on the overstuffed chairs in the lobby. The one, an elderly woman, waited for a ride. Beside her were a tapestry suitcase and a bag with leather handles to match. She looked at her watch and peered out the window. The other person, a dark haired gentleman in a dark suit, was busy reading the newspaper.

As Michael and Edgar walked up to what was the original desk, the clerk looked up from his work.

"May I help you, gentlemen?" he asked.

"Yes, we have two rooms reserved for Global Connections Consulting Firm," said Michael.

"Yes, sir, we've been expecting you," he said handing each a card. "Would you please fill these out?"

The clerk busied himself as the gentlemen filled out the cards. When they finished they handed them back.

"Mr. Reinholdt and Mr. Braedon?" asked the clerk looking at the information on the cards. He looked down at the floor plan and then back up. "Mr. Reinholdt, you are in room 718. Mr. Braedon, you are in room 720."

"Thank you."

"Here are your keycards," he said double checking them as he handed them over. "Mr. Reinholdt, 718, Mr. Braedon, 720." Then he pointed across the lobby and both men turned in that direction. "You can take the elevator over there to the seventh floor."

"Thank you."

The two gentlemen picked up their bags and took the elevator to the seventh floor. They turned left off the elevator and went down four doors to their rooms.

"I'm going to put my things in my room and check in with Gabrielle," said Edgar. "I'll come to your room when I'm finished."

"Good. That'll give me time to call the office and Laura."

Gabrielle Reinholdt was glad to hear from her husband. There was so much to talk about and many things to do for the Gala. She insisted she needed Edgar's help. He promised he'd come home as soon as he had a chance. He quickly checked in with his secretary, Erika, to tell her that he and Michael would be in soon.

Edgar looked around his room. Although it had all the amenities that were required of a hotel room, it was quite small. He thought briefly about putting his things in the drawers and then decided he might ask about possibly switching rooms to a larger one. Ever since he was a child, he hated closed-in spaces and this hotel room gave him that closed-in feeling.

Michael left the door of his hotel room open while he called Laura and the office. It was something he did no matter where he stayed. He was so used to the openness of his homes and during the daytime, he didn't see any reason to have the door closed. While he was on the phone to Laura, he noticed a dark haired man in a dark suit walk down the hallway. Although he was listening intently to what she had to say, he also listened to see where the man stopped. From what Michael could hear, he didn't stop at all.

"Did you get all of the cards done for the wedding?" he asked.

"Yes. Thank goodness we had the guest list done before we left to come to Paris," she said. "I'm so glad we decided to have them all printed. I finished the last address when you called."

"Are you mailing them today?"

"As soon as we're done talking. Then I'm meeting Margo and we're going to see a designer."

"A designer?"

"For my wedding gown, Michael."

"Have a good time. I'll talk to you later. I love you."

"I love you, too."

Michael smiled and shook his head when he got off the phone. Somehow he knew once his partners heard about Laura not being able to find what she wanted in the States, they'd insist she see a designer. Things were moving right along and now they were committed to having the wedding in Paris. The idea pleased him more and more. He called the office and was ending that call when Edgar walked in. He looked around the room.

"When we go down to the lobby, I'm going to see if there's another room I can switch to," said Edgar.

"Is there something wrong with your room?"

"It's quite small," said Edgar. "This one's much bigger."

"Really."

"Yes. I hate to complain, but ever since I was young, I've hated small closed-in spaces."

"Would a room this size be alright?"

"Yes, this would be much better."

"Why don't we just switch. In my travels, I've gotten used to just about anything."

"I don't want to inconvenience you."

"It's not an inconvenience at all."

"If you're sure you wouldn't mind."

"Not in the least. I didn't get very far in unpacking," said Michael pointing to his suitcase.

"I didn't get any further either."

"I'll just switch you cards. They're both in the firm's name. There's no need to trouble the front desk about this."

When Edgar came back with his suitcase, he and Michael switched cards. Michael went to the other room and unpacked.

"Edgar wasn't kidding," said Michael aloud as he looked around the room.

Michael unpacked and met Edgar in the lobby. They drove to Reinholdt International where Edgar introduced Michael to Albert Paxton his Chief Operations Officer. Through his conversations with Mr. Paxton and other workers, Michael began putting together a picture of the business as well as its founder. Before they realized it, the work day ended and Michael and Edgar returned to the hotel for dinner.

Michael went over the notes he had taken. He was anxious to put all the information into the computer so everything would be clear when he talked to Edgar and when he actually gave his report back at the office. He took the time to write down some questions he had; questions he didn't want to ask Mr. Paxton. When he finally looked up at the clock, it was time to meet Edgar in the hotel dining room.

"Edgar, I'm very impressed with your operation," he said when they finally had a chance to relax. "Everything runs very efficiently."

"Thank you."

"I was wondering about a few things. Building One seems to have more sections that are off limits to most personnel."

"More top security work is done there and only those with the highest security clearance can enter those areas if they have permission. If we mutually agree that your firm will work with my company, then those who will work in Frankfurt will have to get clearance in order to move freely about the buildings and only if they have permission."

It had been less than two days since the last communication and now he had in his hand what he had been waiting for. All that was left was for the others to get there from various parts outside the city. Then they'd be ready to leave.

He opened the right-hand drawer of his desk and took out a piece of paper. He went over the list one item at a time, thoroughly thinking about it. There was no room for error. The timing had to be perfect. He was thankful for all the followers he had and how diligently they worked towards the same common end.

One by one they arrived and took their seats in front of his desk. Just like a classroom in school with a seating chart, each knew his exact place. To them it made no rhyme or reason, but to him, it made perfect sense. When they all were seated, there was absolute silence.

"The communication has arrived," he said addressing them. "We will leave immediately. Each of you knows what is expected. Our contact will meet us at the appointed place."

"Yes, sir," they said in unison.

"We cannot fail. This is vital to the success of the Cause."

"Yes, sir."

During the second day at Reinholdt International, Michael toured the rest of the complex. Before returning to Building One, Michael asked Mr. Paxton to look at the buildings they were in yesterday one more time.

Michael sat at the desk reviewing his notes when Edgar came in.

"I have some information I think is extremely critical to your operation," said Michael concerned.

"What is it?"

Michael showed him a sheet of paper with the words *Check Security*.

"We just..." said Edgar and he stopped when he saw Michael place his finger to his lips. He looked at Michael quizzically. "Right now, I have to go home. I promised Gabrielle I'd help her with a few things for the gala. Would you like to come with me?"

"I think I'd like to finish making my notes and then go back to the hotel."

"I'll come to your room when I'm finished and we'll definitely discuss this."

Shortly after Edgar left, Michael returned to the hotel. He walked through the lobby to the elevator and pressed the button for the seventh floor. He wanted to go over all the things about Reinholdt International's security that needed addressed. *I can't believe I didn't catch that the first day. I usually see that kind of thing. I think I'll call Henri about it. If anyone would know about this, it's him.*

He stopped outside his room, took out his keycard, and opened the door. As he walked in, the light from the hall shone in the room. Chairs were overturned and the dresser drawers and their contents were strewn over the floor.

"What the hell!" he said staring at the mess.

Out of the corner of his eye, Michael saw a man dressed all in black. Before he could react, another man hit him over the head. Everything went black and Michael fell unconscious to the floor.

"Quickly, tie his arms and legs," the leader hissed. "Put the hood over his head. Tie it securely."

The men bound Michael's arms and legs. Then they put a hood over his head and secured it around his neck with rope.

"You," barked the leader pointing to one of his men, "check and make sure no one is in the hall."

The man opened the door and looked up and down the hallway. He quickly moved out of the room signaling for the others to follow. Another man raced down the hall and opened the door to the stairwell. Two men came out of the room carrying a bound and hooded Michael. Blood seeped through the hood as they carried him into the stairwell and disappeared. The leader strode down the hall with an air of confidence. He turned back only once to make certain they had missed no one. The last man out of the room quietly closed the door and headed for the stairwell.

It was the middle of the afternoon and the Reinholdt residence was relatively quiet. Gabrielle worked on some of the centerpieces as she waited for her husband to come home. She had on a light blue dress that brought out the blue in her eyes. Her long wavy blonde hair hung halfway down her back. She reached for a clip on the corner table and pulled her hair back.

The committee had just left and would be returning after dinner. They all knew this would be a late night. They were nearing the gala and there were many items that needed finished. Marie, the Reinholdt's maid helped Gabrielle secure some ribbons to the centerpieces when the doorbell rang.

"Marie, would you please get that?" asked Gabrielle twisting the ribbon into a bow. "Mr. Reinholdt may have forgotten his keys."

"Yes, Ma'am."

Marie walked to the front door and opened it. No one was there. She looked around and saw no one anywhere. She was about to close the door when she noticed an envelope on the step. She stooped down, picked it up, and saw it had Mrs. Reinholdt's name printed on it. Taking one more look around, she turned and walked back into the house closing the door behind her. She felt uneasy and stopped for a moment to check to make certain the door was locked. Then she went into the living room.

"Excuse me, Mrs. Reinholdt," said Marie holding out the envelope. "This was on the step for you."

"For me? Thank you, Marie."

Gabrielle smiled and took the envelope.

"If you'll excuse me, I'll be back in a moment," said Marie and she walked out of the room.

Gabrielle looked at the envelope, opened it, and took out the piece of paper.

WE HAVE TAKEN YOUR HUSBAND. IF YOU EVER WANT TO SEE HIM ALIVE AGAIN, YOU WILL DO EXACTLY AS YOU ARE TOLD.

Gabrielle clasped her hand over her mouth and collapsed into the chair behind her. The envelope fell to the floor. Her mind raced through all sorts of scenarios, one blending into the other. She knew she should do something, call someone, but she sat frozen. She looked again at the words on the paper, all printed in capital letters by hand. *Why would anyone want to do this to you, Edgar? Why?*

Before long, keys jingled in the lock and Edgar opened the front door.

"Gabrielle, I'm home," he shouted as soon as he stepped into the foyer.

There was no answer.

"Gabrielle," he shouted again.

Again, there was no answer. He knew she was home. She would never go out with the gala this close. Besides, she told him she was working on the centerpieces. He walked into the living room and saw his wife sitting in the chair. She was ghostly white with a terrified look on her face. In her hands was a piece of paper.

"Gabrielle, what's wrong?" he asked, kneeling on the floor in front of her.

She handed him the note. He read it and was puzzled.

"Where did you get this?" he asked.

"Marie found it on the step outside when she answered the door."

"This must be some kind of sick joke. I'm right here and I'm fine," he said touching her cheek. "A man in my position is bound to draw some crazy people. Sweetheart, don't worry about it, please."

"Edgar, promise me you'll be careful," she whispered. Her voice quivered. "You won't take any chances."

"Sweetheart, I promise," he said as he kissed her. "Are you alright?"

"Yes, Edgar," she said automatically. It was the answer that had always been expected from her and one she said without thinking.

Edgar looked around the room. It was obvious more had been accomplished in his absence.

"These centerpieces are beautiful," he said getting up. "You must be working day and night. What can I help you with, Sweetheart?"

"I need some of these hung on the hooks so we can finish putting the ribbons and cascading flowers on them. I want..." She was unable to finish her sentence as tears came to her eyes.

"Honey, what's wrong?"

"I can't get that note out of my mind," she said shaking her head. She wiped away a tear and looked up at him. "Are you sure everything's alright?"

"I'm positive. I'm right here," he said taking her in his arms. "No one has tried anything. I haven't seen anything suspicious. No one has contacted me or threatened me."

"Please, Edgar, promise me you'll be on guard."

"I promise. I won't take any chances," he said and he kissed her.

"I don't know what I'd do if anything happened to you."

"I promise it won't."

Marie walked into the room and stopped. Edgar motioned to her to get some tea. With Edgar's calm reassurance, Gabrielle was soon ready for him to help her with the centerpieces.

He sat down at the corner of the table with his wife when Marie brought in a tray with tea and some biscuits. She poured tea for both of them and then went back to the kitchen.

"I think this is your best work ever," he said looking at everything around him.

"This committee is very dedicated to getting things done and going the extra steps to make it wonderful. We have new members who have had some wonderful ideas. They're so full of energy."

"It shows in the beauty of all this work," he said. "You're teaching them well, Gabrielle. They've caught your spirit."

"I hope so, Edgar."

He looked at his watch.

"Gabrielle, I hate to leave, but I need to meet Michael at the hotel. Are you going to be alright?"

"Yes, I'll be fine. The committee will be coming soon."

"If you need me, call me. I'll come right home."

Edgar walked into the foyer. Marie was setting a vase of flowers on the small table under the mirror.

"Marie, please keep an eye on Mrs. Reinholdt for me until the committee gets here. She's had quite a scare."

"Yes, sir. We'll work on some other things for the Gala. She'll be fine."

"Thank you. If anything else happens, call me immediately."

As Edgar drove back into the city, he couldn't help thinking about the note.

"What crazy person would ever do such a thing?" he said aloud to himself. "This has to be a joke, a cruel joke."

To play it on his wife was unconscionable.

He returned to the hotel and went directly to the seventh floor. Edgar knocked on Michael's door, but there was no answer. *Come on Michael, answer.* He knocked again and when Michael didn't answer this time, he called the office. Erika told him Michael left shortly after he had. He thought perhaps Michael had fallen asleep so he went down to the front desk.

"Ah, Mr. Reinholdt, how can I help you?" asked the clerk.

"May I please have a keycard to room 718," asked Edgar. "I seem to have lost mine."

"Yes, I know," said the clerk without hesitation. "Didn't the other person who came earlier give you the keycard?"

"What are you talking about?"

"A man came, saying you had lost the keycard to Room 718 and offered to come down to get it for you because you had so many packages. I made it for him earlier this afternoon."

"I see," said Edgar hesitantly.

The clerk sensed Edgar was puzzled and quickly said, "Perhaps I was mistaken, Mr. Reinholdt. Let me make another for you right away."

"Thank you."

Once again Edgar took the elevator up to the seventh floor. *It must have been Michael. He probably did some shopping before he returned to the hotel.* Edgar went to room 718, opened the door and switched on the light. He gasped when he saw the chairs, lamp, and end table turned over. The room was a mess. All of a sudden he broke out into a cold sweat and chills shot down his arms and legs. The words of the note rang though his mind like the toll of a funeral bell. He backed out of the room, turned out the light, closed the door, and hurriedly went downstairs to the desk.

"Excuse me, what time did you make the other key?" he asked the clerk.

"It was around 2:30 in the afternoon, sir."

Edgar Reinholdt turned white and his stomach churned. He turned and walked quickly towards the door.

"Mr. Reinholdt is anything wrong?" the clerk called after Edgar.

Edgar raised his right hand in the air as if to wave the question away.

Mr. Reinholdt, is there anything I can do for you?"

"I…I don't know yet."

Chapter Five

He couldn't remember driving home. It seemed his car knew the way to go. Edgar walked into the living room. His face was as ghostly white as his wife's had been earlier. He stood looking at Gabrielle, trying to find the words.

"Edgar, you're home early," she said with a smile, but when she saw his face, her expression changed. She touched his cheek. "Edgar, what's wrong? Talk to me. I thought you were staying in town."

"Gabrielle, the note," he started and paused, "it may not have been a cruel joke."

"What do you mean?" she asked putting her hand on his arm. "Has someone threatened you?"

"I think whoever sent the note may've taken Michael Braedon…by mistake."

Gabrielle shook her head in disbelief. The color was once again draining from her face. She put her hands to her mouth.

"What are you talking about?" she asked her voice unsteady. "Why would you think that?"

Edgar told his wife everything that happened at the hotel.

"Have you called the police?"

"No. I want to call his office to see if they know anything."

"Edgar," said Gabrielle rather sternly, "whether they do or not, someone broke into that room and ransacked it."

"I know, Sweetheart, I know" he said picking up the phone. "I'll call the police as soon as I speak to Pierre."

As the workday came to a close, the activity at Global was finally settling down and everyone was getting ready to leave for the evening. Lizbeth walked into Pierre's office.

"Pierre, Mr. Reinholdt is calling."

"Thanks, Lizbeth," he said picking up the phone.

"Edgar, how's everything going?"

"Have you heard from Michael?" asked Edgar ignoring the question.

"Nothing since last evening," said Pierre. "Why? I thought he was visiting your complex."

"He did," said Edgar and he proceeded to tell him everything that happened that afternoon.

"Can you fax a copy of the note to me?" asked Pierre leaning forward, picking up a pen, and making notes on a pad in front of him. "Then make several copies immediately and put them somewhere safe."

"I can do that."

"Edgar, contact the police as soon as we're finished. Even if we're wrong about what we suspect, I'd much rather apologize later than lose valuable time," said Pierre. "In the meantime, I'll check both Michael's private and business accounts to see if there's been any activity within the last few hours. If there hasn't, I'll call you and the authorities both in Paris and the U.S."

"Pierre, I'll call you after I've spoken to the police."

What Pierre heard from Edgar was hard to believe, yet he knew in the world today it was highly possible.

"Pierre," he said quietly, "before you go jumping to conclusions, take it one step at a time." He walked out to the reception area and up to Lizbeth's desk. "Lizbeth, has Michael called from Germany at all today?"

"No, sir."

"When was the last time he called?"

"Last evening," she said. "Is something wrong? Mr. Reinholdt sounded rather frazzled when he called."

"Possibly, Lizbeth, quite possibly," said Pierre hitting the ledge gently with the palm of his hand. "Please tell all the partners I'd like to see them in the conference room."

"Yes, sir."

"If anyone has left, call them, and tell them they have to return immediately."

"Yes, sir."

"One more thing, I want you in this meeting."

"Yes, sir."

Pierre went to the fax machine and picked up what Edgar sent. He read the contents as he walked back to his office. He sat at his computer and accessed Michael's accounts. Between the news from Edgar and the information gathered from the banks, Pierre knew he had enough to warrant a call to the authorities.

He took a minute to look over the notes he made, added a few others, and then picked up the phone. The calls took much longer than he had anticipated. Although he didn't have a great deal of information, it was enough for them to take him seriously.

Pierre got up from his chair, took a deep breath, and picked up the note. He was still trying to sort out exactly what had happened. Once again he thought he might be jumping to conclusions, but something in the pit of his stomach told him this was real...all too real!

It was a very solemn Pierre that walked into the conference room and faced his partners.

"What's up, Pierre?" asked George leaning back in his chair. "Why the late meeting?"

"I've received some disturbing news from Edgar Reinholdt," he said taking his seat next to his wife. "It seems Gabrielle received a note from someone claiming to have taken her husband."

He handed the note to Margo. She read it and passed it on.

"Edgar said Gabrielle was very upset by the note and he tried to reassure her it was nothing. A little while later, he went back to the hotel for a meeting with Michael and when Michael didn't answer when he knocked on the door, he went to the desk clerk and asked for a keycard to the room. The clerk told him it was the second one made. Edgar thought it was Michael who had asked someone to get it. When he got to the room, he found it had been ransacked. He went back to the desk and asked the hotel clerk what time the key was made. He knew Michael couldn't have asked for the key because he and Mr. Paxton were meeting with other people in the organization. It was then Edgar first realized Michael may have been taken. He called to find out if we heard from him. I told him no. When he told me why, I asked him to contact the authorities. I contacted the authorities in Paris and the U.S. I also checked the activity on Michael's accounts and there's been none."

"Have you told Laura?" asked Gina jiggling nervously in her seat.

"No," said Pierre. "I wanted to wait until we had something a little more concrete."

"Now what?" asked Robert.

"Edgar's going to call as soon as he's through with the police. The authorities here and in the States will be getting in touch with the Frankfurt authorities. I pray all of this is a mistake and Michael will turn up soon."

"You need to call Mark and Gwen," said Margo touching her husband's arm.

"Right now, they're on their way back to Pittsburgh," said Pierre patting Margo's hand. "I'll call the airline and ask them to give a message to Mark to call me immediately." He looked around the table. "Now we wait."

Once Edgar finished talking to Pierre and faxing the note, he called the police. He was transferred from one office to another and answered the same questions over and over again. He realized what he was telling them sounded far-fetched and he tried hard not to lose his patience. When they finally put him through to Captain Swagen, he was able to convince him that what he was saying was at least plausible. The police arrived at the Reinholdt home and were shown to his office.

"Mr. Reinholdt, I'm Captain Swagen and this is Officer Braken."

"Gentlemen, thank you for coming," said Edgar. "Please have a seat."

"Thank you," said Captain Swagen. "Now, Mr. Reinholdt could you please start at the beginning and tell us what happened?"

Edgar reiterated the story as he knew it. Captain Swagen stopped him numerous times to ask for clarification. Edgar showed them the ransom note his wife received and told them Michael's Paris office had been notified and he was waiting for a call concerning any sort of activity on Michael's accounts.

"Would it be possible for us to talk to the maid?" asked Captain Swagen looking at the note again.

"Of course," said Edgar getting up from his chair. "If you'd please excuse me, I'll get her."

When Edgar left the room, Captain Swagen looked at Officer Braken.

"What do you think?" asked Captain Swagen quietly.

"He seems to be genuine," said Officer Braken. "No matter what you asked, he hasn't deviated in the slightest from his story."

"I thought so, too," said Captain Swagen. "Let's see what the maid has to say."

"I think we should also talk to Mrs. Reinholdt."

The officers stopped their conversation and stood up when Edgar and Marie entered the room. Edgar introduced Marie to the officers and Captain Swagen asked her to tell him what happened. Marie told the story from the time she was helping Mrs. Reinholdt until she gave her the envelope.

"Has anything like this ever happened before?" asked Captain Swagen when she finished.

"No, sir."

"Thank you, Marie. You may go," said Captain Swagen. "Mr. Reinholdt, may we speak to your wife?"

"Certainly. Marie, would you ask Mrs. Reinholdt to come in?"

"Yes, sir."

The room was silent for the few minutes it took for Gabrielle to come to Edgar's office. When she walked in, Edgar introduced her to the officers.

"Mrs. Reinholdt," said Captain Swagen, "could you tell me what happened concerning the note?"

Gabrielle told the Captain everything that transpired that afternoon. Her recollection matched identically with Marie's

"What did you do after you read the note?" asked Captain Swagen.

"I collapsed in the chair. I was terrified. I didn't move until Edgar came home."

"How long was it before your husband came home?"

"Only a few minutes."

"Have you ever received notes like this before?"

"No, sir."

"Thank you, Mrs. Reinholdt," said the Captain and Gabrielle left. "Mr. Reinholdt, the next thing we need to do is examine the room at the hotel. I think it'd be best if you went with us."

"Certainly," said Edgar and the phone in the office rang. "Excuse me, Captain," he said picking up the phone. "Hello."

"Edgar, this is Pierre. There has been no activity on any of Michael's accounts at all today."

"I'll let Captain Swagen know. He's here and we're going to the hotel, now."

Just like any other hotel in the late afternoon hours, the number of guests waiting to check in and out was nearly non-existent. So when Edgar Reinholdt, Captain Swagen, and Officer Braken walked up to the desk, they had no line to wait in.

"Ah, Mr. Reinholdt, you've returned," said the desk clerk looking past Edgar at the police and then back to him. "Is everything alright?"

"We'd like to speak with the manager, please," said Captain Swagen showing his identification.

"Yes, sir, just one minute," said the clerk a little flustered. He turned and walked to the back.

A blonde haired gentleman with blue eyes and a mustache hurriedly walked to the front desk. He appeared to be in his late forties and his suit jacket bore the insignia of the hotel.

"Gentlemen, I'm Mr. Heilman, the manager of this hotel. How may I help you?"

"Mr. Heilman, I'm Captain Swagen," he said showing his identification once again. "Is there some place where we may speak in private?"

"Of course," said Mr. Heilman, "We can use my office. Please, follow me."

He led the way.

"Please have a seat. Now, what seems to be the problem?"

"We have a very serious matter," said Captain Swagen getting to the point. "Mr. Reinholdt believes one of your guests may have been kidnapped."

"Kidnapped!" Mr. Heilman gasped and hurriedly got up to close the door. "Kidnapped? I've never had anything of the kind happen at my hotel. How could that be? There must be some mistake." He took a handkerchief from his pocket and began dabbing his forehead and his mustache. "We're very careful here. That just couldn't happen."

"Mr. Heilman," said Captain Swagen. "none of us likes to believe things of this nature might take place in our establishment."

"Kidnapped," he said again as though the word and the thought behind it were distasteful.

"I'm sure you understand that we must investigate such a serious issue," said Captain Swagen trying to get the manager's attention again.

"Yes...yes...of course," said Mr. Heilman. "Investigate...of course."

"Mr. Heilman, we need to see the room," said Captain Swagen.

"I'm sorry. Which room was it?" he asked completely preoccupied. "Kidnapped?"

"Room 718," said Edgar.

"Just one minute, I will get a keycard for it."

"I have one," said Edgar.

"Okay, gentlemen," said Mr. Heilman, "follow me and we'll go see the room."

Mr. Heilman led them to the elevator and then to the room. Edgar handed the keycard to him and he opened the door.

"Please don't touch anything," said Captain Swagen as they entered the room.

He switched on the light. The nightstand and lamp were upturned on the floor in front of them as well as the chairs across the room. A further look into the room revealed that the drawers had been ransacked and taken out of the dressers as though it was a robbery. Officer Braken spied a heavy object. He bent down to examine it closer and then brought it to the attention of Captain Swagen.

"There looks as if there might be blood on it," said Officer Braken pointing to the edge of the object. "See...right here."

"Blood!" gasped Mr. Heilman clutching his chest. "Oh dear, look at this place." He put his hands up to his mouth and looked around the room. "How could anyone...why would anyone...kidnapped?"

"Mr. Heilman," said Captain Swagen, "are there cameras in the hallways?"

"Cameras? Yes," said Mr. Heilman still quite distracted by the state of the room. "All activity in the hallways is recorded. We should be able to see what may've happened...at least in the hallway." He stopped for a moment before continuing. "We don't have cameras in the rooms. We're a reputable hotel...not one of those kinds if you know what I mean."

"Mr. Heilman, could we please see those security films?"

"Of course. Right this way."

Mr. Heilman took the group to the security office. There were multiple monitors showing the various floors in the hotel. While the cameras continually recorded, the monitors showed a random sampling. The hotel security officer was sitting in front of the monitors writing in the log.

"Alex, this is Captain Swagen, Officer Braken, and Mr. Reinholdt. We need to see the security films from the seventh floor starting at two o'clock this afternoon," said Mr. Heilman. "Alex, as usual, whatever you see or hear goes no further than this room. Do you understand?"

"Yes, sir. I'll have that in a moment. I'll put it through this monitor," he said gesturing towards the one to his left.

He fast forwarded it until there was some action. As they watched, they saw men totally clothed in black come onto the floor from the stairwell. They converged on Michael's room where one gained entry using the keycard. After they disappeared into the room, Mr. Heilman asked the security officer to fast forward it until there was more activity. He stopped it as Michael got out of the elevator.

"That's Mr. Braedon," said Edgar pointing to the screen.

They watched him walk to the door and open it using his keycard. Within a few minutes, a man dressed in black opened the door, looked up and down the hallway, and motioned for the others to follow. A second man left the room and headed toward the stairwell. Then two men came out of the room carrying Michael with a bloody white hood over his head. Mr. Heilman gasped. Two more men hurried from the room to the stairwell. Then they watched a man confidently walk down the hall, turn around, and wait until the last man emerged from the room closing the door behind him. They disappeared into the stairwell.

"I'll need a copy of that recording," said Captain Swagen.

"Of course," said Mr. Heilman. "Alex, mark that to be copied."

"Yes, sir," said Alex making some notes on a piece of paper.

"Excuse me, but is the lobby also recorded?" asked Edgar.

"Yes," said Mr. Heilman. "Why?"

"The clerk told me a man came for the keycard to room 718 around two-thirty," said Edgar. "Both Mr. Braedon and I were at the office at that time."

"Would you please find the recording of the lobby?" asked Mr. Heilman.

Alex backed it up to a little before two-thirty. A distinguished man walked up to the desk. As they watched, they saw the clerk make a keycard and hand it to him. He walked out of range. They began talking amongst themselves and Alex called their attention back to the screen. The man walked back in front of the desk and left the hotel.

"There wasn't enough time for him to go upstairs and back down," said Edgar, "even if he ran up the stairs or someone held the elevator for him. And another thing I think he was in the lobby the day I checked in with Mr. Braedon. Could I see that one more time?"

"Of course," said Alex. He went back to where they started watching. He paused it when there was a good shot of the man."

"I'm sure of it," said Edgar. "He was in the lobby. I remember because there were only two people. The other was an older woman with her bags, waiting for a ride."

"Mr. Reinholdt, I'll check with the clerk that was on duty when you registered. Maybe he'll remember seeing him, too," said Mr. Heilman picking up a pen and writing in a little notebook.

"When did you check in, Mr. Reinholdt?" asked Alex.

"Yesterday morning around nine," said Edgar.

"Now, Alex, could you please find the recording that would show where the man went?" asked Mr. Heilman.

Within minutes, Alex had the recording cued. They watched the man walk into the range of the camera and go to the stairwell, open the door and put the keycard into a hand covered with a black glove. He then turned and walked out of range again.

"Where does the stairwell lead?" asked Captain Swagen.

"To all of the floors including the basement and to the back parking lot," said Mr. Heilman. "You can get out, but you can't get in."

"Are those doors also on closed circuit?" asked Captain Swagen.

"Yes. We're very conscientious of our guests' safety," said Mr. Heilman emphatically.

Alex quickly found the recording from that camera. The door opened from the inside and seven men entered. He fast forwarded it until the time when Michael was taken. The door once again opened and two men exited, one waved madly. A dark blue panel van backed up to the door. The two men opened the back doors and climbed in. Two men carried Michael out of the door and handed him over to the men in the van. They dragged him into the back. The others climbed in and closed the door. The van drove off. Edgar sat there with his head in his hands.

"Oh my God, that was supposed to be me," said Edgar staring at what was happening on the monitor. "That was supposed to be me."

"Mr. Reinholdt, why don't you let one of us take you home," said Captain Swagen. "There's nothing you can do here."

"Thank you. I'd appreciate that. I only wish at least one of Mr. Braedon's partners could've seen those films."

"If they want to see them, they can certainly contact my office," said Captain Swagen, "and we'll make arrangements."

"Thank you. I'll let them know."

"There will definitely be an investigation," said Captain Swagen to Mr. Heilman. "From what we've seen, it's obvious that Mr. Braedon has been kidnapped. I need you to compile a list of people who were working as well as those who were staying as guests on the floor. I'll also need copies of each of those security sections we just watched."

"I'll take care of everything immediately. Alex, please make copies of all those for Captain Swagen."

"Yes, sir," said Alex and then he addressed the Captain. "Captain Swagen, will you be waiting for these copies?"

"I'll send an officer for them in about an hour. Will that give you enough time?"

"Yes, sir."

The four men went back to Mr. Heilman's office. There, Captain Swagen outlined for him what to expect during the next several days. Mr. Heilman assured Captain Swagen that he and his staff would cooperate fully with any request the police might have. Once they had finished, the men walked out to the lobby. As they were getting ready to leave, Alex came running after them.

"Mr. Reinholdt, I'm glad I caught you," he said. "You forgot your envelope."

Edgar started to say something but caught Alex's look."

"Thank you. I would've been looking for these contracts later. Officer Braken, would you please drop me off at my office. I almost forgot I have some work to finish."

Once safely inside Building Number One, Edgar opened the envelope and took out the contents. Amid blank sheets of papers, he found five DVDs marked Lobby 1, Lobby 2, Hallway, Parking Lot, and Check-in with a post-it-note on it, *"I think you're right."* Edgar smiled.

"Thank you, Alex," he said quietly.

He made a note in his day planner to find a suitable thank you gift for the young gentleman when this was all over. Then he set to work making copies to send to Pierre.

With the news about Michael, no one left the office. Almost two hours passed before the phone rang.

"Edgar, anything new?" asked Pierre.

"I just came from the hotel with the police. I don't know how to tell you this. We were able to confirm that Michael has been taken. They have it all recorded. The police have asked for copies of the security recordings."

"There's no doubt?"

"No doubt at all. I watched the films myself."

"Nothing has reached the news or the internet as yet."

"Perhaps it's too soon. He was taken sometime after three o'clock. The police will be able to figure the exact time once they look at the recordings again."

"Any idea who did it?"

"None at all. The only thing is, Pierre, the man who came to get the keycard this afternoon I could swear was in the lobby the morning Michael and I checked in. The manager is going to ask the clerk who was on duty. Pierre, I'm so sorry about this. It should've been me. You have no idea how I feel."

"Edgar, this isn't your fault."

"I just can't help feeling responsible. Listen, I'm sending the contracts overnight so you'll have them by morning. Please open them immediately and make sure I've signed them all correctly."

"Edgar, the contracts can wait. Really they can."

"No, Pierre, I want to get them to you right away…before anything else happens and they get misplaced. Remember. Open them immediately."

"I'll do that."

"Immediately."

"Immediately, Edgar. I promise."

Laura looked at the clock in the kitchen for the tenth time. She was certain she told Gina she was cooking and they were invited to dinner. It was unlike them not to call to say they'd be late. Michael hadn't called either. She shrugged her shoulders, looked around and decided to finish dinner.

When the doorbell finally rang, she hurried to answer it. Usually they arrived two at a time, but when she opened the door, they were all there.

"Come in, I thought maybe you had forgotten," she said. "Dinner's ready." She looked around at their faces, shut the door, and followed them into the living room. "Has anyone heard from Michael? I thought he'd have called by now."

Almost collectively their heads went down and she could hear deep breaths being inhaled and exhaled. Several of the men put their hands in their pockets and nervously shuffled their feet.

"What's wrong?" she asked looking from one to the other. There was a sudden sense of fear in her voice. "Tell me…now."

Angelique told her the story with all of the details of the note and Gabrielle's shock. In her mind she struggled over how to tell her the rest. The last thing she wanted to do was alarm Laura or be cruel.

"Is Edgar alright?" asked Laura with her hand against her chest.

"Yes," said Angelique.

"Michael told me Edgar didn't like his room and so they switched," said Laura. "I'm really glad Edgar's alright. Are you ready to eat? We can talk about this at the table."

"In a moment," said Angelique touching Laura's arm. "Why don't you sit down?"

"I'm fine," said Laura. "Is there something else?"

"Yes," said Angelique.

"Go on," said Laura looking her in the eyes.

"There's no easy way to tell you this," said Angelique. "Laura, Michael's missing."

"What do you mean missing?"

"Laura, he's been kidnapped," said Paul and everyone cast a glare at him.

"Actually, they came to take Edgar, but took Michael by mistake," said Angelique.

"Wait a minute," said Laura shaking her head. "Who took Michael?"

"We don't know," said Gina.

"What's being done?" asked Laura looking around at the faces of Michael's closest friends, that journalistic side of her coming through.

"Edgar notified the authorities and an investigation is underway in Frankfurt," said Henri. "That's why we were late. We were waiting for Edgar to call with more information."

"I've also notified the authorities in Paris as well as the United States," said Pierre. "They assure us they'll be working with the law enforcement agencies in Germany."

"Has there been any contact with the kidnappers?" asked Laura.

"Aside from the note to Gabrielle, we've heard nothing," said Angelique.

"How was she supposed to contact them?" asked Laura.

"The note said she was to do what she was told," said Pierre.

"Now it's a waiting game," said Paul.

Laura stood stunned. She and Michael decided there was no reason for her to go with him. He planned to pack his days with visits to Edgar's facilities and there'd be little time for anything social. Besides, her time could best be spent working on the wedding plans. Her mind was going in all different directions.

"Laura, are you alright?" asked Gina.

"Yes," said Laura focusing once again on what they were saying. "Could this be a mistake? Could someone else be missing and not Michael?"

"There's no trace of Michael," said Pierre. "He hasn't contacted Edgar, the office, or you. There's been no activity on his accounts and he's not booked on any flight anywhere. Edgar says they have proof that Michael has been taken. They just don't know who did it."

Laura stood perfectly still and silent. Suddenly she caught a whiff of the aroma from the kitchen. "Oh dear God," she said, "my dinner's going to be ruined."

"I'll help you," said Brigit getting up and following her to the kitchen.

"I thought she'd be more upset than this," said Robert.

"She is upset," said Nicole. "Just because she's not wailing and screaming doesn't mean she's not upset."

In a few minutes, Brigit came from the kitchen. "Dinner's ready," she said.

The mood at the table was somber. Any attempt at trivial conversation seemed to fizzle. Laura pushed her food around her plate with her fork more than she ate. Unless someone was talking directly to her, she was in her own world…a world where her heart was breaking…a world where Michael was missing. After dinner the couples left one by one. Pierre and Margo were the last ones to leave.

"Laura," said Margo, "why don't you come home with us."

"No, thank you, I'm fine. I want to be here in case Michael calls or comes home. I don't want him to worry if he comes home and I'm not here."

"Then let me stay here with you," said Margo.

"No, really, I'll be fine."

"If you need any of us for anything, call us, please," said Pierre. "We'll be here right away."

"Thank you," she said as she walked them to the door.

After they left, she locked the door and stood with her back against it for a few minutes. She looked up and said a silent prayer and then closed her eyes. *Lord, please make this all have been a mistake. Please let him come through the door right now.*

Laura walked into Michael's office and sat at his desk. She made a list of anyone she could think of who might possibly be able to help. She opened the top right drawer and took out her address book. She looked and found as many phone numbers as she could. Now she knew the importance of all the connections she had cultivated over the years.

Laura looked at the clock on the desk. *It's still early in the States. Someone has to know something.* One by one she called each of the names on the list and asked them for help. Every one of the calls ended the same way. All of them 'wished there was some way to help, but their hands were tied.' When she was done calling, she sent follow-up emails. Even though she got the answer she knew she'd get, she refrained from sending the reply she wanted to send...the one that would've told them exactly what she thought of them at that instant, where they could go, and what they could do with themselves when they got there.

"Fuck you all! I certainly hope none of you ever finds yourself in this position," she said looking down at the list of names she had just called and emailed, "If by some chance you do and you have the unmitigated nerve to use your power for your own gain, I will drag your name through the mud. I will make your life a living hell...even more than mine is right now. You will rue the day you ever said no to me or anyone else."

She was so angry words couldn't even describe it. She meant every word she just uttered and then some. Someday she knew she'd find herself coming face to face with those people on that paper and it'd be them who'd feel uneasy.

"I hope I get the chance to see every one of you bastards squirm."

Laura turned out the lights knowing she had done everything she could tonight. She changed into something comfortable, sat on the side of the bed, and gently got under the covers. She reached over to Michael's side, grabbed his pillow, held it close, and sobbed.

Chapter Six

Michael awakened in the back of the van, heard talking, but understood nothing. He tried to move his hands and realized his arms were tied behind him. It was pitch dark and he opened his eyes wider and tried to focus. He moved his head slightly and could feel the cloth covering his head. With every turn and bump he jerked around. His head pounded. He tried to remember what happened. He remembered meeting with Edgar and coming back to the hotel. He slowly walked through his actions in his mind; opening the hotel room door and walking in…then nothing. *How long have I been out? Where am I? What's this all about?*

As much as he wanted to know the answer, his head hurt too much to even care right now. He closed his eyes and drifted off to sleep.

When he woke again, he was being carried out of the van and into a building. The hinges of the door creaked as it opened and he was tossed inside. Then the door was slammed closed and locked. He lay there listening, trying to decide whether anyone was in the room with him. It was deadly silent. He started thinking about what was happening and his thoughts turned to the others who found themselves in this situation. *It can't be. This has to be a bad dream. I'm going to wake up soon and find myself lying next to Laura.*

Somehow, he knew that wasn't the case. He was in real trouble and no one knew where he was. He didn't dare utter anything. He heard the key in the lock and the hinges creak again as the door opened. His heart started to race. Hands grabbed him and made him kneel. The hood was removed and the bright lights blinded him. He squinted and looked around to see he was in a bare room with a simple wooden floor. Everyone in the room was wearing, long robes with cinctures and boots. He felt the butt of a gun at his ribs.

"Good morning, Michael Braedon," said the leader. "Why were you going into Mr. Reinholdt's room?"

"It was my room," said Michael somewhat confused.

The man brought the gun butt hard into his ribs. Michael gasped in pain and doubled over. A guard grabbed his hair and pulled him up.

"The registry said it was Mr. Reinholdt's room, not Mr. Braedon's," said the leader angrily. "Why?"

"Mr. Reinholdt didn't like the other room, so we traded," Michael said breathily.

"I see," said the leader bringing the volume of his voice down. "Did you tell the front desk?"

"No."

The man brought the gun butt down on Michael's shoulder. Again Michael gasped and doubled over. A man pulled him up by his hair.

"Why not, Mr. Braedon?"

"We thought it was a simple change and didn't need to bother anyone with it."

The man took the gun butt and rammed Michael in the stomach.

"Does it still seem like a simple change?"

"No," Michael said hardly audibly.

The man grabbed Michael by the hair and pulled his head back. The leader walked up to Michael and put a knife to his throat. Michael could see the knife blade glistening from the lights.

"I could kill you right now. I have that power over you, Mr. Braedon," said the leader through clenched teeth. "I have the power to kill you or allow you to live. Do you want to die Mr. Braedon?"

"No." said Michael.

The leader pressed the knife harder against Michael's throat. "Perhaps, Mr. Braedon, I may just let you live for now...until I'm tired of you," said the leader. "Or perhaps I'll just kill you a little at a time." He looked Michael straight in the eyes trying to find the fear in him. He lowered the knife slightly and addressed him again, his eyes glaring. "Why didn't Mr. Reinholdt come back to the hotel?"

"He had to go home to help his wife with something."

The leader gestured and the man holding Michael let go of his hair, pushed him over on his side and kicked him multiple times in the back.

"Kneel, Mr. Braedon," commanded the leader and pointed to a spot on the floor directly in front of him.

Michael tried to move, to back away. Two of the other men grabbed him, raised him to a kneeling position, and dragged him to the spot in front of the leader.

"Bow to me, Mr. Braedon," said the leader with disdain.

Michael remained firm. The leader grabbed his hair and pulled him down until his head cracked against the floor.

"You will learn," said the leader. "Yes, Mr. Braedon, you will learn."

He let go of Michael and motioned to the others. They dropped Michael on the floor, kicked him, and followed the leader out the door.

Michael lay in a fetal position. His mind began to wander. *What do they want? Why did they want to know about Edgar? How did they know which room Edgar had? Who are they?*

Michael's thoughts turned to Laura. Did she know? Did she know how much he loved her? What was he going to do if he never got to see her again?

He knew beyond a doubt that this was real. Somehow he had to get hold of everything. He needed to straighten out his thoughts, think clearly, and find some way to get out of this mess. Right now his mind was so jumbled he couldn't make sense of anything. He closed his eyes trying to block the pain. He knew this was just the beginning.

The office was plainly decorated. Only the necessities were there. The floor was wooden and the walls made of a sort of stucco. The oversized old-fashioned metal desk separated the leader from the followers who were seated on old desk chairs.

"How could this have happened?" asked the leader raising his voice and slapping his sword against the top of the desk. "Did our contact not check on the room arrangements personally?"

"Yes, sir, he did," said Sadik getting the courage to speak. "He heard the desk clerk assign Mr. Reinholdt and Mr. Braedon their rooms."

"Are you certain that he heard correctly?"

"Yes, sir," said Sadik. "He checked the registry himself, as soon as the clerk went to the back."

"Sir, he went up to the floor immediately after and saw Mr. Reinholdt come out of Mr. Braedon's room and go to his," said Gehran. "He even walked down the hallway and saw Mr. Braedon sitting in his room and heard him talking on the phone. He was very thorough."

"Then," said the leader walking and coming to a stop right in front of Gehran, "how do you explain Mr. Braedon in that room and not Mr. Reinholdt?"

"Sir, you heard Mr. Braedon say that they switched rooms," said Qadir trying to get the leader's attention away from Gehran. "They must have switched rooms after he had done all the checking. No one would expect them to change rooms."

"Why would this happen?" asked the leader looking up. He raised his hands in the air. "Why would the Divine One do this?"

"The Divine One has his reasons," said Sadik softly and calmly. "You know that, sir. You of all should know. After all, you are the Chosen One. You are the leader of the Faith."

"Yes, Sadik, I am," said the leader calming slightly. He paused to reflect on that thought. He was indeed the leader, the Chosen One. "Sometimes the Divine One's ways do not show his reasons clearly at first."

"Yes, sir," said Sadik, "that is why we must have faith."

"We could still take Mr. Reinholdt, if you want," said Qadir trying to appease the Chosen One. Qadir knew what the Chosen One could do if things did not go his way and he did not want to see a display of his wrath against any of those present.

"That would not be wise," said the Chosen One shaking his head. "Not wise at all." He turned and walked over to a wall covered with pictures and maps. He tapped the picture of Mr. Reinholdt. "He will be very watchful now. Mr. Reinholdt is a very intelligent man. He will soon know that Mr. Braedon was taken and will notify the authorities. Any attempt to get Mr. Reinholdt right now could prove disastrous."

"Sir, perhaps Mr. Reinholdt will negotiate for Mr. Braedon's release," said Gehran trying to salvage the operation.

The Chosen One walked back to Gehran and looked him in the eyes once again. Gehran sat perfectly still and did not turn his gaze away from the Chosen One.

"Perhaps, Gehran, perhaps," said the Chosen One. He walked back behind his desk. "If not, we will have to find new ways of getting what we want. Make no mistake, we will get what we want," he said hitting his fist against the desk. "No one will stop us!"

"Yes, sir," said Gehran calmly. "We will get everything we need. The Divine One will see to it."

"Yes, Gehran, the Divine One will see to it," said the Chosen One sitting calmly in his chair. "And, we will use Mr. Braedon. Perhaps, when his family and Mr. Reinholdt witness how we deal with him, they will be all too eager to part with our prize."

Laura awoke to the sun shining through the bedroom window. She was still holding onto Michael's pillow. She could smell him on it, almost feel him beside her, holding her, but he wasn't there and he wasn't going to be. Maybe he never would.

Every time she thought about him, her heart ached and her eyes welled up. She looked at the ring on her hand, the one he had given her when he proposed. With that ring, he promised to marry her. Somehow, someway she knew he'd keep that promise. She gently put Michael's pillow on his side and got out of bed.

"Laura Darmer," she said aloud, "you have to get hold of yourself. You're not going to get anywhere if you resort to crying. Something has to be done…and you know that no one who has the power to do it is going to do anything. They told you so last night…those bastards!"

It was time to pick herself up and do something, anything. She walked over to the dresser to get her clothes and looked in the mirror.

"Now, what're you going to do about it? You have to find some way to bring Michael back. You know that and somehow you'll find the answer. Now, pull yourself together and think."

Laura looked one more time at her reflection, picked up her clothes and went to shower.

"Maybe a nice shower will help me think a little more clearly," she said aloud. It seemed to make her feel better to hear her own voice.

All the time she was showering, she thought about everything she and Michael had talked about over the past few days. Was there any clue in what he said to her, any reason whatsoever that someone would want to take him and from a hotel in Frankfurt of all places? She diligently went through the conversations, but hard as she tried, the only thing she could recall was talking about the wedding and how much he loved her.

If it wasn't personal, it had to be business. That was the only answer that made sense. And if it was business the only ones who could possibly know the answers would be Michael's partners and the logical place to start was at the office.

The atmosphere at Global Connections Consulting felt different when Pierre walked into the office. There was an ominous feeling. He walked up to the desk and didn't even have a chance to greet Lizbeth before she handed him an envelope.

"Mr. Reinholdt called to remind you to open the package immediately and look over the contracts," she said.

"He's really insistent about looking at the contracts," said Pierre looking at the envelope.

"Very insistent," she said. "Have you heard anything else?"

"Not a word."

"Everyone's waiting in the conference room."

"Thanks, Lizbeth. Hold the calls unless they're directly related to Michael."

"Yes, sir."

They were deep in conversation when Pierre came in the room. George leaned back on his chair and yawned. Monique poured another cup of coffee and sat back down. Robert was busy checking different sites on the internet.

"Did anyone get a good night's sleep?" asked Pierre sitting down next to his wife Margo.

"No," they said almost in unison.

D. A. Walters

"The package from Edgar arrived and he's insistent that it be opened immediately," said Pierre holding the envelope for them to see. "He even called again this morning."

"What could be so important about these contracts that we have to take care of them right away?" asked Jacques.

"I have no idea," said Pierre as he opened the envelope. He reached in and pulled out a stack of papers. "These aren't contracts. They're nothing but blank sheets of paper," he said leafing through page after page of blank paper. Finally, he came to a paper with the words *Watch These*. He removed the paper and found five DVDs.

"What are these?" he asked as he sorted through the DVDs; "Lobby 1, Lobby 2, Hallway, Parking Lot, Check-in. They must be in this order for a reason."

Pierre walked over and handed the five DVDs to Robert. He took the first one, put it in the computer, and projected it. As it was about to start, the door opened and Laura walked in.

"How are you?" asked Margo getting up and giving her a hug.

"About as good as all of you are from the looks of you," said Laura. "What're you doing?"

"Edgar sent five DVDs with a note saying 'Watch These,'" said Pierre.

She took Michael's seat next to Pierre.

"Let's watch," she said.

"That must be the man who asked for a keycard to Edgar's room," said Henri.

They watched him go off screen.

"Where did he go?" asked Gina. She got up, curled her leg underneath, and sat back down.

Then they saw him come right back past the desk and leave the hotel.

"What floor did you say they were on, Pierre?" asked Paul.

"Seventh," said Pierre.

"There's no way he had time to go to the seventh floor and back down," said Jean.

Robert took the disc out and put in Lobby 2. They saw the man walk to the stairwell and open the door. A gloved hand reached out and took the keycard from him. Then he turned around and walked out of range.

"Who is he and why did he do that?" asked Laura shifting in her seat.

"After we watch these," said Pierre to Robert, "see if you can get a really good still picture of him and print it."

"Not a problem. Are you ready for the Hallway?"

"Yes," said Laura.

They watched as the kidnappers came from the stairwell and entered Michael's room. Robert fast forwarded it until they saw Michael getting off the elevator. They watched as he used his keycard to open the door and walk in. Within minutes, they saw him being carried out; his hands and legs tied and a bloodied hood over his head. The group watched in horror as he was carried into the stairwell. Laura sat there with her hand over her mouth.

"Laura, are you alright?" asked Monique.

Laura nodded. Robert took out the Hallway and put in the parking lot. They watched as the outside door opened and the men loaded Michael into the van and drove away. The group sat there speechless.

"As Edgar said, there's no doubt that Michael has been taken," said Raquel. "The key to who did it seems to be the man…if he even knows."

"Why did he include the one marked Check-in," asked Gina picking up the disc.

"Edgar thinks the man who asked for the keycard was in the lobby the day they checked in," said Pierre.

"Let's see," said Robert.

The resemblance was uncanny.

"I'll make some good prints," said Robert. "I think Edgar's right."

"Definitely," said Raquel. "I wonder if he was a guest at the hotel or just someone posing as one."

The door to the conference room opened and Lizbeth came in without knocking.

"Ladies and gentlemen you need to look at the internet."

She walked over to the computer and put in the web address. Laura gave a cry. There was Michael kneeling, hands and feet tied. One captor had the gun butt at his chest. It was evident from the way he was kneeling that he was in a great deal of pain.

"Mr. Braedon, you tried to trick me, did you not?" asked the Chosen One. "No one tricks me, do they?"

The captor hit Michael in the chest and Michael gasped and doubled over. Laura's hands trembled and tears trickled down her cheeks. Jean got up out of his chair, walked over to Laura, and put his hands on her shoulders.

"I will get what I want one way or another," said the Chosen One looking into the camera. "Mr. Reinholdt, you may think you are safe because you escaped me, but you are not. I give you my word that I will get what I want. Will I not, Mr. Braedon?"

The Chosen One grabbed Michael's hair and shook his head up and down.

"See, Mr. Reinholdt, even Mr. Braedon has seen the light."

He let go of Michael's hair.

"Bow to me, Mr. Braedon."

Michael knelt upright. The Chosen One grabbed Michael's hair and pulled his head down until it hit the ground. The entire group jumped as they heard the crack.

"You will learn to respect me."

The screen went blank and Laura sobbed so hard her shoulders shook.

"Why are they doing this?" she asked through her tears. "They don't even want him. They want Edgar. Why don't they just ask for what they want and give him back?"

"That's not what they do," said Jean as he knelt beside her chair and put his arm around her.

"How do you fight against something and someone you don't know?" asked Brigit.

"There's no reason why, no logical reason at all," said Paul. "None of this makes any sense."

"Listen!" said Henri. "No one's even on the same conversation. We need to focus." He waited until he knew he had everyone's attention. "Look, my friends, if we're going find Michael, it's going to take one hell of a lot of research."

"Where the hell do you propose we start?" asked George with a tinge of attitude. "You can't just Google terrorist and find them listed."

"No, but we start with what we have and follow up on everything no matter how slim it seems to be," said Henri pointing to the image on the wall. "Scrutinize every part of every picture, every word Michael's captor uttered, everything Edgar's found out. Don't let up. If something doesn't make sense and you think something's missing, push until you get the answer you need."

"Robert," said Laura, "could you make a copy of everything for me? I want it all, no matter how useless it may seem. I'll take the time and do whatever needs done to get Michael back."

"I'll do that," he said. "No matter what we find, we need to share it. Fifteen pairs of eyes are definitely better than one."

"First of all, what we just watched wasn't the whole thing," said Margo. "There has to be more. Michael looked too beat up and in too much pain for this to be the first interrogation with them. There has to be a previous one. I want to see it all. It's like coming in during the middle of the movie and not seeing the beginning. You miss the important stuff. Someone online has to have it. Find it!"

Chapter Seven

Michael lay in the room trying to think of anything but what was happening. He had no trouble remembering everything that happened before this trip. He could even recall what he ate the morning he left for Frankfurt. He could remember everything up to that point when he concentrated, but every time he let his mind wander, he'd wind up on one subject, Laura.

Michael heard the key in the lock and froze in mid thought. The door opened and a woman came in carrying a large tray. On the tray was a porcelain water basin, torn cloths, a white towel, a jar of salve, a white ceramic cup, a pitcher of water, and bread. She and the guard helped Michael to a sitting position. She took the jug of water, opened it, and poured some into the cup. She put the cup to his lips and told him to drink. Michael drank, a little at a time. She fed him the bread, a small piece at a time. When he was finished, she bathed him and put salve on his wounds.

She leaned closely to him and whispered quietly so no one else would hear. "Answer respectfully, talk nicely, do what they say, and it will be alright."

Michael looked puzzled.

"What does he want?" he whispered back, his voice raspy.

"Your respect," she said not missing a motion in what she was doing. "He must have your respect."

"Why did he take me?" Michael asked.

"Remember," she said looking him in the eyes, "why is not as important as how you speak to him."

She continued to make sure his needs were met. She took her time and he relaxed as he listened to her speak.

"How do I address him?" asked Michael. "I don't even know his name."

"His name is not important to you," she said. "Address him as you would anyone you would show great respect." She smiled at him. "Do you understand?"

"Yes," Michael whispered.

She folded the cloths, carefully closed the salve, and placed the pitcher back on the tray. She stood up, picked up the tray and walked to the door. She knocked on the door, the guard opened it and she left.

Laura walked into Michael's office. She stopped just inside the door and looked around, then walked over to his desk and sat in his chair. On the desk were pictures of her, of them. She picked one up and ran her fingers over the glass and clutched it close. It brought back memories of the day it was taken.

"Oh, Michael, I love you so much," she whispered as the tears came to her eyes. She looked at their picture. "I don't know what to do. I can't bear to see them hurt you. I can't bear to even think about it."

She put the picture down where it belonged, pulled the chair closer to the desk, and turned on his computer. When the password screen came up, she put it in. She looked at all the icons on his desktop and found a folder marked Laura. She clicked on it and there were hundreds of pictures of them. She set it to show the pictures one after the other and leaned back into his chair and just watched as the pictures changed. Somehow it made her feel closer to him. There were all of the memories coming to life before her eyes. She knew there were many more she wanted to make with him. Right now, she watched and remembered.

Time seemed to be suspended and Laura didn't even hear the knock on the door. Lizbeth opened the door slightly and peeked in. She walked over to the desk.

"Excuse me, Laura," she said quietly. "There's a call from Mark."

"Thanks, Lizbeth."

Laura picked up the receiver.

"Mark?"

"Laura, how are you?"

"Numb. How are you?"

"I'm in a fucking nightmare. I called everyone I could think of to try to help get him back."

"You got the same answer didn't you?"

"We don't negotiate with terrorists."

"I know," said Laura, "I tried last night, too."

"You can bet your life if it was one of theirs they'd be doing whatever it takes to get him back," said Mark with venom in his voice.

"But he's not one of theirs, is he?" said Laura. "He's just a number, a nine digit number."

"It makes me so damn mad."

"I know. I was really nice on the phone, but when I hung up, those four, five, and seven-letter words were flying everywhere," said Laura. "God forbid it ever happens to one of theirs and those bastards do something. I'll cause such a media nightmare for them that they'll wish it was them instead of their loved one."

"Laura, I know you would."

"They make me sick."

"Listen, I've contacted all of our U.S. and foreign offices and told them to be alert for anything that might remotely be related. I also told them that starting immediately the doors are to be locked and all visitors are to be buzzed in."

"Good, they need to be on their guard," said Laura. "There's no telling what these people might do."

"I want the offices secured. I don't want anything happening to our first line personnel like Maggie and Lizbeth."

"I agree, Mark," said Laura. "Do what you think is best. For me it would be a security officer at the door and new locks."

"Not bad ideas," said Mark.

"Then do it," she said. "You know your brother wouldn't even think twice about spending the money to protect everyone.

"You're right," said Mark. "I just wish I knew what the hell they wanted."

"Mark, I have no idea. That's why I want to go to Frankfurt," said Laura. "I want to go to the hotel. I want answers and I think it might be best to start at what I think is the beginning."

"I don't want you going alone," said Mark. "Gwen and I are coming to Paris and then the three of us will go to Frankfurt. I want answers, too. I don't understand how something like this could happen. Let me make the arrangements to get to Paris and then call you back."

"Listen, take care of the security. I'd feel awful if something happened to anyone else."

Laura put down the phone, took one last look at the computer before shutting it down.

"That's enough wallowing," she said aloud to herself. "You need to do something constructive."

She left Michael's office and walked down the hall. When she came to Margo's office, the door was open, so she knocked on the frame.

"Come in."

"Hey, Margo, sorry to interrupt. I just got off the phone with Mark. He and Gwen are coming. They'll probably be here tomorrow. Then the three of us are going to Frankfurt."

"I'm glad they're coming. We can call Edgar so he can arrange for you to get access into the hotel rooms," she said looking up from what she was doing. "Pierre should be able to do that, but I also think someone else from here should go, too."

"That's good," said Laura. "Mark said he contacted all the offices and told them to be on alert. He wants to change things so clients are buzzed in."

"I didn't think of security," said Margo.

"I didn't either until he mentioned it. I told him I'd change the locks and get a security guard for the door."

"Laura, we have to protect our staff," she said. "We can't put them in danger."

"Exactly," said Laura.

Margo picked up the phone while she was still talking. "I'll take care of this right now."

"Yes, Margo," said Lizbeth.

"Lizbeth, please get in touch with the locksmith we used last month and ask him when he can come to meet with me and also that security firm we use for our functions. I'd like to meet with the head of that firm as soon as possible, too."

"I'll do that immediately."

All the while Margo was talking Laura looked down at a paper with a list of dates. "What're you working on?" she asked when Margo was through.

"I've been researching the other hostage situations."

"Find anything interesting?"

"There are a lot of similarities," said Margo with her hands on her hips, "but in the others, the perpetrators were the same. In this one with Michael, they seem to be different." She stopped and looked at Laura. "I think we're dealing with an entirely different group. Even the room seems to be different. The rhetoric is definitely different. Come and see."

The two of them sat in front of the computer and started to compare footage. Margo pointed out all of the things she had found. Laura was amazed at how much she had done in such a short time.

"Can we have some still shots made?" Laura asked.

"You know Robert can do anything when it comes to this stuff," Margo said and she picked up the phone.

"Yes, Margo."

"Lizbeth, could you please ask Robert to come to my office?"

"Right away. Margo, both Mr. Billings, the locksmith and Mr. Hurley, the head of the security firm will be here in an hour. I thought it would be better if they were both here together."

"That's excellent, Lizbeth," said Margo. "Please let me know when they arrive."

A few minutes later, Robert came through the door. Anytime Margo sent for him, it had something to do with a computer. Margo was so exceptionally bright, but when it came to computers, she had absolutely no patience.

"You need something?" asked Robert.

"You know me so well," said Margo smiling. "We need some still shots."

"Not a problem," said Robert "Why do you need them?"

"I think we're dealing with a new group of terrorists," said Margo looking up at him from her chair. "From what I can see, no one's the same in Michael's abduction as in the other kidnappings."

"Where did you find all this?" he asked.

"On the internet," said Margo. "There's just so much out there."

"I'm impressed," said Robert.

"If you think that's impressive, look at this," she said and she clicked onto a file folder she made. Inside were other folders each dated and containing a different video she found.

"Wow!" said Robert.

"See," said Margo. "I do listen."

Margo got up from her chair and allowed Robert to sit down. He sent the files over to his computer so he could work on them. Before long the rest of the partners had filtered into Margo's office and were looking to see what she found.

"Why don't we put a copy of everything we have in the room with the magnetic boards" said Jacques, "displayed and spread out so that whenever we have time, we can go in and look at what we have? You never know what might stand out some time that you didn't see before."

"There's a computer in there, too," said Robert.

"I'd like to help with that," said Laura. "I need to do something."

"Let me show you the room," said Gina.

"I'll bring the pictures as soon as I'm finished," said Robert.

"Robert, could you isolate this area on this shirt?" asked Margo pointing to a spot on a picture. Robert moved closer to the screen, looked, and then made a note of what Margo wanted.

"It looks like an insignia," said Margo. "Make it as large and clear as you can."

The guard entered the room with a tray. Michael watched him as he set it down near him. The woman followed the guard through the door, sat down in front of Michael, and began feeding him again. Her manner was calming and peaceful. She had an air of kindness about her.

"Remember what I have told you," she whispered coming very close to him. "You must show him respect."

"Yes," Michael whispered.

"I know it is hard, but he holds your life in his hands."

Michael nodded.

"No matter how hard it is," she said, "answer the best you can and address him with respect."

"I don't know what he wants."

"You will."

The guard stayed near the door. The woman didn't say much and Michael reasoned it was because of the guard's presence. She busied herself in her task and when finished, she picked up the tray, and the guard let her out.

This time, the guard stayed and locked the door with both him and Michael inside. He knew the guard was not one of the men who had inflicted any sort of punishment on him, yet his presence made Michael wary. The guard walked across the floor and then sat down across from Michael.

"What do you do?" the guard asked without so much as an introduction.

Michael looked at him very hesitantly.

"I'm a consultant for companies," said Michael.

"What do you do for the companies?"

"When they have problems that need solved or want to do something else with their business, they call my company for help."

"Why were you with Mr. Reinholdt?"

"My company was doing some work for Mr. Reinholdt and I came to Germany to see what his operations were like," said Michael. Now his curiosity was peaked. "How do you know Mr. Reinholdt?"

"Mr. Reinholdt's company has invented something that is of extreme importance to the Chosen One."

"Do you know what Mr. Reinholdt's company has invented?"

"I do not know," said the guard. "I only know that the Chosen One is in great need of it."

Michael looked at the guard, trying to figure out why he was taking time to talk to him. Obviously it wasn't just to make simple conversation.

"Did you find what you wanted to know?" asked the guard.

"I did get a lot of information, but I know I wasn't finished yet. There were still places I needed to see and people I needed to talk to."

The guard got up without another word and walked towards the door. He unlocked it, went out, and locked it again behind him. Michael sat staring at the door. He knew now beyond a shadow of a doubt that the reason he was taken was because of Edgar and something he had invented. Michael was sure he had no idea about what it was the Chosen One wanted or needed. He closed his eyes and tried to think about anything he had seen at Reinholdt International.

Laura worked displaying all the information on boards in the room. She separated the printed material in folders and organized it the way she thought it made the most sense.

Robert walked in sometime later with a large folder of new material. What started out as a simple request from Margo to make a few still shots became a laundry list. While Laura worked in the room, Margo compiled notes, and Robert tried to keep up with all of her requests.

"I separated everything according to individual incidents," he said handing the folder to Laura. "There's also what Margo wrote about each hostage and what their business was. She included the date they were taken and the date they were executed, released, rescued, or disappeared."

"Thanks."

"You know that person who was in the lobby when they checked in?" asked Robert. "As far as I can tell, Edgar was dead on when he said he thought the man who asked for the keycard and the man in the lobby were one and the same. Take a look."

He put both pictures down on the table in front of Laura.

"Unless they're twins, this is the same man," said Laura. "The question is why was he waiting for them in the lobby?"

"That, my dear, is the ultimate question."

"Then we need the answer."

"It's looking great in here," he said looking around at all the work Laura had done.

"I wish I knew what I was looking for."

"You will. I know you," he said. "If you need anything else, let me know."

"Thanks."

Laura worked for hours putting everything up. When she finished, she looked around the room at everything that was displayed. She started going from one picture to the other mentally matching up the men in each. She stopped, took a few minutes, made a list, and then walked out to Lizbeth's desk.

Once Lizbeth got her what she needed, Laura returned to the room. She looked at the pictures of the other hostage situations and put colored dots on people. She started comparing the first two then the second and third, until she had compared all of them. Soon she was able to match up the cast of characters. However, when it came to the situation with Michael, no one matched.

Several hours passed since Margo was in the room. Pressing business kept her occupied. There was nothing like a client emergency to put things into perspective. As soon as she had everything on an even keel once again, she went back to the room.

"What's this?" she asked looking at all of the dots on the pictures.

"When I was putting them up, I realized you were right when you said the players matched. Then when I was finished, I looked at them again and tried match them mentally. I decided it would be much better if I put the same colored dots on the same persons. There were only a couple of incidental people that didn't match," said Laura pointing to a few of the men who only appeared in one picture. "The main players stayed the same, except in Michael's. No one matches."

"This is amazing," said Margo looking at the pictures. "I recognized a few that were similar, but now it jumps right out at you."

"I know. It's really obvious now."

"With all of these other situations, someone has taken credit for doing it, always the same group," said Margo. "With Michael's, no one has come forward."

"It's as though they don't want to take the credit for this," said Laura. "I don't understand it."

"Aside from the internet broadcasts, there's been nothing," said Margo walking over to one of the first pieces pinned to the wall. "Even the note they left for Gabrielle didn't identify them."

"Whoever they are, we'll find them."

Chapter Eight

Life became a whirlwind for Mark and Gwen Braedon. They hardly had time to get home from their business trip to Sydney when the events concerning Michael came to light. It had been a very rewarding trip business-wise and it enabled them to spend time with their children and some of the other partners' children who ran the Sydney office. They were looking forward to a quiet evening at home when they were given the message to call the Paris office immediately. 'From daydream to nightmare in seconds' is how Mark would come to describe that moment.

He and Gwen spent the evening on the phone to anyone and everyone trying to get help. Needless to say, sleep was not a priority. They both knew that as soon as they could, they'd be on the next flight to Paris. Any other time, Mark would've gladly succumbed to fatigue, but not this time. He was operating on pure will. Even on the plane, when there was nothing he could do, he couldn't relax enough to sleep.

They arrived in Paris and went directly to Michael's house. Mark unlocked the door and put the luggage in the foyer. To look at him, there was no mistaking he was Michael's brother. They had the same brown eyes, dark hair, and were similar in build.

"Laura, we're here," he shouted closing the door behind him.

"Mark, Gwen, I'm so glad you're here," said Laura as she hurried into the room.

Mark hugged her and gave her a kiss. When Gwen hugged her, the two of them became very teary eyed.

"Come into the kitchen," said Laura wiping a tear from her cheek. "I made some breakfast."

"How are you doing?" asked Mark once they were seated and eating at the table.

"Alright, trying to keep busy. How about you?"

"I can't believe this is happening," said Mark. "This happens to other people, not my brother."

"I know," said Laura.

"I watch everything they send over the internet," said Mark.

"I saw the first one," said Laura, "but I just can't bear to watch."

"After we talked, I contacted the police and the FBI again. I called those senators and congressmen and they all had the same thing to say; 'The United States does not negotiate with terrorists.' When I asked them if they'd try to find Michael, they told me it would not be in the best interest of the nation to expend that kind of manpower for one man. I asked them if I could quote them."

"I bet they loved that," said Laura.

"Oh yah, they got really quiet," said Mark, "and then I read it back to them and asked them if I had it right. I was pissed and they knew it."

"Good for you," said Laura getting up and taking plates to the sink. "Their answer to us matches exactly what the families of the other hostages have said."

"I tried to be objective about their position. Looking back on the other hostage situations, I admit I sort of understood it when it was someone else," said Gwen, "but now that it's one of our own, it's a little hard to take."

"I know," said Laura turning around and facing them, "and I'm not letting them off the hook either. I send them an email every day...not a form email, but a personal one. They may not do anything, but they sure as hell will know who Michael Braedon is and that I'm holding them accountable for his well-being."

"Good for you," said Gwen getting up to help.

"We created a room at the office with everything in it. You should see it," said Laura getting another cup of coffee and sitting back at the table.

"I'd like to," said Mark. "I brought some things you and the others might find interesting."

"Really," said Laura.
"Really," said Mark.
"That good?" asked Laura.
"Better…much, much better."

When Mark and Gwen walked into the room, they were overwhelmed at the amount of material that had been collected.

"You gathered all this just since you found out?" asked Mark walking around the room looking at every piece and leafing through the folders.

"Yes," said Laura. "Everyone has been working very hard."

"This is amazing," said Gwen.

"There're things you need to see," said Laura. "We have actual footage of Michael being kidnapped."

"What!" said Mark.

"Come, sit over here," she said gesturing to seats facing the only bare wall in the room. "We didn't dare say anything over the phone. I always think someone might be listening."

Robert had everything set to go. He took the time and put all the footage in order on one DVD so it was easier to access. All it took was a few clicks.

"Where did you get this?" asked Mark sitting on the edge of his seat.

"From Edgar."

"This was definitely planned," said Gwen.

"They meant to take Edgar," said Laura. "If there ever was a doubt, this settled it."

"It's amazing," said Mark. "This had to have been planned for months."

"They were looking for an opportune time and they got it," said Gwen.

"Why did they include the last part?" asked Mark.

"That was from the lobby when Edgar and Michael checked in. Edgar was almost positive that the man in the lobby was the same as the person who asked for the keycard," said Laura.

"Was he?" asked Gwen.

"You decide," said Laura as she handed them two pictures of the man.

"Incredible," said Mark.

"Who is he?" asked Gwen.

"As Robert has said, 'that, my dear, is the ultimate question,'" said Laura. "He may be the key, and then maybe he was just hired for those acts."

"That's true," said Mark.

"Now what did you bring?" asked Laura.

Mark held up an envelope. "Info about Reinholdt International I think you're going to find very interesting."

"Can I make some copies of it so we can all look at it together?"

"As long as it stays only with us and is shredded and burned as soon as we're done," said Mark very seriously.

"Shredded and burned?" asked Laura raising her eyebrows.

"This can't get out."

"Really!" said Laura. "That good?"

"Better."

Although business had to be conducted as usual, no one's mind was one hundred percent focused on company dealings. When Laura went to ask them to come to the conference room, they were all too eager for a diversion. When all were present, Laura handed out the packets of information.

"It seems Reinholdt International has developed a communication system that's so complex and so sophisticated it's made it a target for legitimate and illegitimate sources," said Mark.

"Why?" asked Pierre as he started leafing through the packet.

"It'd actually enable anyone who possessed it to control any satellite in space, any nuclear weapon, as well as listen to conversations even in a highly secured area," said Mark. "It has the ability to negate security systems currently in place, change them, assign new security codes and allow only the person who possesses the device or software to access the satellite or area."

"Wouldn't it have to have the address of the satellite?" asked Robert.

"It can detect and display exactly which satellite it is and what it does. Then it can gain access to that satellite. It literally can make the satellite give it the access code."

"Is this common knowledge?" asked Paul looking up from the papers.

"No, definitely not."

"Where did you get this information?" asked Jean.

"I have sources that keep abreast of rumors…especially those that have a potential threat to the national security of the United States," said Mark pausing for a few seconds. "This, people, is a threat to national security for every country. The United States as well as the other powers involved were interested in getting Mr. Reinholdt to suspend development of the system and destroy the plans or at least seal them so no one would be able to duplicate it."

"But if they were able to develop it once," said Angelique, "what makes you think someone won't do the same thing in the future."

"It was a freak mistake that enabled the system to be developed to this sophistication. They were merely trying to develop a more covert communication system when they stumbled upon this," said Mark. "With this system, any group, no matter how small, could bring the largest countries to their knees. Someone in the Reinholdt organization must have leaked the information that the system existed to this group. Weren't they actually targeting him?"

"Yes," said Laura, "the ransom note, the keycard, the manner they treated Michael in those first internet appearances all points to Edgar."

"If this is what they want, they'll do whatever they have to, even using Michael, to try to get to Edgar," said Mark. "Michael is nothing to them unless they think they can somehow make this mistake work."

"Do you think they'll kill him?" asked Brigit.

"I don't know," said Mark. "Michael has no idea what they're after, unless they tell him and I don't think they will."

"Where does that leave us?" asked Nicole.

"In possession of knowledge," said Mark, "but absolutely no way to do anything about the situation right now."

There was silence as the group looked over the information more carefully. Proposed on those pages was a real life Armageddon...not some farfetched author's notion.

"Why do you want to go to Frankfurt?" asked George.

"I want to see the hotel," said Mark. "I want to know how this happened. What hotel would allow just anyone to get someone else's room key? Who was their contact? Why did he do it? Maybe Frankfurt has those answers."

"That's a lot to expect," said George.

"I know, but we're never going to find the answers if we don't start somewhere," said Mark. "I also want to hear what Edgar has to say about all this."

"I agree," said Pierre. "I talked to him and told him we're coming. He's going to make the arrangements to get into the hotel room."

The Chosen One stood in the center of the room towering over Michael. In his right hand, he held a sword. There was no doubt in Michael's mind that he had every intention of using it. He could tell by the look on his face and the way the Chosen One kept slapping his left hand with it. He gestured and the guards dragged Michael to his feet. They untied his arms and held him tightly.

"Did Mr. Reinholdt know I was coming after him?" asked the Chosen One.

"I don't think so," said Michael.

The Chosen One raised the sword and swiftly slashed Michael's upper right arm. Michael gasped.

"I am not asking you what you think," said the Chosen One angrily with his eyes glaring. "I asked you; did Mr. Reinholdt know?

"He didn't say anything about someone wanting to kidnap him," said Michael.

"How much did Mr. Reinholdt pay you to change rooms?"

"He didn't pay me anything."

The Chosen One raised the sword and swiftly slashed Michael's upper left arm. Again Michael gasped.

"Who told you to change rooms?" asked the Chosen One.

"No one told me to," said Michael, his voice showing strain.

"Did Mr. Reinholdt tell you he did not like the room?"

"Yes, it was smaller than mine."

"Tell me about Mr. Reinholdt's business."

"He owns a communications company."

The Chosen One again raised the sword and swiftly slashed Michael's left forearm.

"I know he owns a communications company," the tone of his voice got angrier. "Do I look like a fool?"

"No, sir."

"Why were you with Mr. Reinholdt?" the Chosen One asked, his eyes glaring and his jaw set.

"Mr. Reinholdt was contemplating expanding his operations. He asked my company for help."

"What is Mr. Reinholdt working on?"

"He has many projects."

With that answer, the leader slashed Michael's right forearm.

"You know what I am referring to."

"Mr. Reinholdt has many projects that deal with national security."

"Now, that is better, Mr. Braedon," said the Chosen One changing the tone of his voice. Instantly, his voice registered compassion whether real or feigned. "Perhaps if you get a little rest, you will be able to elaborate a little more on some specific projects of interest."

"Yes, sir," said Michael with great restraint.

The Chosen One gestured and the screen went blank.

When the stream ended, Mark sat there with his fists clenched.

"What the hell do you want!" he screamed at the projection. "What the fuck do you want!"

"They want to know they can get to Edgar through him," said Margo calmly.

"I don't think Michael even knows what the hell they're talking about," said Mark with an edgy tone. "Hell, I didn't know the system existed until my contacts sent me the information."

"I don't think Michael knows either," said Pierre. "His life doesn't depend so much on whether or not he knows about the system, but on whether or not Edgar might negotiate for his release with the system possibly being the ransom." He looked around at his friends. "As soon as it's apparent that's not the case, is when Michael is in real jeopardy."

Laura entered the room.

"I hear Michael was on the internet again. Is he alright?" she asked hesitantly.

"He's still alive, if that's what you mean," said Mark angrily. "We need to get to Frankfurt. We need answers. We just can't sit here waiting for them to come to us."

"Clean this," said the Chosen One handing the sword to Gehran.

"Yes, sir," said Gehran taking the sword from him.

The Chosen One continued walking down the hall to his office. The length of his stride and the heaviness of his footsteps sent a clear message that he was not to be disobeyed, or questioned, especially now.

"Sadik, I need to leave for a while. No one is to go into Mr. Braedon's room except for the woman," he said and he stopped and turned to look Sadik in the eyes. "Do I make myself clear?"

"Yes, sir," said Sadik quickly.

"Ahmed!" he shouted.

"Yes, sir," said Ahmed hurrying to the Chosen One's side.

"Get in touch with the others. I want a meeting. There are things that must be done in light of these new developments."

"Yes, sir," said Ahmed. "When do you want them here?"

"Three o'clock."

"Yes, sir."

"Now, Qadir," he said quietly, "you and I will take care of a few things. Get the car."

"Yes, sir."

The Chosen One watched as each of his followers left to take care of their duties. He stood by the window and watched Ahmed drive off towards the city. Something bothered him about that man. He had a feeling; a feeling he hadn't had for many years. He knew that ignoring it could mean disaster to the Cause, to him. He wouldn't allow that to happen as he had done in the past. That was the difference between naiveté and experience.

He had learned much since those days. Now, he knew almost instinctively who he could trust and who would betray him. *Ah, Ahmed,*

I will watch you carefully. Something is not right with you. I fear your head is being filled with lies even now. Rest assured I will never allow you to come between me and victory. If it comes down to it, you will have to go.

As he was pondering the situation, Qadir brought the car. He left the office, careful to lock it before leaving the building.

The Chosen One walked out of the building across a small area. Others were busy working in the camp. He paused to look around at the activities and got into the car.

"Where are we going, sir?" asked Qadir once the Chosen One was settled.

"To a new place," said the Chosen One. "Go straight until I tell you otherwise."

They drove in the same direction for quite a distance before the Chosen One broke the silence.

"What I am going to show you, Qadir, you cannot tell anyone. Is that understood?"

"Yes, sir."

The directions took them out into the desert several miles. The entire time, the Chosen One looked in the mirror and even on occasion turned to look to both sides and behind them. When they came upon a small building, the leader told him to stop.

"Sir, if I may say," said Qadir. "We could have gotten here sooner if we would have taken a more direct route."

"True, Qadir," said the Chosen One, "but this is so important that I did not want to take the chance of anyone guessing where we were going."

"Yes, sir."

"So Qadir, I want you to keep that in mind. You must always be careful that no one is following you when you leave camp. You must also make sure that no one begins following you at any other time. If that should happen, you are to go elsewhere and not here. You must make them feel that wherever you stop is your destination."

"Yes, sir," said Qadir, a little confused by this new bit of clandestine activity.

"You will understand soon, Qadir," said the Chosen One.

They got out and walked to the building. The Chosen One unlocked the door and they went inside. It was a very simple building with only two main rooms. Qadir looked around. There were two desks in the first room and several chairs. Along the walls were outlets and ports for phones. The Chosen One opened the next door to his office. It was modestly furnished with everything necessary for him to run his operations.

His desk had been placed near one wall and in front of it were several chairs. Against another wall were cabinets with locks. In this room also were outlets and ports for phones. The Chosen One looked at Qadir.

"Something bothers you, Qadir?"

"No, sir," Qadir said quickly.

"You are thinking...we are in the middle of nowhere and yet, we have electricity and phones, yes?"

"Yes, sir."

"Qadir," said the Chosen One shaking his head, "when will you realize that nothing is impossible when you have connections."

"Yes, sir. What is the purpose of this building?"

"Qadir, there are always those who wish to rise to power, those who do not want the Cause to succeed. I am afraid Qadir that some of those may already be in our ranks. Not everyone we are close to can be trusted. That is why you must be careful, Qadir, very careful."

"Yes, sir." Qadir knew the Chosen One did not trust everyone. That was obvious in what they were asked to do. Lately, though, it seemed that the Chosen One had little trust in Ahmed. With the new warning, Qadir knew he must be very tight lipped especially around him.

"This is going to be a command center, Qadir. From here we will communicate with all of the followers. I have taken the time and spent much money to get it ready. I want you to make certain everything is running the way it should. We are going to bring everything of importance here where our enemies cannot find it. There may come a time when we will have to use this. I want to be ready for that. No one can stop us from getting our message out to everyone."

"Sir, I will make sure everything is ready here," said Qadir realizing the seriousness of such a request. "This is a very good idea."

"Yes, Qadir, it is. Remember, you cannot tell anyone about this. I will tell who I want when I want. Is that clear?"

"Yes, sir," said Qadir. He felt privileged that the Chosen One had such trust in him that he would be the first to see this new place.

"Now, Qadir, let's see what all of this can do."

Chapter Nine

With each passing day, the situation with Michael grew more intense. The desire to go to Frankfurt to see things firsthand was of primary importance. Edgar impressed upon Captain Swagen that sense of urgency and succeeded in getting permission for Michael's family and partners to visit the site.

Pierre, Margo, Mark, Gwen, and Laura arrived at the airport in Frankfurt, Germany and were met by Edgar and Captain Swagen.

"Pierre," said Edgar, "I'm so sorry to be meeting you again under these circumstances."

"Yes, Edgar, I agree."

"May I introduce to you Captain Swagen? He's in charge of the case. Captain Swagen, this is Pierre Lemont from Global Connections Consulting firm in Paris, his wife Margo, and Mr. Braedon's fiancée, Laura Darmer," said Edgar.

"Edgar, I don't think you met Michael's brother Mark and his wife Gwen," said Pierre, "Captain Swagen."

"It's a pleasure meeting all of you," said Captain Swagen.

"Captain Swagen," said Mark, "is it possible to see the hotel room where my brother was taken, first?"

"Yes, Mr. Braedon, we'll go there directly. We're through with the scene and you can take any personal effects with you."

From the airport to the hotel, Mark asked questions about the investigation. It was evident to Mark that although they were doing the very best they could, this was something they never had dealt with before.

Upon arriving at the hotel, Captain Swagen asked for the keycards for rooms 718 and 720. He informed the clerk that they were there to pick up their belongings and had permission to do so.

The group went up to the seventh floor and Captain Swagen handed the keycards to Edgar. Edgar opened the door to 718. He turned on the light and looked in. Captain Swagen looked at his phone.

"Please excuse me," he said, "I must get back to my office. If I can be of any further assistance, please call me."

"Thank you," said Pierre.

"It's exactly as it was that day," said Edgar and for a moment he seemed to be lost in thought. "I'm sorry. While you're in here, I'm going to collect my things. I'll be over as soon as I'm finished."

Two steps inside Michael's Room, there were spots of blood on the carpet where he fell. Mark took pictures of everything. An overwhelming feeling came over Laura as she stood there. Tears streamed down her face when she saw the destruction before her. She could sense Michael's confusion and pain...almost vividly see what happened.

She walked over to the far side of the room and started picking up papers and things from the floor. She placed them on the table. The toe of her shoe hit against the picture frame and she bent over to pick it up. It was the picture of her and Michael the night they were engaged. She held it close for a moment, despite its cracked glass, and then put it down gently on the table. She picked up more things and began to sob. Mark helped her to a chair and she looked up at him.

"These bastards will not destroy my life," she said with anger and determination. "I won't allow it. I'll find him and I'll get him back."

"I know you will and we'll do everything we can to help bring him home safely," said Mark. It was hard for him to hold his composure. The evidence of the violence was all around him. He was so angry and afraid for his brother.

Pierre, Margo, and Gwen gathered the rest of Michael's things and even though every drawer had been emptied, they still checked everything, replaced the drawers, and closed each one as they finished. Surprisingly, Michael's laptop and briefcase were still there. Laura put everything from the table into Michael's briefcase and Mark closed it.

"Mark," said Pierre, "I want to see the stairwell."

"I'll go with you," said Mark making sure he still had his camera.

They went down the hallway and entered the stairwell. As they walked the stairs, Mark took pictures of each flight, the drops of blood on the steps, the doors, and view from the seventh floor to the bottom and from the bottom to the seventh floor. Mark pushed the panic bar on the door leading to the outside. No alarm sounded. He took more pictures of the exit and the parking lot. Then they went back to the room.

The bed seemed undisturbed, but when Laura checked under the pillow she found a small, black, velvet pouch. She drew it out, opened it and poured the contents into her hand. It was a heart shaped locket. She turned it over and on the back was engraved *Laura, I will love you forever, Michael*. She clutched it in her hand.

"Oh Michael, I will love you forever." she whispered.

Gwen and Margo took everything off the bed to make sure Michael didn't hide anything else. Their search turned up nothing. They folded the bedding and placed it neatly at the bottom.

"Let's go," said Gwen as she gave Laura a hug. The ladies walked out of the room followed by Pierre and Mark. Laura looked back as they shut the door.

The Reinholdt home stood quite secluded on the outskirts of Frankfurt. The shrubbery and wrought iron fencing had been added as merely something ornamental Gabrielle liked. The car took them through the gates and up the drive past impressive flower gardens and a perfectly manicured lawn. Edgar instructed the driver to stop in front of the house.

Gabrielle was waiting for them when they arrived. Hot tea and coffee were readied to calm the nerves and an assortment of pastries was arranged on a plate. She invited them to join her.

"Oh, my dear, Laura," she said, "how are you doing? Are you sure you're comfortable?"

"I'm doing fine and yes, I'm comfortable, thank you."

"Edgar, I know you've talked about what happened the day Michael was taken," said Mark, "but we were wondering if you'd mind going over some things with us."

"Of course."

Edgar and Gabrielle told the story about what happened the day Michael was taken. Even though they knew most of it, it helped hearing it from them.

"Edgar, do you have any idea why these people would want you?" asked Pierre.

"Not really."

"We know you were the intended target," said Margo, "which makes this unlike any of the other kidnappings. This one also had a note and the others didn't."

"I have no idea what they wanted with me," said Edgar quite insistently.

"I'm sorry to interrupt, but I must excuse myself," said Gabrielle getting up from the table. "My committee members are arriving."

"Thank you for everything, Gabrielle," said Laura.

"If you have time, I'd love to show you what we're doing."

"We'll be in shortly."

Mark watched as Gabrielle left the room. When he was sure she was gone, he turned his attention to Edgar.

"Can you tell me a little about the new communication system your company is developing?" asked Mark.

"Mark," said Edgar, "we work on many new communication systems."

"Yes, Edgar, I know," said Mark leaning forward in his chair. He brought the volume of his voice down to almost a whisper. "I want to know about the one that could possibly bring a country to its knees."

The color drained from Edgar's face. "The work on the one I think you're referring to has been terminated due to matters of national security," said Edgar looking around. "How did you find out about it?"

"I asked some people who always have their fingers on the pulse of what's happening in the world concerning issues vital to national security," said Mark. "I called a friend and asked him what it might be that Reinholdt International had that would be so important to a militant group that they'd go to such lengths to kidnap its President and CEO.

One simple question like that gave me an answer I had not expected." Mark paused and sipped his coffee. "I had no idea Reinholdt International was dabbling in such an area."

"It happened so innocently," said Edgar shaking his head. "We were given a government grant to develop a simpler more effective way of activating and commanding satellites in space. It was to be an extremely secure system, so foolproof no one could get into it. So, the SecReSAC System was born. SecReSAC System stands for Secured Remote Satellite Activation and Command System. What happened was the opposite. By a sheer mistake, the inverting of some figures and codes within a series of formulas and commands, a system was developed that could take over a satellite, any satellite, reprogram and command it. It made the satellite identify itself, tell what its purpose was and also what it could do. Needless to say, I ordered the suspension of the program. I also ordered all files, information, programs, diagrams, communication, and everything else to be sealed and vaulted."

"What about the grant?" asked Margo.

"I notified the leaders of the countries involved about the situation and told them I had suspended and vaulted everything. They thought it best that for the time being, nothing was done in that area. We were hoping to revisit the project at a later date and begin again from the ground up."

"How did the information get leaked?" asked Pierre.

"I don't know," said Edgar. "Until now, I was unaware that anyone outside of the small circle of interested parties even had an inkling of the project's existence."

"Who worked on the project?" asked Mark.

"There were approximately fifteen people who worked on various stages of the project."

"Was there any one person who knew everything about the project?" asked Margo.

"No!" said Edgar emphatically shaking his head.

"Do you have the names of the persons who worked on it?" asked Gwen.

"The information is at the office. If you'd like, we can go there."

"That'd be a big help," said Pierre.

"I'm not sure what you're looking to find," said Edgar. "Everyone involved in the project was thoroughly screened."

"I'm sure they were, Edgar," said Pierre. "We're hoping to find someone connected in some way to this group."

The telephone at Reinholdt International had been ringing all morning and Erika was doing her best to handle all the calls. While there were the usual calls concerning business, the majority of the ones she took dealt with clients checking on Edgar and expressing their relief that he was safe. Even though the kidnapping attempt happened days prior, it was just now permeating into the mainstream media.

"Good afternoon, Erika," said Edgar as he approached her desk.

"Good afternoon, Edgar."

"Erika, I'd like you to meet Pierre Lemont and Mark Braedon from the consulting firm."

"It's very nice to meet you," she said.

"It's very nice meeting you, also," said Mark.

"Have there been any calls?" asked Edgar.

"Yes, sir. There've been quite a few," she said picking up two piles.

"All those?" he asked looking at the stacks. In all his years in business he had never been presented with that many call sheets.

"Yes, sir. These deal with business matters," she said handing him the smaller of the two stacks, "and these are from clients who are so relieved you're safe."

"I'll make sure I attend to the business ones and I'll also send each of these a thank you."

"Yes, sir. I'll have their addresses for you by the end of the day."

"Thank you. Would you please get me the employment files for everyone who worked on SecReSAC?"

"I'll have those in a moment."

Erika walked down the hall. Her blonde hair was just below chin length and was cut to frame her face. She dressed and carried herself like the picture-perfect secretary in all the movies. She had been with Reinholdt International since its inception as a fledgling communication company. After she retrieved the files, she walked back to her desk and handed them to Edgar.

"When you're done," she said, "I'll put them away."

"Thank you. We'll be in my office."

Edgar's office was pristine. There was nothing out of place and not one piece of paper could be seen anywhere. He invited them to be seated.

"What information do you need, gentlemen?"

"Their names, how long they worked for the company, where they worked before, what degrees they hold and where they got them, and pictures if you have them," said Pierre.

"What are you looking for?"

"If this was a very secretive project, no one outside of the company, really outside of that inner circle, should've known anything about it," said Mark. "Obviously other people did know about it and not just our kidnappers. My friend also knew about it. Therefore, the leak had to have come from the inside."

"I can't believe someone on my staff would do such a thing," said Edgar looking up from the papers.

"Edgar, from what I understand," said Mark, "some would've been willing to pay billions for it."

"I guess when you're talking about something worth billions of dollars," said Edgar, "loyalty means nothing."

Edgar made one copy each of the pictures and information sheets. He carefully blacked out any sensitive, personal information, and then made additional copies.

"I'm still not sure what you're looking for," Edgar said.

"Anything that might give us a clue about who we're dealing with," said Mark, "any connection no matter how remote or thin it may seem."

"Why are you doing all this when the authorities are working on it?" asked Edgar.

"I have the highest regards for the police and other law enforcement agencies," said Mark, "but they've never been able to solve the hostage situations in the past. That's why none of them have ever been rescued unless they had military connections. Everything connected with these situations is so clandestine and intricate, it's virtually impossible for them to use conventional methods to solve them. I don't want my brother winding up as one of those statistics no one remembers except those of us who love him. I'm not about to sit back and wait."

"When you put it that way," said Edgar putting all of the papers into a folder and into his briefcase, "that may be why Alex gave me the discs." He called for Erika and asked her to put the files back.

"Do the areas where the work is done have security cameras?" asked Pierre.

"Yes, of course they do."

"What happens to the footage?"

"Everything that had to do with SecReSAC was sealed. That was one of the first things we thought about."

"Have you reviewed those records?"

"There was never a reason to."

"I think there's definitely a reason to do so now," said Pierre.

"What would you be looking for?" asked Edgar.

"Perhaps someone taking information out of the facility," said Mark.

"That's impossible," said Edgar assuredly. "We have a foolproof method. Everything is counted every day, even the pieces of paper in the lab. No one brings anything in and no one takes anything out."

"You know, there was this kid named Roger in my class in high school," said Mark looking from Edgar to Pierre. "Roger wasn't all that smart and he hated to study. Instead, he went to great lengths to cheat. Oh, sure, he got caught with his crib sheets and opening notebooks, things like that, but then Roger got really creative. He'd always go to the bathroom and get some toilet paper to use as tissues. So on the night before the test, he'd take some of that good school toilet paper home and write the answers on it. The next day, he'd go to the bathroom as he always did and get toilet tissue. Then he'd substitute the cheat tissue for the new tissue. Never got caught. No one wants to touch anyone's tissue. Maybe you had a creative worker like Roger."

Edgar thought for a moment and then shook his head.

"To answer the question you're thinking," he said, "we don't count toilet tissue or facial tissue. Never would think to do that."

Edgar Reinholdt's security system was as good as any Pierre and Mark had seen at other companies. The system was varied and complicated. One thing was certain, if anyone needed to get into these inner rooms, they must do so with a deliberate concentration. Edgar negotiated the maze of security with determined ease and once inside he offered them a seat.

He went into another part of the room and came back with a small box. He set it down and opened it.

"I figure we need to start at the moment the mistake is made and we realize what's happening, at the end and work backwards, or at the beginning of the project," said Edgar. "What do you think?"

"I think if we start at the end, we may find something faster," said Pierre, "and then it'll be easier to look for more when we know who it might be."

"There was a meeting with the staff when it was decided the project was going to be put on hold."

"Let's start with that meeting," said Pierre.

Edgar went through the box, looking at the labels. He found the one he wanted and started it. They watched intently the reactions of the team as they were told. After they finished watching it, Mark asked him to show it one more time, just the part where they were told. As they watched, Mark pointed out a worker who seemed to be slightly agitated.

"It may be nothing, yet, it may be something," said Mark. "Do you know offhand who he is?"

"That's Dabir," said Edgar. "He's been with the company over ten years."

He started the record of the last day in the lab. As they watched it was obvious that something bothered Edgar.

"What's he doing?" he asked finally. He started the record again and pointed to one of the workers. "Watch him. He glances up, then turns around and starts fidgeting with something. Then he turns back."

"What's he looking at?" Pierre asked.

"I don't know," said Edgar, "but he does it several times."

"It's like he's looking to see if anyone can see him," said Mark.

"Is there a window up there that you use to watch what's going on in the lab?" asked Pierre.

"No. There are no windows, only surveillance cameras," said Edgar.

"Maybe that's what he's looking at," said Mark.

Edgar shook his head. "We have new cameras like they have at the hotel. They're hidden and the workers have no idea where they are. They're quite small, but they can cover the entire room."

"So what's he looking at?" asked Mark.

"Wait a minute," said Edgar. "We haven't taken down the old cameras yet. The new system still has a few flaws, so we're using the old ones as well. I wanted to make sure we were recording everything."

"Do the old ones scan the room?" asked Pierre.

"Yes. There are several in the room. A red light comes on when that particular camera is recording."

"Could he have been waiting for the camera to stop recording?" asked Pierre.

"Maybe."

"Who is he?" asked Mark.

"I can zoom in for a close up," said Edgar. It's Ghassan. I think we have time for one more."

As they watched, nothing of interest was seen. Mark made a mental note of the names of the two men Edgar identified. He wanted to make sure he wrote them down when he got back to the hotel.

"We can begin at this point in the morning," said Edgar. He picked up the box and put it back where he found it. As they left the area, Edgar diligently made sure each door was securely closed and alarmed.

Michael heard the keys in the door and sat in terror of who was on the other side. When it opened, Sadik came into the room again. Michael breathed a silent sigh of relief. Sadik sat down as he had before.

"Mr. Braedon," he asked, "how long have you known Mr. Reinholdt?"

"Just for a few weeks," said Michael.

"Did you ever see Mr. Reinholdt's company?"

"Yes, I visited his facilities."

"What are they like?"

"Each one has offices and work areas. There are labs and assembly rooms."

"Mr. Reinholdt must be very smart."

"He must be," said Michael, "but everyone's smart in their own way. What do you like to do?"

"I like my job," said Sadik, "and I also like to be home with my family."

"Do you have children?" Michael asked.

"Two boys and a girl," he said smiling.

"How old are they?'

"Three, six, and eight," he said, "Do you have any children?"

"No. I'm not married, yet."

"Are you planning on getting married?"

"We were hoping to get married in the near future," Michael said smiling. "How long have you been married?"

"Ten years this September. Where do you work?" asked the guard.

"I have my own business with my partners. We have a consulting business. We work with other companies to help them solve problems."

"Do you like what you do?" asked Sadik.

"Yes."

"Why?"

"It never gets boring. I get to travel and meet a lot of people and I find people and business fascinating," said Michael. "Why do you like your job?"

"It is always exciting and I get to work with the Chosen One."

"What do you do?"

"Whatever I am told."

Chapter Ten

The next morning Pierre, Mark, and Edgar continued looking at security films. The work was slow and tedious, but they knew the price for not doing a thorough job would be astronomical. They scrutinized anything that looked the least bit suspicious.

"Is there any way to isolate the instances on the films where there's questionable activity without jeopardizing security?" asked Mark running his fingers through his hair. "Everything's beginning to run together."

"What you're looking at really doesn't show anything of a classified nature," said Edgar. "It's impossible from these distances to really read anything and even if you could, you'd never have the complete formula or code and it'd be meaningless."

Pierre got up and walked around the room stretching out his arms and legs. He massaged his neck. After a few minutes, they began watching again, this time marking sections.

"I would've never thought any of this activity was suspicious," said Edgar. "However, now that I'm looking at it, I can see there's obviously something going on. I wonder what else I've missed over the years. We need to take care of security in addition to what we've already discussed."

"Getting your security totally functional needs to be done, immediately," said Mark. "You may not be out of harm's way yet. If these people want what we think they're after, you're the only one who can give it to them."

"They'll be more careful about getting you the next time," said Pierre. "They'll make sure they have the right person."

"If they take me," said Edgar, "they'll never have the entire project, because I don't know everything. I just know where to get it."

Edgar finished working on the computer in the room and the three left and went back to his office. Once there, he retrieved the file and made a copy for Pierre.

"As far as our computers are concerned, they have the latest security system and we constantly monitor for any attempts at sabotage," said Edgar sitting behind his desk with his hands folded. "We made certain nothing can ever be retrieved in its entirety with one attempt. Information is separated into numerous files. Some projects are so sensitive that if they fall into the wrong hands, it could mean death for hundreds of thousands and in some cases millions of people. For SecReSAC, the numbers are catastrophic."

"That's why they want it," said Mark. "To possess it would put the fate of the world in their hands."

The partners from Global Connections found themselves pushed to the limits with a morning packed with meetings and an afternoon with none ahead. After the last client, they went to the "war room" as they called it and looked at everything that was hanging. Some of them walked systematically from one end to the other, while others went back and forth between several distinct pictures.

"Do you see what they're wearing?" Raquel asked, pointing to some of the pictures. "There's something about the attire that's so familiar to me. I think I remember it from something I studied a long time ago. It may mean nothing, but then again..." her voice trailed off as she began to think.

"Let's see what I can do with this," said Robert, "and besides, if it meant nothing, why did Margo ask for it before and why are they all wearing it in the same place."

"Did anyone notice that when they were carrying Michael out, one of the abductors lost a glove and someone else picked it up?" asked

Gina, looking carefully at a select few pictures. "And if you look closely, there's something on his hand."

"Where?" asked Paul walking over to his wife.

"This is the one I noticed it in," she said pointing to the spot. "See?"

"We need a good picture of that hand," said Brigit.

"Let me find one," said Gina.

"How did you find that?" asked Jean. "I mean just glancing it looks like all the others."

"I know. Every time I walked down the hall past the room, I'd go in and look around," said Gina. "Something kept popping out like it wasn't supposed to be there. When I had a few minutes, I looked at the pictures a little harder and there it was…the hand. At first you don't notice it. You assume it's part of the hood. That's what was throwing me."

"I would've never caught that," said George getting close to the picture.

Robert sat at the computer, trying to make the magic happen as the rest liked to call it. As he got further along, no one could be any more surprised than he was at what was coming together before his eyes.

"Well, if that insignia doesn't mean anything, why does our guy have it tattooed on his hand?" asked Robert as he looked at the enlarged print.

"What!" said Raquel.

"Look," he said as he placed the prints one beside the other down on the table ending with the hand.

"That's incredible," said Jean. "Now, the question is…what is it?"

The door opened and the Chosen One came in with two of his guards. Michael immediately recognized them from the treatment he had received at their hands. His body stiffened…he knew what was about to happen. His heart raced and he felt that undeniable trembling of fear rise inside him.

"Mr. Braedon, it seems no one even cares about where you are or what is happening to you," said the Chosen One. "How can that be?" The Chosen One gestured with his hands as he walked closer to Michael.

"You have talked to your guard and he has told you what a loving family he has. Have you no family?"

"Yes, sir, I do," said Michael trying to keep the tone of his voice as even and respectful as he could.

"Do they not care about you?"

"I'm sure they do, sir."

"I am not so sure about that," said the Chosen One shaking his head. "No one has even tried to contact us, to find out where you are. How can that be? Perhaps we have been too nice to you."

With a nod of his head, the first guard took a knife and thrust it into Michael's upper leg. Blood spurted from the wound when he removed it. Michael tried hard not to flinch.

"Mr. Braedon, we know there are people who know what we want," said the Chosen One, his eyes glaring at Michael and his teeth clenching as he spoke, "and if they ever want to see you again, they will make every effort to get it for us."

He nodded again and the other guard thrust his knife into Michael's calf and drew it downward. Michael's legs buckled and he fell to the floor.

"Mr. Braedon, at the rate your family and friends are moving, there will not be a part of your body that will not be bearing my signature," said the Chosen One emphatically. He paused and looked Michael in the eyes. "Hope and pray, Mr. Braedon, that someone out there cares. I am losing patience. You do not want to see me when my patience is gone." He paused for a moment to let that sink in. "We will talk again soon."

The Chosen One turned and walked out followed by the guards. Michael drew his leg up as close to his torso as possible. He was desperately trying to stop the bleeding. There was no way he was going to bleed to death in this cell...not if he could help it.

The keys rattled in the door and Michael froze. *They can't be coming back again! What the hell do they want?* As the door opened, Michael caught sight of the woman. She was followed by his guard carrying her tray. The guard placed the tray beside Michael and the woman worked at cleaning and taking care of his wounds.

Michael looked puzzled. Nothing made any sense.

"The Chosen One is not without compassion," said the woman quietly as though she had read his mind. "You have been very respectful to him and he appreciates that. He had to give an example to your family and friends. The Chosen One needs what they have and he needs you to get it. I will make sure you are taken care of and comfortable. That is my job. You must rest so your mind will be clear to answer his questions. There is no way to do this without hurting you. I am sorry for that."

Michael leaned back against the wall and allowed the woman to do her job no matter how much it hurt. He kept thinking back to what the Chosen One had said. *How can that man ever think that the way he's treating me is nice? Dear God, give me strength.*

Michael played over the conversation with the Chosen One in his mind. He started to think intensely about what he said. *What if they don't care about what's happening? Are they even trying to find me?* He stopped dead in his thoughts.

Michael Steven Braedon! he said to himself in the sternest tone possible. *Of course they care. You know they're doing everything they can to find you. They have no idea where you are or who these people are. Hell, you have no idea who these people are. All you know is that this leader is the Chosen One... the Chosen One of what? Who the Hell chose him! You also know the others do everything he tells them to do. That's what you know and you're here...right here with them. If you don't know who they are, how do you expect them to know?*

"That's good," said the woman. "Rest and relax. I will return in a little while."

"Thank you," said Michael as he smiled at her.

She smiled back, picked up her tray and knocked for the guard.

Laura, Gwen, and Margo sat quietly in the sitting room of their suite in the hotel. They worked on the computer and went through everything they had found in Michael's room. They emptied his briefcase paper by paper again and reread all the files on his computer. Gwen worked on the internet trying to find anything she could on terrorist organizations and anti-Semitic groups.

"One thing keeps appearing over and over again on every page of notes Michael wrote," said Laura. "It says check security." She looked up and put the papers on her lap. "Why would he write that?"

"I don't know. Keep looking," said Margo. "There has to be a clue somewhere."

"I'll look again in a minute. I need to get up and walk," said Laura uncrossing her legs and getting up from the chair. She walked out of the room and into her bedroom.

"I downloaded information on some terrorist groups," said Gwen. "I don't know whether or not it's valuable, but then again I don't know exactly what we're looking for. I even found some that are based on ancient cults. I downloaded those, because of my own…Jesus!" Gwen said. "Margo come here!"

She hurried over to the computer.

"Dear God!" she said as they watched Michael. Gwen and Margo wiped tears from their cheeks when Laura walked back into the room.

"Alright! What's going on?" she asked apprehensively.

Gwen took a deep breath and told her what they saw leaving out the anguish they had seen on Michael's face. Laura looked at them with determination and anger.

"Those fucking bastards! How dare they say we don't care!" she said raising her voice. "Who the hell do they think they are! They're the ones hiding. Damn them! There has to be an answer somewhere as to their identity. We have to find it," she said looking from one to the other. "We have to get him back! We need to be able to talk to the others in Paris. I feel like we've been out of touch forever."

"As soon as Pierre comes back, we'll figure that out," said Margo wiping another tear from her cheek. The scenes with Michael were embedded in her mind. She knew Laura was right, but everything was clouded by what she just watched.

"Did they give any time limit?" asked Laura.

"No," said Gwen.

"We need to start asking anyone and everyone. Hopefully, if they see we're making an attempt maybe they'll leave him alone," said Laura in a pleading tone. She looked up. "Oh, God, please let them leave him alone."

Mark and Edgar made a list comparing the notes they took from the security films and the log on Edgar's Computer. The list had very few holes because of Edgar's detailed entries.

"How's it going?" asked Pierre as he sat down.

"We were able to compare the log and the notes we made and figure out what they have," said Mark.

"The pieces in themselves mean nothing," said Edgar trying to convince himself as well as Mark and Pierre. "There are critical parts missing. It also hinges on whether these men remembered anything and supplied additional information."

"That's why they want you," said Pierre. "They must think you know every part of SecReSAC's development. For them, you're the missing piece, the critical link."

"But I'm not," insisted Edgar. "I only know how to get the information."

"I know that, Edgar," said Pierre calmly. "Now, the question is, what can they do with what they have?"

"If they're able to acquire the electronics necessary, they could possibly interrupt transmissions, even scramble them," said Edgar. "That, while it'd be an inconvenience, could be rectified and it's possible to guard against that. They can also take command of stations and ultimately link them according to region. They can get their message to millions." He stopped for a moment. His mind was far ahead of what he was saying. "What I'm really worried about is that they have the potential to get into the systems that have a direct bearing on national security of many nations."

"How potentially dangerous could this be?" asked Pierre. He had an idea, but needed Edgar to spell it out.

"If they're able to put the commands together, they could start a war between and among nations," said Edgar taking off his glasses signaling just how important the matter was. "It's imperative that the leaders take measures to safeguard those systems. This group needs to be stopped without thinking anyone is interfering with their efforts and I'm the only one I know who can do that."

"You know by doing this, Edgar, you'll be creating a need for them to try again to get you," said Mark and he paused, "or to use Michael as a pawn to get the information they lack."

"As I see it, if they're successful, they'll have no need for Michael and may choose to get rid of him," said Edgar. He couldn't bring himself to use the word kill. "This way, he's still useful. I want to do whatever I can to buy as much time as possible."

"We appreciate that," said Pierre. "Before we return to the hotel, I'd like to call the office?"

"Of course. Use the phone in my office."

Pierre sat at Edgar's desk. He was suddenly anxious to discuss their findings and also curious about what the partners had been doing and what they had found in his absence.

"What's going on there?" asked Pierre when Robert answered.

"Taking care of business as well as working on the other project," said Robert. "Raquel and Gina have found something really interesting. Can't wait for you to see it."

"Neither can I," said Pierre. "Did you see Michael?"

"Yes. To say we're worried would be an understatement. Are you finished there?"

"We have Michael's briefcase and computer and what appears like all of his paperwork and notes. I think we're going to come back in the morning, unless there's a flight tonight," said Pierre looking at his watch.

When Pierre finished he walked over to Edgar and Mark.

"Edgar, thank you again for everything," said Pierre. "We'll be returning to Paris as soon as we can get a flight."

"Erika, please check to see when the next flight is to Paris," said Edgar.

"Yes, sir."

"If there's anything you find out or need to discuss with us, please call," said Pierre.

"I will. In the meantime, if you need me for anything, call me at the office, or use my private home number," said Edgar. "If I'm away, Erika will be only too glad to get you what you need."

"I appreciate that," said Pierre.

"Excuse me, Edgar, there's a flight leaving at 7:20 this evening. Would you like me to make the reservations?"

"Please," said Mark.

Chapter Eleven

It was almost nine o'clock by the time they reached Paris. The lights were on in the house and when Mark unlocked the door he was greeted by a wonderful aroma.

"Now, this is what I call a welcome home," said Mark walking into the kitchen.

"This is the most relaxed I've felt since this whole thing began," said Laura. "Maybe it's because I can feel Michael all around me."

"His presence is very strong," said Gwen smiling at her.

"I've taken hundreds of pictures of every inch of the hotel where Michael was that day," said Mark after they finished eating.

"We have security footage from Reinholdt International. There's someone who seems to be engaging in activity that isn't normal," said Pierre. "After seeing it, Edgar realized his security has been compromised and needs to be dealt with in addition to the new system he's already adding. Henri, you're the best person I know to deal with this."

"I'll get on it," said Henri making a note.

"Robert, we were only able to do so much with the footage. You need to go over it all. The last thing we want is to have missed something."

"No problem," said Robert.

"Now what have Raquel and Gina found?" asked Mark rubbing his hands together.

"Well, we found that everyone had something printed on the clothing they were wearing. It was an insignia," said Raquel handing the picture to Gwen. "Gina also found a picture of the bare hand of one of the abductors."

"The hand has the same insignia tattooed on it," said Gina.

Gwen looked at the insignia and got a puzzled look on her face.

"I think I've seen this," said Gwen, picking up a picture and looking at it intently.

"Are you serious?" asked Raquel getting excited. "I thought I had seen it once also."

"Yes," said Gwen, "I've been going on the internet looking at information about terrorist organizations. This wasn't from a bogus site. I think it's one of those ancient ones."

"Where are your downloads?" asked Gina.

"In my computer case on my flash drive," said Gwen. "Let me get it."

"This is going to be a long night," said Laura getting up from her chair. "I don't want to stop right now. Maybe this'll be a break, or a direction, or at least something."

"I agree," said Margo. "We need to keep going. We have to find who they are. We have to make them understand we want Michael back. We can't allow them to torture him because they think we don't care."

"The United States Government issued a statement saying the family had come forward to ask for help, but that the United States does not negotiate with terrorist groups," said Robert. "I found it on the internet on several prominent sites."

"That'll at least show we cared enough to ask for help," said Mark. "Now we have to find them and try to negotiate with them ourselves."

"We need to use everything," said Laura, "websites, social networks, and anything else we can think of. Let's put it out there on everything we have. See what happens."

"I'll put it on the home page," said Robert.

"We all have different contacts," said Laura, "and so do they. Let's ask if anyone knows anything about Michael's kidnappers and also ask them to pass it on to all their contacts on every site they're on as well as their email contacts."

"I'll write the email and forward it to all of you," said Angelique.

"Thanks. Let me get some of these things put away and I'll be back to help," said Laura picking up a suitcase.

"Let's start with the security films," said Pierre putting the disc in the computer.

After a while, Jacques got up to refill his glass with ice water. "It seems to be the same person throughout," he said.

"He's always in the same position in the lab," said Pierre. "When he turns, he's still slightly turned towards the camera."

"What's he writing," asked George, "and what's he writing on?"

"Whatever it is, he brought it into the lab with him and it was undetectable," said Pierre. "Every piece of paper was counted before anyone came in and before anyone left to ensure that nothing was taken out of the lab."

Robert froze the frame, copied it, cropped it, and enlarged it until it filled the screen. Then he did what he could to make the image clear.

"It looks like a napkin, or a tissue," he said.

Pierre looked at Mark with a look of disbelief. Mark shrugged his shoulders.

"Roger lives," said Mark with a raise of his eyebrows.

"What?" asked George.

Mark took a few minutes to reiterate the story of Roger he had told Pierre and Edgar.

"That's amazing," said Henri.

"What did he write on that napkin?"

"Looks like some numbers and letters," said Robert.

"We're going to have go frame by frame to see what he got," said Paul. "We have no choice."

"Does he always wear gloves?" asked Gina chewing on the end of a pen.

"What's with you and hands?" asked Paul.

Gina got up, walked over to the wall, and used the pen to point to a very blurry marking under the glove. "What's that on his hand?"

"The Glove?" asked Robert.

"Or is it just a shadow?" she said almost talking to herself.

"Don't know that either," said Robert. "This'll be much easier to deal with on the computer in Michael's office."

Although it was quite late, Edgar knew time was of the essence when it came to protecting the security of the nations he had as clients. He knew he had to impress upon the leaders the gravity of the situation without causing a general widespread panic. He also knew it was imperative to keep it just between him and the leaders. He took a deep breath, picked up the phone and made the first call.

"Office of the President," said Ms. Harlan.

"This is Edgar Reinholdt of Reinholdt International."

"Yes, Mr. Reinholdt, this is Ms. Harlan, how may I help you?"

"Ms. Harlan, I need to speak to President Bartram. It is of the utmost urgency."

"Can you hold, please?"

"Yes."

She put him on hold, got up from her desk, walked over to the office door, and knocked.

"Come in," said President Bartram.

"Mr. President, Mr. Reinholdt of Reinholdt International is on the phone. He said it's of the utmost urgency that he speaks to you."

"Thank you, Ms. Harlan."

Ms. Harlan walked out of the office and closed the door behind her. President Bartram picked up the phone.

"Mr. Reinholdt, this is President Bartram, what can I do for you today."

"Mr. President, I'm sorry to bother you, but there has been an incident at my company and information has been pirated…information that in the wrong hands could be a threat to national security as well as world security."

"I see," said President Bartram trying to sound calm. "Mr. Reinholdt, what can we do about this?"

"Several things, however, it's going to take the cooperation of all the countries involved to get it done."

"I'm afraid I don't understand. If it deals with national security, why can't it be dealt with individually?"

"Different countries share the same satellite. If they don't agree on a course of action, nothing can be done."

"I see," said President Bartram. "You know, we can handle this one of two ways. You can play an exhausting game of phone tag trying to get all parties to agree, or we can invite them to come together and solve this."

"I'd prefer to do it the second way," said Edgar with a slight bit of relief. "That way everyone will hear the same thing. They'll be able to ask questions, come to an agreement, and we'll then have a course of action."

"I agree. There'll also be no ill feelings about being the last one told."

"Exactly."

"I'll gladly host those meetings," said President Bartram looking down at his calendar.

"I'd appreciate that."

"I know I can impress on my colleagues the necessity of meeting as soon as possible."

"The sooner the better," said Edgar. He knew every day that passed gave the pirates more time to try to access security areas.

"I'll also make the calls to set up the meetings. That way I can coordinate their arrivals and schedules."

"That would be very gracious of you."

"If you could email or fax a list to me, we can be certain no one is overlooked."

"I can do that immediately."

"I'll call you with the arrangements as soon as I have them."

"Thank you, sir."

"Mr. Reinholdt, don't worry, I know we'll be able to do this."

"Thank you. I look forward to your call."

Edgar sat back in his chair and gave a sigh of relief. Just a few more minutes rest and then he'd make some quick notes about the meetings and finally get some much needed sleep.

Chapter Twelve

It was early morning before everyone made it back to the table. One by one they filled their coffee cups and sat down. On the table in front of them were stacks of pictures and documents. Laura kept leafing through the pages in Michael's portfolio. As she did she kept shaking her head and the expression on her face was one of puzzlement.

"Before we get started again maybe one of you could answer something for me," said Laura. "When I was going through the papers in Michael's briefcase, every page where he was meeting with Edgar or going through one of the complexes had the same message, check security. I read a few pages, but I didn't see a correlation."

"I have no idea," said Jacques. "May I see some of the notes?"

As Laura looked around the room, it was apparent they all seemed puzzled by what she said so handed each of them several pages of notes.

"What could Michael have picked up on when he was visiting the complexes that we didn't see?" asked Pierre after he had read his pages.

"Don't forget, we were only at the main office," said Mark. "Michael visited all of them."

"We may need to see the recordings for the time Michael was in those buildings," said Jacques. "He usually doesn't doodle."

"The fact that he wrote it on every sheet of paper he used for notes sent up a red flag," said Laura. "If it was just a suggestion, it would've found itself as a note somewhere on a line in the notes, not in the margin where it calls it to your attention as soon as you look at the paper."

"You're right," said Jacques.

"I'll call Edgar and ask him," said Mark. "We need to send those new pictures, too."

Raquel kept looking at the pictures of the insignia. She was trying to figure out where it was that she had first it. She stopped for a moment and looked over at the others.

"Gwen, how's it going?" she asked.

"It's going slowly, but it's going."

"Now Gina for your hand," said Robert handing her the picture. "Here it is. No glove."

"What's on his hand?" asked Gina.

"It's the same tattoo," said Robert.

"Okay. Now we're getting somewhere," said Jean. "There was someone on the inside. We need to know who he is."

"Margo, the area you pointed out the other day, I found that picture. Sorry it took so long, but here it is," said Robert.

"Good God, it's the same," said Margo.

"What about the man who asked for the room key?" asked Laura.

They found the security footage of the lobby and as they watched, there seemed to be no connection.

"All we see is his right hand," said Brigit. "The tattoos are on the left. Does he ever show that hand?"

They watched as he walked towards the door. He was getting ready to leave, when he saw a woman waiting to come in. He raised his left hand, placed it on the door, and pushed it open so she could enter. Then he left. Robert went back to the spot where he raised his left hand and placed it on the door. As he worked to isolate the hand, everyone held their breath. From the distance the picture was shot, it was impossible to tell. However after Robert was finished, there was no doubt. The tattoo was there.

"Now we need the answer to the question," said Monique. "Who are they?"

"They're members of a secret sacred society that dates itself back before the organization of Islam. They believe they're the true religion and Islam is the corrupted form of the one true religion, theirs. This is going to take some time to go through. The document is well over 300 pages. Look at this," Gwen said turning the laptop around. "Does this look familiar?"

"It's the tattoo and the insignia," said Raquel. "Now, I remember. There was an article that alluded to them a few years ago in a magazine I was reading."

"If we're going to have any chance of getting Michael back," said Paul, "we need to know everything about these people. Margo, what about the other hostage situations? Does that insignia show up in those also?"

"None of them," she said. "They were all from a more mainstream religion."

"These people who have Michael are true fanatics of an ancient religious cult," said Gwen.

"Okay, now we know who they are," said Mark. "We also know what they ultimately want, which is SecReSAC. Now, how do we use it to get Michael back?"

Mark sat at Michael's desk talking to Edgar. He had Michael's notes in front of him.

"We're trying to find out what Michael meant by check security," said Mark. "We were only in your main building."

"I know what you're referring to. We were supposed to discuss it the evening he was abducted."

"Is there any way to get the footage from the security cameras for the days and times Michael was in the other buildings?"

"I'll make sure I get those for you."

"Did you have a chance to check your email?"

"I'm doing that now. Dear God," he exclaimed as he looked at the pictures.

"Is this what you thought was taken?"

"Some of it, yes, but there are more formulas and codes I didn't count on them having. Mark, they can do so much more than I thought they could. This isn't good. What else did you need?"

"We were wondering if anyone from the team quit, got fired, hasn't shown up, or has been late?"

"I'll have Grace in HR run a report from each building. Mark, if this would've occurred at any other time under normal circumstances I would've invoked company policy. They would've been terminated and prosecuted for such behavior. However, I think it's better to keep the status quo and act as though nothing has happened. I want to be able to keep my eye on them. I know my enemies and that becomes my advantage."

By mid-afternoon, Edgar had the security recordings sent. They went through much of what was shot when Michael was there and noticed nothing.

"What is it he sees that makes him question the security?" asked Robert. "I don't see it."

"Just watch the footage and don't think," said Gina getting that tone of mysticism to her voice. "Let your mind process it. Don't forget, Michael was right there. He was seeing first hand. We're trying to get inside his head to see what he saw instead of pretending we're there first hand and are seeing things as he did."

"Gina, where do you get this?" asked Paul clearly surprised by her seemingly lackadaisical attitude towards something he thought was critical.

"It's just how I think."

"Maybe you should try it," said Brigit trying to give credence to what she proposed. "After all it did work for her."

"Gina, with as logical as you are when it comes to dealing with client matters, how can you be so illogical when it comes to this?" asked George shaking his head.

"There's a time and place for logic and this is not that time," said Gina standing up with her hands pressed on the table. She made sure everyone was paying attention to her and she looked at them with glaring eyes. "These people we're dealing with are anything but logical and if we're even going to have a prayer of gaining Michael's release, we better realize that. They don't play by the rules. They don't play fairly. They play by their rules and they change the rules to suit them. If we expect them to put everything in a nice neat logical package, we're already defeated. They're not going to send us a letter telling us exactly what to do to make them happy. They're going to make us work for it. As someone said, the answers are all around us, we just have to find them. If that means stepping out of our nice neat little logical world where every step has a contingency plan if something goes awry, then so be it. But I'm warning you, we better step well and begin to think on our feet and God forbid use our gut instinct, because that's what they're using."

"I don't know about you, but I'm done being reactive. I'm not saying we should leave the emotions behind, because it's all that emotion that's going to be the catalyst for being proactive. We'll solve this. We'll get him back. We're damn good at giving ourselves deadlines. We've never allowed a client to give us one and I'm not about to wait for these assholes to set one. Either they give Michael back or we kick their ass. Better yet, they give Michael back AND we kick their ass."

"How do you propose we do that?" asked Pierre sitting back in his chair.

"Find them damn it!" she said pounding her fist on the table. "We have the best of everything here. Use it! We have connections everywhere in this world. Use them! We can make or break corporations if we so choose. We could even systematically destroy a country's economy if we wanted to. But we're going to allow these bastards dressed in black, wearing insignia's and having tattoos to take our aggressiveness away. I think not. You know, I've been in shock, I've cried, I've gone the poor me, poor Michael, poor everyone else route, and now I'm mad as hell! They had no right taking him and someone's going to have to teach them a lesson. They're going to have to pay for what they've done. If these big governments aren't going to do it because frankly they don't give a damn about just one person, then those of us who do give a damn about that one person better get the job done."

"You know how you beat them," she asked glaring at each one of them individually as if boring a hole in them, "you make it harder and harder for them to move about freely. You make it harder and harder for them to deal with anyone else except you. You dry up their sources. They want this information badly enough, then they're going to have to deal with us. And guess what. They're not going to like the final outcome. I'll have Michael and they'll consider themselves blessed if they die before I'm done with them."

No one moved as Gina finished. Her facial expression showed how convicted she was. Laura looked at Gina, nodded her head, and smiled. From the rest of the room a collective exhale was heard.

"Dear God, Gina! Where the hell did that come from?" asked Paul. "I've been married to you for years and never saw that side of you."

"I'm angry and frustrated, the same as the rest of you are," she said lowering her tone a little and finally sitting down, "however, no one was saying anything. We've been doing things, but not nearly as aggressively as we would if this were a client in trouble. Think about the day after we found out. Margo had a client in trouble and the world stopped until that company's problem was solved. Well, this is more important than any client we have. Michael is our friend and partner. He deserves at least the same effort from us that we'd give to a client. No, he deserves more."

Chapter Thirteen

Sadik stood for a moment, fixed his uniform, and then opened the door to the Chosen One's office. He had no idea why he was summoned, only that he was. For him, there was no choice. He was one of the chosen and he had promised to do whatever the Chosen One asked.

"You called for me, sir," said Sadik standing in front of the desk.

"Yes, Sadik," said the Chosen One. "Please sit down." He waited until Sadik was seated and then continued. "There is something I would like you to do."

"Yes, sir."

"I would like you to go to Mr. Braedon and untie him. After all we have put him through I do not think there is any threat of him escaping."

"No, sir."

"Sadik, I also would like you to talk to him some more. There are things we need to know. Perhaps you will be able to find them out for us."

"Yes, sir. What is it you want to know?"

"Listen very carefully, Sadik, very carefully."

The Chosen One took his time and explained exactly what he wanted him to do. He made Sadik repeat back to him multiple times the questions he wanted him to ask and the information he wanted him to illicit. When their conversation was finished, Sadik went first to the kitchen. The woman handed him a tray without saying a word. Then he went directly to Michael's room, unlocked the door, entered, and locked the door again.

"The Chosen One is not without compassion," he said placing the tray on the floor in front of Michael. "He has asked me to untie you."

Once Sadik untied him, Michael moved his arms slowly and grimaced. It hurt from being tied in one position for so long. He rubbed his wrists and they stung as the feeling began to come back slowly.

"Thank you," he said to Sadik, "and please tell the Chosen One how grateful I am to be untied."

"I will tell him."

Sadik sat down, poured some tea, and offered him a cup. Michael gratefully accepted it.

"Can you tell me something?" asked Michael initiating the conversation.

"Perhaps," said the guard.

"Why would you want to abduct Mr. Reinholdt?"

"Mr. Reinholdt has something the Chosen One wants and only Mr. Reinholdt can give it to him."

"How did the Chosen One think that Mr. Reinholdt would be able to give it to him?"

"The Chosen One was going to ask for the information as ransom for Mr. Reinholdt."

"I see," said Michael sipping his tea. "What would happen if only Mr. Reinholdt had access to that information? How would the Chosen One get it?"

"I do not know that, but I am sure that the Chosen One had a plan."

"I thought the Chosen One would have a plan, because when a project is as important as this one seems to be, there are always contingency plans. Smart people always have more than one plan and the Chosen One is a very smart man."

"Yes, he is."

"How is your family?"

"They are good," said Sadik. "Do they work on the same things in all of Mr. Reinholdt's buildings?"

"No, they work on different things."

"Do workers from one building ever work in another building?"

"I don't think they do. Usually people who work in this capacity are specialized. So they are placed in the building where they work in their specialty. They would have to have special security clearances to work on some of the projects."

"Do you have security clearances to go into Mr. Reinholdt's buildings?"

"In some places I could go because I didn't need clearances. To go into the other parts I'd have to get clearances."

"I see. Mr. Reinholdt must protect his buildings."

"Yes, he does."

"Does he have cameras in his buildings?"

"I did see security cameras when I was there."

"That is good."

"You need to have them when you work with sensitive material."

The woman knocked at the door and was permitted in. The guard left the two of them. Even though Michael was no longer bound, she made sure he was taken care of with great gentleness and compassion.

"I am proud of the way you are answering the Chosen One," she said quietly. "Keep talking to the guard and tell him how smart they are especially the Chosen One. Tell them things that will help them. As long as he can use you, you will be safe. You may not be unharmed, but you will be alive."

"Thank you."

With everything she said, Michael tried to put into place the cast of characters that were surrounding him, the woman, the guard, and those who seemed to be nothing more than body guards or enforcers. He knew that whatever this organization was, it was much larger than the few he came in contact with. In any other circumstance, he would've asked. In this one, he knew quite well that asking the wrong question could spell certain death.

When the woman finished, she gathered everything and walked to the door. She knocked, the door opened, and she left.

The Chosen One took down the pictures and maps from the wall. He placed them on the desk and started looking at each one intently. All the time, all the planning, and now he had to start over. He took out papers and started making notes. On the maps, he updated the number of chosen in each area and added new places. This was the bright spot to the day. The number of chosen was growing every day and that pleased him.

The next thing he needed to do was update the number of chosen on the website. He logged in and changed the number and smiled. Then he checked his mail. Each of the operatives knew he had to check in and update the Chosen One daily. He took the grid and began checking off the names as he read their mail. He copied the information he needed and made note of the names of those interested in becoming chosen. He answered each email separately letting them know they were indeed appreciated.

He clicked to open another folder and put in the password. It opened to display multiple folders each of which needed a different password to open it. Each contained information that was vital to the Cause. He systematically went through each one, reading their contents, changing anything that was not of importance anymore and adding new items. Here is where he planned what would happen to the Faith and the Cause.

He came to the folder detailing the Reinholdt project. He read over the plan. What was certain was that it had been well thought out, researched, and planned. Yet, with all that, it failed. Now came the time to decide who to take next. He doubted that Mr. Reinholdt would trade anything to release Mr. Braedon. He scrolled down and found a picture of Mrs. Reinholdt. A smile came over his face. If he couldn't get Mr. Reinholdt, perhaps he could take his wife. What man wouldn't give the world to save his wife, especially one who was as beautiful and captivating as Mrs. Reinholdt? Ah, yes, he would certainly enjoy that. He made a few notes, closed the folder, and sat back and prayed.

D. A. Walters

Chapter Fourteen

Edgar Reinholdt boarded a plane for the United States for a series of meetings with the heads of world powers. The leaders unanimously accepted the invitation of President Bartram to have the meetings at secure undisclosed location. This gave distance and secrecy to the discussion concerning a potentially catastrophic situation. Edgar knew his job was to calm fears, sell the package that would enable the nations to safeguard their systems, as well as keep clients that were necessary for the viability of his company. All of the preparation had been done; all he needed to do was sell it.

That was easier said than done. He knew in the past that things could get bogged down in committee for years as the politicians used it for their own agendas and political gain. That couldn't happen this time. This was far too important to go to committee.

If someone got wind of a security breach, the internet would be filled with rumors. That wouldn't go well for him, his company, or Michael. He hoped to impress that sense on the leaders.

President Bartram had done the bulk of the work thus far. He spoke to the leaders individually and they were apprised of the urgency of the matter. All knew Mr. Reinholdt and his reputation. For the most part, they knew him as a quiet man who was as steady as a rock. For him to be this exact in his wording, 'a threat to world security,' made each leader listen and take the matter seriously.

After Edgar landed, he retrieved his luggage and made his way into the public section. He looked around trying to find the person he was to meet. A gentleman walked up to him.

"Mr. Reinholdt?"

"Yes."

"I'm Agent Sampson of the Secret Service," he said showing Edgar his identification. "The President has asked me to escort you to the meetings."

"Thank you."

The two got into a waiting limousine. Edgar sat quietly during the ride. It took quite some time to get from the airport to the meeting location. The limousine came to a stop in the middle of a rocky, hilly area. Agent Sampson opened the door and escorted Edgar to the entrance hidden in the hillside. Once inside, they walked down a hallway. Uniformed people were walking down corridors and in and out of rooms. Edgar and Agent Sampson entered an elevator. Agent Sampson put a key in the slot and the elevator moved. When the door opened, a young woman was waiting.

"Welcome, Mr. Reinholdt, please follow me," she said. "I'm Kara. I hope you had a pleasant journey."

"Very pleasant," said Edgar.

They walked down another corridor and stopped outside a room. Kara opened the door and turned on the light.

"This will be your room, Mr. Reinholdt. I'll be back in a few minutes to show you the way to the conference room."

"Thank you," said Edgar. Kara closed the door and Edgar looked around. The room was spacious, much to his liking, and he took the opportunity to freshen up after his long trip. He had finished putting his clothes away when Kara returned.

They walked left down the hall and turned right at the next. She opened the door to a reception area.

"Please make yourself comfortable. The President will be with you in just a moment."

"Thank you."

As he looked around he saw that the dignitaries had arrived. Mr. Fairfield, the Prime Minister of England, walked over to him. He was a tall distinguished looking man who was dressed impeccably. His manner was a dead giveaway to his English heritage.

"Mr. Reinholdt, it's so nice to see you again," said Prime Minister Fairfield. "How is your wife?"

"Fine. And yours?" asked Edgar.

"She's well also. It was so nice of the President to offer to host this meeting."

"Yes, this way it will be so much easier on me and everyone will get the information at the same time."

President Bartram entered the room and greeted people as he passed. He was the epitome of graciousness, but by the same token was not a man who could be walked on. His track record as governor and in the Senate showed how assertive he could be. As President he had brought a new spirit to the country...a no nonsense approach. His diplomacy opened doors once closed by past administrations. For the most part, he involved his office only when necessary. Because of that, when he addressed any of the world powers, they knew to listen carefully to what he had to say.

"Mr. Reinholdt, thank you for coming," he said shaking his hand.

"You're very welcome, Mr. President. Thank you for hosting this."

"You're most welcome. I've had the room set up with everything you requested."

"Thank you."

"Shall we get started?"

"Yes."

"Ladies and Gentlemen," said President Bartram addressing the group, "if you would all make your way into the conference room, we'll get this meeting started."

They filed in and took their seats. President Bartram addressed the group first.

"When Mr. Reinholdt contacted me concerning this problem, I immediately asked if he'd like to meet everyone at once. He said he'd prefer it. Everyone will hear the same thing at the same time and be able to ask questions. That'll enable us all to learn and understand. As you know, ladies and gentlemen, time is of the essence. I want to thank you for clearing your calendars and meeting on such short notice. Mr. Reinholdt, I turn this meeting over to you."

"Thank you, Mr. President," he said as he walked to the podium. "A little over two weeks ago, there was an attempt on my life. I was supposed to be abducted; however a business associate was taken mistakenly. That led to an investigation by local and international police, as well as an investigation launched by my company and the company of the man who was taken. What we soon discovered was that the security in my lab had been compromised and information had been taken out of the facility. While no one person has every piece of every project, isolated pieces can still cause havoc. We were able to ascertain that formulas and codes were smuggled out of the lab by one of the members of the team working on a secret satellite project. The project, as you know, has been halted for reasons of national security, more accurately, world security. However, what was taken can definitely compromise the safety and security of nations on more than a communications level."

"Mr. Reinholdt, if I may interrupt?" asked Prime Minister Fairfield.

"Certainly."

"How is it possible that these formulas and codes were smuggled out?"

"We thought we had a foolproof method. No one brought anything into the lab except for themselves and perhaps a tissue. Every piece of paper used in the lab was counted before the team entered and again before they left to make sure that not one piece of paper left the lab. If it hadn't been for the new security system, we probably still wouldn't have detected it."

"I'm afraid I don't understand," said President Bartram.

"With our old system, the cameras would slowly move side to side to record the activity in the lab. When the camera was turned the other way, a person would have the time to write a few notes. The new system doesn't have that type of camera. The cameras are so small and hidden so well that the workers don't even know they're there. Even though the new system is in place, the old system is still operational. So the person in question would look up to see where the camera was. When he was out of its shot, he'd turn slightly and make notes on a tissue. He has no idea we know."

"How do you know what he took?" asked Prime Minister Marshall of Canada.

"We isolated those frames and enlarged sections making it as clear as possible until we could read what he had written. Many of the formulas, codes, and diagrams are so distinctive that even small sections can tell us which one it is. We then matched what was taken with the log for the lab for that day. That way we were able to confirm our findings."

"How much of the project was he able to get?" asked Prime Minister Masada of Spain.

"He's quite far from replicating the main project; however, what was taken can disrupt communications without you even knowing it. Anything personal, business, private, or classified can be intercepted by them, decoded, unscrambled, and read as though they are reading a newspaper. They'll also be able to reply to whatever is sent making it appear that it came from the intended receiver. You'll have no idea if the intended person received it until it may be too late. They can even send false orders moving whole armies."

"Won't that take time for them to be able to do that?" asked Prime Minister Fairfield.

"Once they find out what they have and what it can do, they'll start experimenting." Edgar paused for a few seconds. "It won't take them long."

"What has happened to the man who did this?" asked Prime Minister Masada leaning forward in his chair.

"Nothing. I thought it best to make him think he has been successful so far. This way, I know where he is. As long as he thinks he can get more information, he won't disappear and I'll also know whoever he's working for doesn't have everything he needs."

"Okay, Mr. Reinholdt, how do you propose we handle this situation?" asked President Roelini of Italy.

"I'd like to put forth three options and the reasoning behind each."

Edgar pulled up a page on the computer and projected it on the wall. The participants turned their attention to what was being shown.

"One is to immediately secure the communication satellites to guard against any type of tampering. This will ensure national security on all levels with respect to the embezzlement of intellectual property in question as well as all other communications. This will secure everything."

"The second is to do nothing and allow the activity to continue. This will give us an idea of what they have at their disposal and how far they're able to take the information and utilize it. This would put national security in jeopardy and open everything up to them."

"The third suggestion is to do a partial securing of the communication satellites. Secure all those areas vital to national security and allow all other areas to be manipulated. This will give them a sense of satisfaction that their contact person was successful. It'll also make them want additional information taken that will enable them to get into those areas that we've already secured."

"Please feel free to ask as many questions as you need to. I want to remind you that you're the only ones who can make the decision and the decision must be unanimous since different nations share satellites."

"Mr. Reinholdt, do you have one option you prefer over the others?" asked President Mason of Germany.

"Yes, however, I want you to think about each of these options and then we can discuss and debate them. Make no mistake, if you don't choose the option I'm in favor of, I'll lobby for it long and hard."

They all laughed.

"Mr. Reinholdt, do you have these itemized on paper. Sometimes, I think better when things are in front of me," said Prime Minister Fairfield.

Laura sat on the couch with her feet curled up; Gwen was in a big chair; and Mark was in the kitchen fixing something for breakfast. This was the first time they had an entire night's sleep since it all began. While everything was pressing, there was something about the day that warranted a slower start.

"If you were the people who took Michael and you thought you had Edgar, how would you go about getting the information you needed?" asked Laura finally breaking the silence.

"Somehow, I'd have to get to him," said Gwen putting down a book she was reading.

"How would you do that?"

"Well, I could always try to take him again or maybe I could take someone he cared about. If I did that, he might trade the secrets for the safe return of that person."

"Do you think he'd do that?"

"I don't know. It would depend upon who they took."

"Would Mark do it if they took you?"

"He better. Hey Mark!" Gwen yelled. "If they'd have taken me and you were in Edgar's position, would you give them what they wanted?"

Mark walked in from the kitchen.

"Yes, then I'd do to them every little thing they did to you and then I'd fuckin' kill them…slowly…very, very slowly."

"What if things had been reversed and they had taken Laura instead of Michael?" asked Gwen.

"Michael wouldn't stop until he had them," said Mark. "He'd give them anything they wanted to get Laura back and then he'd deal with the consequences later. I don't know anyone who wouldn't. Why?"

"Do you think they know if they had taken Edgar it would've been a mistake?" asked Laura.

"That's really the big question, isn't it?" said Gwen. "What if they know now that Edgar's the only one who can get them the information? Now what?"

"I don't know," said Laura. "I mean, how could we make Edgar give up something that's his in order to save someone we love?"

"If it was a woman, Edgar would do it," said Mark gesturing with the spatula in his hand. "For a man, I don't think he would."

"But isn't that the way it always is?" asked Gwen. "Men are supposed to be able to get themselves out of any situation without help."

"Yah with a paper clip, a piece of chewing gum, and some pocket lint," said Laura.

"Isn't that the truth," said Gwen, "while the women cry and squeak 'Help me, please help me.'"

"That paints a picture doesn't it?" said Laura.

Mark laughed and shook his head. "Yah, only it doesn't contain any of the women I know."

Gwen took off her slipper and threw it at him and he ducked.

"You know, I don't think Edgar has thought past the fact they might take him," said Laura.

"Seriously, he probably doesn't even think his wife might be in danger," said Gwen.

"I think that's the last thing on his mind right now," said Mark.

"I wonder where everyone is," said Laura. "I thought they'd be here by now. I don't know why they just don't stay. I mentioned it, but I don't think they want to impose."

"I'd call them, but someone has to finish breakfast," said Mark turning to go back to the kitchen.

"Now aren't you little Betty Crocker," said Gwen teasingly, "and did I tell you how sexy you look in that apron?"

Just then, the doorbell rang. Mark walked to the window, pulled the curtain back slightly, and looked out. He walked to the door and opened it.

"Good morning," said Mark. "Come in."

"Laura, is the invitation to stay here still open?" asked Margo.

"Of course. Put your things wherever," said Laura smiling.

Sadik sat in front of the Chosen One. He went over everything he heard Michael say. He didn't want to leave anything out when he was asked. He waited patiently while the Chosen One finished writing in his book.

"Well, Sadik, tell me how our Mr. Braedon was," said the Chosen One.

"He was fine, sir," said Sadik. "First, he wanted to thank you for allowing him to be untied. Then he asked why we wanted to take Mr. Reinholdt and I told him that Mr. Reinholdt has something that you needed."

"Good, good. Then what did he say."

"He asked me what you would have done if you had taken Mr. Reinholdt, but only Mr. Reinholdt had access to the information."

"And…"

"I told him that you would have had a plan for that. He said he thought you would have had a contingency plan," said Sadik.

"Yes, I see," said the Chosen One. The fact that only Mr. Reinholdt had access to everything never crossed his mind. Now he knew he had to find another answer. He was thankful he had begun thinking in that direction earlier.

"Then I asked him about the workers," said Sadik. "He said that they worked in only one building. He said they worked in the area of their specialty. It was what they had clearances for. I also asked about the cameras and he said there are cameras in Mr. Reinholdt's buildings."

"Very good, Sadik," said the Chosen One smiling. "I knew I could count on you to get Mr. Braedon to talk. He has given me much to think about."

"Yes, sir," said Sadik.

"Sadik, speak of this to no one," said the Chosen One.

"Yes, sir."

In a little while, Mark called them to the kitchen. While they ate, Laura asked each of them about the kidnapping of p;their spouse and the answers were all the same. One thing they all agreed on was that Edgar would be more apt to relinquish some sort of information if the hostage was a woman.

"You know, Edgar wouldn't part with that information to save himself," said Gwen.

"Why would you say that?" asked Nicole. It was inconceivable to her that you wouldn't do everything possible to save yourself.

"He's a man of integrity and if he gave over that information even to save himself," said Gwen, "he'd better close the doors to his business, because no one would do business with him after that."

"To save the one we love, we'd do anything…to save ourselves is something different," said Pierre.

"Well, I know we can't make Edgar give them what they want to get Michael back. I also know no government is going to come to his rescue. If Michael is going to be found and released, it's up to us," said Laura. "Now, for some reason, I can't explain, I know we can, will, and have to do it. There's not one flicker of doubt in my mind that if the situation was reversed, he'd do everything in his power and then some to make sure the person came home safe and sound. That's nothing more than we should expect of ourselves."

After hours of discussion among themselves, the group of international leaders was no closer to making a decision. They needed more input from Edgar. They ordered the selections according to their priority and what they felt was in the best interest of their countries. Edgar once again took his place at the podium.

"How can I be of help?" he asked.

"Mr. Reinholdt, we've gone over these suggestions and have debated them feverishly. For us, the least attractive and the one that is absolutely not acceptable is doing nothing," said Prime Minister Fairfield. "It would be ludicrous to jeopardize everything."

"I couldn't agree more," said Edgar.

"Then why did you even propose it?" asked President Mason.

"Because I wanted you to have all the options," said Edgar.

"The most acceptable of the three selections is the complete securing of all satellite functions, so they cannot use anything," said Prime Minister Marshall. "I know I would've done that."

"I thought so, too," said Edgar. "If it was only one country, it wouldn't be this complex."

"The third selection, the securing of vital functions while allowing the possible tampering with other areas is possibly doable," said President Mason, "however not everyone is in agreement."

"Mr. Reinholdt, what are your thoughts on the subject?" asked President Bartram.

"If we completely secure all satellite functions, then we've lost the opportunity to discover who's behind the espionage," said Edgar. "It's not so important that we know there's a person within my operations who is the one actually stealing secrets. He's nothing more than a small insignificant part of this whole project."

"What we really want to do is find out who's behind this. If we cut off every avenue, they'll try to find someone else who can give them the information they want and need. Right now, we know who their contact is and we can make sure he gets the information we want him to have. We can also make sure he doesn't have access to any information that could be catastrophic in nature."

He paused, took off his glasses, and looked at each of them. He knew what was on their minds and it was up to him to quell their fears.

"Ladies and Gentlemen, I wouldn't be suggesting this course of action if I thought it would in any way jeopardize the security of any nation. If they find they have access to most areas of communication, then they'll figure it's only a matter of time before they can crack the rest of the communications network via newly acquired codes."

"Then what happens, Mr. Reinholdt?' asked Prime Minister Fairfield. "When they acquire those codes, will it once again put our national security at risk?"

"I have no intention of giving them the codes they'd need."

"How can we be sure they don't already have the codes?" asked President Mason.

"Those codes will be newly generated and heavily guarded."

"If we do what you ask, Mr. Reinholdt what does that do to you personally?" asked Prime Minister Honomito of Japan.

"That makes me the same as I've always been...their target."

"How can we be sure you won't give them what they want?" asked Prime Minister Masada verbalizing what was on more than one leader's mind.

"I make confidentiality and integrity the main focus in my business. I have never sold anyone out and I do not intend to begin now. There's no one person who knows every piece of every project. That includes me. That's what's called a safeguard. Even if they had me and I told them everything I knew, the project wouldn't be complete. With regards to where we are now, no matter what they do, I'm the one who can counteract it. I give you my word on that."

They sat at the dining room table. There were piles of documents and information, but none of them blatantly held the key to getting Michael back.

"All this information from the internet needs to be substantiated," said Gwen. "We need to find legitimate sources, like books from a library or perhaps from someone who teaches Islamic History."

"Good idea," said Angelique.

"I'll do that. I'll contact Pitt," said Laura, "and get in touch with the professor who teaches it."

"We also need to know what parts of the world would be important to them," said Brigit. "Is it the same as mainstream Islam or perhaps it has changed from ancient times? That information may give us a lead to a location."

As large sheets of paper were filled with notes, Nicole tore them off and George hung them on the walls of the room. They hoped it would be easier to keep track of the information they had or needed and add other information as it was found.

"I'm still baffled as to why Michael was so insistent on checking security," said Pierre. "I've watched those records repeatedly trying to see what he saw and couldn't see anything."

"Maybe you're trying too hard," said Laura. "Whatever it is, Michael noticed it more than once and at more than one location."

"I keep thinking about what Michael could possibly have seen from his vantage point," said Pierre obviously frustrated.

"Well, maybe instead of looking at it that way," said Gina, "one of you needs to look at everything as a whole, while each of the others chooses one person and watches their activity. Then maybe someone could watch to see if there's anyone who comes in and out of the work area; someone who really doesn't belong in that place. Sometimes when we watch something so much, we miss little things. "It's time for a new perspective."

The meetings between the leaders were beginning to take on the feel of strained diplomacy. This wasn't the time to be accusatory. However, hard as they tried to see things from another's perspective, it was getting tiresome. Some of the leaders seemed to be indecisive and argumentative just for that sake. Several times the meeting had to be stopped to give the participants a chance to cool down and 'check their notes.'

If nothing else, all agreed that the first order of business was to ensure that national security wasn't compromised in any way. That, after all, was the goal of this meeting. The second part was to ensure they stayed in control of what was happening. It was important to know the contact person. Blocking everything would cause them to use someone new. By the time they found out who the new contact was, the terrorists could be in control of everything.

"We cannot afford to give them the upper hand," said Edgar adamantly. "The option with the least question marks is the one in which we give them only what we want them to have." He paused and looked around the table.

"Mr. Reinholdt, regardless of which of the two options we choose," said President Bartram, "those aspects of this problem that deal with national security must be protected."

"I think we're all in agreement as far as that's concerned," said Prime Minister Masada looking around the table at the others nodding.

"Is it possible," asked Prime Minister Fairfield, "to immediately protect all those things vital to the national security of our countries and then debate the rest?"

"That's definitely doable," said Edgar. "I can certainly secure those areas vital to national security as outlined in your contracts. There are papers in the packet in front of you that will give me permission to do so. Once they're signed, I'll take care of everything I can. I took the liberty of itemizing those things that are covered under the term 'national security.' These are lists that your countries had placed in the contracts from the first contract you signed with my company until the present."

Once the contracts were signed and Edgar left, the leaders started looking over the papers he had given them. There was silence for several minutes. Although he had quite thoroughly outlined everything, many of them were more than a little skeptical of one man's ability to keep everything in line…especially something of this magnitude.

Chapter Fifteen

The morning brought the promise of a new perspective. The men tried Gina's suggestions and it wasn't long before they had a break through.

"I think, I'm finally seeing what Michael may have seen," said Jean. "Can you back up to the part where there's a flash on the screen?"

"Sure," said Robert as he returned to that section.

"Now can you set it to repeat after about 30 seconds?" asked Jean. They watched the section.

"There, see it? Watch this guy," said Jean excitedly walking up to the wall and pointing at one of the workers. "He must be there to keep a pictorial record of everything that goes on in the lab."

"That's not unusual," said Pierre. "A lot of companies have those people."

"True, but look," said Jean. "He takes two pictures, one with the camera that's issued for that purpose and one with what seems to be his own."

"I noticed the flashes on other sections, but I just thought it was the camera passing a light," said Jacques.

"At first so did I, but then I noticed it was a double flash," said Jean. "It took me until now to see that the person was changing the camera."

"I wonder if that was happening at the other places," said George.

They went through the records again, this time making notes of when the flashes appeared. Robert took the time to capture those segments and put them in a folder.

"This had to have been what Michael was seeing," said Paul. "From what I can see, they're all different people."

"Are they connected?" asked Jean.

"They have to be connected," said Mark. "It'd be too coincidental that every one of these historians would take two pictures with two different cameras."

"Now we need to know what's on those pictures," said Pierre.

"Well, if they turned them in, Edgar should have a copy," said Mark.

"Let's see if Erika can give us some information," said Pierre picking up the phone.

Sadik walked into the room carrying a tray with two cups and some bread. Once he sat down, he offered some to Michael.

"Thank you," said Michael breaking small pieces of bread to eat.

"You are welcome," said Sadik taking a sip from his cup. "Mr. Braedon, what does Mr. Reinholdt's company do?"

To Michael, this seemed to be the tenth time he was asked the same question. He knew the Chosen One was testing him to see if he'd give some other answer. Without hesitation Michael answered as he had done many times before.

"I know that Reinholdt International works with governments on very sensitive matters of security. They also devise vast networks of communication."

"How much do you know about the importance of satellites?"

"In regards to what?"

"Communications."

"I know that the use of satellites has made it possible for more complex methods of communication."

"Does Mr. Reinholdt work with communication satellites?"

"Yes, Mr. Reinholdt's company deals with communications carried out using satellites. I also know that Mr. Reinholdt is embarking on a new communication project. He and his company were beginning to work on it when I was there."

"How important is your company to the project?"

"Our company is not directly involved in that project."

"Then why did Mr. Reinholdt have you at his facility?"

"Mr. Reinholdt wants to move into the public sector. Right now he deals only with government contracts. He hired us to research all the aspects of the industry to see if his facilities could accommodate such a move and if there was a market for it. He wanted unbiased answers."

"Like what?"

"We were checking out everything that had to do with the competition that Mr. Reinholdt might have if he went into the public sector. Then we were also trying to find out what Mr. Reinholdt would have to do to separate what he does for governments from what he would do for other companies. It's important that the two stay separate."

"Do you think Mr. Reinholdt would negotiate for your release by using information the Chosen One wants?"

"I have no way of knowing that since I don't know what pieces of information the Chosen One would be asking for. It might be possible that I have some of those answers. What is the Chosen One trying to do?"

"I do not know exactly what the Chosen One wants."

"How do you know what questions to ask then?"

"I am given specific questions to ask and then based on the answers, other questions."

"What do the answers have to do with the treatment I receive?"

"As long as you cooperate to the best of your ability or what the Chosen One believes is the best of your ability, then you have nothing to worry about. The minute you give wrong information or try to give information that would sabotage the Chosen One's efforts, the treatment will become unbearable," said Sadik. He paused and looked Michael in the eyes. "Make no mistake about that."

The guard stood up, picked up the tray and left. Michael thought about everything he had seen, heard, and researched about Reinholdt International. He wondered just how much information he actually had that the captors would determine to be pertinent information. How long could he spread that out and how long could he keep the treatment benign. He made mental notes about what he said in the conversation. He was positive the Chosen One was trying to find out whether or not he was telling the truth. He had no other choice but to tell him the truth…at least the truth as he knew it. Anything else would mean his immediate execution.

What was once a very tidy house had become somewhat cluttered. Throughout the downstairs there were papers piled on every available flat surface. They had been leafed through and their contents perused many times. Large sheets of paper decorated the walls and post-it notes were on anything that would hold them.

The ladies went through everything concerning the hostage situation with Michael as well as researching the group responsible for the abduction. It was imperative for them to construct a profile of the society members that held him. The more information they could find, the better job they'd be able to do finding the members who had infiltrated the Reinholdt organization. There in the living room of Michael's home in Paris, they began piecing together certain aspects of personalities and beliefs the group looked for in members.

Paul walked into the room and sat on the arm of the chair next to his wife. He bent down and gave her a kiss on the cheek.

"Did you find anything, yet?" asked Gina.

"We found the security problem," said Paul, "thanks to you."

"What was it?" she asked putting down the papers she was reading. The others looked up from what they were doing to listen.

"It seems Edgar has what we call historians who record the activities in the workplace. The people Edgar has in these positions aren't only taking pictures using the camera provided by the company, but also their own. On the surveillance records, we could see two flashes. Several times, we could actually see the person taking the first picture using the company camera and then his own. We spoke to Edgar's secretary and she's faxing us their information

"What about the pictures the historians took?" asked Margo.

"Those should be here in the morning," said Pierre. "It might give a clue about what else they're looking for."

"We know their goal is to spread their religion, the true religion," said Gwen. "SecReSAC will give them the ability to spread the religion to every part of the world. In an extreme case, literally shove it down everyone's throat with the threat of annihilation if there's resistance."

"Having SecReSAC in itself will mean nothing if they don't have the equipment necessary to implement the program," said Mark.

"Start making a list of what you think they'd need," said Brigit. "Then search the internet to find every company that sells each piece of equipment. After that, get in touch with their purchasing department and find out who has bought that particular piece of equipment in the past ninety days. We're looking for patterns."

"As for those that need a government requisition, we're looking to see if any unusual countries are requesting the equipment," said George. "You know, third world and very small countries that really wouldn't be looking to purchase something of this caliber."

"Robert," asked Gina playing with the pen in her hand, "how hard would it be to find out if there had been any sort of break-ins at government complexes that might use these things?"

"Not a problem. The more they try to cover it up, the easier it is to find."

"As I've said before, we need to make them come to us," said Gina. "We need to make it impossible for them to find anything without our help."

Diplomacy had all but run its course. Tension was in the air and with Edgar away from the table and out of the room, the leaders felt free to express their doubts and concerns to one another in relationship to the option that wouldn't secure all communications.

"What bothers me most is not that those public communication networks could be compromised, but that Mr. Reinholdt himself is still somewhat of a target," said Prime Minister Honomito. "As long as they don't take him, he can undo what they do, or prevent them from going too far. What happens, however, if he's taken? How could we be positive they wouldn't be able to get into the secured communications?"

"I understand what you're saying and that certainly was true when they decided to take Mr. Reinholdt in the first place," said Prime Minister Fairfield. "He's only good to them if he can deliver what they want. If they take him, they can't get it."

"We know that, but how can we be sure that the people who took Mr. Braedon know that?" asked Prime Minister Honomito.

"We can't," said Prime Minister Marshall.

"How can you be so sure that a man of Mr. Reinholdt's intelligence doesn't possess all of the pieces of the puzzle?" asked Prime Minister Masada.

"I think Mr. Reinholdt is smart enough to know that knowing everything would make him the ultimate target," said Prime Minister Marshall.

"Each of us knows how dangerous that is," said President Bartram trying to be the voice of reason. "That's one way of protecting the leaders from certain abduction. The same is true in Mr. Reinholdt's world. The position he has created for himself is one that makes him more valuable alive than dead and more valuable free than captured. As long as those who are in possession of the information realize this, we have nothing to worry about. Mr. Reinholdt will be able to protect our interests as well as his own."

"What happens if the situation changes?" asked Prime Minister Masada. "Let's say they decide to release Mr. Braedon and take Mr. Reinholdt's wife instead. Would he crumble under the pressure and deliver to them exactly what they're asking for?"

"We have no way of knowing that," said President Roelini getting up from his chair and walking around. "That could be disastrous!" he said waving his hands. "What happens if he decides to negotiate with them for her release?"

"Look, we have no way of knowing how each of us would react if our spouse or child were taken," said Prime Minister Fairfield. "It's easy to sit here and pass judgment, but until you're in that situation, you have no idea how you would react."

"That's exactly what I'm talking about," said President Roelini. "If we don't know how each of us would react, how are we to know that Mr. Reinholdt wouldn't give them everything they wanted to get his wife back."

"Look, they haven't made that move," said Prime Minister Fairfield, "and they've made no indication they will."

"They're not going to tell us what they're going to do!" said Prime Minister Honomito raising his voice to be heard. "They're just going to do it. We need to plan for that. We need to know that Mr. Reinholdt will stand firm."

"I agree," said President Bernuit leaning forward and placing his arms on the table. "Tell me something, President Bartram, has the family of Mr. Braedon come forward to ask for help in this matter?"

"Yes, they have." said President Bartram. "As soon as it happened and multiple times since then...every day as a matter of fact."

"And what was your answer?" asked President Bernuit.

"Our answer was the same as it has been in every hostage crisis. We do not negotiate for the release of a citizen. You should know that as hard as it is to say no, we must hold firm."

"What if they're persistent," asked Prime Minister Masada. "Will that change your mind?"

"No. We don't put the rest of the nation at the mercy of terrorists," said President Bartram and he paused and shook his head. "Now we're at their mercy and still can't act. If we were to decide to negotiate now, we'd have to admit that we know that secrets had been taken that could compromise national security. That would undo everything we're trying to do here."

"I'm the person who knows the least about Mr. Reinholdt," said Prime Minister Strickland of Australia. "I understand our country has dealt with him many times before. It would seem to me that if countries repeatedly do business with this man, his dealings must be ethical."

"I have no problem with Mr. Reinholdt. His reputation is beyond reproach," said Prime Minister Honomito. "My concern is the situation and..."

"Not being in control," said President Roelini finishing Prime Minister Honomito's thought. "I feel I'm the only one who knows what is best for the citizens of my country. That's why I'm in charge. I don't like handing over control to anyone."

"I understand how frustrating this is," said Prime Minister Fairfield, "however, we need to give Mr. Reinholdt enough respect to address our doubts."

"I have a few more questions for him when he comes back," said Prime Minister Honomito. "I'm still not convinced that this is a prudent choice."

Chapter Sixteen

Michael woke as the morning dawned. He had been so exhausted that he was able to sleep despite the conditions. His dreams were a mixture of pleasure and pain, both of which contained Laura. He worried about her and what she must be going through. He wondered what the day would bring; however, he knew that worrying was useless. He learned to put out of his mind anything he had no control over and in this instance especially, if he began to worry or what if, he'd drive himself crazy. That was no way to survive. In order to survive, he had to tell them what they needed to know and somehow figure out what they were talking about. What was it Edgar was working on? What was it that was so important to them?

Michael tried to pull himself up, but his body ached from the beatings and slashing. What he wouldn't give for a hot bath. Keys jingled in the lock, the door opened, and in walked the eight abductors. He immediately began to fear what this morning's interrogation would bring. The Chosen One, stood in front of him. One of the men moved out of the group and began recording the proceedings. The leader barked the order to bring Michael to his feet.

"Where are Mr. Reinholdt's facilities located?"

"All of Mr. Reinholdt's facilities are centered in Frankfurt and the surrounding areas." "What type of business does Mr. Reinholdt engage in?"

"It is a communications business."

"What is Mr. Reinholdt's area of expertise?"

"Mr. Reinholdt is at the present time working with governments exclusively."

"What do you mean by at the present time?"

"Governments are the only clients that Mr. Reinholdt has right now."

The Chosen One nodded his head and the men on either side of Michael held him tautly upright. The Chosen One took the gun he was holding and hit Michael with the butt in the ribs. Michael gasped in pain. The men let go of their grip and Michael doubled over. The Chosen One nodded again and the men pull Michael to an upright position.

"Do you think I am stupid?"

"No, sir," said Michael gasping.

"What are Mr. Reinholdt's plans?"

"He is initiating a move that will expand his operations by offering his services to corporations that are not connected with the government."

"What does Mr. Reinholdt hope to accomplish by this?"

"Mr. Reinholdt hopes to expand his business, add clients, and diversify to other areas. He feels that there's a need in the business world for modified versions of his communication devices and programs."

"Will he offer the same things to the private corporations that he offers to governments?"

"No. He will offer them communication products that will enable them to compete more advantageously in today's market. There will be nothing that will even come near to the caliber that is offered on a government level."

"Would a person, if they were able to obtain the corporate communication devices and programs be able to modify those programs and perhaps be able to rival a government's communication system?"

Michael looked up at the Chosen One. It was obvious that the question took him by surprise. "To be honest, I never thought about it in that way."

Again, the Chosen One nodded. The two men raised Michael to his feet. This time the Chosen One took the gun and hit him in the legs. Michael lost his balance and fell face forward on the ground with his face at the feet of the Chosen One. He put the barrel of the gun on Michael's back.

"Perhaps you need to do a little thinking, Mr. Braedon," he said with clenched teeth. "I will expect an answer when I return."

After the Chosen One raised the gun and his hand, he gave a backhanded upward gesture. Two men lifted Michael up to a sitting position and leaned him against the wall. He watched as they left and locked the door behind him. He closed his eyes and shook his head. What did he say that was so wrong? How could he answer something he didn't know about? What was it going to take for them to leave him alone? Michael sat on the floor and leaned his head against the wall. He tried to think of something, anything other than this place, these people, Edgar, and the situation. His thoughts went to the one person he knew could take his pain away.

As he thought about her, he could feel her touch on his skin, see her face, the tears in her eyes. He knew that every time the leader walked in with his entourage, he was on the internet. *Baby, I hope you didn't watch this. I can't stand to think about you being upset. I know you're going through hell and I want nothing more than to be able to walk through the front door of our house in Paris. I want to take you in my arms and hold you while we both cry. You are the love of my life, Laura, and I had to wait so long to find you. I want to kiss you, touch you, and make love with you. Oh, God, Laura, I need you now.*

The more he thought about her, the more real she was. At that moment, he felt he could reach and touch her. He allowed his mind to wander to a place where he was safe and loved.

Mark covered his face with his hands. The treatment of his brother was beginning to take its toll. He watched Laura's face as she listened to the questions and the answers that Michael gave. The seconds of silence followed by the gasps of pain were more than she could handle. The tears streamed down her face. She walked into the kitchen and stood holding onto the counter. *How much more can you go through? I'm so worried, Michael. I love you.*

"Oh, Michael, I will find you," she cried. "I promise I'll find a way to find you and make them release you. And then I'll make them pay." She pounded her fist on the counter. "I will make them pay."

Mark walked into the kitchen.

"Are you alright?"

She turned to face him and shook her head. He put his arms around her and she sobbed.

"It's going to be alright. I know it doesn't seem so right now, but it will be. We're going to find him. We're going to bring him home." He said those words not only for Laura's sake, but for his own. He tried to convince himself, but the reality of the situation was staring right at him.

"What do they want from him?" she asked wiping her eyes. "What the hell do they want!"

"They want answers to their questions about Edgar. They want to know how much Michael knows so they can find the best way to get Edgar to give them what they want."

"I don't think Edgar's going to give them the information to save Michael."

"Neither do I. I think they may now realize that if they had taken Edgar, it would've been a mistake. We know he wouldn't have been able to give them what they wanted even to save himself. If they've figured that out, they need to find what it'll take for Edgar to retrieve the information and deliver it to them."

"I agree with what you said earlier, Mark. I think if they had a woman, Edgar might do it," said Laura reaching for a tissue to wipe her face again.

"Why are you still thinking about that?" asked Mark looking her in the eyes. "Just get that out of your mind." The very thought of a woman, any woman, being taken sent chills up his spine.

"Mark, the closest person to Edgar is his wife. He absolutely adores her. Even when she was pestering him about the gala, you could tell how much he really loved her," said Laura leaning up against the sink. "I think if they threatened to take her he'd give them whatever they wanted."

"But, would they release Michael if they had her?"

"If they thought Michael was of no use to them, I think they'd release him," said Laura, *or kill him.* "The problem is, how can we be sure?"

"With them, I don't think we can. I think it depends upon how badly they want the information and the secrets."

"Well, that's something we have to figure out now, don't we."

It was early morning when the leaders returned for the second day of deliberation on the problems that faced them and their countries. The looks on their faces showed that sleep was a luxury none of them really enjoyed the night before. Coffee cups and plates with half-eaten breakfast pastries sat in front of most of them. President Bartram walked into the conference room and greeted them.

"Ladies and Gentlemen, I hope you slept well."

"Not really," said Prime Minister Honomito. "I feel as though we have no options in this matter."

"Oh, we do have options, three of them," said President Bernuit.

"Those are the options Mr. Reinholdt put forth," said Prime Minister Honomito. "Those are not the options we would have chosen."

"How do you know that?" retorted Prime Minister Strickland. "What would your options be?

"In my country we would find these people," said Prime Minister Honomito raising his voice. "It's the only way to end this."

"I agree that's important," said Prime Minister Fairfield trying to calm Prime Minister Honomito while not alienating the others, "but not as important as taking measures to secure our countries first. We must think of the welfare of our citizens."

"Don't you think I know that!" said Prime Minister Honomito becoming somewhat agitated. "These people must be brought to justice!" He hit his fist against the table.

"Yes, Prime Minister Honomito, you're right in that respect," said Prime Minister Marshall. "However, there isn't anything we can do in this situation right now. If we go after them in any manner and they find out about it, nothing will be safe. They'll ultimately get the information somehow and we'll never know." She paused for a moment. No one at the table uttered a sound. "Like it or not, at least this way, we can still monitor what's going on and counter it."

"What I find frustrating is that we have the world's best armies and intelligence agencies at our disposal," said Prime Minister Masada, "but we're powerless when it comes to this."

"Powerless? I think not," said President Bartram. "Powerless means we have to do exactly what they want us to do. That's not what's happening. What we have here is a chance to use our own intelligence wisely. All of us are so dependent on counsel. We continually defer to this agency or this organization or this person when a decision has to be made. We're coached on how to answer questions at press conferences and never give a speech our speech writers haven't written. We are the leaders of the free world as they like to term it. We're supposed to be the brightest and the best at what we do. It's now our time to show why we were elected."

Now that he had their undivided attention, President Bartram continued. He brought his voice down and looked around at all of the leaders engaging them in what he was saying.

"You see, the only person in my country who can make a decision concerning this is me, no one else. I can't chance allowing anyone else in on this. Even though I trust those people closest to me with my life every day, I can't entrust to them the lives of every one of the citizens of my country. I'm the only one I trust with that job and I have to do that job the best I can."

"I agree with you totally," said Prime Minister Fairfield. "We've made the decision to secure the systems vital to national security. Now, we have to decide how to handle these pirates."

"What about the consulting firm that's working with Mr. Reinholdt?" asked President Roelini. "Where do they come into all of this?"

"We have used that firm and I can tell you that their confidentiality is second to none," said President Bartram. He knew exactly what was on their minds. "They also have just as much if not more to lose. They have one of their own in harm's way. As tempting as it is to go against past practice and get involved in this hostage situation, the United States must stand firm on its no interference stance. Any movement to the contrary would signal that we know something more than we're letting on."

"Then, Mr. Braedon has become a pawn in this," said Prime Minister Masada smoothing his moustache.

"More like a means to an end," said President Bernuit.

"As long as they feel he's useful, they won't kill him," said President Bartram. "He's a very intelligent man. I've met him on numerous occasions and have been amazed at his wealth of knowledge on just about any subject that arises in conversation."

"Let's hope his wealth of knowledge is enough to keep him alive until a solution is found," said Prime Minister Strickland.

"What happens if his colleagues decide to try to find him?" asked President Roelini.

"Then, besides us, we have many more pairs of ears and eyes trained on the subject. There's no way they'll jeopardize his welfare," said Prime Minister Fairfield. "They'll do whatever they have to do to gain his release. They'll never sell out any of us. They make a living being ethical. It's a way of existence for them." He paused a moment and looked at his colleagues. "At this time, we cannot and will not do anything to interfere with what they're doing, if indeed they're doing anything. If we do so, we'd have to explain why we'd be getting involved with them and that's not an option."

"I agree," said President Mason.

"I still cannot understand why a covert operation launched to specifically target this group would in any way endanger our efforts," said Prime Minister Honomito, "or be a danger to Mr. Braedon for that matter."

"This group we're dealing with is most likely everywhere," said Prime Minister Fairfield, trying to keep his patience. "You know as well as I do that there's no possible way to assure that even the most dedicated agents in a covert operation are not dual operatives. All of us have seen our share of traitors. We've also seen how costly it has been for everyone when what you're trying desperately to resolve blows up in your face and the ramifications must be dealt with swiftly."

"This situation would be catastrophic if a covert operation proved to be infiltrated by those very individuals we're trying to counter. Those are numbers I'm not willing to risk. We cannot in good conscience put the world at risk while we sit around waiting for news."

"I couldn't agree more," said President Roelini and he turned to face Prime Minister Honomito. "Mr. Prime Minister, while I and probably all the others in this room would love nothing more than to storm this group's fortress, so to speak, we must put those wants and desires on a back burner and take care of our citizens. While this group assumes that they will sooner or later have us all sitting on a ticking time bomb, the measures Mr. Reinholdt is putting in place will have diffused that bomb. Then when the time is right, I'll gladly join you and the others and together we'll put an end to this group's tyranny."

"President Roelini, that will please me greatly," said Prime Minister Honomito.

Laura sat curled up in the chair in the living room with her laptop. She looked over the website for the University of Pittsburgh and was determined to find the information they needed. Finally after some time, she found the name of the professor and his contact information.

She picked up the phone and called.

"Good morning, Professor Laban's office."

"May I speak to Professor Laban?" asked Laura.

"May I tell him who's calling?"

"Yes, this is Laura Darmer. I'm a freelance writer and I need some information for an article I'm writing."

"Just one minute please."

There was silence on the other end as she was put on hold. In some ways she was glad not to have to listen to elevator music or constant information overload.

"Ms. Darmer, this is Professor Laban," he said finally breaking the silence. "How can I help you?"

"Professor Laban, first of all, thank you for taking my call. I'm writing an article on the ancient religious group that claims to be the ancestral line of Islam and therefore the only true religion. I was hoping to be able to set the record straight concerning this ancient group. There seems to be such controversial material written about them."

"Yes, Ms. Darmer. How can I help you with that?"

"I'm a bit confused concerning this. I see no ties whatsoever to Islam when it comes to this ancient group."

"Ms. Darmer, you're correct. The faction of this religious group that has surfaced is hoping to attach credibility to itself by claiming to be the original forerunner of Islam. However, there are definite philosophic differences that cannot simply be swept away. Those who have chosen to buy into this do so with the blind naiveté of a child and this new resurgence has been taken to a level of cultism."

"There is one leader, one person to listen to, no questions asked. This leader has claimed that he was led to a cave where the real writings of the prophets were kept hidden until the most worthy of servants was of age to receive their teachings. It was during the time he was in the cave that the white light enveloped him and he was given all of the teachings of the prophets, the holy words, the laws, and the mission he was to undertake. He was then told to write down all he knew and give it to the new followers."

"Those who came to him would be those who were chosen. They'd then be given the holy words and the laws. When they were ready, they'd be allowed to know what the mission was. Only those who were chosen would be allowed to know the mission."

"Professor Laban, do you have any idea how many followers there are of this Religious group?"

"A conservative estimate would put it at less than ten thousand."

"Do you have any idea what the mission is?"

"Yes, it's to bring the entire world to the one true religion. In order to do this, they're to use any means to communicate the word."

"How are they proposing to do this?"

"There have been instances where they've been able to take over small local radio stations and small local television stations. The leader is a very personable man, very charismatic. That's how he was able to add to his ranks. Sources close to him say that the success he has achieved on a small level has made him want to try a much larger endeavor, but wouldn't expound on it."

"Professor Laban, I've tried to find them on the internet, but every time I search, I only get the historical information concerning the ancient religion itself."

"At first, that was all I could find also until I realized that the message was only meant for the chosen. So in order for me to find them, I had to either query as though I was one of the chosen, or find one of the chosen to give me the site."

"What did you do?"

"I queried. I wanted to know the process first hand."

"How long did it take?"

"It took the better part of a year. They're very careful about who they allow to be chosen."

"That doesn't exactly make sense if they're trying to bring everyone to this one true religion."

"It would seem so, but in his way of thinking, you can never be too careful. You see, it's in its infancy stage and cannot withstand any attacks from the inside."

"So you're telling me if I want to find out everything I can about this organization, I'm going to have to query and it'll take approximately a year?"

"Oh, no, Ms. Darmer, you can't query. Women aren't chosen. They were never part of the original religion. Women don't count in their world. Women are only a means to justify an end. They're to be used to get what you want. Women are only needed to increase the membership, to keep the members fed, clothed, and sheltered. The only other way women are useful is to be able to get information that's critically needed when someone won't give it up. The leader will order the woman to seduce a man to get what the leader wants."

"Professor Laban," said Laura rather apprehensively, "are you one of the chosen?"

"No, Ms. Darmer, I'm not," said Professor Laban. "I was only for research purposes. Although it was strictly forbidden to print out any of the documents they placed online, I did it anyway. I use passages from them for my classes where we compare the real religions with the cults that rise out of them. It's interesting to find out just what some individuals are able to do and how they're able to convince others it's in their best interest to believe in their God. Ms. Darmer, I'd be glad to send you copies of everything I was able to retrieve online as well as what I use for my class."

"That would be wonderful."

"Once you've had the chance to read everything, call me and we can discuss any questions you may have."

"I'd appreciate that."

"Now, where can I send these?"

"Professor Laban, if you could tell me when you'll have them ready, I'll send a courier to pick them up. At the present time, I'm out of the country."

Laura smiled as she hung up the phone. That went better than she ever expected. At least in a matter of days, they'd have some real information about the group.

"Who were you talking to?" asked Gina looking up from her laptop.

"That was Professor Laban. He's a professor of philosophy and religious studies at Pitt. I thought I'd call and ask some questions concerning the group that has Michael," said Laura.

"What did you find out?" asked Gina.

"Professor Laban was very enlightening. He told me that the leader has been chosen to receive the word, the law, and the mission. He was told to write down all he was told, to find those who were chosen to help him, and ultimately to bring the entire world to the one true religion."

"That's quite a mission," said Angelique.

"Professor Laban said he queried as though he was one of the chosen and it took him nearly a year to get the information. When I expressed amazement that if I queried it'd take a year to get information, he told me I couldn't query because I was a woman and women aren't chosen. As he put it; women are a means to justify an end."

"Now what?" asked Angelique.

"He's going to send me everything he has about the group along with materials from his class. He said he thinks I'll find it interesting. Now I need to call Maggie and have her arrange a courier to pick up the package tomorrow at two o'clock," said Laura. "Is there anything that needs to be brought here maybe from the office?"

"I don't know," said Gina moving her laptop to the lamp stand next to her and getting up. "Let me ask Pierre if there's anything he needs from the Pittsburgh office. I know for a fact there are things that have to go back there, so this'll be good."

Gina knocked softly before walking into the study where Pierre was working.

"Pierre, I'm sorry to bother you, but Laura is having some documents brought here by courier from Pittsburgh," she said. "She wanted to know if there was anything you needed the courier to bring. She's getting ready to call Maggie to have her arrange it."

"As a matter of fact, I have a list of things we need," said Pierre getting up from his chair and walking over to Michael's desk. He picked up a folder and opened it. "Tell Laura I'll be there in a minute."

Laura placed the call to Maggie. It was the first time they had spoken since Michael had been taken. She remembered their last conversation when the other hostage was killed. She often thought of what Maggie said that day, *"Sometimes I wonder what I'd do if it was someone I knew."* She shuddered every time she thought of it. How could they've ever imagined it'd really happen to someone they knew. Somehow she knew Maggie probably thought about that many times, too.

"Hi Maggie, how are you?" asked Laura after she answered the phone.

"Holding up, Laura. It's so hard. I just can't believe this is happening. All I can think about is our conversation."

"I know. I thought about that, too."

"Who would have ever thought..." said Maggie, her voice starting to break, "and then for it to be Michael."

"I know Maggie."

"When I talked to my mother, I told her I thought it was my fault. I told her I put the thought out there and it happened."

"Surely, Maggie, you don't believe that?"

"I don't know what to believe," said Maggie sniffling. "All I know is that it haunts me."

"Maggie, you had nothing to do with this," said Laura trying to reassure her. "Remember, they weren't even after Michael. They took him by mistake."

"I know, Laura, I know and I know you didn't call just to talk. What can I do for you?"

"Maggie, I need a favor?"

"Sure, what is it?"

"I need for you to arrange to have a courier go to Professor Laban's office in the Cathedral of Learning to get a package for me. I emailed his address to you already.

"I'll get that as soon as we're through. Anything else?"

Pierre also needs him to come by the office to get some things from you. He'll be on the phone in a minute."

"Good. I need some things from the Paris office also."

"Maggie, take care. I promise I'll call you sometime just to talk."

"I'd like that."

"Here's Pierre," she said and handed the phone to him.

Pierre's conversation with Maggie took less than five minutes.

"What did you need the courier for?" Pierre asked Laura handing the phone back to her.

"I'm having information brought about the group that's holding Michael."

"Are you serious? Where did you find it?"

"A professor at Pitt is sending it to me."

"Does he know who you are?" asked Pierre with concern.

"I told his secretary I was writing an article and needed information. If they check my name, they'll see that I've written for various publications on a number of diverse topics. When I talked to him, I kept the conversation to the religious group and nothing else. I figured the courier would be the quickest way to get the information to me."

"That's fine," said Pierre. "It also gives us a chance to take care of business, too. Michael and Mark always took care of the back and forth document shuffle. Now, we need to take care of it in a more conventional way. Imagine that."

"Pierre, I hope we never become so conventional."

"Me too, Sweetie." He smiled, took her hand in his and patted it.

The Chosen One stood looking out the window of his office. He watched as his followers scurried around doing everything they were asked to do. He felt that surge of power move through him. This was indeed worth waiting for. It was worth everything he endured in the past.

He learned from the best and the worst. He knew their mistakes and now that power was his, he wouldn't make those same mistakes. The mark of a true leader was how well he could take the past, learn from it, and use it to create his future...the future he wanted.

He was there, he knew it. Everything was falling into place...some things a little slower than he'd like, but falling just the same. He knew whatever happened, good or bad, he must turn into an opportunity to use to his advantage.

Now his followers were coming into the office. This was the second meeting since Mr. Braedon was taken. This wasn't usual. Sometimes weeks would go by between meetings and everyone knew they were only called when it was of some importance. Today, all those who were close to the Chosen One were present.

"We are getting closer to the time when I must address all of my followers," the Chosen One began. "It is imperative that they be able to see me and hear the holy words spoken to them. I have much to say in the message."

"Yes, sir," they said in unison.

"We have been working on getting the information that we have been blessed to have received from those who work for Mr. Reinholdt," he continued. "We are discovering new things every day. It is only a matter of time. Gehran have you heard any more from Dabir."

"Yes, sir, he and the others are still getting pieces of information for the projects they are working on."

"Did you impress upon him that we need the information as quickly as possible?"

"Yes, sir. He has assured me that he and the others are working as quickly as they can to get you what you need."

"There have not been any problems, have there, Gehran?"

"No problems, sir, but he has heard that Mr. Reinholdt is going to put in a new security system. He does not know when it will be operational. They are trying to find out. If the new system goes in, it will slow things down for a while."

"We cannot allow that to happen, Gehran," said the Chosen One emphatically. "We cannot afford to have our progress slowed."

"Yes, sir."

"Perhaps Mr. Braedon might know something about that system," said Sadik.

"Yes, sir, perhaps," said Gehran. "After all, he had been in Frankfurt with Mr. Reinholdt."

"And at the facilities, sir," said Sadik. "Perhaps Mr. Reinholdt told him about it."

"Yes, Sadik, perhaps. We may just have to pay Mr. Braedon a visit. Let's hope that our hospitality has in some ways made him a little more cooperative."

"Yes, sir."

The leaders were discussing their options and amendments to those options when Edgar entered the room. He quietly sat in his seat and didn't interrupt.

"Have you been able to take care of everything?" asked President Bartram when he noticed Edgar's presence.

"Yes, Mr. President."

"I secured everything that had to do with the safety of the citizens. I didn't, however, secure other nonessential communication networks, television, radio, and the like. Those I felt would be the first things they'd try to control or take over. It's important for them to think they've succeeded. They'll try to take over radio and television broadcasts without the networks knowing it."

"Their objective will be to broadcast their message before anyone at the network can possibly stop them or trace their signal. When they get better, they'll learn how to do this in such a foolproof manner that the network won't be able to stop their transmission. From everything we know about them, communication is their prime objective."

"Mr. Reinholdt, what happens if they're able to somehow take over one of the communication satellites?" asked Prime Minister Masada. "Will they then be able to access our computers and take over all levels of communication and thus put national security in jeopardy?"

"Absolutely not. The safeguards I've put in place will alert us long before they're able to get to anything remotely connected with national security. As I was making the necessary adjustments and putting into place those security measures, I kept thinking of other scenarios. Perhaps this was a blessing in disguise. It's giving us a chance to reassess what's listed on those pages dealing with national security."

"You're exactly right Mr. Reinholdt," said President Bernuit. "Things have changed drastically during the last few decades, even the last few years. We need to take these new issues into consideration. If we don't we're letting ourselves open to sabotage by just about anyone who's technologically savvy."

"This may be an opportune time to do this," said Edgar. "I'm not sure what your schedules are like, but I for one, will clear my schedule for this. The way I see it, there can't be anything more important."

"A week ago I would've never dreamed it'd be possible for someone outside of the government circle to take over a satellite and tell it what to do," said Edgar adding emphasis to the problem that lay before them. "When you think about it, if I say the word terrorist to you, I bet you have a notion in your head as to what a terrorist looks like. Part of our problem is that we've put a face to terrorism and along with that face comes the idea of what terrorism involves, most of which are bombs, planes, and transportation."

As he looked around the table the leaders were nodding. It was evident they also had that misconception of terrorism that was overplayed by the media.

"Who'd ever think of a terrorist as being someone in a three piece suit with glasses, a pocket protector, and a love for computer jargon? Yet, that's one of the most vulnerable areas we have and an attack on our information systems is terrorism."

"I think we need to vote on whether or not to stay," said President Bartram. "Since no one should feel pressured, I think it should be just a simple yes or no written on a piece of paper and we'll ask Mr. Reinholdt to count them."

Prime Minister Fairfield passed around a cube of paper he used for doodling during meetings. Each person took a sheet and wrote either yes or no and folded it. Edgar looked around the room and saw a crystal bowl. He picked it up and circulated it among the leaders. When it reached him, he took the pieces of paper out one at a time and read each aloud as he unfolded them.

"It's unanimous, all yeses."

Laura loved to cook and bake, especially for Michael. He always appreciated everything she did. Even though he wasn't there, she found herself wanting to make the things he loved the most. Whether the rest of them were aware of it didn't matter. She did it to feel that connection, that bond. She looked at the table one last time and then called the others to come to dinner.

"You've been in that room all day," she said as they took their places. "What've you been doing?"

"We've been going over films and documents," said Pierre. "Edgar put people in positions he thought were the best for the job. The problem, as I see it, is that this group must've been planning this for years. They had to get people into Reinholdt International and they had to prove themselves as exemplary employees. They chose Reinholdt International because they were after their cutting edge communication methods. They weren't originally after SecReSAC. SecReSAC was a bonus, the answer to their prayers."

"It'd enable them to be heard everywhere at the same time and if they were ruthless enough enable them to strong arm everyone into accepting their religion or die. They could threaten annihilation of an area if everyone doesn't comply. What would result would be mass chaos. People who dare to say no could cause the destruction of whole areas. Therefore, anyone who dares to say no will probably be killed by others in his area."

"That's horrible!" said Margo.

"Exactly," said Pierre. "The more we find the more bizarre it is."

"How do we get Michael back without giving them the keys to everything?" asked Gina.

"I don't know," said Pierre. "We need time and we need Edgar to buy it."

"What good is time going to be if Michael can't hold out?" asked Laura.

"Don't even think that way!" said Gwen.

"He'll hold on as long as it takes," said Jean.

There was silence for the first time at the table as they ate.

"Laura," said Mark breaking the silence, "what's so important that you needed a courier?"

"I talked to Professor Laban from Pitt," she said. "He's sending detailed information on the religious faction that's holding Michael. He was very informative on the phone and he's going to send me his first hand information when he asked to become a member. He had to prove he was chosen. It took nearly a year. When I asked him if it'd take me that long once I had all the inside information, he told me women aren't chosen. The only thing women are good for is a means to an end."

"Talk about being back in the stone ages," said Monique.

"That's what we're dealing with," said Gwen. "This is a resurgence of an ancient religion."

"This time it's being resurrected in order to fulfill a dream of the leader," said Laura. "No matter how you look at it, no matter what label you give it, what he really wants is power. He wants to take over the world."

Chapter Seventeen

Laura placed the package from Professor Laban on the dining room table and opened it. On top was a note.

Ms. Darmer,

I hope you will be able to use this information. I know how much this means to you. I wish you the best of luck in your efforts to get Mr. Braedon back. If I can be of any further assistance, please call me.

Sincerely,

Allister Laban.

A smile crossed Laura's face. Gina looked at her.

"What is it?" she asked.

She handed Gina the note.

"How did he know?"

"I don't know," said Laura. "I never said a thing about Michael."

Laura began taking the items out of the package. The contents included textbooks, notes for his class, the information he found when he researched the group, all of the information he received when he "joined" the organization, and pictures of the members with their names. There were multiple pictures of the leader of the group.

"What's all of this?" Nicole asked as she looked at the table.

"This is what Professor Laban sent," said Laura. "This should tell us about our abductors."

"Let's get started," said Gina.

The Chosen One stood in front of Michael. This time only two guards were with him. Although there always had been at least five before when he was tortured by them, he knew three of them could still mean pain.

"Mr. Braedon, what can you tell me about the new security system in Mr. Reinholdt's operation?" he asked.

"I know there's a new security system, but the old one is still operational while the new system is being brought on line."

"When will the new system be in place?"

"The new system still has some problems and according to Mr. Reinholdt, it should be fully operational in the main complex within the next three months. Until then, the only system that is operational is the old one."

"Have they put the new system in any of the other complexes?"

"They've started putting the hardware in the first of the other four complexes; however the hardware has not been completely installed and therefore isn't connected yet."

"Is there an estimated time for the hardware to be finished?"

"When Mr. Reinholdt and I talked about it, he told me the hardware in Complex Two will be completed within sixty days. Once that's finished, it'll take another sixty days to do Complex Three. Complexes Four and Five will take approximately ninety days each because they're larger buildings with more complexities."

"What are we talking about as far as bringing the new security system on line in all of the buildings?"

"It'll take at least three hundred days to get all of the hardware installed. After that, it'll depend upon how much will be similar to the main building. Once they have the bugs ironed out in the first building, the others should go a little easier."

"Do they have to have the first building operational before they install the hardware in the second building?"

"No, they're working on getting the hardware in building number one operational while they're installing the hardware in building number two. The workers who are installing the hardware will move to the next building when the one they're currently working on is finished. Another team is brought in to make the security system interface with the computer system. That's where all of the problems lie. They need to make sure that the computer can control the system while sending a live feed to a security office as well as recording the activities so that they're able to go over them if they need to."

"Right now, do they have that capability?"

"Not really, they only get what the camera is facing at the time. The cameras are set to pan the area. When the camera is recording something on one side of the room, the activities on the other side of the room are not being recorded. That's why Mr. Reinholdt wanted the system updated. He wants to be able to record everything that goes on inside the complexes, especially in the classified information areas."

"That, Mr. Braedon is how I want you to answer. You see how nice I can be when you answer me respectfully and completely?"

"Yes, sir."

"Thank you, Mr. Braedon for your honesty."

"You're welcome, sir."

As they left, Michael leaned against the wall and sighed.

Mark and Robert looked at one another. This was the first time Mark was breathing a sigh of relief at the end of an interrogation of his brother.

"He just handed them a crock of lies and they bought it," said Mark leaning back and running his fingers through his hair.

"He sounded like he knew what he was talking about," said Robert.

"From what he said, they'd assume Edgar trusted him," said Mark. "They're probably also thinking that the treatment they put him through must have had some bearing on how he answered."

"We need to make sure Edgar leaves the old system alone so they don't find out the new system is operational," said Robert. "We already know what to look for when they're trying to take information out of the complex."

About fifteen minutes later, the telephone rang and Mark got up and answered it.

"Hello."

"Hello, Mark?"

"Yes, Edgar. Did you see the latest?"

"I can't believe they're broadcasting my security plans on the internet. How am I supposed to make my complexes impervious to break-ins? There's not a hell of a lot I can do about it either. I can't even begin thinking about it."

"Listen, Edgar, Henri has already started implementing changes. Let's put it in his hands. What I'm worried about is what they'll do to Michael if they find out the new one is working."

"I called my office and told my head of security that both systems were to be working, but if he's asked, only the old system works. If they check, the only thing they'll see is what the old system is sending. The new feed is going to the computer."

"Good."

Mark walked back into the dining room and sat down,

"Henri, you need to step up those security measures for Edgar."

"In light of this last interrogation we can't wait," said Henri.

"It's one thing to find out that your company is the project of a militant group," said Robert, "and quite another for your security system to be the subject of open conversation for anyone to pick up."

"We can't afford for someone else to get an idea to steal anything," said Mark. "We have enough to worry about with Michael."

Laura came into the room and sat down at the table.

"I hear Michael was on again," said Laura. "What did they do to him?"

"They asked him questions and he was able to answer them to their complete satisfaction," said Mark. "They thanked him for the information and for being honest and respectful."

"Did he really answer honestly?" asked Laura.

"Sort of," said Mark. "He told them that the new security system wasn't up and running and that the old one was. So, Edgar ordered the old system to remain operational until further notice."

"What happens if they find out?" asked Laura picking up a pen from the table and playing with it.

"They won't," said Mark.

"I think they're going to check the security office," said Laura nervously clicking a pen. "If it was me, I would."

Laura walked back into the dining room. Nicole was trying to organize the material Professor Laban sent. She set the pictures aside and Laura picked one up.

"Who is this man?" she asked aloud. There were more than a dozen pictures him, some with his followers and several alone. Laura looked at each one studying him. "I know he's the leader of this new religion and the leader of the abductors, but who is he?"

"Doesn't Professor Laban say who he is?" asked Nicole.

"He says his name is Moukib Mustafa, but that's not his real name," said Laura as she looked at them. "That's his assumed name for religious purposes. I want to know what his real name is."

"Let me get Robert," said Nicole. "I know he can find his name."

Nicole left the room and within minutes came back with Robert.

"Do you have a good clear picture of him?" he asked.

"Pick one," said Laura.

She laid out the pictures in front of him. Robert looked them over and picked one up.

"This one's good. It's generic enough that it doesn't let on who it is or rather whose persona he's assumed," said Robert. "Let me scan this and put it out there. Someone has to know who he is."

"How are you going to do that without them finding out?" asked Laura her legs shaking from nervousness.

"I'm only going to ask people I know who are up on these sorts of things," said Robert. "I'm not going to send it out randomly. I'm not going to take any chances."

"I'm sorry. It's just that when it comes to Michael, I don't want anything going wrong," said Laura.

"I know you don't and neither do we," he said. "I promise it'll be fine."

"What else did you find?" asked Gina after Robert left.

"These people are male oriented," said Laura. "Women have no purpose except for biological necessities and use as pawns to get what they want. What I find interesting is that as much as they say that women aren't important, every major decision in the history of the group involves a woman. Battles were won because of women, territories relinquished to them because of women. In every one of their quests, they've used women to gain knowledge, land, skills, wealth, and sovereignty.

"So, when we speculated that we thought using a woman would be to their advantage, we weren't far off," said Gina.

"No. In light of this, if Michael can't make Edgar deliver what they want, they may try to take Gabrielle," said Nicole. "That's if they still hold by the ancient teachings concerning women."

"When I talked to Professor Laban, he indicated that women have no rightful place in the group. They are not chosen," said Laura. "Whether or not they're chosen and whether or not they want to admit it, women are the most important part of their societal structure."

"Would they attempt another abduction?" asked Gina leaning forward and putting her arms on the table. "Would they be that brazen to go after Gabrielle?"

"Who would Edgar give up the information for?" asked Margo. "I mean if someone's life was on the line, who would be the one he'd part with the information to save?"

"We already know we're looking in terms of a woman," said Nicole. "They won't try to kidnap another man."

"Gabrielle's the obvious answer," said Gina picking up a pen and writing Gabrielle's name on a piece of paper.

"Who else?" asked Gwen.

"Does he have any daughters?" asked Monique.

"Not that I'm aware of," said Gwen. "He has three sons, but they're not married."

"We're back to Gabrielle," said Brigit.

"What about someone connected with Reinholdt International, but not related?" asked Laura.

"Like one of us?" asked Nicole "They already have Michael and Edgar isn't parting with the information."

"Because Michael is a man," said Laura. "I'm talking one of us." She pointed to each of them including herself.

"What would make him give in for one of us?" asked Brigit.

"Guilt and fear," said Laura, "pure and simple."

"If they take one of us and he doesn't give in, he'll know Gabrielle will be next," said Angelique.

"Do you really think they'll release the person once they get what they want?" asked Monique.

"From what I'm reading, yes," said Laura. "They're not predisposed to murder. From ancient times, the accounts don't point to a murderous trail. Torture, yes. Is everyone else in the other room?"

"They're finishing up," said Margo, "and getting things together to go back with the courier."

"We need to talk about what we found," said Laura.

It took a lot longer than they thought to go through everything Maggie had sent. Contracts had to be signed and specifications for projects reviewed. Other documents had to be retrieved from the office and everything packed and ready to go.

When they were all together, Laura didn't waste any time or words telling them what this group was like. She spelled out very plainly what she thought was going to occur.

"You really think they're going to be bold enough to try to take Gabrielle," said Jacques.

"If they can't get what they want with Michael," said Nicole. "If they want SecReSAC, then they'll have to have a plan to get it."

"This is insane!" said Jean. "They really believe that women are only a means to an end?"

"Yes. It's documented throughout their history," said Laura putting pile after pile of papers down on the table. "There are stories here about kings who gave up their entire regions in order to save the women they loved. The stories are filled with the horrible tortures and torments that the women had to endure. Even back then, they were masters of negotiation. They made sure the king followed their instructions to the letter. Any deviation resulted in more horrific treatment of the woman. According to the documentations, they never lost. They always got what they wanted."

"I thought Professor Laban said that there was very little of the ancient left," said Margo.

"As far as the laws and teachings are concerned, yes," said Nicole. "Don't forget, it had to be updated. At the time, the known world was that small area around the Fertile Crescent and into Egypt. Nothing else mattered. Word of mouth was the manner of communication. They were able to spread themselves quite far for that era by conquering people using one woman at a time."

Nicole picked up a pile of papers and lined them up on the table one after another.

"Take a look at these maps," she said. "These are in date order. Until Rome moved in, they were unstoppable. What makes it so unbelievable is that they did it without a formal army. They died off, because they couldn't compete with Rome."

"Today, the emphasis is on communication not war. They believe that only those countries that can't or won't come to the table and talk enter into warfare. I believe they'll have no choice but to go the route of the ancients and use a woman for the purpose of gaining their objective. Any other way would be just too costly and risky."

"So what are you saying?" asked Henri knowing very well that there was something more to this than information.

"We're saying they're going to do exactly what we're doing now," said Nicole. "They're trying to decide who will be able to get them the information they want. We came up with our list. First, there's Gabrielle."

"Edgar would never stand for his wife being in jeopardy," said Gwen. "I've seen just how much he loves her."

"Second would be one of us," said Nicole. "That would be purely out of guilt. If I had to put it in an order, it'd be Laura first, since it was the room switch between Michael and Edgar that started this. We already know Edgar feels guilty. The problem is, we don't know who they'll choose, nor do we know when or where. Only they know that."

"The only way we could know that," said Gina, "is if we were able to construct the situation and make them buy it."

"That's ludicrous!" said Pierre raising his voice. "There's no way we're going to put another person's life in danger!"

"That's the only way we have of controlling most of the variables," said Laura. "We'd control who, when, where, and how."

"No! No! No! Absolutely not!" Pierre yelled standing up and walking to the wall that served as the screen for the projector. "We couldn't control the treatment. We could never guarantee her safety. We couldn't guarantee that Edgar would cooperate."

"If he was part of this we could," said Laura standing up.

"How could we ask a man who is trying to calm the leaders of major nations to give up a secret that could undo everything he's been working to achieve?" asked Mark.

"He's a very intelligent man," said Laura. "If he knew what was at stake, he could actually give them a bogus program and through his connections, make it appear as though they had actually been able to take over the satellite. Remember, communication is their objective."

"They want to take over the world for God's sake!" said Pierre emphatically. "You said it yourself. I still say no. It's much too risky. I couldn't put anyone in that much danger and live with it."

"When Edgar gets back, we'll talk to him," said Mark, "and make sure he has such a plan ready."

"That may be too late," said Nicole. "This leader's going to run out of patience. When's the next time you'll be able to talk to Edgar?"

"He's to call and update me," said Pierre.

"You need to broach the subject then," said Nicole, "even if it means going to the States to meet with him there."

"We have to have a plan," said Gina. "Like it or not, Edgar is the key to this right now. Leaders or no leaders, he has to be part of this. He has to be made to understand what's at stake. They're going to come looking for someone else and we'll have no say in that matter. They'll take whomever they want. What happened to being proactive in this?"

"Not when it comes to another life!" said Pierre.

Laura reached into her pocket and took out a piece of paper. She looked at it, folded it again and put it back in her pocket. She leaned up against the sink in their bathroom, turned her head, and looked in the mirror. She took her phone and keyed in the numbers.

"May I speak to Professor Laban?" she asked.

"This is Professor Laban."

"Professor Laban, this is Laura Darmer, you said if there was anything I needed."

D. A. Walters

Laura sat in front of her computer. Her task seemed simple enough. Set up two new accounts with free email services. Once completed, she sent off her first email and waited impatiently for the reply. Within fifteen minutes, she had it. Using the contents of the email, Laura began sending out emails using the second account. She shut down the computer and went out to the living room.

"You alright, Laura?" asked Gwen.

"I just needed to stop reading that for a little while. I went and cleared out my email," she said. "I haven't done it for such a long time. I have a few notes from friends that I need to answer. I just stuck them in my saved mail. I'll get to them later. I just don't know what to say."

"Do you think they expect you to write back?" asked Gina.

"I don't know...maybe not."

"Just take it easy right now," said Brigit.

Laura looked at a picture of Michael and her on the table.

"I'd do anything to get him back."

"I know you would," said Gwen.

"I don't know how," said Laura.

"None of us knows exactly what to do," said Raquel. "We just have to trust that we'll find a way."

"Laura, you know that no one here is going to let anyone hurt you," said Margo suddenly realizing what Laura must be feeling. While each of them had someone to turn to when something scared them, Laura had no one.

"I know," said Laura trying to smile.

"What we'd really like to do is just talk to them and make them give Michael back without having to give them anything in return," said Monique, "but it doesn't work like that. No one gives something for nothing."

"That's what's so exasperating about this," said Brigit. "We know what they want, but we can't give it to them because it's not ours to give."

"Laura, did Pierre's outbursts shock you?" asked Margo trying to find out what so drastically changed Laura's mood.

"A little," said Laura. "I never meant that we had to decide right then who it'd be," she stopped for a minute. "I would never suggest putting anyone else's life in danger. I would never do that. He has to know that. All of you have to know that."

"Honey, we know that," said Angelique touching her hand.

"We were just trying to think like they would, that's all," said Laura. "It's the only way to be prepared for what they might do."

"You're right. Pierre doesn't like the choices. None of us do," said Margo. "I know they're thinking about what we said and it's scaring the hell out of them."

It was obvious by the mood in the study that the men were also shocked by Pierre's outbursts. Although there was work in front of them, no one was doing much of anything. Jean was fumbling through some papers trying to concentrate, but for the most part, they had their eyes cast downward.

"Just how would you decide which woman to send?" asked Pierre finally breaking the silence. "Would we draw straws and the one with the shortest straw would go? Damn it!" He slammed his fist on the table. "Which one of you would send your wife into that situation to get Michael back?" He got up and started walking around the room. "Did you read or listen to what has happened in the past? How could I send my wife, put her in danger. How could I watch them," his voice became almost inaudible. "How could I watch them rape her? What would I say to our sons? There has to be another way."

"We may not have a say in this," said Henri. "If they make their decision and make their move, we'll have no choice but to deal with it."

"I think that's what they were trying to tell us," said George. "Now we're certain they're not going to go after Edgar. If they're going to take anyone, it'll be one of the women."

"Look, Pierre, no one's suggesting we draw straws to see who'll go. No one wants to put their wife in that situation," said Mark. "And I know some of you are thinking that if anyone should have to go it should be Laura. After all she's Michael's fiancée." As he said it he looked around at their faces. Faces that were once looking directly at him were now downcast. He knew he hit a nerve…had spoken aloud the unthinkable that some of them were thinking. "Well, I'm sure as hell positive that Michael wouldn't want Laura in that position either," he said quietly, "but unless we find a way to solve this, we may find that one of those women we love more than life itself may be snatched from our midst."

"They're not going to come in asking if they can have one of them," said Jacques pointing out the obvious. "They're going to lay in wait for their opportunity."

"Then from now on, they go nowhere by themselves," said Pierre. "They'll get in and out of the car in the garage. When you're out, if something looks the least bit suspicious, get out of there immediately."

"What about Gabrielle?" asked Paul. "Is Edgar taking the same precautions with her?"

"He's taking no chances with regards to his wife or his company, especially with being out of the country," said Mark. "The only place Gabrielle may be in any danger is at the gala, but with the amount of security they already have for the event, it seems highly unlikely."

"Pierre, we'll do whatever we can to keep everyone safe," said Paul, "but we still have our main objective and that's to get Michael back safely. We have to think about that. That's what we need to work to achieve."

"We have to be able to do that without jeopardizing anyone," said Pierre.

"I'm afraid if we think along those lines, we may be living in a fairy tale world," said Jacques. "Everything comes with a price."

"Sacrificing one person for another is ludicrous!" said Pierre.

"No one is suggesting sacrificing anyone," said Jacques. "All I'm saying is that we may have to use everything at our disposal to make this happen. I'm certainly not advocating trading one of the women for Michael. I still think there's a solution to this," he said trying to offer a different approach. "We're making great strides, but this is going to take patience, something we have very little of at times."

"We also have a business to run," said Jean. "That package from Maggie was a real eye-opener for me at least. If business in the States is that brisk, what's it like here? We need to lay out those contracts right now, get back to business, and formulate a schedule we can live with."

"I was thinking the same thing, too," said Paul. "We need to get back on track time wise with those contracts."

"When we make the schedule, we have to find some way of freeing up one or two of us to work on Michael's situation," said Henri.

"Is that agreeable?" asked Pierre. "Then, let's get the rest of the partners in here and get this schedule done."

It was eerily quiet throughout the rest of the house with everyone meeting about the business. Laura went through the rooms straightening them and collecting all the glasses and plates that had been left. She smiled as she went. They were so wrapped up in what they were doing they'd leave one area to go to look at what someone found somewhere else without giving a thought to what they were leaving behind.

She spent a lot of time in the kitchen just getting everything in order and as she did, she thought of nothing but Michael. She looked at the refrigerator and there held up by a magnet was the list of what they needed for the wedding. She had been systematically checking things off as they were done. Now, it existed in suspended animation. She didn't dare hope that everything would go on as planned because she just wasn't sure, yet she didn't dare lose hope because she knew everything was possible.

Laura walked to their bedroom on the other side of the house. She turned on the computer and checked her email…nothing. She knew it was going to require patience, but she had little of that. She wanted everything now.

"Michael," she said as she picked up his pillow, "it's the only thing I know how to do."

Chapter Eighteen

Several days passed and Michael began wondering why neither the guard nor the Chosen One had returned. The only one who came to his room was the woman. He no sooner finished the thought when he heard the door. The Chosen One and two guards entered.

"We've checked out what you told us, Mr. Braedon," said the Chosen One. "It seems that you were absolutely correct in your assessment of the current situation. Our contacts tell us that they are indeed working on everything one building at a time, at Mr. Reinholdt's insistence. It seems that he does not want to allow that many outsiders in his buildings. That is very wise of him, would you not say so?"

"Yes, sir."

"Now, Mr. Braedon, you were with Mr. Reinholdt in Frankfurt, were you not?"

"Yes, sir."

"And you did say that you visited those facilities, did you not?"

"Yes, sir."

"What can you tell me about each of the facilities?"

"Sir, in regards to what?"

"In regards, first of all to the work that's done at each one."

"Each of Mr. Reinholdt's facilities are numbered. Number One is the main facility. It houses the main offices, conference rooms, and records for the company. It is also the facility where any classified work is done that needs the highest security clearance. It contains many work areas that can only be accessed by workers with proper credentials.

Nothing is permitted to be taken into the work area and nothing is permitted to be taken from the area. Anything that must be catalogued or filed from that area is done after the workers have left the building. The records are then taken to another area where there are many electronic checking points. In order for Mr. Reinholdt to get into the area with the highest security, he must pass through upwards of ten check points."

"Would you say that the work done in that area would have to do with communication systems vital to national security of one or more countries?"

"I think that would definitely be a fair assumption."

"Has Mr. Reinholdt always been involved in this type of work?"

"Mr. Reinholdt's business started as a small communication business that serviced telephones. The business began to expand. Mr. Reinholdt was always meticulous about his work. He knew how to keep the confidences of his clients. This began to lead to other types of communication work, much of which was used by governments. Now he deals exclusively with government contracts."

"What can you tell me about Facility Number Two?"

"Number Two specializes in special computer hardware and software."

"Can you give me an example?"

"Yes, sir."

"The software that is used to keep all the life support systems aboard the space shuttles and space stations working at optimum performance was designed, tested, and implemented in prototype devices. It also deals with radar, sonar, and other various transportation needs."

"Is there any high security area in Number Two?"

"Yes, there is a high security area in each building. None of the others, however, is as extensive as the area found in Facility Number One. Facilities Three, Four, and Five work on various projects. When I was there, Facility Number Three was working on a way to triangulate and locate someone who is only able to give off a split second signal. Four was working on a project that will revolutionize the communication system and tracking system in underground mines and tunnels. It will be so sensitive that it'll be able to pinpoint exact locations, formulate a rescue plan as well as be able to be accessed by the trapped persons in order to help them navigate to the best possible place to sustain life and be rescued. Facility Five's project dealt with the ability for the leader of a country to address the entire country with the utilization of a single program from a single location."

"Mr. Braedon, is there anything else that you can tell us about these facilities?"

"Not that I can think of right now."

"Were you able to get into the work areas?"

"Some of them, but not all of them. Most of them require clearance and I don't have that type of clearance."

"Did Mr. Reinholdt suggest you get that type of clearance?"

"When Mr. Reinholdt decides to do the project, he'll insist that anyone working on the project get such a clearance."

"Is there any reason why you would not be able to get such clearance?"

"No, sir, none that I can think of."

"Very good, Mr. Braedon. You did well today. You see, I can be quite the gentleman when I am given the answers I seek."

"Yes, sir."

"Relax Mr. Braedon. Perhaps we will talk again tomorrow morning."

"Yes, sir."

As the door closed and locked, Michael put his head down, closed his eyes and breathed a sigh of relief. His head shot up as he heard the keys in the lock of the door. As it opened, the woman came in. Once again Michael breathed a sigh of relief. As long as she was there, nothing would happen to him. She smiled as she came and sat near him.

"You are doing well. Do not worry. You are showing him great respect and he appreciates it. He is finding out what he wants to know. He is finding you to be an honest man. That is also good."

"What happens when I can no longer tell him what he needs?"

"Do not worry about that. He will find what he needs, if not with you, with someone else. As long as you are respectful, you are safe."

"And as long as I have answers."

"You will have all that you need. Trust in that."

The sun had come up only minutes before Laura got out of bed. She immediately showered and dressed. Once she dried and brushed her hair, she sat down at her desk. She logged onto her computer and was greeted by a flashing signal telling her that she had mail waiting.

To the one who seeks to find.

I can perhaps get you one step closer. Try sending an email to the person whose address is listed at the end. Tell him that you received his name from me. Do not forward this email. Do not use my email address. It is not to be given to him. Use only my name. Be watchful. Be careful.

Darius

Laura stared at the email. She was unable to move for several minutes. She copied it and placed it in the folder she created the day before. Next she wrote:

I received your name from Darius. He said you may be able to help me. I'm seeking to find the leader of those who have taken Mr. Braedon. I would like to be able to contact him in order to speak with him. I understand that perhaps you may be able to get me one step closer.

Please, if you have any information, send it to me at this address.

Thank you.

She paused a moment and pressed send. She copied the email and also put it into the folder. Whatever she found concerning Michael, she wanted to keep in one place so she'd be able to find anything quickly. She heard voices and clicked out of her email and folder. Nicole knocked lightly and then walked in.

"You're up early," she said.

"I couldn't sleep," said Laura.

"Did you see Michael this morning?"

"No. How did he look?"

"He looked alright."

"Did they hurt him again?"

"No, they asked him questions about the work that was going on in Edgar's facilities when he was there. He was able to answer them very calmly. They told him they checked out what he told them about the security system. It's just a good thing Edgar took care of things immediately. I know they'll be checking on what Michael told them today."

"Do you think he was telling the truth?" asked Laura.

"Michael has no reason to lie," said Nicole. "He told them what he knew."

"What's going to happen when he doesn't know?"

"I don't know. When we met last evening, we devised a plan so the business can continue and we can also work on finding Michael," said Nicole. "We have to divide ourselves so we can do both. Today Henri, Jean, Raquel, and I will be here. The others are working on the Worthington project."

"That sounds like a good idea," said Laura. "I need to get out of here just for a little bit. I don't care if it's just to go to the store."

"We can do that. We just have to go with someone," said Nicole.

"When I get nervous I cook and bake."

"We're going to weigh three hundred pounds by the time this is over," said Nicole laughing.

Laura picked up her credit card and license and put them in her pocket.

Pierre reached over the ledge and hung up the phone. Margo came quietly up behind him and stole a quick kiss.

"What's going on with Edgar?" she asked.

"He was concerned about what Michael said today. He said there was a lot he left out. They checked out the security. It happened close to the end of the shift. He was thankful he had the chance to make the changes."

"So now we know they're checking on what Michael says," said Margo.

"They're going to find out he didn't tell them everything," said Pierre.

"Dear God, I hope they ask him if there was anything else they were working on," said Margo. "What about the meetings?"

"They chose the third option."

"What about Gabrielle?" she asked.

"So far, everything's fine. I'm going to send him some of the information we received from Professor Laban. I want him to be aware of what this group is like."

Jean pulled into the garage and closed the door. The three of them got out of the car and Nicole opened the door to the house.

"Hey, can the two of you help unload?"

"Sure," said Henri. "What did you buy?" He looked in the trunk of the car and saw all the bags crammed together. "Is there anything left at the store?"

"The freezers are empty," said Laura. "While things are quiet, I thought I'd cook so that when things get hectic, all we have to do is thaw and heat."

"Believe it or not, that makes sense," said Raquel picking up a bag.

"As long as I get to eat some of everything when you're making it," said Henri, "I don't care how much you bought."

"I promise. Tonight will be a little of everything," said Laura.

"Now, that sounds wonderful," said Henri with a big smile on his face.

After his conversation with Pierre, Edgar made his way back to the conference room. The leaders had been discussing things since early morning and had decided to work late into the night. He was grateful they were cooperating as well as they were. The situation was stressful enough without them being at odds with one another. When he came into the room he took his seat.

"Mr. Braedon seems to be able to appease his captors at the present time," said Prime Minister Fairfield.

"Yes, he has."

"Is it true Mr. Braedon couldn't get into the classified areas," said President Mason.

"That's true. He didn't have clearance, so I wouldn't permit him access to the classified sections."

"His company has done work for our government before," said President Roelini. "They have the highest clearance we give."

"That goes for our government too," said President Bartram.

"Obviously those who have Mr. Braedon don't know that," said Edgar. "They asked him if there would be any reason why he couldn't get clearance."

"So, now they must know that Mr. Braedon can't give them information on specific projects," said Prime Minister Strickland.

"Even I couldn't give specifics," said Mr. Edgar. "I don't possess all the knowledge. No one in my organization does. That way, I'm able to protect the projects and my workers from outside forces."

"So, if they had succeeded in their plan to take you, Mr. Reinholdt, you wouldn't have been able to give them what they wanted," said Prime Minister Masada.

"No. I'm the only one who has access to the information. I make it a practice not to know everything. Now where are we in regards to this matter?" asked Edgar.

Laura spent the rest of the morning and afternoon in the kitchen baking and cooking. Her laptop and printer sat on the only spare counter that wasn't covered in spices and utensils. She was enjoying the quietness while the others were working. After everything she had been through, this was a welcome diversion and gave her a sense of peace.

Whenever he thought he smelled something new being made, Henri excused himself to go to the kitchen. He looked around, lifted the lids of the pots and breathed in the wonderful aromas. He broke a piece of bread from the loaf and dipped it in the spaghetti sauce to sample it. The look on his face and his reaction told Laura he was enjoying every taste. Then he blew her a kiss and walked out. Laura smiled, shook her head, and went back to making cookie dough balls to freeze.

Before she even started, she made a list of everything she wanted to make and put it in order. There were things that could be done and finished quickly while other things needed to simmer or bake for hours. One by one she crossed things off her list. As she finished each one, she separated it into several storage containers, labeled them, and put them in the freezer. As promised, she left out enough for the evening's dinner. She decided to put everything on the counters and everyone could help themselves. Serving dishes and utensils lined the counter tops as soon as all the dishes used in preparation were washed and put away. To look now, no one would believe the disaster zone it had been.

The quietness of the house seemed to dissipate as the rest of the partners came back from work.

"Something smells wonderful," said George as soon as he walked through the door.

"Laura's been slaving in the kitchen all day," said Raquel giving her husband a kiss.

"The freezers were empty and I thought while it was relatively quiet I could get some cooking and baking done," said Laura.

"Did you leave anything out for us?" asked Mark.

"Of course I did," she said. "If you're hungry, we can eat in about twenty minutes and then we'll have the evening ahead of us for whatever needs to be done."

"Sounds good," said Henri.

Around the dinner table, the Worthington account was the main topic of conversation. All through the conversations could be heard "mmm's" and "oh's" as they tasted different dishes.

"Mon Dieu, Laura, I don't know which I like most," said Henri, getting up from the table to help himself to some more of everything.

"Laura, everything is delicious," said Gwen.

"Thank you."

Within minutes Henri's plate was clean. Brigit watched her husband wipe his mouth with his napkin and sigh like a contented puppy.

"Well, darling," she said teasingly to him, "which is your favorite?"

"They all are," said Henri. "I can't make up my mind."

She patted his stomach.

"If you'll excuse me, I want to check my email to see if we've had any response to our inquiry about the identity of the leader," said Robert getting up from the table.

"We're almost finished compiling the list of the members of the faction that have infiltrated Reinholdt International," said Jean. "When we're finished it'll be complete with names and pictures."

"What about the information Professor Laban sent?" asked Margo.

"I still have quite a bit of reading to do," said Laura. "Some of it's difficult to read. Sometimes I just have to stop, put it down, and do something else."

"I asked Edgar about Gabrielle. He hired additional security," said Pierre. "She's also not permitted to go anywhere alone. I want to send him copies of some of what Professor Laban has sent. I'm not convinced he believes his wife might be in danger. Laura, if you can get some of it together, I'll send it. It doesn't have to be a great deal of information, just enough to make him take notice."

"Anything yet?" asked Mark.

"No," said Robert.

"Give it time," said Monique.

"Jean, if you can put these names and faces together along with the other information," said Paul, "we can run them."

Laura came in with the copies to be scanned and sent to Edgar.

"This should give him a good idea. I left out the graphic descriptions. If he asks for more, we can send it later."

"Take a look at these," said Paul as he handed Laura the sheets they finished running.

"These are great. Their faces are so clear," said Laura leafing through the sheets.

Gwen took one of the sheets from Laura and looked at it.

"Well dear, Halim," she said, "welcome to the Braedon-Reinholdt 'most wanted.' Just in case you're wondering, we will get you."

Chapter Nineteen

Now that the Worthington account was well underway and several others were also being taken care of, true to the promise, the group spent more time working to find a solution to Michael's dilemma. Everyone was reading, plotting, drawing, whatever was called for when a smiling Robert came into the dining room.

"We have success," he said holding up the picture.

"What're you talking about?" asked Pierre looking up from a diagram.

"We have a name to go with that face," said Robert. "Afmad Yamani is his real name."

"Does that mean anything to anyone?" asked Pierre. They look puzzled.

"Should it?" asked George.

"I don't know him," said Jean.

"It doesn't mean anything to me," said Jacques.

"If I remember correctly, he was second in command to the Ayatollah back in the eighties," said Laura. "There was talk about him plotting to overthrow the Ayatollah. When this was discovered, he was exiled."

"Where did he go?" asked Mark.

"No one actually knew," said Laura. "Those closest to him said he fled to Africa. You see, they threatened him with death if he was ever seen in the country again."

"So that's why the person who responded wanted to know where he could be found," said Robert. "They still want him. What was his issue with the Ayatollah?"

"They didn't see eye to eye on philosophy," said Laura. "While the Ayatollah was the supreme ruler and a stickler for the law, he interpreted it in a manner that would be in his best interest. Yamani was a purist. He believed the religions of the region were becoming more and more corrupt and therefore none of them was the true religion. He even started telling people they were never going to be saved because they had no religion if they followed the religion of the Ayatollah. People began questioning what the Ayatollah was doing especially when it didn't go along with the teachings. It got to a point that when anyone questioned the Ayatollah or his authority, the person was arrested and promptly executed…no questions asked. Go on the internet and search for the Ayatollah. There should be quite a number of pictures available. Yamani is always on his right."

"How in the world do you know this?" asked Margo.

"I can remember my parents talking about the Ayatollah. It was a topic of conversation every night. I think someone my father knew had been held hostage by him, or an organization in his country. I remember the name Yamani because I liked to say it. I'd ask my father to point him out when they would show the Ayatollah and his entourage on television, or if there was a picture in a magazine. In our house, the only magazines were those that dealt with domestic and world affairs. I learned to read those for enjoyment."

"Which one's Yamani?" asked Paul.

Laura looked at the picture projected on the wall. She walked over to it and pointed to the man on the right of the Ayatollah.

"Are there any other pictures?" asked Monique.

"About fifty," said Robert.

They started going through them. None of them showed his face really well.

"Well now, look at that," said Paul.

Shining on the wall was a picture of Afmad Yamani. He was obviously having a conversation with another member of the entourage. The picture was a head and shoulders close-up. There was no doubt that the man projected on the wall was the same man who was holding Michael. The only difference was age.

"Can you print that?" asked Laura.

"Of course," said Robert.

He handed the copy to Laura.

"Well Mr. Yamani, I feel like I've known you all my life," said Laura smugly. "I guess that's a plus for me. I wonder if anyone else has made the connection."

"Do you think Professor Laban knows who he is?" asked Gwen.

"I'm sure he doesn't. If he did, he'd have told me," said Laura. "Let me tell you this. If his identity becomes public knowledge, there'll be no safe place for him to hide. As far as your source is concerned, tell him you found the picture and everyone was arguing about who it was. Please don't let on who he really is."

"Not a problem," said Robert.

"Once I have Michael back, I'll deliver Yamani to anyone who wants a piece of him. "

"Laura, I said it before, I'd never want to be in his shoes once you get to him," said Mark.

As they were talking Robert took the photograph of Yamani he just found, the new picture sent to him by his contact, as well as the other picture of the leader of the new religious faction, sent to Laura by Professor Laban, and put them on the screen side by side.

"That's amazing. Print that, please. I want it," said Laura. "I know this sounds crazy, but I actually feel a sense of power."

"In what way?" asked Nicole.

"We know his secret," said Laura. "There's a chink in his armor."

"Can we use it?" asked Paul.

"Not yet. If we do, he just may kill Michael and flee again," said Laura. "The longer he feels safe the better it is."

Edgar finished reading through the information Pierre had sent. His hands trembled as he made the call. When Pierre answered the phone, Edgar didn't even say hello.

"Is this true, Pierre?" he asked.

"Is what true, Edgar"?

"What you sent me?"

"Yes."

"Is this who we're dealing with?"

"Yes."

"Are these descriptions accurate?"

"Yes. I'm afraid those only scratch the surface. Laura felt that you didn't need to read the graphic accounts."

"Dear God," gasped Edgar. "After I read through the first page, I called my wife. I impressed upon her that she wasn't to go out alone, ever, not even to the yard. This makes my skin crawl."

"We did the same thing here. The women go nowhere unescorted."

"Is there any evidence they'd hurt Michael?"

"The leader demands respect. As long as Michael is respectful the punishment seems to be less severe."

"I don't exactly call their treatment of him respectful. Pierre, I'm good at what I do. Whatever they're able to fabricate, I'll be able to counter. No one has checked on what Michael told them yesterday," said Edgar. "It could be there's so much it'll take a few days for them to verify everything. I'm sure they'll be meticulous about it. It seems for them, there's so much at stake."

"He has very much at stake; mainly his credibility and the growth of his organization."

"How much do you think they want?"

"I think he wants it all," said Pierre. "He started out wanting to be able to reach new members. Now, I think he can sense the power he could have."

"Pierre, usually I love what I do because there's always a sense of excitement, but frankly, this is a little too much excitement. Now, with the information you sent, I can't even conceive of what I'd do if they had my wife."

"I can tell you each of us has thought about that, too."

"I just don't know how to resolve this. I don't know what I can do short of giving them everything in return for Michael and I can't do that. Pierre, I can't help but wonder, if they had taken me, would they've let me go, or would I be dead by now. I have nightmares about it."

"I can't imagine what you're going through. It's so easy to tell you to be thankful."

"Believe me I'm thankful."

"How much longer do you think these meetings will last?"

"We should be finished here in two or three days," said Edgar. "Have you made any arrangements for coming back?"

"No, not yet."

"Edgar, do me a favor. Don't make any arrangements until you hear from me."

Pierre walked into the kitchen where everyone was having coffee.

"Well, we've succeeded in frightening Edgar," he said taking his seat next to Margo. "He should be finished in two or three days. If it's alright with you, Laura, we can send William and James to pick him up and drive him to Pittsburgh."

"That's fine," she said.

"I thought if Mark, Gwen, Paul, Gina, and perhaps you would go to Pittsburgh, you could all fly back together. While you're there, you can tend to whatever has to be done at the office, as well as whatever personal things you need to do. The same thing will hold true there. No one goes anywhere alone."

Once the majority of them left for the office, Laura cleaned up the kitchen and performed her daily ritual of straightening up. Today she gave everything a quick once over. She was anxious to check her email. As soon as she could, she signed in on her computer.

You wanted to talk to me. Talk.

Laura stared at the screen. She pressed reply.

Are you the one who has Mr. Braedon?

Within minutes another email appeared.

Yes, I have him.

Again she pressed reply.

How do I know you have him?

She waited.

Because I said so.

Laura typed

I want proof. I want pictures. Not the ones from the internet either.

She paused to think. Then she continued typing.

I want pictures of Mr. Braedon without his shirt on, one of his chest and one of his back.

As she waited, she started to tap on the desk.

That will take a little time. Will you wait?

She pressed reply.

Yes, just do it.

As she waited, she got things ready to pack.

The Chosen One shut down the computer and walked to the door.

"Sadik!" he yelled. "Get the woman immediately."

"Yes, sir," Sadik answered and ran off.

"Gehran, get the camera from my desk."

"Yes, sir."

"We must have photos of our Mr. Braedon...special photos."

"Yes, sir."

Michael heard the keys in the door and stiffened. As it opened, the woman walked in followed by the Chosen One and two guards.

"Mr. Braedon, we are in need of pictures," said the Chosen One.

He addressed the woman.

"Unbutton his shirt and slide it down his arms."

She did so.

"Stand, Mr. Braedon."

Michael struggled to stand up and the Chosen One gestured to the guards to help him.

"Look at the camera, Mr. Braedon."

He took the picture.

"One more, a closer shot. Please turn around."

He took two shots.

"Thank you, Mr. Braedon. You may sit down. You can tend to him now. Just let the guard know when you are finished. Have a pleasant day, Mr. Braedon."

Michael looked surprised. *Why would anyone want pictures of me without my shirt? What the hell's going on?*

The woman looked at him and smiled.

"Relax, Mr. Braedon, all is well."

It seemed like an eternity to Laura. As she waited, she paced the floor not being more than a few steps from the computer at any given time. When she heard the signal, she rushed to the computer and opened the mail.

Is this proof enough?

She opened the attachments.

"Oh my God, Michael. Oh my God," she whispered putting her hands over her mouth. She moved the pictures to her folder, then went back to the email and pressed reply.

Yes.

She waited for the next email.

What do you want?

I want to make a deal. She replied.

When she opened the next email all it said was

Click the link.

Laura clicked the link and entered a chat room.

What kind of deal?

I want you to release Mr. Braedon.

Sorry, I cannot do that.

What is it you want?

Something you cannot give me.

Who can?

Mr. Reinholdt.

Do you think he'll give it to you to release Mr. Braedon?

Maybe.

I didn't think your religion allowed men to be put in this type of situation.

What do you mean?

Men are never used as pawns. They're negotiated with. They're respected.

We do respect Mr. Braedon.

Do you call physical abuse respect?

He needed to know we were serious about what we wanted. Now he speaks to us with respect.

What do you want from Mr. Braedon?
As much information as he can give us.
What if he doesn't know what you want?
We will have to get it another way.
Does that mean you'll take someone else?
That is a possibility. Whatever it takes to make Mr. Reinholdt give us what we want.
What will you do with Mr. Braedon?
That remains to be decided.
What if I offer you a more viable way of getting the information from Mr. Reinholdt? Will you release Mr. Braedon?
It would depend upon what it was and if we were certain Mr. Reinholdt would divulge the information.
What if it was someone very close to Mr. Braedon?
How close?
Very close. Someone he'd do anything for.
How would that help?
If he was released he could and would make Mr. Reinholdt give the information.
How are you so sure?
According to your religion, women are a means to justify the end.
How do you know this?
I did my homework. I know quite a bit about your religion. I know that throughout its history, your religious leaders used women to make men give up land, power, and riches.
Meet me here in one hour.
He was gone. Laura stared at the screen, copied the conversation, and then clicked out of the box. She opened the folder with Michael's pictures and as she sat there as the tears ran down her cheeks.

Laura took a cup off the shelf and poured herself coffee. Her eyes were so irritated from crying. She thought a cup of coffee might settle her down a little as she waited. Gina walked in, took one look at Laura, sat down on the chair at the side of the table, and took her hand.

"Honey, what's wrong?" she asked.

"I can't seem to get the thoughts of those women and what those men did to them out of my head," said Laura.

"Are you afraid?" asked Gina, pouring a cup of coffee.

"I don't know."

"No one's going to let anything happen to you. You know that. That's why we're being so careful. We don't want anything happening to anyone."

"I guess I'm on edge."

"Mark and Gwen are on their way. When they get here, Paul and I are going home to get some things. We'll call you when we get there and then when we're leaving. Jacques and Nicole will still be here."

"I think they should go with you. Once Mark and Gwen are here, there'll be three of us. I'd feel better if they went with you."

With Mark and Gwen getting things organized for the trip, Laura went to her room. She sat in front of the computer, opened her email and moved all of the correspondence to the folder. She opened the pictures of Michael and stared at them. She got up and made sure the door to the bedroom was locked. Then she printed everything, put it in a folder and tucked it into her briefcase.

"Oh, Michael, I will get you home. No matter what it takes, I will get you home. Michael, please pray I have the strength. I love you."

She kissed her fingers, touched the screen, and clicked out.

Are you there?

Yes. Have you decided?

There are conditions.

What types of conditions?

The name of the person.

Only if it's kept secret.

That can be arranged.

Mr. Braedon can't know.

He will know nothing of this or any other conversations dealing with this matter.

I'm Mr. Braedon's fiancée.

Does Mr. Braedon's fiancée have a name?

Laura Darmer.

You know I will check this out. Was it in the papers?

Yes, the society page of the *Pittsburgh Post Gazette*. March 12.

Laura had no patience for waiting and every minute seemed like an hour.

You are a very beautiful woman.

Other conditions?

Once I have you, then I will release Mr. Braedon.

No! Mr. Braedon is to be released before you get me.

That gives you a chance to back out.

That gives you a chance to keep both of us.

How do I know I can trust you?

I went through all the trouble to find you. I have to be serious about this.

I will be back here in one hour.

It was so quiet Laura almost forgot there were other people in the house with her. When there was a knock on the door, she jumped.

"Laura?" asked Mark. "Are you alright?"

"Yes. I'm trying to do some work. Since we're going to be back in Pittsburgh for a few days, I thought I'd try to get in touch with a couple of clients and also maybe do an interview or two for that project I have coming up. That way I'll have material to work on when I get back here."

"If you need anything I'll be in the office."

"Thanks."

Laura sat wringing her hands and staring at the computer screen. She was getting impatient with all the waiting.

I have made some decisions.

What are they?

We need a mediator. Someone who will make sure no one reneges on their part of the bargain.

Who do you have in mind?

That has to be up to you to suggest and me to agree or disagree. The person has to have access to the media, but not too visible.

So anyone from the national or syndicated news shows would not be acceptable.
That is correct.
What about a newspaper reporter?
No.
Why not?
They do not reach enough people. It has to be someone who can reach a vast audience if necessary even though he might not do that all the time. We do not have those types of people in...
Where?
Did you think I would tell you where?
Not really. What about someone in radio?
Is he local?
Yes.
Can he command national attention?
Yes, he has on numerous occasions.
His name?
Tom Richards.
Radio Station?
WXDX
Is he a man of his word?
He never minces words. He says exactly what's on his mind. What's more, he keeps his word. If he promises something, he'll do it.
Do you know him personally?
No.
How do you know about his character?
I've seen evidence of it in his work and his dealings with others.
I want to check him out. I need time. Give me a day.
I need a promise.
Who are you to ask for promises?
I am Mr. Braedon's fiancée. The one who is going to get you what you want. That's who I am.
What do you want?
I want you to leave Mr. Braedon alone. No more abuse of any kind.
As long as we communicate there will be no more abuse.
What time?
Where are you?

D. A. Walters
I will be in the Eastern United States.
Tomorrow at 11:00 A.M. your time. Agreed?
Agreed.
Laura copied the conversation to the folder and picked up her phone.

Chapter Twenty

For some reason, the house felt very empty. She had been in it before when Michael was away, but now there was a loneliness, a sadness.

"Ms. Darmer, I'll take your bags upstairs," said William.

"Thank you, William," said Laura.

She walked into the living room. Michael's presence was everywhere. All of the memories made in the house. The parties, holidays, and special quiet intimate times all came flooding back. She closed her eyes and could almost feel Michael holding her.

"Laura, William is going to take me to the office," said Paul. "Are you going to be alright here with Gina?

"Yes. Where is she?"

"She's lying down upstairs. She never seems to sleep on the flights. Call if you need anything. Gwen will be coming back with William."

"That's fine," said Laura. "When's Mr. Reinholdt coming?"

"William will leave to get him tomorrow," said Paul. "He's supposed to be here tomorrow evening."

Laura looked at the clock and got her laptop out of its case. At eleven o'clock she entered the chat room.

Are you there?

Yes.

Did you check out Mr. Richards?

Yes. He is what you say he is.

Then he's acceptable?

Yes. Now you must get him to agree.

I'll do my best. I have to be able to tell him what's expected of him.

He will bring you to an undisclosed location and leave you. He will then go to a rendezvous point, receive Mr. Braedon, and take him to the embassy courtyard. Then he must go to the television station and report that Mr. Braedon has been released. You will see that broadcast. He will then come to get you and take you to the rendezvous point, hand you over to us, and leave. Once Mr. Reinholdt has given us what we want and we are convinced that it is the genuine article, Mr. Richards will be called. He will once again meet us at an undisclosed place to receive you and broadcast to the world that you have been released. I warn you...If you do not stay at that place while Mr. Richards receives Mr. Braedon, we will kill you. If he decides not to hand you over, we will kill you and him. You will be watched. Do you agree?

Up to this point, yes, but I'll want it in writing. If you're a man of honor and your word is good, you'll have no problem doing that.

We will discuss this once you have talked to Mr. Richards.

Now I'm the one who needs time. I'll contact you at two o'clock tomorrow my time. Agreed?

Agreed. Miss Darmer, you have a week, seven days to make this happen, or I will not be responsible for the condition of Mr. Braedon.

Laura Darmer opened the door to the offices of WXDX Radio and walked up to the receptionist at the desk. Linda immediately looked up from her work when she heard the door.

"May I help you?" she asked.

"Yes, I'm Laura Darmer. I have a twelve o'clock appointment with Mr. Richards."

"Ms. Darmer, please have a seat and I'll tell Mr. Richards you're here."

"Thank you."

As the receptionist turned and walked up the hall, Laura looked around the room. She took notice of all the awards and pictures of the DJs with famous groups and singers and then settled herself into a dark blue tapestry covered wing-backed chair. She placed her briefcase on

for Love and Ransom

the floor beside her and folded her hands in her lap. She went over what she was going to say to Mr. Richards when they met. She hoped she had chosen the right words to convince him to help her. What would she do if he didn't want to do it? She'd be back to square one and have to find someone else of his caliber that both she and Michael's captor could agree on.

As she thought about it, she prayed silently that the captors wouldn't move up the timetable. She needed every minute to make sure this would work. She also needed his solemn promise that their conversation would go no further. If the government or any of the team members found out, she knew they'd do everything in their power to stop her. That just couldn't happen.

She was still in deep thought when Tom Richards walked into the reception area. His attire was his usual faded blue jeans, Metallica T-shirt, and sneakers. He ran his fingers through his jet black hair and walked over to Laura.

"Ms. Darmer?" he said extending his hand. "I'm Tom Richards."

"Mr. Richards, I'm very glad to meet you." said Laura, standing and extending her hand to shake his. "Thank you for seeing me."

"It's my pleasure. I understand by our previous conversation that this meeting is of a sensitive nature."

"Yes, it is."

"Let's go back to my office. It's right this way."

She picked up her briefcase and he led her down a corridor to the third door on the left. He opened the door and allowed her to enter before him. The room had a dark wooden desk with report sheets strewn. Laura looked around. There were matching file cabinets and a computer station along with other electronic equipment.

"Please have a seat," he said as he closed the door behind him.

Laura sat on the chair in front of the desk and placed her briefcase on the floor beside her. Tom walked around to his chair and sat down.

"What can I do for you?"

"Mr. Richards, I need your help. My fiancé, Michael Braedon, has been kidnapped by mistake by an ancient fanatic religious group and is being held hostage. He's the one you see on the internet," she said as she gestured to the computer on the workstation to her right.

"I'm very sorry to hear that, Miss Darmer," he said getting up, walking over to the workstation, and turning off the monitor. "What do you mean by mistake?"

He returned to his seat behind the desk.

"The intended person was a businessman from Frankfurt, Germany, who my fiancé was meeting with. When the client's room wasn't up to his expectations, Michael offered to change rooms with him. It seemed simple enough. So simple, they didn't even inform the desk the switch had been made. The kidnappers, not knowing of the switch, took Michael instead."

"Why did they want the other man?"

"He's a very prestigious businessman in Germany whose company deals in communications. The group had a specific target in mind, because he could give them the details of a secret project his company was developing."

"How do you know he was the intended target?"

"A note was sent to his wife just shortly before he arrived home. When he realized what must have happened, he contacted Michael's office in Paris."

Laura reached inside her briefcase and took out a folded piece of paper. She unfolded it and handed it over to Tom. He took the paper and read it.

"Did they ever contact her for the ransom?"

"Once they discovered the mistake, ransom was no longer an option. They viewed this as a trick of sorts to make them look foolish."

He handed the paper back to Laura. She folded it carefully and put it back into the case.

"Alright, now, Ms. Darmer, what does all this have to do with me? How can I possibly be of help to you?"

"Mr. Richards, the United States government won't deal with fanatic religious groups or terrorist groups for the return of a hostage. It's just not in the best interest of the country according to them to negotiate for one individual and put the lives of thousands of others on the line. Michael's brother, Mark and I sent letters, emails, made phone calls. We've pleaded with everyone: Senators, Congressmen, the President and nothing."

She produced a folder containing numerous letters for Tom to review. As he did so, she searched his face for some sort of clue as to what his reaction might be, but found none.

"Did any of this surprise you?" he asked handing back the folder.

"Not really," she said as she took the folder from him. "It's the same answer they've given every family member and friend who's interceded on behalf of a hostage. Each no I received was just another checkmark in the defeat column. However, I'm a woman who doesn't accept defeat gracefully."

"Something told me that, by the manner in which you set this meeting and the conviction in your voice," he said smiling at her. "So for a woman who doesn't accept defeat, what was next?"

"We knew if anything was going to be done, we'd have to do it ourselves. We sat down and thought everything out very carefully. We knew we needed to know everything we could about Michael's captors. We talked with professors of Islamic History, authorities on international affairs, searched the Internet and read every book, article, and news story we could find on the psychological and religious nature of this group."

"Once we finished the research, we began to query over the internet into various chat rooms and any avenue we could find, to try to find out who these people were. We wanted to talk to them. We wanted to state our case for Michael's release to them personally."

"Ms. Darmer, first of all, who are we?"

"I'm sorry. We, refers to Michael's business partners and me. His brother's also a partner."

"Now, why would you want to contact them and plead your case?"

She leaned forward placed her arms on his desk and looked him directly in the eyes.

"We wanted to open the lines of communication. We wanted to be able to do whatever needed to be done to get Michael back."

"Pardon me for asking, but how did you ever expect to find them yourselves?"

"I had no idea how we were going to actually connect with them. I was always told where there was a will; there was a way. I received an email from a professor giving me a lead. I emailed that lead who put me in touch with someone else. That someone else was able to get to the leader of the group. The leader then contacted me."

"How did you know it was them?"

"He had to prove to me that he was the one holding Michael. I asked for pictures...specific pictures. He sent pictures to me that no one has seen on the internet."

Laura reached into her briefcase and pulled out a folder. From the folder, she took four pictures of Michael and placed them on the desk in front of Tom. He took each picture in hand and looked at them.

"They're really careful not to show too much background in these pictures, aren't they?"

"They don't want anyone being able to pinpoint where they are."

He turned a picture around for her to see.

"Why did they send you a picture of his back?"

"I asked for that picture. As you can see, Michael has a distinguishing tattoo that would prove his identity to me," she said pointing to the tattoo on the picture. "They would have no idea he had a tattoo. I thought it'd be a foolproof way of making sure it was Michael. Needless to say, they've confirmed his identity to my satisfaction as well as theirs."

"What do you mean by that?"

"I wanted to know I was dealing with the right people and not some impostors who were going to take me for a royal ride and waste what precious time I had. There's much too much at stake...Michael's life."

"Okay, now that you're convinced they're the real deal, what's next?"

"I made them an offer."

"What type of offer?"

"Me, in return for the safe release of Michael."

"You!" he exclaimed, his mouth dropping. "Ms. Darmer, are you serious? Surely, you don't trust these people."

"Not completely."

"How could you even entertain such a notion?"

"Mr. Richards, there's something they want and I feel Mr. Reinholdt will give up the information if I'm involved."

"But Ms. Darmer!"

"I've thought very carefully about this. There are terms and conditions on both sides that must be fulfilled before this deal can be done. Part of that deal is a mediator. It has to be someone who's known; but not so well known his or her notoriety would get in the way of the message these people want to convey. I put forth several suggestions including you. You were the one he accepted."

"Why me? Why would you choose me? More than that, why would he choose me?"

"They value communication and you give them a valuable outlet. I've never known you to mince words. With you, what you see is what you get. There's no pretense. You don't believe in it. While you're a local radio personality, you also have connections in the national arena. That combination is important. The fact you're local enables this to stay quiet until the switch is made. You'll be able to move through the obstacles and meetings unobtrusively. You have the ability to remain quiet and secretive and when the entire ordeal is completed you also have the ability to create national news."

"I'm flattered by the confidence you have in me. Just what is it you're asking me to do?"

"I'm asking you to help me pull this off and save both Michael and me."

"How can I possibly do that?"

"According to the terms you're to accompany me to an undisclosed location in what I believe to be a Middle Eastern country, leave me there, go to another location and receive Michael when they release him, deliver him safely to the courtyard of the United States Embassy, and report that news via the television of that nation. Then you'll return to me, take me to an agreed upon location and deliver me to the captors. You will then get Michael out of the country and back to Paris and then return to the United States and your job until you're notified by the captors of their intent to release me. You'll return to the release point on the agreed upon date and time, accept my release and deliver me safely back home. My identity is not to be disclosed until after my release. That's what I'm asking you to do."

"The first part I can do with no problem. Delivering you to the captors, I don't think I can."

"If you don't, they'll kill me. It's just that simple. When you take me to that place and leave me, they'll be watching. You'll have only so much time to accept Michael, deliver him to the embassy, make the newscast and return for me. If you don't return, they'll kill me."

"And if I do deliver you, they may also kill you."

"That's not what they do. They use women to get what they want. According to their religious beliefs, women are a means to justify the end. They need what Mr. Reinholdt has. Up to now he's been reluctant to give it to them. What's made this deal so attractive to them is that by taking a woman, it'll force Mr. Reinholdt to give up what they want."

"How's that possible?"

"I know Michael's partners are intelligent people. It won't take them very long to realize I'm the person who's taken Michael's place. This'll create pressure on Mr. Reinholdt to release the information they want. Once Michael has found out, Mr. Reinholdt will release it, mainly out of guilt."

"How do you know a woman would make a better hostage for them?"

"Throughout their history, they have used women hostages to make men give over wealth, land, and power."

"How?"

"They tortured them until the man gave in. A professor sent this to me. Perhaps you might want to read it," she said handing him a few papers.

When he finished reading them, he looked at her.

"Miss Darmer, what they did to those women was brutal."

"Can you imagine if the woman you loved was taken hostage?"

"I'd be devastated. I can tell you that right now."

"Yet, if a man is taken and tortured, the world says, 'Oh well, isn't that terrible,' and goes on."

"How would Mr. Braedon feel if he knew you were going to do this?"

"He'd be totally against it."

"Then what makes this a better situation for you to be in than him?"

"I have read the documentations of every situation. At the end, the woman was always returned to her family. Never does it document the death of a woman at their hands. Never is there documentation of a man being taken hostage. What other recourse do they have? Their religion doesn't condone homosexuality so raping Michael wouldn't happen. I've already seen them torture and abuse him. I can't bear that. When I asked them what they'd do to Michael if he couldn't get them what they wanted, the leader told me it hadn't been decided yet. I don't want to find out."

"Tell me something. How do you feel about this?"

"What do you mean?"

"Are you scared?"

"Yes, Mr. Richards, I am. I'm scared to death."

"Then why are you even entertaining the notion?"

"Because I just can't sit back and watch them torture Michael and do nothing. I love him. I want to spend the rest of my life with him. I want the plans we made to come true. Do you understand that?"

"Yes, I can understand that."

"What would you do if it was your wife, or your fiancée?"

"I don't know. I pray I never have to find out."

"I pray you never have to either. I pray no one ever has to find out."

"Are you prepared for whatever they may do to you?"

"I know what they've done in the past and I'm trying not to think about it."

"It's something you have to consider."

"Honestly, every time I think about it, I get physically ill. Somehow, I'm hoping and praying I'll be able to find the strength to withstand whatever they do to me."

Tom leaned back in his chair, lowered his head, and looked at his hands. Neither of them spoke. After several minutes, he looked up at Laura.

"What has to be done next?" he asked.

At two o'clock, Laura made an excuse and went to her room. She turned on her computer and began typing.

Are you there?

Yes. Did you talk to Mr. Richards?

Yes. He has agreed to mediate.

Does he know what is expected of him?

Yes. As far as we've talked, he's been apprised.

Does he understand that the least foul up can mean death to you and to him?

Yes. He understands. I need another assurance from you.

What is that? I have already promised that I will not abuse Mr. Braedon nor will I order his abuse.

I need your word that you will not make any attempt to take Mrs. Reinholdt.

I give you my word that she will remain safe and will only become an option if you are unable to make Mr. Reinholdt deliver what I need.

Agreed.

I will work on the details and notify you by email when I am ready to talk. I will give you a time and you will be there.

Please know I will only be in the States for two or three more days. After that, I will be in Paris.

When you arrive in Paris, you are to email me. I want no mix-ups on time. Agreed?

Agreed.

Once she copied the conversation to the folder, she began making other notes…notes on what she remembered about Yamani. What type of person he was. What his principles were. While the religious organization he headed now was of importance in the scheme of things, a man rarely disregarded the principles that had been ingrained in him throughout his past.

Laura turned off the computer and went down to the living room where Gina and Gwen were sitting going through some of the material they had brought with them from Paris.

"I need to go to the library," she said to them.

"Why?" asked Gina.

"I want to look up some old articles on Yamani. I want to know more about that man."

"How about some company?" asked Gina.

"I'd love some," said Laura. "Gwen, are you coming?"

"Sure," she said. "Let me call Mark and tell him where we're going. Maybe we can meet them for dinner later. That way we don't have to cook."

It seemed to be her day all around because Laura was able to find a parking place quite near the entrance of the Library.

"This doesn't happen every day," she said to the others. "Usually I have to walk across the bridge."

They walked up the steps and into the old building. Laura went to the librarian in charge of periodicals and asked her to see copies of *Newsweek* and *US News and World Report* dating back to the eighties. The librarian told her they were available in two forms, on the computer or the old magazines. Laura told her she wanted to see the old magazines. The three women sat down at a table and the librarian brought the first stack. Gina asked where they could find information on ancient religions and the librarian directed them to another floor and wing.

"We'll be back in a few minutes," she said to Laura.

"That's fine."

Laura took out her pen and notebook. She began leafing through the magazines looking for articles. When Gina and Gwen returned, they were carrying several books containing information about ancient religious groups. It was more than an hour before anyone spoke.

"There's just so much information," said Laura. "There are things that might be important." Laura walked over to the librarian and arranged for the information to be sent and then came back to the table.

"Did you find anything interesting in the books?"

"Plenty," said Gwen.

"Are they books we can check out?"

Gwen opened the front covers.

"Yes they are."

"What's so interesting?" asked Laura reaching in her purse and pulling out her library card.

"Do you know the name of the leader?" asked Gwen.

"Yes, Afmad Yamani," said Laura.

"No, his chosen name," said Gwen.

"Yes, it's Moukib Mustafa," said Laura. "It was in the notes from Professor Laban."

"Now, listen to this," said Gwen. "The first one chosen to begin this religion was given the name Moukib Mustafa. Notice on his name, he's not saying the second or anything the way the Popes are listed. Now in this book, which documents the new resurgence of the group, it states that the Divine One has once again sent the Chosen One back to earth. Yamani has his followers believing that he's the actual ancient Chosen One. The drawings of the Chosen One in the books are so general that it could be anyone."

Once those articles come, we'll have a lot of reading to do tonight. Then if we need to get any more information, we can come back tomorrow," said Laura.

The change of scenery was definitely doing everyone some good. It was also nice to eat out for a change. Over the past weeks, aside from the time they were in Frankfurt, she and the others had done nothing except eat at home. After dinner, they returned to the house. Mark and Paul worked on contracts while the ladies read over what they had brought from the library and what was sent. With every article, the three women constructed more of the personality of Yamani.

"It amazes me that you remember him from these days," said Gina. "As I'm reading these accounts, I can see he was, even at that time, leaning towards this ancient religion. It's so evident. Back then, no one would've connected it. Now, it's blatant. That's hindsight for you."

"Our key to Yamani is knowing everything we can about the religion and what he believes," said Laura. "He didn't adopt everything the religion professed. He modified it and molded it to what he actually wanted. He's smart enough to keep the parts of the religion where the truths lie, but he's brought it into the modern day culture in order to make it attractive. While other religions denounce much of the Western Culture, Yamani embraces it, especially technology saying it's a good thing because it can be used to spread the word and ultimately bring everyone to the one true religion. He's even able to sell that to his followers."

"Even though I've gone through everything the same way you have," said Gwen, "there's still one large question mark."

"What's that?" asked Gina.

"Is he capable of killing someone?" asked Gwen.

"There isn't any basis for murder or even justifiably killing someone for the sake of the religion in the ancient teachings," said Gina.

"However, since Yamani has modified the religion to suit himself, there's no guarantee he won't kill."

"All throughout the documentations we read, there was never any mention of abuse of men," said Laura. "Look what he's doing to Michael. I think they've broadened their scope."

"I think they still believe their treatment of women is the means that justifies the end. However, I don't think women are their only target now," said Gina. "They'll do whatever it takes to get their word out and complete their mission."

"At least now, we're not up against an unknown assailant. We know who he is, what he's like, and what he's capable of doing," said Gwen. "That gives us an edge. He has no idea we know who he is. The only thing he knows about us is whatever Michael has told him."

"In that case, he may know Michael has business partners and I'm his fiancée," said Laura. "Aside from that, there's no way he's going to be able to construct personal profiles of us the way we're able to do with him."

"From what we have, is there still anything we need to research tomorrow?" asked Gwen.

"I'd like to be able to find ancient maps and see if we can find the place where this religion began. I think that's important," said Gina. "Every religion has its holy land. Where's this religion's holy land?"

"Do you think they may be holding Michael somewhere in connection with that?" asked Laura.

"It's possible," said Gina. "Then again, it could be anywhere that was important from Yamani's past."

"Well, for right now, why don't we make a list of those places," said Gwen.

"We can find some of the places in these articles and books and everything we brought with us," said Laura.

"What we need is a map," said Gina

"We need several. This area of the world changes so often, that we may not be able to find cities or towns from the 1980's," said Gwen. "Let me go online and see what I can find, while the two of you make a list."

The three of them worked the rest of the evening on the project. When it was time for bed, Laura climbed the stairs to their room. For the first time since Michael's capture, Laura would sleep in their bed. She pulled down the covers and climbed in. She clutched his pillow close to her. She could smell him as though he was beside her. As she closed her eyes she could see him lying there; could feel his presence. She held his pillow as tightly as possible and prayed…for Michael…and for herself.

Chapter Twenty-One

In the morning, before Laura came downstairs, Mark and Paul left to check out some work sites. Gina and Gwen were working in the study. As she came down the grand staircase, she saw William in the entry hall.

"Is there anything you need me to do before I leave, Miss Darmer?" he asked.

"No, William, nothing I can think of. You are taking James with you to get Mr. Reinholdt."

"Yes, I am. Mr. Lemont was very emphatic about it."

"William, please don't take any chances. We have no way of knowing how much these people know. We also don't know how extensive their organization might be. I'd like you to call me when you get to the rendezvous. That way, I can tell Mr. Reinholdt exactly where you are. Then, I'd like you to call once you have Mr. Reinholdt and are on your way back."

"Yes, Miss Darmer. James and I thought we'd make sure the car is properly serviced before we pick up Mr. Reinholdt. That way, we shouldn't have to stop until we're home."

"When I talked to Mr. Reinholdt, he said they'd be finished around noon." She walked over to the lamp stand and took a piece of paper from it and gave it to William. "Here is all the information about where to pick him up along with a contact number for him. I gave him your phone number and James' as well."

D. A. Walters

Laura walked from the foyer into the study. Gina and Gwen finished taping maps together and Laura walked around the desk to look at the map.

"We tried to make them bigger so we could actually see the names of the cities without a magnifying glass," said Gwen.

"Why don't you take them down to the office supply store and see if you can get them printed on one sheet of paper. Maybe they can even darken the lettering," said Laura running her fingers over the taped seams.

"Good idea. Are you coming?" asked Gina rolling up the maps.

"I think I'll stay here. I need to get some work done," said Laura. "Could you also stop at the store and get some things for dinner. I thought since Edgar will be here earlier than expected, we could cook something."

"Laura, don't go anywhere," said Gwen.

"I promise I won't."

The house was very quiet and with everyone away, Laura used the time to get things together. Once Edgar arrived, she most likely wouldn't get another opportunity. All those pieces of information she knew she'd need were somewhere in her desk drawers and she rifled through them in earnest. There was also the matter of all the letters explaining her actions. She knew no one would really understand her motive. To them it just didn't make sense. Pierre made it extremely clear and she knew the others would agree.

Never had she meant for them to send one of their own wives into this situation. That was incomprehensible and she didn't blame them. Not one of them would expect his own wife to trade herself so he could go free, so why would they condone trading one of them to get Michael back. That didn't make good sense. She could only imagine what went on behind the closed doors with all of the men after Pierre's outburst. Although she'd never ask them, she knew most, if not all of them, felt it should be her who should go if it ever came to it.

No matter how they felt, she couldn't allow their doubts and opinions to cloud her judgment. The decision had been made and now she was working towards that end. She had just finished putting some notes in the folder when the doorbell rang. Laura walked down the hall, through the living room and into the foyer to answer the door.

"Mr. Richards, please come in. How are you today?" she asked.

"I'm fine. Please call me Tom."

"You haven't changed your mind, have you?" she asked searching his face for a clue.

"No, I haven't. Actually, I've spoken to my boss and told him I'd have to take a trip with relatively no notice. He told me it wouldn't be a problem. Have you heard anything?"

"Nothing. I won't hear anything until I'm back in Paris. That'll be several days from now. I'll call you to tell you exactly when I'll be leaving. They're going to contact me once all the details are worked out on their end. After I see what their plan is, I'll negotiate with them so that if it isn't slanted in our favor, it'll at least be even. When the plan has been agreed to, I'll send for you. Once you're in Paris, we'll make the rest of the plans."

"You're still determined to go through with this."

"Yes. The only way I won't, is if they release Michael first and I don't foresee that happening."

"I wish there was another way."

"Me, too, Tom, but this is the only way I know to appease them and get Michael back. Edgar Reinholdt will be arriving late this afternoon and when he gets here I know we'll have a lot to discuss."

"Miss Darmer,

"Laura"

"I know you've given this plan a great deal of thought, but I want you to know I'm still not a hundred percent sure this'll work."

"Tom, it has to," she said adamantly. "I'm counting on it. I'm only hoping Edgar will swiftly come to the decision to give the information so he can gain my release."

"Laura, just so you know, I've started writing down what we talked about and decided. Don't worry, it's not where anyone can get access to it. I even put a different password on it; something none of the guys would ever guess."

"That's fine. I do that too. It's on my computer in an embedded file. Before I leave…for the exchange…I'll make sure you have a copy of everything. From now on, I'll also send you everything I receive from them."

"Good."

"Do you have an email address no one knows about?"

"No, but I can create one."

"Please do that. I'll feel better knowing no one can read what I send." She picked up a piece of paper from the end table and wrote down her email address. "When you've created your new account, email it to me at this address. You're the only one who has this. They have a different email address and also a special chat room. I'll also make sure I give you those. Knowing the leader, he'll want to use those to keep in touch."

"Somehow I think this might be easier if we knew the identity of the leader."

"We do."

It had been a grueling week for all involved, but one that had gotten more accomplished than would've happened in a year going through committee. For the first time, all of the dignitaries were in the sitting room relaxing. The sense of relief was evident.

"Mr. Reinholdt, it's been a pleasure," said President Bartram. "Please let us know if there are any further developments."

"I will," said Edgar. "I'll make sure everything we talked about is covered as soon as I possibly can."

"Are you returning home?" asked the President.

"In a few days. I have meetings to attend elsewhere," said Edgar. "It's a very busy time."

"This is probably something you really didn't have time to deal with," said President Mason.

"It's all part of our business," said Edgar. "I wish each of you the best of luck as you deal with your governments. Hold a hard line."

"As agreed, Mr. Reinholdt, we will say and do nothing until Mr. Braedon has been released and these perpetrators have been brought to justice," said President Bartram. "Then we'll inform our governments that we'd been apprised of the situation from the beginning and handled it in the best interest of national as well as world security."

For more than fifteen minutes, neither of them spoke. The news of the leader's identity sent shockwaves through Tom Richards. He finally looked at Laura with a stunned look on his face when he finished looking at the material.

"Do you know who this man is, Laura?"

"Yes, I do."

"Then you know how conniving he can be," said Tom emphatically. "He almost turned an entire nation against its leader. He would've if it hadn't been for outside interference."

"Can you imagine what this world would've been like with him at the helm of a country?"

"I don't know and I also hope I never find out."

"As you can see there's much more at stake than just Michael. However, he's the most important part of this as far as I'm concerned," said Laura. "Tom, it's extremely important no one finds out what we know."

"They won't hear it from me."

There was very little time between Tom's leaving and Gina and Gwen's return, however, there was no sign that Tom Richards or anyone else had been there. They took the cardboard cylinder into the study and the three of them hung the maps.

"These are so much better," said Laura looking at the large clear versions of the maps they had made. "I can actually read the names of the cities."

"They're in chronological order," said Gina, "and they made them all the same size. They actually fit one on top of the other."

"We got a second set made on transparencies so we can overlap them," said Gwen "That might give us more of a clue as to where they may be."

"Let's get started," said Laura.

The three women worked for hours, looking through material and making notes of clues to the location of the holy land. When they heard the keys in the front door, Gwen looked up at the clock and Mark and Paul walked into the study.

"What're you girls doing?" asked Mark as he kissed his wife.

"Trying to find Michael," said Gwen giving him back a kiss.

"How's it going?" asked Paul.

"Well we've narrowed it down at least. There are three areas that keep repeating," said Gina. "We found them in the ancient writings, in Yamani's history, and in some of the accounts in the last decade. When we overlay these, they match up."

Laura got up from her chair, walked over to the desk, and opened a drawer. She searched until she found what she was looking for. Then she walked up to the map.

"You know, my mother always said the world was made of triangles," said Laura. "No matter what you look at, you can divide it into triangles."

"Okay, where're you going with this?" asked Paul as though Laura had said something so foreign, so bizarre.

"Well, we have three points. If we connect them, we get a triangle," she said as she took a straightedge and a dry erase marker and connected the points. She continued talking as she drew. "Now if we bisect each leg and draw a line from the opposite vertex through the bisect we'll get a point of intersection," she said.

"And that point of intersection means what?" asked Paul.

"That's where they are," said Gina as though the answer was obvious.

"How do you know that?" asked Mark.

"Take a look at some of the major religions. The triangle is a vital part of it. Just look at Christianity for example. The triangle represents the Trinity. In many churches, there's a stained glass window or a painting of a triangle with the eye of God in it. The pupil of the eye is at that point of intersection. It's the center of all," said Laura turning around to face them. "Yamani would want to be the center of all. This point of intersection falls in Iraq."

Paul walked up to the map to get a closer look. "That's one hell of a point of intersection."

for Love and Ransom

Edgar Reinholdt arrived shortly after five o'clock and Mark showed him to his room. When he came downstairs he joined Mark and Paul in the dining room. Mark offered him a drink which he gratefully accepted.

"Dinner will be ready in a few minutes," said Gwen when she, Gina, and Laura came into the room and sat down.

"How did things go?" asked Mark. He couldn't wait any longer to find out.

"Better than I had anticipated," said Edgar.

"To be honest, Edgar, I didn't think it would take this long to address the situation," said Paul.

"It didn't," said Edgar. "We had decided the first step on the first day. Then as I was taking care of shoring up national security for each country, the leaders began talking amongst themselves. They came to the realization that national security needed to be reassessed particularly in regards to technology. They realized they were vulnerable. The next days were spent identifying and deciding how best to protect them. They'll introduce this to their governments at the appropriate time."

"When is that, Edgar?" asked Gwen.

"After we have Michael back and the perpetrators have been brought to justice," he said. "They'll inform their governments they knew about this since the beginning and have taken steps to further ensure national security at many new levels."

"How the hell did you get them to agree to that?" asked Mark.

"I hold their best interest in my hands," said Edgar smiling.

After dinner Paul wanted to check out some of the new things Michael had added to the game room since the last time he was there and Mark went to make a call to Pierre to update him on what was going on.

"I haven't seen anything on the internet or on the news about Michael," said Mark. "I don't understand what's going on. It seems the only time they show him is when they're abusing him."

"Maybe they're leaving him alone," said Pierre.

"It's making me nervous. What're they up to?"

"I don't know. When're you coming back?"

"I think we're leaving tomorrow evening. We went over contracts and paperwork yesterday and did site visits today. Tomorrow, we're meeting with the clients to allay their fears."

"Sounds good. We're doing that here, too."

"One or two of us need to come to the Pittsburgh office at least every two weeks or so. There's so much work happening here."

"Is there anything that we can do here to help out?"

"Not really. The actual work can't be done from Paris."

After the call, Mark came out into the living room.

"Where's Edgar?" he asked.

"In his room," said Gwen. "I think he's exhausted."

"This can't be easy for him," said Gina.

"He can relax for the most part tomorrow before we leave," said Paul.

"Are you going to be able to meet with everyone and still make the flight?" asked Laura.

"I think we'll make it with time to spare," said Mark. "There're four of us."

"We need to pack all of this up to take with us," said Gina.

"There's way too much to take," said Laura. "Why don't we just have it sent along with anything you need to take from the office? I can do it when I take these books back tomorrow. I just need to drop them off and take care of a few errands while I'm here. I'll be back as quickly as possible."

It was getting late and with the busy day ahead of them, they went to bed. Laura sat at her desk and made a list of the things she needed to give to Tom before she left. Among her errands included getting money for him to cover the cost of the plane fare and hotel in Paris. She didn't want any questions asked. As she thought about it, she put everything in logical order. The more she thought, the more her hands began to tremble.

"What am I doing?" she asked and she looked over at Michael's picture.

She closed her eyes and took a deep breath. As she thought about what would happen if she didn't do it, she knew there was no other way.

Chapter Twenty-Two

The Chosen One knew how important the deal was he was making. The last thing he wanted was to be taken for a fool. The Cause was too important. He needed some way to reassure himself that she was who she said she was. The only one who could tell him was Michael.

The guard opened the door and the Chosen One walked in. Then the guard locked the door from the outside. The Chosen One stood in front of Michael. Today he came alone.

"Well, Mr. Braedon, I have not seen you for several days," said the Chosen One. "I wanted you to know that I have not forgotten about you. I did check out your story and everything you told us was true. There were other things being worked on at the time, but the ones you told me about were by far the most important ones. I know that you were only in some of the areas very briefly which accounts for not knowing in detail what they were working on. I am pleased with the way you are cooperating, Mr. Braedon. I want you to keep thinking. I want every little detail when I ask about something. It is very important that you hold nothing back. If you keep this up, I may be forced to keep you around longer."

He then took a few steps towards Michael and leaned in closer to him. "If, however, you get sloppy in what you tell me and you leave out important things, I will have no choice but to try to jog your memory. You know, Mr. Braedon, I have many ways of helping people cooperate. I am sure you will not like any of them. I have to leave to take care of some very important business, but I promise I will return on another day and we will chat." He turned and started walking towards the door. "Oh, by the way, Mr. Braedon," he said as he stopped and turned around, "your fiancée, Miss Darmer, is it? She is a beautiful woman…a very beautiful woman indeed. I should really enjoy talking with her one day."

With that, he smiled, turned, and left.

Michael looked with apprehension at the door. *How does he know about Laura? How does he know what she looks like? What does he mean talking with her? What's he going to do?* Michael sat there contemplating what he meant. Did he mention Laura to anyone? He was sure he was careful not to let anything slip about her. With new purpose, Michael began to run through his mind every minute of his encounter with Edgar.

Edgar Reinholdt rose early in the morning. His bags were packed from the day before. He saw no reason to disrupt everything in his suitcases, so he packed whatever he needed in his carry-on piece. Once he closed that, he'd be ready to leave.

He needed to touching base with his office, to make certain everything was running well. Although Erika was the epitome of organization and Albert Paxton could handle any type of crisis, neither of them was aware of the pirating of information that was going on in the buildings. He was anxious to get everything taken care of, especially the provisions of the new contracts he had with the countries. After all this was over, that would be top priority.

Once again, he looked in the mirror and began to think about where he'd be, if they had been successful. It never occurred to him that anyone would want to kidnap him. He never thought of his job as being the least bit dangerous. He enjoyed what he did; enjoyed it from the first day. This was certainly a wake-up call for him, both personally and within his business.

Edgar stared at his reflection. With everything he had seen Michael go through at the hands of his captors, he wondered if he, himself, would've been able to withstand the treatment. It was a test of character he never wanted to experience. He hoped one day he'd be able to talk to Michael and tell him how sorry he was for all this and how much he admired him.

A knock at the door brought Edgar back to reality and he answered it.

"I thought I heard you moving around in here," said Mark. "I was wondering if you wanted to come to the office for a while. You can use the computers there and phones to get in touch with your office."

"I'd like that," said Edgar.

"Have you spoken to your wife?" asked Mark.

"Yes, I called her when I arrived here, yesterday. I'd like to call her again if it's alright," he said.

"Call her as often as you like. Perhaps she might like to join us in Paris."

"I think she'd like that. All of this is causing stress for her and I'd like to have her close to me."

"Is there someone who can come with her, or would you like us to send someone for her?"

"Her friend has family in Paris. Perhaps they'd like to travel together."

"When you're ready, we'll be in the kitchen. Please join us for breakfast."

"Thank you."

Once everyone left for the office, Laura took all the information about Yamani and copied it in Michael's office. She put the copies in a folder and put it into her briefcase. Then she went and gathered all the papers that needed to be sent.

She was almost finished when she remembered the box. She ran upstairs to the bedroom and went into the closet. Way in the back were all of those things they just couldn't part with. They were the memories of their past. She and Michael would get one or two of them out every so often and tell stories about themselves when they were younger. She finally found the box and took it downstairs.

She went into the study and took one more look around so she didn't forget anything. Carefully she took the maps down from the wall, rolled them neatly and put them back in the tube. William walked in carrying the box she asked for and the two of them packed it.

"Hopefully, whatever has to go from the office will fit in here."

"It may be a little snug, but we'll make it work somehow," said William. "If you're almost ready to go, I'll pull the car around."

"Yes, William, I'm just about ready."

The first stop was at the office as she promised. William parked in front of the building and watched her walk through the doors. As soon as Maggie saw Laura, she came from behind the desk. The two of them embraced.

"How are you, Maggie?" asked Laura wiping a tear away.

"I'm alright. I just wish they'd let him go."

"Me, too. My mind just keeps replaying that conversation you and I had."

"So does mine. You know one of the last things we talked about was your wedding. He wanted to know if I'd go to a wedding in Paris."

"What did you say?"

"I told him if my boss was being nice, maybe he'd give me the time off."

"Oh, Maggie," said Laura smiling, "the two of you love teasing each other."

"Yes we do. I have everything ready for you," she said as she wiped a tear from her cheek.

Maggie walked to her desk and picked up a fat envelope. She handed it to Laura.

"I made up the label for you. I put your Paris address on it."

"Thanks, Maggie. The next time I see you, I'll be with Michael. I promise."

"I'll be waiting."

Tom Richards had just finished his morning drive show when Laura arrived.

"How are you, this morning?" asked Tom closing the door to his office.

"I'm doing well," she said, "and you?"

"I just keep thinking about all this"

"Please don't get cold feet," she pleaded.

"Don't worry. I won't."

"I have some things for you."

Laura placed her briefcase on his desk and opened it. She took out all the information she had gathered on Yamani and the religious faction.

"This should make some interesting reading until we're contacted," she said as she handed him the folder. "I also have money for you. There's enough here for plane fares, hotels, meals, and probably whatever else you need. It's cash, because I didn't want it traced." She took the envelope from her purse and handed it to him.

"Cash is fine."

"Whenever they call, whatever the timetable is, I want to meet ahead of time to work everything out. I don't want anything to go wrong."

"I'm nervous about the whole time limit thing," said Tom. "What if I can't find a street, or get lost, or there's traffic."

"He's not about to leave anything to chance. He'll make sure you have explicit instructions and directions."

"I know you're right."

"Remember, I told you I put the file on my computer?" said Laura handing him a piece of paper. "This is the password for that file. I want you to memorize it so once the switch is made, you'll be able to tell Michael and his partners how to access it. I'm writing letters to them explaining why I did it. Tom, there's going to be a letter in the folder that has to be given to Maggie."

"Who's Maggie?"

"She's Michael's secretary here and one of my best friends. Please make sure she gets it."

"I will. Are you sure about going through with this?" he asked looking her in the eyes.

"Yes, I've been taking my time and thinking quite clearly. When I'm making the plans and making sure everything is going to be taken care of, I'm calm. It's only when I think of what they might possibly do that I start to stress." She stopped and took a deep breath. "I'm hoping Edgar will part with the information so they'll release me as quickly as possible."

"For your sake, I hope you're right," said Tom trying to muster an encouraging smile.

"We're leaving this evening. I'll call you from Paris when I get there."

"Then I guess the next time I'll see you will be in Paris."

Chapter Twenty-Three

Laura took one more look around the room and then walked through the hallway. She just reached the foyer when the front door opened and Gabrielle walked in followed by Joseph.

"Gabrielle," said Laura, "it's so nice to see you again."

"Laura," she said, "thank you for inviting me."

Let me show you to your room.

"This is just lovely," said Gabrielle walking into the room.

"After you're settled, please join us in the living room," said Laura. "I hope you brought pictures of the gala."

"I did," she said. "I thought you might want to see them and then Edgar told me you asked me to bring them."

"I've been dying to see them. I saw everything in bits and pieces. I've been curious about how everything went together."

"I'll bring them out with me."

"Everyone will be here shortly. I'll tell Edgar you're in your room if he gets here before you come out."

"Thank you."

Laura went back to the living room and began straightening things a little. It seemed straightening had become her great diversion. Nothing else was really as mindless.

"Honey, what're you doing?" asked Margo.

"I don't know. Trying to straighten things a little," said Laura stopping what she was doing. "What's Gabrielle going to think when she sees all this?"

"She's going to think we're working to get Michael back. Remember when we went to her house. There were things everywhere for the gala."

"I guess you're right."

They heard the door to the garage open and Mark yelled in.

"We're in the living room," said Laura.

"Has Gabrielle arrived?" asked Edgar as soon as he came in sight of Laura.

"She's in your room."

Edgar walked into his bedroom and closed the door behind him. He walked up to Gabrielle, put his arms around her, and kissed her.

"I've missed you, Gabrielle."

"Oh, Edgar, I've missed you, too."

"How are you, sweetheart?" he asked.

"I'm fine. I'm so glad you asked me to come here. I so wanted to be with you."

"I've wanted to be with you, too. I hate being away."

"Edgar, how are things, really."

"We're doing everything we can, sweetheart."

"Do you think they're going to release Michael?"

"I don't know. We're going to try everything we can to make it happen."

"Laura must be beside herself. I know how I felt when I got that note…and you were safe," said Gabrielle reaching up and touching his cheek. "I can't imagine what it would be like if they had taken you."

"Right now, I don't want to think about any of that. I want you to tell me what you've been doing. I want to hear everything."

He sat down with her on the loveseat.

for Love and Ransom

When Edgar and Gabrielle came to the living room, he introduced his wife to those she hadn't met. Then he joined the rest of the men in the study. The ladies began looking through the pictures. Each one showed some detail of just how spectacular the event was. Gabrielle's face beamed with pride when she talked about it.

"Gabrielle, how long does your committee work on this?" asked Nicole.

"We give ourselves about two weeks off after the gala and then begin meeting for next year's. We first make a list of what we liked and what we didn't like and more importantly why. We never repeat a theme. We're always learning. We want to attract new people to our group, so we have to constantly change and grow. We always try to recruit young members. If we can get them excited and keep them excited then our group will last and we'll be able to do more good things."

"Do you always work at your home?" asked Monique.

"Oh yes. My dear husband puts up with all of that," she said smiling. "I don't know another man who would."

"How did you find out about the organization?" asked Raquel.

"I started it. Many people start businesses, like my husband. I chose to start a philanthropic organization."

"Do you draw a salary from it?" asked Brigit.

"No, my dear, no one who works for the organization draws a salary. Ours is a very simple bookkeeping idea. Whatever we take in, minus what we had to pay for, equals what we're able to donate. Believe me; we try to get as much donated as possible. This year, we paid out less than ten percent of what we took in. We did very well."

She told them every detail of the gala and it was evident to everyone that for Gabrielle, this was a labor of love.

The group decided once they had Edgar back in Paris they'd work on a plan aimed at getting Michael released. They knew the most important step of the plan hinged on Edgar's willingness to cooperate. After all, what the abductors were after only Edgar could deliver.

221

"Edgar, I know you've had quite a time lately," said Pierre trying to be as diplomatic as possible. "We need to talk to you about Michael. I realize you've made a promise to the leaders that you'll do nothing to jeopardize national security. There has to be some way to keep that promise and somehow dupe the captors into letting Michael go. I know if it had to do with my area of expertise, I'd be able to put together something that would allow them to think they could succeed with what we were giving them. I don't know if that's possible from your end."

"I can honestly tell you I haven't thought about it," said Edgar. "I've been so busy trying to make sure they can't access certain systems."

"With what they have now, can they be a formidable adversary?" asked Henri.

"With what they were able to take," said Edgar taking his time to think a little, "if they can find out how to utilize it, they can be quite formidable."

"To a point where it'd be impossible to stop them?" asked Robert.

"No," said Edgar quickly. "I can always stop them. The trick is to anticipate what they're going to do. If that can be done, I can stop them before they even start."

"But, can you stop them and still make it seem to them that they're succeeding?" asked Paul.

"Gentlemen, that's being devious!" said Edgar looking from one to the other. "I've never done business like that."

"We know that, Edgar," said Mark. "Under normal circumstances, we'd never suggest it. Right now, it's very important they think they're being able to get their message out to everyone."

"As I've said, if we can anticipate, we can do it," said Edgar. "However, if they've been able to proceed undetected, we're going to have to scramble to do damage control."

"That's a position we don't want to be in," said Pierre.

"Then we need to know everything they can do with what they already have," said George.

"Obviously, it's not enough," said Robert, "because they keep asking Michael for more information."

"They want it all," said Edgar shaking his head. "They want SecReSAC."

They created a list of what Yamani could do and a time line of how they'd most likely proceed.

"What if they don't start at the beginning?" asked Paul. "What if they eliminate those insignificant accomplishments for bigger ones? Then you'll always be behind them."

"Unfortunately," said Edgar, "we don't know where they are on this line."

"If I were them, I'd want to see results quickly," said Jean. "I'd want to see what all this got me. I'd try to take over a small television station and transmit my message in place of their programming without them knowing. Then I'd try to link two or three until I was able to take a region."

"Can they do that?" asked Paul.

"They have the knowledge," said Edgar.

Michael sat facing the Chosen One. This was the first time the Chosen One sat in the room. Michael knew whatever he wanted must be important to him, as well as something he didn't want others to know. The only one who accompanied him today was his personal guard, Sadik.

"Mr. Braedon, it is nice to see you again. I apologize that it has been several days. Now, what do you say about this. I think one day, I should like to meet your Miss Darmer. She sounds like an exquisitely lovely person. I bet you think about her quite a bit." He watched Michael's face for a reaction. He could tell he was puzzled. "Oh, by the way Mr. Braedon, I was wondering if you could answer a few questions for me. Remember, think carefully and give me your best answer. I certainly would not want anything to keep you from seeing Miss Darmer again. The work that Reinholdt International is doing in regards to the satellites, can it make communications between let us say television stations easier?"

"Yes, sir."

"Can you tell me anything about it?"

"I heard them talking about the ability of being able to link stations together."

"How many stations?"

"They were initially talking about linking two or three. Then, they were talking about having the potential to link all the stations in a particular region."

"I see."

"There was even one person who proposed that it might be possible for the ruler of a country to take over all of the stations at one time in order to broadcast emergency information."

"Would the ruler need to have the permission of the stations?"

"No. It'd be done through commands sent through the satellite."

"Would there be any way for the station to know that the president had taken over the broadcast?"

"They were discussing that. One person said it couldn't be done because the stations would know what they were broadcasting. Another person said the station wouldn't know. They'd be broadcasting and the signal would be intercepted after it left the station and redirected. So those at the station wouldn't know."

"What about the televisions they use to monitor what they are broadcasting?"

"Those are direct feed lines. They don't leave the building."

"So, you are telling me that it is impossible for the stations to know their transmission has been interrupted."

"Not impossible. There's always the possibility someone will call the station to complain that their program has been interrupted by the president again."

"How can that be stopped?"

"If you can take over the transmission of television stations, you should be able to divert their calls also."

"You know, Mr. Braedon, you never cease to amaze me. You have given me much to think about and much hope. I think you may have just bought yourself another day or two…that is, if I can get these things to happen. I am sure Miss Darmer will be glad you have answered so well. Whenever I am finally able to meet your wonderful lady, I will tell her how well you cooperated."

Michael sat in awe for the second time. *How could he possibly know about Laura?*

While the ladies discussed the gala and the men discussed pressing business, dinner was cooking. Laura went to their bedroom without anyone even missing her. She turned on the computer and logged onto the internet.

Miss Darmer.

Yes.

Ah, you are there.

Yes. How's Michael?

He is well. He did very well today. I told him that he may just have bought himself another day or two.

Have you come to any decisions?

Yes, I have. However, I need to try these ideas that Mr. Braedon shared with me before I give you any details. Everything must be in place before any trades can be made.

How long will that take?

Patience, my dear Miss Darmer, patience. All in due time. I promised you that no harm will come to Mr. Braedon while we are talking. I intend to keep my promise. I will contact you in a day or two…or so.

What do you have to do?

There was no reply. Yamani ended the conversation. Laura put her head in her hands. Now, all she could do was wait and the waiting was nerve wracking. She picked up the phone and called Tom.

"I've heard from them again," she said.

"Do we have instructions?"

"Not yet. He said he talked to Michael this morning and he did very well. He told him he may have just bought himself another day or two."

"What does he mean by that?"

"I don't know. I have his word that he won't harm Michael while we're talking. He said he had to try out the ideas Michael gave him."

"What ideas?"

"I don't know. He ended the conversation saying he'd be in touch in a day or two…or so. All we can do is wait."

"I know this has to be frustrating the hell out of you. It's frustrating me."

"More than you know. I just want it to be over."

"I found some interesting things about him when I was searching for more information. I told some of my colleagues I've been asked to put together a documentary. You should see what they sent me. Is there any way I can get this to you?"

"Is it too much to email?"

"Much too much."

"Then box it and I'll have Michael's secretary, Maggie, pick it up and overnight it to me."

"I can have it ready in an hour. Call me when you're finished reading it, or if they contact you before that, or if you just want to talk."

"Thanks."

Laura hung up the phone, logged out, shut down the computer, and walked to the study.

"I'm sorry to interrupt, I know how busy you are, but is there anything you need sent from the Pittsburgh office? I know we were just there a few days ago, but I thought I'd ask," she said. "A friend of mine has uncovered some interesting information about Yamani and it's entirely too much to email. I'm going to call Maggie to pick it up and send it overnight."

"As a matter of fact, there is," said Mark. "Let me get a list ready and then we'll call her."

"You told someone about Yamani?" asked Robert glaring at her.

"No, I told him I needed background info for an article comparing him to more contemporary men ascending to power," said Laura. "I'd never jeopardize anything concerning Michael. You should know that."

"I'm just making sure," said Robert in an unusually curt tone.

"What do you mean by that?"

"You know exactly what I mean," said Robert. "We're doing everything in our power to keep this under wraps and I'm not about to let you destroy everything we've done for some journalistic whim."

"Listen here," she said, "I trust my contacts as much as you trust yours. You asked me to trust you, now you need to trust me."

"All I'm saying is I want you to be sure they can be trusted," he said raising his voice. "You're spending your time reading in there and we're busting our asses coming up with a plan to get Michael back."

"You know what?" Laura said, hardly believing what Robert had just said. She walked in front of him and leaned in until her face was really close to his. "No matter what it takes, I will get Michael back.

You can take that to the bank." With that, she stood up, turned on her heels, and walked to the door. She turned to face Mark. "When you're ready to make the call, come and get me." Then she stormed out of the study.

Robert's face was beet red and the others sat there speechless.

D. A. Walters

Chapter Twenty-Four

Mark put the box down on the couch, opened it, and took out the envelopes for the business. There was a small envelope with Laura's name on it. He handed it to her and she opened it.

Laura, I hope you find this as informative as I have.
Tom.

"Who's Tom?"

"Tom Richards, he's a D.J. for WXDX. I've known him for some time. I asked him to see if he could find out anything about Yamani for an article for me as a favor. I told him to keep my name out of it. He asked some of his connections in the broadcasting industry for information telling them that he had been approached about doing a documentary on the Ayatollah's right hand man. This is what they sent him. He made copies of everything for me."

"Wow. It looks like you'll be really busy," said Mark.

"How're things coming with Edgar?" asked Laura.

"Better. We have a list of what they can do with what they have. So we might be able to come up with a plan to anticipate what they're going to do so we can be ready."

"Maybe whatever's in this box will help you narrow it down further."

"In that case, start reading," he said. "We can use any bit of help."

With Gabrielle visiting with her friend and her friend's family, the ladies were able to dig into the information Tom sent. The only sounds that could be heard were the turning of pages and an occasional 'Good God.'

"This man's a monster disguised as a religious man," said Gwen slapping some pages against her lap.

"He's the one who took care of anyone who had any objections to what the Ayatollah was doing," said Laura. "It was Yamani who had all those people killed preceding the war."

"Was he told to do it or did he act on his own?" asked Nicole.

"According to this, the Ayatollah gave no such order," said Monique. "In fact, his order was to try to bring them together by talking. Once the order was given by Yamani, it was the beginning of the end for him."

"What did Yamani have to gain from those actions?" asked Angelique.

"Credibility," said Laura. "He was trying to discredit the Ayatollah. He had made claims that the Ayatollah was moving the people away from the one true religion and if that happened, they'd never have their rewards in the afterlife. The people didn't believe him. The Ayatollah was their spiritual leader, their supreme leader and wasn't to be discredited."

"Yamani's actions were performed in the name of the Ayatollah, so the people thought the Ayatollah was working against them. Those who stayed loyal to him vowed to protect him. That's when the fighting broke out. When the Ayatollah found out what had happened, he knew Yamani was behind it. He had him exiled. When the Ayatollah died, Yamani was free to return."

"There are accounts here of people being tortured at Yamani's hands," said Brigit. "He also gave orders for the torturing of others. He became a person to be dreaded and feared. When he finally disappeared, the people experienced a sense of peace."

"He remained in hiding until recently when he resurfaced as the Chosen One," said Gwen. "What he has done so far gives his followers no indication he's anything like the man he was during the reign of the Ayatollah. As a matter of fact, aside from the horrific treatment of women, he's doing everything to be the opposite."

"Then how do you explain his treatment of Michael?" asked Angelique.

"Up to that time, he hadn't done anything," said Laura. "Now with this new twist, some of the old Yamani may be shining through."

"How long do you think it'll be before he falls back into his old ways?" asked Nicole.

"I don't know. I think he's already started down that path with Michael," said Margo. "The first days of his confinement brought a form of punishment. Now it's become much more. Now it's not only physical, but psychological. He has threatened to kill him, but hasn't said when."

"Every time he shows Michael, you can tell that there's always that threat of death," said Gina, "even if he doesn't say it."

"I know. Michael's life hangs in the balance day by day," said Gwen. "I'm not sure how much time we have."

Silence fell over the group as they once again pored over the documents. As she read further, Laura's face turned ghostly white. She became agitated and her stomach began to churn. All of a sudden, she put down the papers, clasped her hand over her mouth and hurriedly ran to the bathroom. She returned several minutes later.

"Are you alright, Laura?" asked Gwen.

She took a deep breath.

"Part of Yamani penchant for torture involves women," she said. "There are detailed accounts of mutilations, abuse, and rape and how they were done. He can't be permitted to take Gabrielle. She'd never survive anything that's in here."

"May I see that?" asked Margo.

Laura picked up the papers and handed them to Margo.

"Oh, dear God," she said after a few minutes..

After she finished reading a page, she handed it to Nicole.

"This makes me sick to my stomach. How could they do that to anyone?" asked Nicole. "How could you treat another human being that way? I don't know how those women stood that treatment. I could never do that."

"Not even if it was for your husband?" asked Laura.

"As I'm looking at it right now, I have my doubts," said Nicole. "If I was faced with my submission being the only way to save him…that may prove to be different. I don't know. I honestly don't know."

"Please tell me you're not thinking about that," said Margo.

"How could I even get in touch with them?" said Laura.

"If you could, would you?" asked Margo.

"I don't know," said Laura. "I guess you have to be faced with that decision to know how you'd make it."

Even with the intense nature of things, there was still much more that had to be covered. It was evident by the demeanor of the group that patience was wearing thin.

"How else can we prepare for this, Edgar?" asked Jean.

"We've covered everything we can think of as far as this is concerned," said Edgar. "I think we have very good tactics outlined."

"We still don't know what he's going to do," said Jacques playing with his pen, "nor do we know at what point he'll start."

"True, but the way we have it set up," said Edgar, "we can jump in at any point and make the damage minimal."

"Edgar, there's something else we have to address," said Pierre. He'd been waiting until the time was right and now was just as right as any.

"If you're addressing the job I'm hiring you to do, I think we need to put that on hold until this is resolved," he said putting the papers in front of him in a neat pile.

"I couldn't agree more," said Pierre leaning forward. "Michael is only going to be able to appease them a little while longer. At that time, they're going to have to find another way of getting the information they need. We've done extensive research on this group and our wives are doing even more as we speak," he said gesturing towards the living room. "What we can tell you is this…if they can't get what they want from Michael, they'll find someone to take his place. That someone will most likely be a woman."

"What are you saying?" asked Edgar putting down the papers and taking off his glasses.

"What I'm saying is that they're going to go after someone who will be able to make you give them what they want," said Pierre.

"Are you trying to tell me that my wife is in danger?" asked Edgar looking from one to another.

"It may be your wife, or it may be someone else's wife," said Pierre. "Whoever it is, you need to be prepared for that. Just what are you willing to give? Are you willing to part with the secrets of SecReSAC?"

"No!" Edgar said raising his voice.

"Are you willing to hold the line while he abuses and tortures your wife or someone else's wife?" asked Pierre raising his voice. Lately he had been having trouble keeping his temper totally under control.

"Giving them SecReSAC is basically giving them the keys to every country and welcoming him with open arms," said Edgar taking out a handkerchief and wiping his brow.

"Well, Edgar, that's what he's going to ask for," said Pierre quietly.

"What is it you want?" asked Edgar.

"What is it you can do that'll give him SecReSAC on your terms?" asked Pierre. He paused and looked at Edgar. "How can you modify it so they're led to believe they have the real deal so they'll release the person they choose to take?"

Edgar put his head in his hands and shook it. After a few moments, he folded his hands as though in prayer and touched his lips.

"I don't know," he said. "I never thought of this before."

"Well, Edgar, I wholeheartedly suggest you begin thinking," said Pierre. "He hasn't come asking for anything yet, because Michael's been able to give him things he needs. When Michael stops being useful, he'll come asking. If you say no, then he'll begin looking for someone who just might be able to persuade you to give in."

"I have my wife very well guarded," said Edgar almost trying to convince himself of the fact.

"Yes, Edgar, I know that," said Pierre tapping the table with his index finger. He continued addressing him spelling out the obvious. "Remember, you also thought you had a foolproof method at your complexes, too. Yamani knows no boundaries. He gets what he wants. He's been waiting for this for a long, long time. Even though he made a mistake by taking Michael instead, in reality, he made the smart move. He now knows if he had taken you, he wouldn't have been able to get what he wanted. Even his mistakes turn out to advance his strategy."

"Knowing what we know now, I don't believe you're in any danger. None of us are. Our wives, on the other hand, are. If he does take one of them, I want to be able to give him what he wants as soon as possible in order to get her back. Do I make myself clear, Edgar?"

"Abundantly clear."

As the ladies read through the material sent by Tom, distinct piles were forming. A lot of the material included things they may've read about before or surmised, but now were corroborated.

"Here's something interesting. It seems Yamani had a plan for taking over all of the television and radio stations back in the eighties," said Laura. "It was quite an elaborate plan which called for tens of thousands of people. He would've had to coordinate these forces worldwide. At that time, there was no way of doing this in an easy way. It would've had to have been done on a relay system which would've taken so much time that there was a possibility someone could've intercepted a message and caused the chain to be broken."

"How important was taking over the stations?" asked Gwen.

"It was number one on his list," said Laura.

"Do you think it's still number one?" asked Raquel.

"Most likely," said Laura. "It's the only way to reach the vast majority of people. Take a look at this. It's the speech he planned to give."

"Anything interesting?" asked Angelique sitting down beside her.

"Read it yourself," she said, handing it to her. "I think it's bizarre."

Angelique sat reading the more than five pages of text. "It's bizarre alright," she said. "If this is the way he felt back then, it only serves to reason that he's much more prepared to carry out what he outlined in this speech." She stopped talking and looked at each of them. "This man has to be stopped. He can't be allowed to do this."

After the intense conversation between Edgar and Pierre, the room became silent. Several of them used this opportunity to leave and get a change of scenery. Mark came into the living room. He walked behind Gwen and put his hands on her shoulders and started massaging her.

"Find anything interesting?" he asked quietly.

"Oh, yes," she said. "What do you want to know? How he abuses, mutilates, and rapes women? Or perhaps you want to read his plans to take over the television and radio stations. Or maybe you'd like to read the speech he planned to give."

"Whoa," he said stopping the massage. "What're you talking about?" He walked around the chair and faced her.

"Mark," she said pointing to a stack of papers, "this pile tells what he did to women to make sure their men gave him what he wanted. Let me warn you, it's very graphic. These pages contain his plan to take over every television and radio station in the world back in the eighties. It's a very detailed, aggressive, interesting plan, and the number one objective on his list. This is the speech he planned to give when he took over the stations. The rest of this we haven't had a chance to go through yet and we aren't going to do it now, because frankly, we need a break."

Mark bent down and kissed his wife, picked up the piles, and hurriedly returned to the study.

"Well, we know where he's going to start?" he said as soon as he was through the door.

"What do you mean?" asked Jacques.

"You know that package that came from Laura's friend?" asked Mark. "Well, so far, they've uncovered three distinct things." He put a pile of papers on the table. "First, this pile tells very graphically, Gwen says, what he does to women. This second pile," he said putting it down, "outlines his plan, during the eighties, to take over every television and radio station in the world. This one," he said holding it up, "is the speech he planned to give. She said that taking over the television stations was his number one objective."

"Well, then, are we to deduce from this that he would most likely stay with his original course of action?" asked Robert.

"I think it's a fair assumption," said Mark.

"Did she say why the plan didn't work?" asked Edgar.

"No, I think they want us to read this for ourselves."

Chapter Twenty-Five

Michael sat with his back against the wall. It had been days since he had seen his captor. He was beginning to understand the importance of thinking clearly, taking his time, and answering as completely as possible, even if it meant only making an educated guess. As long as he made it sound intelligent and plausible it would be accepted. It was nearly two months since he had been taken and he still couldn't put some of the details together. He began to wonder if that information had been lost forever or if it'd only take something to trigger it. Michael looked up suddenly as the key rattled in the lock. The Chosen One walked in.

"Mr. Braedon, I do apologize for not coming to see you sooner," he said, "but we were trying some experiments. You see, some of our members own television stations. They agreed to allow us to experiment. We were able to take over a total of five stations without them knowing it. It was so successful that two of the members called asking when we were going to conduct our experiment. We told them we already had and they were shocked that they didn't know it happened. The others knew. They had phone calls concerning the interruption of their broadcast. I call that somewhat of a success. It was not even difficult to do. It only took a few simple commands. Now, Mr. Braedon, we need to address the problem about the telephone calls. Do you have any suggestions?"

"I think you can handle this one of three ways. First, you can divert all calls to a central call center where you'd have people answer the calls and apologize for the interruption of their favorite program and promise to get everything back on as soon as possible. The second would divert all calls to a central call center where the caller would hear a recorded apology. The third would be to have all calls diverted to a central call center where they would receive a busy signal. People would feel there were others who were also frustrated."

"Those are three excellent ideas. The first would take many men and planning. Do you not agree?"

"Yes, I do agree. You'd need to find people to staff the center as well as know the language in order to carry on a conversation and reassure the customer that everything that could be done was being done. You'd also have to know the point of origin for the call so it could be directed to the proper staff member."

"That would be a long and involved process would it not."

"Yes it would."

"What about the second one?"

"As with the first, you would need to know the point of origin in order to know the proper recording."

"Now, tell me about the third one."

"With the third one, there's no need to know the point of origin since all calls will receive a busy signal. That, by far will be the easiest and most cost effective of the three solutions. The trick is to intercept all calls to television stations during your broadcast. What may be even better is to interrupt all telephone calls, both regular phones and cell phones no matter where they're going. This will take care of the problem of identifying and screening for certain calls."

"Ah, Mr. Braedon, it is easy to see why people pay for your services. You give problems a great deal of thought."

"Yes, I do, sir."

"Once again, you have done very well. As usual, we will be doing some experiments to see whether or not your ideas have merit. If they work as well as the last ones, you will once again have bought yourself time. Miss Darmer will be much relieved. Perhaps, Mr. Braedon, when this is all over, we may even meet socially."

Michael watched as he left. *Why does he always mention Laura? There's no way I can protect her from him.* He knew he had to rely on those close to him to make sure no harm came to her.

Laura awoke to the sun streaming in her window. Although the day was beautiful, somehow it wasn't as glorious without Michael. She made their bed and got dressed. When she finished, she sat in front of the computer. She wanted to see if there was anything else from Tom. She was greeted instead by Yamani.

Miss Darmer, are you there?

I'm here.

We are getting closer, Miss Darmer.

Are we?

Yes, I have to check out the information that Mr. Braedon provided this morning. Once I do that and it works, of course, then we will be ready. Please tell Mr. Richards to be ready to move in just a few days. It will be so nice to finally meet you. I am sure you are just as excited as I am.

I'm excited to get Michael back here unharmed.

He will be able to go back, unharmed, I assure you. Then once I have you, I intend to show you just how glad I am to have you in his place. I guarantee you that you will never forget me...even long after you have returned to your life. Let us just hope that you will be able to gain for me all that I want and need...for your sake.

Do you have any instructions?

There was no answer. Laura stared at the screen, she was suddenly nauseated. She copied the conversation to the file and emailed it as well to Tom. She started to pick up the phone, but couldn't.

When Gwen walked into Laura's room she found her vomiting.

"Honey, what's wrong?" she asked grabbing a washcloth from the closet and wetting it. She pulled Laura's hair back and started wiping her neck with the cloth. She helped Laura up and looked at her face. She saw terror in her eyes and tears streaming down.

"It's going to be alright," she said putting her arms around her. "You have to believe that. Let me run a shower for you and get you some clean clothes. Then we'll talk."

Laura stood in the shower trying to relax. Gwen went into the bedroom and got new clothes for her. She took towels out of the closet and when Laura was finished, she helped her dress. Then she helped her back into the room and they sat on the couch.

"What happened?" asked Gwen.

"I had a dream," said Laura trying to control her emotions. "I was in that cell."

"With Michael?"

"No, with Yamani. He kept telling me I'd never forget him. Then he…" She started gasping. Gwen took her hands.

"Take it easy, honey. You're right here with us. He's not going to get you. We won't let him. I know Michael. He's counting on us to make sure you're safe until he's able to be back with you."

"Gwen, I want him so badly," she said. "I'd do anything to get him back."

"I know that, sweetie," said Gwen, moving the hair out of Laura's face. "We have to be patient. It's only a matter of time before Yamani contacts us to get what he needs from Edgar."

Laura nodded.

"I just want Michael to be safe," she whispered.

"I know."

"I think all of those papers we read have made this so much more real," she said, her voice shaking. "It's not just hearsay what he does to people, especially women. It's fact. I don't know how much more I can read."

"Honey, you don't have to read any more if you can't. I know we're going to read through the rest of it. We need to make sure there isn't anything we're missing that could help us find Michael and bring him back."

"I'm sorry, I just can't," she said her eyes welling up.

"Honey, it's alright," said Gwen handing her a tissue.

"My head's pounding."

"Do you want to lie down for a little while? I'll fix your bed for you?"

"I know this sounds silly, but I don't want to be alone," said Laura looking up. "Could I lie on the couch?"

"Honey, this is your home, of course you can."

"There're extra pillows and blankets in the hall closet," said Laura.

"Will you be alright for a few minutes while I get it ready?"

"Yes."

Gwen walked out into the hall and then brought blankets and pillows from the closet to the living room.

"What's going on?" asked Angelique.

"Laura's not feeling well," she said.

"Let me help you."

"I went into her room and she was vomiting. She had a dream that Yamani had her. He told her she'd never forget him. She couldn't even finish telling me the rest. I've never seen her like this," said Gwen as she stopped what she was doing. "She doesn't want to be alone."

"I'll go and make her a cup of tea."

Gwen looked up from finishing the couch and saw Mark.

"Could you please help me bring Laura out to the couch?" she asked him.

"What's wrong?"

"I'll tell you later."

He followed Gwen into Laura's room. One look told him what this ordeal was doing to her.

"Laura, honey, what's wrong?" he said tenderly. "Let me help you."

Mark helped Laura up and put his arm around her while Gwen held her from the other side.

"We're going to move everything from the dining room to the living room so we can be together. Angelique's making some tea."

They made sure Laura was comfortable on the couch.

"Thank you," she said as she looked around the room. Angelique brought a cup of tea to her and Laura sat sipping it. Mark helped Gwen and Angelique bring piles of papers into the living room. Laura reached and put the cup on the coffee table, leaned back, and closed her eyes.

"If you find anything, bring it to us, please," whispered Mark to Gwen. "We're trying to stay one step ahead of this man. What you gave us yesterday was a great help." He gave his wife a kiss. "I love you."

"I love you, too," said Gwen. "Where's Gabrielle today?"

"She's at a friend's estate. Her friend's interested in the work she's doing. So interested, she's called a meeting of about twenty of her closest friends. They're going to be working on starting a chapter of Gabrielle's charity work here. It'll be the first such chapter outside of Germany. Edgar said she's very excited about the prospect."

"She should be," said Gwen. "She's worked very hard to get this to the point it is today."

"Edgar says he's never seen his wife so happy. This gives her so much to think about other than the reality that she and her husband are in danger. I better get in there," said Mark. "Come get me if you need me."

"I will."

Edgar finished the plan that would minimize the effects of Yamani's actions.

"This should do it," he said.

"Now, just what will this do?" asked Jacques.

"It'll allow him to believe he has successfully taken over whatever radio and television stations he chooses," said Edgar.

"How do we know he doesn't have followers in other areas monitoring what's going on? How are you going to keep them from telling him?" asked Robert.

"All calls going to Yamani are going to be rerouted," said Edgar. "They'll receive a busy signal and think someone else is calling to alert him. All we need is his number and we can get that."

Laura slept on the couch while the others read through the material. They discussed among themselves any new findings. They found it amazing how much detail there was and how much thought and planning Yamani put into every detail.

"This is interesting," said Brigit. "I'm reading the notes Yamani made. These date back to the 1980's and two numbers keep repeating throughout. He talks about finding the Divine One and salvation in this place, the holy place. He says that the ground has been consecrated by the Divine One for his chosen ones. The chosen ones are to live in this place. There is to be a holy pilgrimage from one's home area to the holy place."

"Where is this holy place?" asked Nicole.

"It is 32 and 44," said Brigit.

"What's 32 and 44?" asked Monique.

"I don't know," said Brigit.

"Do you think we can find the holy place on a map?" asked Gina.

"I can try doing an internet name search to see what the numbers mean," said Angelique.

"Wherever it is, the center of the city is what is most important. "Listen to this," said Brigit and she read aloud from Yamani's notes.

"For in the center of this there shall be found a place where one may only step foot if summoned by the Chosen One, for so sacred is the ground. And upon returning to one's own kind, may never utter one word concerning one's experience or what was witnessed. For if one should be remiss and forget the warning, sudden and painful death will follow with certain exile from the rewards of the afterlife." She stopped reading and looked at the others. "That has to be where Yamani is."

When Laura awoke, the girls were huddled over a table they had set up in the center of the room.

"That's unbelievable," said Margo. "How could one think they could possibly hide someone in Iraq?"

"I'm not sure," said Nicole.

"There are so many little towns there," said Gina. "When we were reading the other papers and books, they kept mentioning three different places, remember Gwen?"

"Yes, and then Laura drew a triangle and found the point of intersection and it was in Iraq also."

"What are you talking about?" asked Laura sitting up on the couch.

"We're sorry, did we wake you?" asked Gwen.

"It's alright. I feel a little better," she said. "My head isn't pounding. Now, what has you so interested."

"We found two numbers repeated in Yamani's writings. We think we found what the numbers meant. They indicate a region in Iraq. We pulled a map and found a number of towns. We also found a warning about the center of that region," said Brigit.

"A warning?" asked Laura.

"Yes," said Brigit picking up the paper. "Listen to this."

"For in the center of this there shall be found a place where one may only step foot if summoned by the Chosen One, for so sacred is the ground. And upon returning to one's own kind, may never utter one

word concerning one's experience or what was witnessed. For if one should be remiss and forget the warning, sudden and painful death will follow with certain exile from the rewards of the afterlife."

"What's in the center of that region?" asked Laura.

"We don't know," said Gina. "We're not sure which city."

"May I see it?" asked Laura getting up from the couch.

"Sure," she said moving to let Laura in beside her.

"Is this the place, where the circle is drawn?" asked Laura looking at the map.

"Yes, as far as we can tell," said Margo.

"There used to be a great city there. It doesn't exist in that way anymore," said Laura. "It was Babylon."

"Babylon!" said Margo.

"Yes, Babylon," said Laura.

"Why would he choose Babylon?" asked Angelique. "It's an ancient city in ruins."

"Once it was the center of civilization in that region," said Laura. "If Yamani's going back to an ancient form of a religion, he may just be picking and choosing what he likes from various religions. Maybe with the Babylonians he liked the city. Babylon was a sacred city in ancient times. They have reconstructed some of it, but the reconstruction ended before the U.S. invasion. There was a U.S. base there and international forces so I don't think Yamani would be directly in the city. He'd be somewhere near."

"Michael's in a building," said Margo. "It doesn't look like the ruins of an ancient building."

"Remember, Yamani has had many years to put this together," said Laura. "What he's doing now isn't something he decided to do a few months ago. He's been planning this for years. Everything had to be in place for him to succeed."

"How could he carry out his mission from there?" asked Gina.

"He can't," said Gwen. "He has to rely on being able to get to a city that has the technology he needs. It has to be close enough so he can still have control on what is going on in Babylon. Have any idea where that might be?"

"Closest major city would be Baghdad," said Gina.

"He wouldn't use Baghdad," said Raquel, "He can't risk being identified."

"How many people do you think can identify him?" asked Gina.

"In that area, a lot," said Laura. "He must think he's relatively safe or he wouldn't have been involved with the actual kidnapping."

"I think he's the type of man who doesn't trust his minions to do his work," said Margo. "If it's that important, he'll make certain nothing can go wrong. If that means he has to be personally involved, so be it."

"Look at the situation with Michael. Whenever he's questioned, Yamani's the one doing it," said Laura. "You may not be able to see his face all the time, but you know it's him. He's present when any type of abuse or torture is administered. Sometimes he's the instrument of torture. I know if any of us are taken, it'll be Yamani who'll be the instrument of torture for us."

Margo shuddered. "Don't even think about that," she said.

Mark, Edgar, and Pierre came into the room. They looked exhausted.

"Laura, how're you feeling?" asked Mark sitting down beside her.

"A little better, thank you for asking," she said.

"We think we found something interesting," said Brigit.

"What's that?" asked Pierre.

"Throughout his writings, Yamani mentions two numbers 32 and 44," said Brigit. "He refers to it as a holy place. When we found it, it's in Iraq."

"Iraq?" asked Pierre. "What holy place is he referring to?"

"Laura thinks it's the ancient city of Babylon. It was a holy city and it matches 32 and 44," said Brigit.

"Can someone get that tube from the dining room" asked Laura. "It has the maps in it that we were using back in the States."

"Sure," said Jean walking into the dining room and picking up the tube. He brought it back into the room, took the maps out, and spread them out on the table.

There on the map was the triangle that Laura had drawn using the three reference points from the other material they had from the library.

"What did you say those numbers were again?" asked Laura.

"32 and 44," said Brigit.

"Can I have that ruler and a marker?" asked Laura.

Gwen handed her both and Laura went to work drawing the point of intersection for the numbers 32 and 44.

"Now look at this," said Laura.

"Amazing," said Paul. It's exactly in your point of intersection.

"As I said before," said Laura, "Yamani wants to be the center of it all."

"Okay everything points to Babylon, but he can't complete his mission from there though," said Pierre. "It's in ruin."

"He can't possibly have any way to connect to the internet from there," said Robert.

"Yes, but it makes perfect sense. If someone finds where he's holding a hostage, his mission is still safe. If someone finds the central control for his mission, he still has his hostage," said Edgar sitting in one of the big overstuffed chairs.

"Great, now where's central control?" asked Mark.

"Anywhere he wants it to be," said Edgar. "If he has transportation, it could be anywhere."

"What does he need?" asked Pierre.

"Phone lines and electricity at the least," said Edgar.

"As resourceful as he is, he probably has tied into some small city and has strung the wiring to some remote location," said Angelique.

"I never thought about that," said Mark.

"I thought about our place in the country," said Angelique. "We're miles from anyone, yet we have both electricity and phone because we paid to have those services brought to us."

"Yamani wouldn't pay," said Pierre. "He'd take."

"And no one would know," said Laura.

"Why do you say that?" asked Nicole.

"He'd never put up poles and string wire," said Laura. "You can bet if he did bring electrical lines and phone lines from the city, he had them buried."

"If that's the case, he could be anywhere," said Gina.

Chapter Twenty-Six

"Good Afternoon, Mr. Braedon," said the Chosen One. "I thought you might like to know how the project is going. We have had great success with your suggestions. We were able to take over ten stations without any of them knowing it. We kept their programming off the air and ours on for an hour. Even though many tried to call to report what was happening, all they heard was a busy signal."

"So, you were able to control two communication mediums."

"Yes we were. Mr. Braedon, do you know what that means?"

"Not exactly."

"It means that you have done better than I could have hoped. I am smart enough to know that you do not possess the ultimate knowledge I desire. You also cannot get it for me. To get that, I will need someone else. Someone who can be persuasive. Someone who will be able to make the person who has the knowledge give it up. Once that is worked out Mr. Braedon, I will return you to those who love you. Relax, Mr. Braedon, I will return when the time is right."

Michael began thinking again. *Who is he talking about? Who can get him what he wants? Who is it who will make Edgar give up the secrets?* Certainly not him. If he could, Edgar would've already done it. He knew Edgar wasn't the target because he was the only one who had access to the information. Michael felt sure he made certain the Chosen One knew that. *He can't be thinking of taking Gabrielle. Edgar has to have a lot of security surrounding her.* Michael knew this leader would never release him until he had that person. There was no way to warn them to be on their guard.

Laura sat in front of her computer waiting. It had been two days since there was any communication. What was he doing? She knew right now Michael was safe. At least Yamani was keeping his promise about not hurting him. She knew Mark was worried because there hadn't been anything about Michael on the internet. She'd like nothing more than to tell him Michael was safe, but she knew she couldn't. The waiting was unbearable, but at least she knew something was going on. She was just about to get up to get something in the kitchen when she glanced one more time at the screen.

Miss Darmer? I assume you are there.

Yes, I'm here.

Well, Miss Darmer, in two days, you and Mr. Richards are to take a plane to Baghdad. Once there, you will pick up the car I rented for you. I have sent instructions to your email. Please tell Mr. Richards that he will need to help Mr. Braedon walk. Mr. Richards will report Mr. Braedon's release from a television station. I have also sent a copy of what he is to say to your email. When I am ready to release you, he will be contacted. Remember, if you deviate in anyway, I will kill you.

I understand.

Miss Darmer, I am looking forward to having you as my guest. I am sure that your time with me will be quite memorable. Oh, Miss Darmer, Mr. Richards is not to tell Mr. Braedon that I have you until they are back in Paris and they are with those he loves. I promised I would return him. And once I have what I want, I promise to return you to the man you love...even though you may not quite be the same as when you left. I assure you, Miss Darmer, you will never forget me. I will be in contact again before you leave.

Laura quickly copied everything and put them in her folder. She then sent an email to Tom. Once she finished, she picked up Michael's picture and held it close.

"Michael, you'll soon be back here safe. Please don't be angry with me. I had to do this to get you back. Oh Michael, please tell me you'll love me no matter what."

When she returned to the others her eyes were still red from crying.

"Are you alright?" asked Gina.

"I'm just having one of those days," she said. "I'm spending more time in tears than doing anything constructive."

"You're allowed to," said Monique. "I'm surprised you've held together this long."

"I was thinking about all those women," said Laura. "Were there any interviews with them in those papers?"

"We haven't found any, yet, but that doesn't mean there aren't any," said Brigit. "Why are you interested in that?"

"I've been thinking about them and what they went through," said Laura. "How did they endure it? What secret did they have? I don't know what I'd do if I was one of them."

"I'd think about how much Henri loved me," said Brigit. "I'd probably say his name over and over again. I think I'd concentrate on happy times we had. I'd try to put myself somewhere in those times so I couldn't feel what he was doing to me." Brigit shivered. "The thought of that man makes me cringe."

Henri came walking into the room carrying a stack of papers.

"We need some help," he said.

"What do you need?" asked Brigit.

"We have the phone records of all of Yamani's contacts within Reinholdt International. We need you to go through the call logs and find any numbers that are the same. As we figure it, there has to be one number that's going to appear on all of the call logs."

"Well, that'll be a diversion for us," said Brigit. "Whose number are you looking for?"

"Yamani's."

"Yamani's?" asked Brigit.

"Yes, we need to make sure that none of his minions, as Mark puts it, can call him to tell him we're thwarting his plan. We figure there should be similar numbers on the logs from them calling one another, or even Reinholdt's number. However, all of them should have to check in with Yamani. He doesn't trust anyone to take messages for him."

"You know this'll take some time," said Brigit.

"We promise to be patient," he said handing the stack to her. "We'll be in the study when you find it."

"Where's the list of the dates when information was taken from Reinholdt?" asked Margo.

"In its folder," said Gina. "Let me find it."

"We can use that as a frame of reference," said Margo. "I figure after they took secrets, they'd have to tell Yamani what they had."

"Good idea," said Angelique. "It may narrow it a bit."

"We also need the dates they questioned Michael about the security cameras and what they were working on," said Gwen. "Remember, Yamani told Michael he checked into it to see if he was telling the truth."

"That's good," said Margo. "We should see that number come up as an outgoing and an incoming."

Within minutes, Brigit walked into the study.

"We have it," she said.

"That didn't take as long as we thought it would. How did you compare all those numbers so quickly?" asked Henri.

"We didn't," she said. "We only needed to use the dates when the secrets were stolen and the dates when they were checking Michael's stories. We have the number outgoing and incoming."

Edgar looked around the room.

"Good thing we gave it to them to find," he said. "We would've taken it one number at a time."

The rest of them laughed.

Chapter Twenty-Seven

With everyone out of the house and at work, Laura left to meet Tom at the hotel. She knew the meeting that had called all of the partners together would be over by one o'clock and she'd have to be back before then. It took all she could to convince them she'd be fine by herself. She promised she wouldn't go anywhere. She knew it was a promise she just couldn't keep.

When she arrived at the hotel, she found Tom waiting in the lobby. He got up as soon as he saw her walk in.

"Tom, it's nice to see you again."

"Shall we?"

"Yes."

There was silence between them as they went from the lobby to his room. Tom unlocked the door, they went in and he locked the door behind them.

"How was your flight?" she asked.

"It was long, but I slept some. I have your email and I downloaded some maps. I was able to outline the route we're to take. It's not that difficult and shouldn't take that much time. I'm assuming he has control of the television station so there'll be no problem with me broadcasting from there. What I'm wondering about is how I'm going to get Michael from the Embassy once he's there. The Embassy's a safe haven."

"You'll have to tell Michael who you are and that you're taking him back to Paris. You have to make him understand his stay at the Embassy will be only a few minutes, definitely less than half an hour. Tell him you'll be coming back for him, but you needed to make sure he was safe."

"Do you have his passport?"

"No, it wasn't in with his things. Michael would've had it with him. I'll make sure Yamani gives it back to him. Once you're back in Paris, bring him to his house. I know everyone will be there. They'll be wondering where I am. Everything's on my laptop. I know you're worried about what they're going to say to you about what you've done. I've made it clear that if it wasn't you, it would've been someone else."

"I'll handle anything they have to say and any questions they may ask. I'm worried about you. What're you thinking?"

"When I read some of what you sent, it made me sick…physically ill. I had nightmares. He keeps telling me I'll never forget him. I can actually hear his voice when I read them. Those words pound in my head," said Laura. Then she took a deep breath before continuing. "What I'm terrified about is that Michael won't be able to or want to love me again."

"Let me tell you something from my perspective," he said taking her hands. "If I was Michael and my fiancée gained my release by trading places with me, I'd wonder how I possibly could've been so blest to have found her. And if she had to endure what Yamani did to her to ensure that I remained safe, once I had her back, I'd never let her go."

Tears came to her eyes and she smiled at him.

Laura sat in front of the computer adding letters of explanation to the folder and making sure everything was in order. What she had worked so hard to accomplish was only hours away. She went over every detail as she knew it, making sure there'd be no foul-ups from her end. She knew the one thing Yamani valued more than anything else in the world was respect. She knew she needed to give that to him unconditionally. As she looked through some of the pictures on her files, she came across a picture of one of Michael's favorite pieces of art…Matisse's "Thousand and One Nights" that depicted the story of Scheherazade. She thought about how she was able to keep herself safe by telling a story and leaving them at a cliffhanger each morning. If only it was that easy.

Miss Darmer?

Yes.

I trust that Mr. Richards has arrived.

Yes.

And you have gone over everything with him thus far?

Yes.

You are to take the morning flight to Baghdad. I have reserved a car in Mr. Richards' name. Once he has completed his tasks, he will pick up Mr. Braedon, return the car and return to Paris on the next available flight.

Please make sure Mr. Braedon has his passport.

I will make sure of that. I want him out of this country as soon as possible. Do you have any questions?

None that I can think of.

I will talk to you when I see you.

Laura picked up the phone.

"Tom, book us on the morning flight."

"You heard?"

"Yes. He's already reserved a car in your name at the airport. You are then to return to Paris on the next available flight after the task is complete."

"I'll book that, too. Are you alright?"

"For the first time in days, I'm actually calm. I'll meet you at the airport at six o'clock."

Edgar was in the kitchen getting a drink.

"How close are you to a solution," asked Mark as he walked in.

"Very close," he said.

"What if you were asked to give up SecReSAC today, could it be done?" asked Mark.

"Not today, but definitely within forty-eight hours," said Edgar.

"How convincing would it be?"

"Extremely convincing. I've configured it so it appears the person executing the sequence is in control of the satellite. From his vantage point, he'll see that he has complete control and can manipulate any form of electronic communication."

"What happens when his minions find out it's not the case?"

"They'll call to tell him, of course, but will feel assured that someone else is telling him because of the busy signal."

"How long can we expect this to work?"

"As long as it has to. That part's in place. What's not in place is the opposite. We have to make sure he can't get to them to ask how it's being received. As far as his own country is concerned, I'm allowing him to take over all of the networks. It gets a little more complicated when you have to pick and choose and isolate certain numbers." Edgar paused. "I've spoken to the leaders I met with and they're most interested in bringing this matter to a close."

"Do they know who they're dealing with?"

"No. I thought it best that his identity remain as much a secret as possible. As long as he feels no one knows his identity, then the hostage will be safer."

Chapter Twenty-Eight

The Chosen One walked into the room followed by the woman. The only other time this happened was the day the photographs were taken. For Michael it was a mixed set of feelings. He knew what the leader was capable of doing, but also knew that when the woman was present there was no mistreatment.

"Mr. Braedon, today is your lucky day," said the Chosen One. "She will get you ready."

Michael looked at him quizzically.

"Today, you are going home. She will make sure you look presentable for your journey. I will be back once she has finished."

After the Chosen One left, she bathed him and put on his clothing again, everything he had been wearing when he was taken. It had all been cleaned and pressed. Once she was finished she gathered her things together.

"Thank you for all your kindness," he said to her.

She smiled, got up, walked over to the door and knocked. The door opened and she walked out and the Chosen One walked in.

"I do apologize, but we have to put the hood over your face again. It would not be good if you knew where you were."

Michael nodded and they put on the hood and tied it.

Laura took one last look around the house. Then she quietly closed the door behind her and got into a waiting limousine.

The trip to the airport was spent in casual conversation with the driver. Because it was so early, there was hardly any traffic. When they arrived, he helped her out and she gave him a generous tip. Laura walked into the airport and Tom was waiting for her.

"Are you ready?" she asked.

"As ready as I can be," he said.

"Do you have everything you need?"

"Yes."

The flight to Baghdad seemed to take forever, but they made the connecting flights with ease. As they sat there, Laura kept running things through her mind. She tried to block out the cruelties she read about. Instead, she thought about what types of conversations she might initiate in order to save herself from whatever Yamani had in mind. Tom reached over and took her hand.

"I know I can't tell you it's going to be alright. I don't know that," he said quietly. "I'll make sure I follow all the instructions to the letter so nothing goes wrong. I promise when I get word that you're to be released I'll be on the very next plane to get you. And after I've delivered you safely to Michael, I'll do everything possible to bring them to justice."

Laura looked at him and smiled. They had formed a bond that'd never be broken. She knew he'd be worried sick until this was all over. She also knew she had put him in this position.

"Tom thanks for doing this. You know how much it means to me. I've made a promise to myself that I will not cave in. I will be strong. There'll be plenty of time to fall apart when this is all over. I will not show him weakness, only respect."

Tom looked at her hands.

"Where's your ring?" he asked.

I left it on the dresser. I didn't want to run the risk that he'd take it from me. I also left the locket there. I'll look forward to Michael putting both of those on me when I return. I'll return, Tom. I know I will."

Tom picked up the car reserved in his name. Inside, on the driver's seat was a detailed set of instructions. As he read them, the route became very clear. When they arrived at the corner where he was to leave Laura, he pulled to the curb, she opened the door and got out. She walked to the front of the store that sold televisions and appliances. She looked around her. She wondered where they were, how they were watching her, and who they were. She knew in a matter of moments Michael would be free.

Tom read the directions. They were the same ones he memorized, but he wanted to make sure there were no changes. He promised her there would be no mix-ups. He drove to the corner, parked the car, put the keys in his pocket, and opened the door. Across the street he could see a black limousine with blackened windows. When the occupants spied him, they opened the door on the sidewalk side and helped a gentleman out. They removed his hood and stood him against the building, got back in the car and sped away. Tom ran across the street to Michael.

"Mr. Braedon, I'm Tom Richards, let me help you."

He put his arm around Michael's waist and helped him to the car.

"Mr. Braedon, I'm taking you to the Embassy. You are to sit there. It's a safe place. I'll return for you in less than half an hour, after I've finished what I have to do. Do you understand?"

"Yes," said Michael.

"Please stay where I put you so I'll know where you are when I return," said Tom, "and please don't tell anyone exactly who you are. I need to get you out of this country and back to Paris."

"Okay."

Tom pulled up to the Embassy driveway, stopped the car, and got out. He opened Michael's door and helped him to a bench near where other people were reading and just enjoying the day.

"I'll be back."

Tom got back in the car, checked the directions, and drove to the television station. He parked the car in the lot and entered the building.

"Mr. Richards?" asked a man.

"Yes," he said.

"We are ready for you."

Tom sat down in a chair behind the desk and took the copy in his hands.

"Good Morning, my name is Tom Richards. This morning I am reporting the release of Michael Braedon, the hostage who was taken from his room at a hotel in Frankfurt, Germany. His captors have negotiated with me for his release. Mr. Braedon is in good condition and will be returning today to his friends and loved ones. I would like to take this opportunity to thank his captors for their good faith negotiations. Thank you."

"Very good, Mr. Richards. Thank you for coming."

"Thank you for your hospitality."

Tom raced out of the station to the car. He checked the instructions and raced back to where Laura was waiting. As he pulled to the curb, Laura came around the car and got in.

"Did you see the broadcast?" asked Tom.

"Yes," she said. "How is he?"

"He looks good," said Tom. "He's weak, but he'll get his strength back. Laura, I don't know if I can do this."

"You have to," she said. "If you don't they'll kill all of us, then everything will have been in vain."

He pulled up to the curb and turned off the car. He got out and walked around to open Laura's door. He helped her out of the car. She started to tremble. He put his arm around her.

"I helped Michael across the street this way," he said.

"Thank you."

"Draw your strength from him. He has much more to give. He loves you. Remember that. I'll be back as soon as possible to get you."

He felt her body strengthen as he let go of her once they were on the sidewalk.

"Tom, thank you."

He turned and walked across the street, opened the door of the car and got in. As he looked to the other side, she was gone.

"Oh, God, what have I done?"

He drove back to the Embassy, parked the car, got out and hurried over to Michael.

"Mr. Braedon, let's go."

He helped Michael up and to the car.

"Where are we going?" asked Michael.

"To the airport."

Lizbeth rushed into the conference room and turned on the television.

"Lizbeth what in the world!" said Pierre.

"Shh!" she warned.

"Good Morning, my name is Tom Richards. This morning I am reporting the release of Michael Braedon, the hostage who was taken from his room at a hotel in Frankfurt, Germany. His captors have negotiated with me for his release. Mr. Braedon is in good condition and will be returning today to his friends and loved ones. I would like to take this opportunity to thank his captors for their good faith negotiations. Thank you."

"I'm sorry, Pierre, but, I wanted you to hear that," said Lizbeth wiping tears from her cheeks.

"Thank you, Lizbeth," he said softly.

"Oh, my God, he released him," said Mark with tears in his eyes.

"Why?" asked Pierre.

"I don't know," said Mark.

"Does Laura know?" asked Gwen.

"Call her," said Mark.

"I wonder when he'll be here," said Margo.

"Where would he be coming from?" asked Paul.

"Laura thinks Baghdad," said Gwen.

Lizbeth walked over to the computer and checked the flights.

"There's a connecting flight due in here early this afternoon," she said.

"No one's answering at the house," said Gwen.

"Maybe she's still sleeping," said Brigit.

"Laura doesn't sleep this late," said Gwen.

"Laura! Laura!" Mark yelled. "Where are you?" He went immediately to Laura's room and then hurried back to the living room. "She's not in her room," he said.

"Where is she?" asked Pierre.

"Oh, God, please tell me they didn't get her," said Brigit putting her hands over her mouth.

"How could they?" asked Henri.

"I don't know," said Brigit. "Why else would they let Michael go?"

"Gabrielle!" said Raquel. "Check with Edgar and see if she's alright. Yamani would never let Michael go unless he has someone else."

Mark picked up the phone and called Edgar. The call took only a few seconds.

"Gabrielle's with her friends," said Mark. "She's quite safe."

"It's Laura," said Gwen coming back into the living room. She held out her hand. "It has to be her. Her ring and locket were on the dresser."

From the time they entered the house, they cleaned and re-cleaned trying to pass the time. When the doorbell rang, Mark hurried to answer it. There standing in front of him was Michael being held up by Tom. Mark reached out and helped his brother inside. He hugged him and tears ran down his face.

"Mr. Richards?" asked Mark after a few seconds.

"Yes."

"Please, come in," said Mark. "Pardon my manners."

"Laura, I want to see Laura," said Michael.

"She's not here," said Mark.

"Is she back home?" asked Michael.

"We don't know where she is," said Mark almost afraid to reveal what they all had been thinking.

Tom looked at Mark and the others.

"Is there somewhere we can sit where I can talk to all of you?" asked Tom.

"We can sit at the dining room table," said Mark.

Although the piles had been straightened, nothing had been put away. Once they realized what might've happened, they knew whatever they had been working on in regards to Michael's release would ultimately have to be used to gain Laura's freedom.

Tom looked at the computer image projected on the wall.

"We set this up, because it was easy for all of us to see what was being shown, or what we'd found," said Robert noticing what Tom was looking at. "I'll turn it off."

"No, wait. May I please? Laura asked me to pull this address up for you," said Tom walking over to the computer. He typed in the address and almost instantly an all too familiar face appeared.

"Mr. Braedon, by now you are safe with your loved ones," he said, "I promised you that I would return you and I did. You see, Mr. Braedon, I am a man of my word. Yet, even though you're home and safe, someone seems to be missing. Mr. Richards is probably just about ready to explain what has happened, but let me introduce you first to my new guest."

The camera pulled back showing both Yamani and Laura.

"I am sure you recognize Miss Darmer. She worked very hard to gain your release, Mr. Braedon. Now, she is my guest and although you have been released, my torture of you still goes on. I am sure I will be enjoying Miss Darmer's stay with me, for as long as it may be. Mr. Braedon, I will not even entertain exchanging you for her. She is much more pleasing for me to look at." He said as he stroked her cheek. "She is very beautiful."

"Please do not worry, Mr. Braedon, whatever I choose to do, I will be discrete…unless you fail to cooperate. You see, Mr. Braedon, no one knows I have her, but you, Mr. Richards, and those you love. I have kept my promise to her, Mr. Braedon, because you know I am a man of my word. Should you fail to do as I ask, I will have no choice but to let the world know she is mine. Oh, Mr. Braedon, I will keep her safe," he paused a moment, "unless you fail me in some way."

As quickly as he appeared he was gone. Tom looked around the room at the shocked faces, the eyes filled with tears.

"Oh, God, Laura," Michael said and he broke down.

"Michael, it's going to work out," said Mark wiping tears from his own cheeks and mustering all the composure he could. "We'll get her back quickly."

Michael shook his head.

"It'll be on his terms and not until he's done with her," he said as he composed himself and then he turned to Tom. "Mr. Richards what did he mean by Laura worked hard to gain my release."

"I'll try to explain the best I can," said Tom. "Could someone please get Laura's laptop?"

Mark left the table and in a matter of minutes returned with it.

"Thank you," he said. "For those of you who don't know, I'm Tom Richards. I'm a D.J. at WXDX in Pittsburgh. When you went back to Pittsburgh for that brief time after Michael's abduction, Laura came to see me." He looked at Michael. "She told me the story about your capture. She told me she had also made contact with your captors. Now, if I can get this to work, I'll show you everything," he said turning on the computer. He continued talking as he tried to get into the file. "Laura saved every conversation she had with them. She knew exactly what she wanted to do. She knew that once Michael outlived his usefulness they'd do one of two things; release him or kill him. For Laura, those odds weren't acceptable. She decided to stack the deck in favor of release."

"When she came to see me, they had already given her a time limit to find someone who'd act as a mediator. Before she even approached me, they had checked me out and approved me. It was then her job to get me to consent. I had no problem going wherever in the world they wanted me to go in order to get Michael, but I told her I wasn't sure I could turn her over."

"By the time she came to me, she already knew who the leader was although she didn't tell me at the time. From that time, we were in contact by email every time they contacted her. I came to Paris once they decided to release you. Yesterday, I met with Laura at the hotel and we went over everything. She knew this was what she had to do. When we talked there were tears in her eyes. He contacted her later that day to make certain of the arrangements and she called me. When I asked her how she was, she told me she finally felt calm. She knew there was no turning back and that resignation gave her peace."

"Today, when it came time to hand her over, I wanted to just run with her as fast and as far as I could, but they would've killed us all."

"Is that where you went after you put me on the bench?" asked Michael.

"Yes. I first went to broadcast your release so she'd know you were safe, then, I went to turn her over. When I helped her out of the car, she trembled for a moment and I put my arm around her waist. I told her I had helped you across the street this same way and to draw her strength from you because you had so much to give and to remember you loved her. I walked her to the place where I found you. I turned and walked to my car and she was gone."

"Michael, as the time drew closer, she was having a very difficult time. She had nightmares. He taunted her as you'll see in these conversations. I asked her if she was alright. She told me about how her head would pound and how nauseated she'd get. She also told me she wouldn't allow him to see she was weak. Somehow she'd find the strength. The one thing she was and is terrified of is that you won't be able to or want to love her after Yamani is done with her. I told her that if my fiancée gained my release by trading places with me, I'd wonder how I could possibly have been so blest as to have found her and that once she was released and with me again, I'd never let her go."

Michael nodded his head and wept. Tom stopped and waited for Michael to regain his composure.

"This is the folder she created," said Tom as he put in the password. "It contains everything. There are messages for all of you here. She knew if you found out what she was trying to do, you'd do everything in your power to stop her. There's also a message for Maggie that I promised Laura I'd make sure was given to her."

Tom knew the messages would be very personal so he walked out of the dining room and sat on the couch. Gwen walked into the living room.

"Tom, thank you for being there for Laura," she said sitting on the chair opposite him. "I know how hard this was and is for you. Now that Michael's here, it's all so clear. When I look back, I can see all the signs. Little pieces of dialogue play in my head. I know now what she was talking about. We all thought she was so afraid they'd come and get her. We had no idea she was contemplating exchanging herself for Michael."

"Does he have any idea who his captor was?" asked Tom.

"I don't think so," said Gwen. "None of us knew who he was until we researched him."

"He will by the time they're finished with the folder," he said. "Much of what's in there, she sent me. She wanted you to know she meant what she said…she'd get Michael back no matter what it took. It makes my skin crawl to think of what he might be doing to her. Now he's going to taunt Michael with those thoughts."

"I'm so grateful to have my brother-in-law home," she said. "I know these people won't rest until Laura's back with us."

The doorbell rang. Throughout this ordeal, the sound of the doorbell would've made them freeze. Now, as inexplicable as it seemed, there was a sense of renewed safety and Gwen got up to answer it. Pierre stopped her before she took more than three steps.

"I'll get it," he said. He looked out to see who was there and then opened the door "Edgar," he said surprised, "did you forget your key?"

"I wasn't thinking."

"Come in."

Edgar walked into the foyer and Pierre closed and locked the door.

"Has Michael returned?" asked Edgar very agitatedly.

"Yes, he's in the dining room right now," said Pierre.

"May I see him?" asked Edgar.

"Of course."

Edgar was steps ahead of Pierre. All he wanted to do was help Michael in any way possible. He had been in constant contact with the others as they grappled with the realization that Laura was gone. Edgar couldn't bring himself to say it aloud, but he knew beyond a shadow of a doubt it could be his wife who was in the hands of that monster.

"Michael," said Edgar quickly. His words seemed to trip over themselves as he said them. "I'm so glad to see you. I'm so sorry for everything. I'll do whatever I can to get Laura back as soon as possible."

"Thank you, Edgar," said Michael quietly and calmly. "Please sit down."

"Thank you," said Edgar as he took a seat.

"Right now, they're in control," said Michael. "We have to wait for them to ask us for what they want."

"Whatever they ask for," said Edgar, "I'll cooperate."

"I know you will," said Michael.

"Edgar, how's Gabrielle?" asked Gina.

"She's fine. She's still at her friend's house. I went there to see her, myself to make sure."

"I'm glad she's safe," said Michael reaching for a stack of papers. "I feel like I'm at such a disadvantage. Everyone here knows so much more than I do. I have a lot to read just to catch up."

"Michael, one thing at a time," said Mark. "Let's start with basics. Let me help you get a shower and some clean comfortable clothes. Then we'll sit down and have something simple to eat. While we're taking care of your personal needs, the others will organize everything so we can bring you up to speed. First thing, we're so glad to have you here with us. Second, we won't stop until we have Laura home. We promise you that."

Mark and Paul helped Michael to his feet and supported him as they walked to the bedroom. Mark ran the water while Paul helped him get his shoes and socks off. That was as far as Michael would allow them to help. He insisted he could shower by himself.

Pierre looked around the dining room and living room at the piles of papers that occupied every inch of flat surface. He walked back into the living room and looked at Tom.

"Tom, would you mind joining us in the dining room," said Pierre. "We're trying to put everything in some semblance of order so Michael might be able to understand what's happened."

"I'd be glad to help."

"How do we tell him everything in such a short amount of time?" asked Pierre.

"We could give him the *Reader's Digest* version first," said Tom, "and then fill in whatever details he asks for."

"That's a good plan," said Pierre. "I like it. Tom, do you have accommodations?"

"Yes, I have a hotel room," said Tom. "It's paid until tomorrow. I'm to return to the United States and wait for Yamani to contact me."

"Once you go back to the States," said Pierre, "we need to keep in touch."

"Definitely," said Tom. "When you go through Laura's things, you'll see that she was meticulous in keeping every conversation and notes on every meeting. She wanted there to be a record of everything."

D. A. Walters

Gwen and Gina were in the kitchen looking through the cupboards, freezer and refrigerator.

"Now, what do you consider simple?" asked Gwen.

"I consider anything we can heat and eat," said Gina.

"What about soup and whatever else is in the freezer," asked Gwen.

"You know Laura prepared for this," said Gina as she put a container on the counter. "She knew the day she did all the cooking."

"Why didn't we see it?" asked Gwen.

"None of us would ever consider it an option."

"Maybe it was because none of us wanted to believe she'd do it."

It seemed that timing was perfect for once. Michael, Mark, and Paul made their way to the kitchen just as the rest of the group finished organizing the piles of information in some sort of order. Bowls of soup, baskets of breadsticks and trays filled with whatever Gina and Gwen deemed part of dinner were on the table.

It was unusually quiet. The mood was extremely somber when they gathered around the table.

"I know Laura made this. She knew it was my favorite soup. It's wonderful," said Michael as he ate another spoonful. "Please, talk to me. I've been away so long and the only ones I talked to were the leader, the guard, and a very kind woman. When Tom picked me up, I was in such shock to have been released I didn't know what to say."

"Tom, thank you for everything you've done. Thank you for caring for me and making sure I arrived back here safely. Thank you for risking your life to help Laura. I know your decision wasn't an easy one. The fact the leader trusted you says much about your character. I hope you'll stay while we're sorting things out."

"I'll be happy to," said Tom.

"I understand you have a room at a hotel," said Michael, "but I'd feel better if you'd stay with us."

"I need to get my things," said Tom.

"Henri and I will go with you," said Paul.

"No one leaves here alone," said Mark and he paused, "if we know they're leaving."

Chapter Twenty-Nine

Yamani stood in the cell in front of Laura. It was the second time he visited her since her arrival. She sat looking at him wondering what to expect. No guards accompanied him, so she knew he was keeping his word about her anonymity. As much as she tried, she couldn't keep her heart from racing at his presence. She only hoped that the fear she felt inside didn't show outwardly.

"Miss Darmer, how do you like your accommodations? They are the same ones that Mr. Braedon enjoyed. In a few minutes, a very nice woman will help you change from your current clothing into something more suitable for your stay," he said. "You are beautiful, Miss Darmer, and if you cooperate, you will stay beautiful," he said patting the knife tied at his side.

"Yes, sir."

Once he left, Laura took a deep breath and closed her eyes. Just hours before, she had been a free woman. Now she was captive. She wondered how Michael was. He was home with everyone who loved him. He knew she had traded places with him to save him. She wondered how he felt about it. Did he find everything in the file? Had he found the letter she left for him? She left it under his pillow. She hoped he'd look.

Laura looked up as the keys sounded in the lock. The door opened and a woman walked in carrying clothing and a tray of items. Laura looked at her and smiled. The woman smiled back.

When Tom returned to the house, he put his things in his room, changed into his usual jeans and t-shirt and met the rest at the dining room table.

"I'd like to know everything you know," said Michael as soon as Tom sat down.

"Michael, we can tell you the story from the time we realized you had been taken to the time of your release," said Pierre. "As we go through the story, stop us if there are things you don't understand."

"One thing I insist on is honesty," said Michael looking around the room at each and every person. "I want to hear everything. I don't want things sugar coated or left out because you feel I'm not up to it. I want to know it all. I promise you…if it gets to be too much, I'll tell you to stop."

One by one, they told Michael the story, adding their unique parts when it came time. While the partners were able to tell most of the story, Tom was the only one who could tell the real story Laura was involved in. As promised, Michael stopped them several times to collect himself. He heard the story of Laura as she journeyed from firm resolve to fear, doubt, and terror, to calmness.

"I realized Yamani had her when I found her ring and locket on the dresser," said Gwen and she held them out for Michael.

Michael took them from her and held them. He touched each one and just stared at them. He knew how much Laura loved the ring and how much it must have hurt her to part with it.

"She didn't want him to have them," said Tom anticipating Michael's question. "She told me she wanted them to be safe with you. She said she's looking forward to you putting them back on her when she comes back."

"I bought her the locket when I was in Frankfurt," said Michael. "I wanted something special for her and when I saw it, I thought about her and had to buy it."

"She cherished it, from the moment she found it," said Gwen.

"Why would he consent to exchange Laura for me?" asked Michael.

"Laura will give him the edge he needs to get Edgar to give over what he wants. Yamani is the head of a religious group that has patterned itself after an ancient religion," said Gina. "In that religion, women were only a means to an end."

"What're the chances we'll get Laura back?" asked Michael.

"If he asks for what we think he wants," says Jacques, "the chances are very good."

"Just what is it he wants?" asked Michael.

"SecReSAC," said Edgar.

"What's that?" asked Michael.

Michael leaned forward in his chair as Edgar told him.

"Edgar, am I to understand you'd willingly give up SecReSAC to save Laura?" he asked.

"Not SecReSAC per say," said Edgar, "but a restructured version."

"I've modified SecReSAC to act like the real one," said Edgar, "to give the appearance in every phase that it's the real thing. However, Yamani won't be able to access anything that has to do with national security. He'll be convinced, however, that he has."

"What if he finds out he doesn't have the real deal?" asked Michael.

"He won't. Only select followers will be able to communicate with him and he'll be able to communicate with them. For all intents and purposes, he'll believe unconditionally that this works. We're allowing it to work in certain areas so it appears to have covered the entire world. Right now, all Yamani is interested in is the communication aspect. He hasn't even thought about what else can be done with the system. Before he does, we want to resolve this by getting Laura back and putting Yamani and those closest to him away. I want my facilities cleaned up so I don't have to worry about them stealing secrets anymore."

"We understand that, Edgar, but we can't run the risk of appearing too eager," said George. "What we want him to believe is that you're having a hard time making the decision to give him SecReSAC."

"I don't want Laura put in any more danger than necessary," said Michael.

"I know that, Michael," said Mark. "We're not proposing putting Laura through any more abuse. We're hoping if you and Edgar appear to be cooperating, he won't do anything to her."

"When I was being held captive, I had no idea who he was," said Michael. "He kept telling me how beautiful Miss Darmer was. How he hoped he'd have the chance to meet her. I never asked him how he knew who she was. I never thought to ask him how he knew what she looked like."

"Do you really think he'd have told you the truth?" asked Mark.

"Absolutely not. He never told me he was in contact with Laura. He only told me, if I cooperated, he'd soon be done with me. I can honestly tell you I didn't think he intended to release me. I thought he intended to kill me the way they killed the other hostages."

"That would've been the case had it been the other terrorists," said Monique. "However, the group that took you had nothing in common with the other terrorists. We do know he'll release Laura, sooner or later. We want it sooner. She knows what he's capable of doing. She knows what he's done in the past, the atrocities he's committed."

"She knew all of this and she still went through with this?" he asked.

"She's in love with you," said Margo. "The only thing she wanted was for you to be free. If it meant sacrificing herself, she was willing to do it."

"Laura felt this was the only thing she could do," said Tom. "She felt she couldn't contribute to the effort on the same level as the rest of you. We talked several times about it. When I tried to talk her out of it, she told me it was the only thing she knew she could do. She didn't have the connections you have. She couldn't pick up the phone and call someone in another country that might be able to do exactly what she wanted them to do the way each of you can."

"But she was doing so much," said Gina. "She's the one who found Professor Laban and you."

"She was afraid of what Yamani might do if Michael was unable to give him any other information," said Tom. "She had seen Michael tortured and was afraid he might just go that one extra step and kill him. She knew it was improbable that Edgar would give over any secrets to save Michael. She was certain Yamani knew it too. She was afraid he'd try to take Gabrielle. If that happened, not only would Edgar have been devastated, but she doubted Gabrielle could withstand the abuse."

"Tom, I know my wife couldn't. It's not in her character," said Edgar shaking his head. "She's such a sensitive person. That's why she spearheads all of those fundraising efforts for children's hospitals."

"I think Laura was afraid you'd give them anything they wanted to get your wife back," said Tom.

"She's right about that," said Edgar.

"Now, however, we have a viable plan," said Pierre.

"Regardless of what we believe Laura should've done," said Jean, "she's given us the time we needed to put this together. Getting inside Yamani's head is going to be the key."

Mark and Jacques helped Michael walk into the bedroom. Mark pulled back the covers and they helped Michael sit on the bed.

"Are you going to be alright?" asked Jacques.

"Yes, thank you," said Michael. "I can't believe how tired I am."

"Call me if you need me," said Mark.

"I will."

It was amazing how empty the room seemed to be without Laura. Even though he had been here many times by himself, tonight it felt so foreign. He slowly and carefully lay down. It was so good to be in a real bed. As he put his hand and arm under his pillow, his hand found the paper Laura left. He drew it out and unfolded it.

My dearest Michael,

By now you know I've exchanged places with you. I had to do it. I couldn't bear to think of life without you. The only way I could make certain you'd be safe was to offer Yamani another suitable hostage. I don't know what he has in store for me. I pray whatever it is, I'm able to endure. The one thing that'll get me through is knowing how much I love you and how much you love me. I only hope that when this is all over and I'm permitted to return, you'll still find it in your heart to love me and want to love me. I left my ring and locket on the dresser. I know you will keep them safe. I hope one day you will put them on me...again. Michael, when you fall asleep, dream of me and hold me close in your dreams. Somehow, I know I'll feel your touch.

I will love you forever,

Laura

Tears streamed down his face and Michael could hardly finish reading the letter.

"I love you, Laura," he whispered. "I will always love you."

He clutched the letter close and closed his eyes.

Margo sat on the bed beside Pierre. She couldn't imagine what Michael was going through. Every time she thought about it, her heart ached for him. She turned and looked at her husband.

"Maybe we shouldn't have told him everything," she said second guessing the decision already made.

"We did what was right," he said. "If we had kept things from him, it would've been very hard trying to explain why we'd do such a thing. He asked for honesty and that's what we gave him. I respect my friend enough to do that."

"I just hope he's alright," said Margo.

"He's not," said Pierre shaking his head, "and he won't be until Laura's back and they can deal with what's happened to the two of them, together." He reached for his wife and held her close. "I love you," he said.

"I love you, too."

Mark awoke suddenly to the sounds of Michael screaming in the next room. He jumped out of bed and ran to his brother's room. He turned on the lamp, sat on the bed, and put his hands on his brother's shoulders.

"Michael, it's alright," he said quietly. "You're home. You're dreaming. I'm here with you."

Michael looked at his brother. He had a look of sheer terror on his face. His breathing was fast and heavy and at times he gasped for air. His hair was wet from sweat.

"Talk to me, Michael."

Michael grabbed Mark and started to sob. Mark put his arms around him. Gwen came to the doorway, looked in, and walked away. Margo hurried down the hall.

"What happened?" she asked. "Is everything okay?"

"Michael had a bad dream, I think. Mark's with him," said Gwen. "I need a cup of tea."

"Want some company?" asked Margo.

"I'd love some."

It seemed like hours before Michael was able to compose himself enough to talk. Finally he released the hold he had on Mark and sat back. He wiped his eyes.

"What am I going to do?" he asked his brother, still hardly able to talk.

"What do you mean?" asked Mark.

"Do you know what he did to me?"

"Only what he allowed us to see."

"What if he's treating Laura the same way he treated me?" asked Michael, his voice trembling.

"I don't know," said Mark. "Tell me what frightened you so much."

"I could see him with her. Two guards were holding her and he took the butt of the rifle and slammed it into her ribs. I saw her double over. I heard her gasp. I saw the guard grab her by her hair and pull her up and then he did it again. I watched her set her jaw so she didn't cry out. I listened as he gave his guards the command to set her down on the floor. I watched her clutch her ribs. I heard him tell the guards to leave. Then I heard him tell her that she would never forget him. He knelt beside her and she tried to move away, but there was nowhere to go. He started to touch her..." He stopped and looked Mark in the eyes. "and I knew he was going to rape her. I couldn't stop him. All I could do was scream."

"Michael, it was a dream," said Mark.

"I know, but maybe he's already done it."

"What happened after you went to bed that started this?"

Michael handed Mark the letter that Laura left for him.

"Mark, what am I going to do if he rapes her? I know me. I'll want just five minutes with him."

Chapter Thirty

Tom and Michael sat in the living room talking before Tom left to return home and to his job. He knew it was what was expected of him by Yamani and he'd somehow know.

"Michael, get in here!" yelled Monique from the dining room.

"What's going on?" he asked as Tom helped him up off the chair and into the dining room.

"Look," she said as she pointed to the wall. .

"Mr. Braedon, how is it to be home?" asked Yamani. "I trust you slept well. It must be wonderful to have everyone you love around you and have dinner with your family and friends. Oh wait…not everyone is there are they? Miss Darmer is missing is she not? And she was who you wanted to see more than anyone else. She would brighten your day, but now she brightens mine. All you wanted to do was hold this beautiful woman in your arms, but you cannot."

Yamani took his hands and ran them down Laura's arms. Then he moved her hair to rest slightly behind her shoulder.

"I know she would like nothing better than to be with you, too. But alas, circumstances what they are, it cannot be so. You know that I can be a compassionate man. When you gave me the answers I was seeking, I treated you very well, did I not, Mr. Braedon? And when you did not give me what I wanted, well, let us just say you will remember those times. The same holds true now. As long as you are able to give me what

I want, I will treat her very well. When you are unable to give me what I desire, let us just say, she will remember those times."

"You are the product of my compassion, Mr. Braedon. I could have very easily disposed of you, but I did not. I kept my end of the bargain I made with Miss Darmer and I released you. Mr. Braedon, being the compassionate man that I am, I will show some of that compassion to you right now. Since you cannot hold Miss Darmer, I will hold her in my arms and comfort her until things work out and the two of you are together again."

As he put his arms around Laura, she visibly became rigid and bowed her head. He brushed her hair with a kiss.

"I will be in touch, soon, Mr. Braedon. I will take good care of Miss Darmer, I promise. Really, Mr. Braedon, you have nothing to worry about…as long as I get what I want."

With that, the transmission ended. Mark stood beside his brother with his hand on his shoulder.

Yamani dismissed his guards and turned his full attention to Laura.

"Miss Darmer, I can be a very loving man, you know," he said.

"Yes, sir."

"That is what I like, respect."

He stroked her hair and kissed it lightly.

"It is alright, Miss Darmer. You can relax. I have no intention of hurting you, unless you do something to disrespect me…or unless Mr. Braedon fails to get me what I want. You will find, Miss Darmer that things will go much better for you if you cooperate."

"Yes, sir."

"I do wish I could stay and enjoy your company all day, but I must take care of business. Perhaps I might return later…tonight. Maybe you would like to get better acquainted." He released her, kissed her on the cheek, and left the room.

Laura closed her eyes. *"Michael,"* she thought, *"help me feel your arms when he's with me. Help me remember what it felt like to be with you. I love you. Please do what he says. I want to come home."*

There were shocked looks on the faces of those who witnessed Yamani's message. Edgar walked into the room where Michael was staring at a blank wall.

"I'm so sorry," he said. "I was in the office and I heard everything. We can give him what he wants any time. It's ready."

"Thank you, Edgar," said Michael finally taking his eyes off the wall, "but we can't give him what he wants until he asks for it."

"You also can't hand it over quickly either," said Raquel. "If you do, he may feel that it isn't what you claim it to be."

"In that case, his treatment of Laura could be far worse than if we make him wait for it," said Brigit.

"Michael, I know this is a lot to ask you to do, but if you have the time and the stomach for it, I suggest you read everything we compiled," said Tom. "It'll tell you exactly what type of man you're dealing with."

"Mr. Richards, I hate to interrupt," said Joseph, "but if we don't leave now, you'll be unable to make your flight."

"Thank you, Joseph," said Tom. "I'm coming right now."

"Michael, while I agree with Tom that there's so much information that gave us a profile of Yamani," said Pierre, "I'm not at all sure you're up to reading it."

"Did Laura read it?" he asked.

"Most of it," said Margo.

"How much is most of it?"

"More than enough to understand what she was heading for," said Gwen.

"If she could read it, I owe her that much…and more."

Tom walked down the ramp to the general area. Cameras began flashing and people started running towards him. He froze and stared trying to figure out what was going on. Two airport security officers grabbed him by the arms and escorted him back to the secured area out of the reach of the cameras and reporters.

"Thank you," he said once they let him go.

"Mr. Richards," said one of the security officers.

"Yes."

"There's a call for you," he said handing him a phone.

"Thank you. Hello."

"Tom, this is Jim Prescott. The media's been in our lobby since this thing broke. Security's going to take you out another way and into a limousine. When you get here, we'll get you in through ProData's security entrance. They've already agreed to help us out. We'll talk further when you get here."

"Yes, sir." He handed the phone back to the officer. "I'm not sure whether he's being understanding or whether he's angry."

The security officers laughed.

"We know what that's like," the one said. "Mr. Richards, let's get you out of here."

Michael walked very slowly into the kitchen holding onto things for support and stopping many times along the way. He carefully sat down at the table and winced as he did. Gina poured two cups of coffee and joined him.

"How's it going?" asked Gina putting a cup of coffee in front of him.

I can't read any more right now. Is that man for real?" he asked rubbing his hands over his eyes.

"Oh, yes, very much so," said Gina sipping her coffee.

"How can you do those things and live with yourself?"

"I guess when you mask it as God's work, you excuse it," she said. "Think about it. This is the God Yamani has fashioned for his own purpose. He's taken an ancient religion, kept what he liked, and mutated the rest of it molding it to be what he wanted. His followers believe whatever he tells them to believe."

"It's just amazing he'd go to such lengths to establish a religion for his own purposes," said Michael.

"He's been trying to do this since he was with the Ayatollah. The atrocities he committed back then earned him exile from his country. He's had a lot of time to put this together. This is a very deliberately calculated endeavor. Laura's convinced his ultimate goal is to take over the world."

"That sounds like something out of a movie," said Michael.

"I know. The difference is this man's dead serious," said Gina. "The whole reason behind stealing the secrets from Reinholdt International is to fulfill the mission of the religion and get as many people as possible to follow the one, true, pure religion. I know he's convinced the men working for Edgar that they're doing God's work."

"I've seen him with his men," said Michael. "It's as though he owns them."

"He does," she said. "He holds the key to their afterlife."

Michael shook his head.

"As I was reading, I kept trying to convince myself he wouldn't do any of that to anyone. Me, the person who experienced both ends of his treatment."

"Michael, we'd all love to believe no one would ever treat another human being with as much disregard as is evident in those papers."

"The truth is, he does. I know that. I have the evidence on my body."

He raised his shirt to show his ribs. She gasped and stood up immediately.

"Michael, you need to see a doctor!"

"Not now," he said putting his shirt down.

"Right now!" Gina said.

"When they see my arms and legs, they're going to want to put me in the hospital."

"Look, let's take this one step at a time," she said. "Let me get a doctor to come here."

"Doctors don't make house calls," he said

"They will for a price."

Tom put his suitcase down in his office and looked around. Nothing had changed here even though he knew everything was different from his perspective. There was a knock on his door and Jim Prescott came in.

"Tom, it's good to have you back," he said.

"It's good to be back," said Tom. "Jim, I apologize for not telling you why I needed to leave. It was part of the agreement."

"Tom, I'm not angry. I'm assuming you can't say anything about this yet."

"You're right."

"I'm assuming this has something to do with that beautiful woman who came to see you a while back?"

"I can't tell you."

"If I were a betting person, I'd bet she traded herself for him."

"I really can't say."

"I understand completely. What about your show?" asked Jim.

"I intend to do it. The hostage release is a subject I won't address at this time. Once everything's over, I will."

"Do you actually believe he'll release her?"

"I didn't say he had her, but I may have to leave again on very short notice."

"I understand. For everyone's safety, I'm not going to ask anything else about it."

"I appreciate that. You know those people aren't going to leave until they talk to me."

"I'm not worried about them. I've dealt with the nuisance media before. You, however, can't talk to them. The front door is locked as well as the door to our offices and studios. People will have to be buzzed in and only if they have appointments."

"I guess this'll be my home until this is over."

"If there's anything you need, one of us will get it. I hope he releases her soon."

Tom smiled and shook his head as Jim walked to the door.

The door to her room opened and Yamani's guard came in followed by Yamani.

"Ah, Miss Darmer, did you miss me?" he asked opening his arms widely. "I told you I would come back tonight. I want to get a little more acquainted."

He gave his guard the order to leave them alone. He sat facing her and reached and touched her face.

"You are so beautiful," he said looking into her eyes. "All you have to do is everything I want you to do and you will stay beautiful." He took the knife out of its sheath and put in on the floor slightly beyond arm's reach. Laura saw the blade glisten and knew beyond a doubt what it was for.

He moved his face close to hers and began kissing her.

"I know it has been a long time since you and Mr. Braedon have been together intimately."

He lowered his right hand following the curves of her body. Laura didn't move. She knew he meant what he said about doing what he wanted. She had seen what he did to Michael; read what he had done to others. As he stroked her body, she could hear his breathing change. He took her robe in his hands and gently took it off.

"You are so beautiful," he said eyeing every inch of her. "Mr. Braedon is a very lucky man."

Laura closed her eyes and tried to remember Michael's touch.

Michael sat in the chair with his feet on the ottoman. He leaned back and closed his eyes.

"Tired?" asked Margo.

"A little. It's been quite a day. I feel drained. I think it's just hitting me now," said Michael. "When the doctor was examining me, it was the first time I really looked at what Yamani had done." He yawned. "I just want to sit here for a few minutes then I'll wash these wounds off and dress them."

"I'll tell you what. You rest and I'll get things together and we'll get you taken care of."

"Are you sure you want to see them?"

"Probably not, but I want you to get well."

When Margo returned, Michael was staring off into space.

"What're you thinking about?" she said as she put the tray down on the coffee table.

"Laura."

"I should've known."

"I keep praying she'll be safe and not have to go through any of this."

"We're all praying," said Margo. "They say if you bombard heaven, God will listen."

Chapter Thirty-One

Laura sat in her cell holding her robe against her. She didn't remember when it was over, nor did she remember Yamani leaving. Now she just felt dirty and wanted to wash him off. The day was dawning already. She heard the keys in the door and gripped the robe tighter. As the door opened, the woman came in carrying her usual tray of things. She looked at Laura and smiled.

"I'm going to help you get washed," she said, "and I brought you something to eat."

She took the rag, dipped it in the water and squeezed it. She handed it to her and as she did she spoke very softly to her.

"I know what he has done. I can also tell that you gave him much respect and did not fight him. It is important to do what he says even if you do not want to."

She continued helping and once she had made her as comfortable as possible, she gave her something to eat.

"You're so kind," said Laura. "Thank you."

"I am here to serve him. I do whatever he asks of me," she said. "He knows I am good with people. I am compassionate like he is."

"Have you known him long?"

"For numerous years, now. I look forward to serving him every day in this life as I look forward to serving the Divine One in the afterlife."

Laura smiled.

"That's what it's all about," said Laura.

"Yes," she said. "I will come later to see you and bring you dinner. Remember, listen and be respectful."

Michael's whole time awake could be divided into two tasks. One was reading as much as possible about the man who once held him captive and the other waiting for word. Right now, he sat in front of the computer expecting a message at any time. To him it seemed logical. From his perspective he was on the internet more than off. For Michael, one time of torture seemed to flow into the other and there was never this much time to get comfortable.

Gina walked into the room with a notebook in hand. She stopped briefly to make a note.

"Michael, I contacted our dentist and optometrist. Each will call to let me know exactly when they can take you," said Gina. "I gave them a time frame and told them it has to be immediately into the chair and out the door."

"How did you do that?" asked Pierre putting down the contracts he was looking over.

"Brigit went through all of the transmissions from Yamani," said Gina. "There are times when he never contacted us."

"Those are sacred times during the day that are to be spent in meditation and prayer," said Michael.

"How did you know about those times?" asked Mark.

"The guard told me about them during one of our many talks," said Michael.

"Did the guard ever ask you about your family?" asked Gina.

"Yes, but I answered in generalities. I never gave specific names or information. I know I didn't. When Yamani kept mentioning Laura by name and telling me how beautiful she was, I was confused about how he knew about her."

"It's all clear, now, isn't it," said Gina.

"Yes. Now he knows he can still get to me through Laura. If we do something, anything to disrespect him in any way, he'll take it out on her. Every time I take off my clothes, I'm reminded of his violent temper."

"Michael, as much as we'd like nothing more than to bask in the great feeling of having you back, we have a lot of work to do and so do you," said Jacques. "Laura worked every bit as hard, if not harder, than the rest of us. You're going to have to make up for the void she left when she took your place."

"What's there to do when you have to wait for him to ask for what he wants?" asked Michael.

"Plenty. He's power hungry," said Robert. "Edgar has been giving him little doses of power through you. He's reaching more people. We've been checking his website."

"His website?" asked Michael. "This man has a website? Are you serious?"

"He has one that gives information and gives a running total of those who've inquired about the religion and want to become chosen ones," said Robert. "That number is increasing with every broadcast. There's a difference if you're the leader of eight people or eight hundred people or eight thousand people. He's been broadcasting within his own country. He's ready to try going outside the boarders."

"Can he do it with what he has?" asked Michael.

"Yes. It's just a time consuming project," said Edgar.

"What's going to make it easier?" asked Michael.

"SecReSAC," said Edgar. "It'll put the world at his fingertips. In its purest uncensored form, it'll give him the world. Now, it'll give him everything that doesn't have to do with national security." He paused for a moment. "I talked to my office and gave an assignment to my premier division."

"What type of assignment?" asked Monique.

"I sent a bogus contract from a government division here in Paris that we've done projects for. They work on government military communication issues. The division is going to develop a component similar to one of the components in SecReSAC. It'll enable Yamani to access an area containing as many as ten thousand stations at a time. With this information, he should see his numbers soar," said Edgar. "This should put them at ease that their cover hasn't been blown. It should also make him even more power hungry for SecReSAC."

"Yamani only acts in the capacity he thinks he can handle," said Michael.

"Let's see what he does with this?" said Edgar.

Michael soon learned his partners were serious when they said that those who stayed at the house worked on the hostage situation. In some respects he found they were much more driven in this arena than they were at the office. He surmised going to the office would seem like a mini vacation in some respects. Those who stayed behind with him today sat around the kitchen table.

Michael read through some of the information on Yamani and as he did, he made notes. Sometimes he'd remember little bits and pieces of conversations that happened when he was in the cell. He knew that anything that happened from the time Laura made the deal to the time he was released was not transmitted. Page after page of yellow legal sheets were filled. The fact that Laura kept a record of everything was inspiration enough.

Margo was getting a cup of tea when the phone rang. She answered it and brought the cordless in to Edgar.

"Yes, this is Edgar Reinholdt," he said.

"Mr. Reinholdt, this is President Bartram."

"Yes, Mr. President. What can I do for you?"

"Mr. Reinholdt, what the hell is going on!" said President Bartram raising his voice.

"Sir, what are you talking about?"

"Are you aware that missiles have been fired inside Iraq?"

"Sir, I'm not aware of that," said Edgar trying to keep his voice as calm as possible. "Perhaps you could tell me a little more."

Pierre, Michael, and Margo looked at Edgar. He quickly scribbled the words *'fired missiles Iraq'* on a piece of paper and turned it so they could see.

"Missiles from three different areas around Baghdad have been fired. We're trying to ascertain their intended target. The Iraqi government contacted us as soon as they were launched to tell us they had not launched them."

"If they didn't launch them, who did?"

"That's why I'm calling you. They said it was as though the missiles were being controlled from somewhere other than the bases. Is it possible these people could have taken control of weapons systems?"

"Not that I'm aware of, unless they were able to get into sectors I haven't been apprised of yet."

"Let's say for the sake of argument that they have," said President Bartram with a great deal of attitude in his voice. "How long until they'll be able to control them with any degree of accuracy?"

"It would take a great deal of practice to achieve any degree of success."

"Mr. Reinholdt, did you allow them to have this?"

"I assure you I did not."

"How can we take it away from them?"

"Mr. President, I can't take away their ability to take over missiles that are in areas they already control. What I can do is make it impossible for them to gain control of anything that doesn't have an Iraqi fingerprint."

"Mr. Reinholdt, I can't impress upon you enough how uneasy this is making all of us."

"Mr. President, I understand. It's making things on my end more complicated and stressful. I assure you I can manage this situation."

Pierre took a pen and quickly wrote on the paper *'person inside' 'glitch in system.'* Edgar nodded his head.

"While we have the utmost confidence in you, Mr. Reinholdt, this has to stop!"

"Mr. President, the fact that the Iraqi's contacted you means they have no idea what's going on. I have no idea if this group has anyone planted in the government. We need to be very careful. If you suggest to them that there must be a glitch in their system, perhaps you can even reason with them that the best way to handle this is not to replenish the supply of missiles at those installations until it's fixed."

"I can do that, Mr. Reinholdt. If we don't work together on this, we stand to lose a great deal."

"I understand, Mr. President. How many people know about this?"

"The President of Iraq notified me and I notified each of the leaders and then you. They've all agreed…this goes no further. I'll ask the Iraqi's to take the position with the media that it was a problem with the system and they're working to correct it."

for Love and Ransom

"Mr. President, I'll begin working on this immediately. Please let me know if there's any other way I can be of service."

"I will, Mr. Reinholdt."

He put down the phone, looked around the table, and shook his head.

"Edgar, missiles fired in Iraq?" asked Pierre.

"I must get to your office," he said. "It has to be him. He's figured out how to fire them."

"How?" said Margo.

"How did this happen?" asked Pierre.

"I don't know," said Edgar. "I need to find out. This is something we didn't expect from him."

"One thing about Yamani," said Michael, "you must expect the unexpected."

"Do you think he knows he fired those missiles?" asked Pierre.

"I'm sure he knows," said Edgar.

"How accurate can he be?" asked Michael.

"It's hard to say," said Edgar shaking his head. "I think with practice he can become quite accurate."

"Joseph will be here in a few minutes to take you to the office," said Pierre hanging up the phone.

"Thank you. I promise, as soon as I'm finished, I'll return and we'll continue our conversation. I only hope I can figure out what they've done."

"If it was my house and he was able to gain access, I'd change all of the locks," said Margo. "What's a logical reaction when someone takes control of your missiles?"

"You change the access codes," said Edgar.

"Can you do that?" asked Margo.

"I can, but the Iraqi's won't be able to access their own system."

"I think the important thing is to change the codes on the rest of their systems," said Pierre.

"Countries follow patterns. That's the problem", said Edgar. "Their codes are labeled in such a way that you know where the installation is that you're unlocking. You need to create a system that's so random it'd take an infinite number of tries to figure it out."

"Did the missiles cause any damage?" asked Michael.

"Not this time. He has to learn how to control them."

"Edgar the phone is for you," said Pierre.

"This is Edgar Reinholdt."

"Mr. Reinholdt, damn it! He's fired them again."

"Did he hit anything?"

"No, but he's coming closer to a main section of buildings."

"Mr. President. I need permission to change their access codes to the rest of their missile sites. He must have someone on the inside."

"Let me contact Iraq's president. Will you supply him with a list of the codes?"

"Yes, but he has to understand he cannot give them to anyone. Changing the codes will keep those other installations out of his reach for a while anyway. Mr. President, they cannot know I'm involved."

"I understand, Mr. Reinholdt. I'll contact you as soon as I have an answer."

"We know he's near Baghdad," said Pierre. "It only stands to reason he'd have someone in the government offices."

"It's just something we never thought about," said Edgar shaking his head.

"He's always full of surprises, isn't he," said Margo.

While the others were discussing the situation Yamani had inadvertently put them in, Michael slowly walked into the other room and sat watching the computer. He kept reading through the letters Laura left and all of the conversations she had with both Yamani and Tom. He kept wondering what was going through her mind as she went through each step. He wondered what she was doing right now. As he was reading, the familiar email notification sounded. He clicked on it.

Mr. Braedon, Click on the link.

Michael clicked and shouted, "It's him. He's contacting us."

Mr. Braedon, are you there?

Yes, I'm here.

How do I know it is you?

The guard who stayed with me told me about his family and how blessed they were to have found you.

I see.

If I may ask, sir, how is Laura doing?
She is doing just fine. She is so beautiful. You are a lucky man.
Yes, sir, I know.
If you do what I want, she will stay beautiful. If not...well, none of us wants that.
You know I'll do whatever is in my power, sir.
Yes, somehow I knew I could count on that. Did you see I am having some fun?
In what way, sir?
I have been able to gain access to the missile system of a country. That is something I did not know I could do?
Neither did I, sir. Do you have total control?
Not yet. That is why I contacted you. What do you think I can do to gain control?
What seems to be the problem, sir?
I am falling short of the target.
If I may ask, sir, what is the target?
It is a group of abandoned buildings.
I see. Could it be the angle at which the missiles are coming out of the ground? Perhaps it's throwing off the intended trajectory. If they're angled more towards the sky, then it would take a greater distance to get them to hit the target. The arc would be bigger.
Ah, Mr. Braedon, that is something I have not considered. Is there anything else?
I don't know if you can adjust the speed the missiles go, or the time they're in the air, but both of those things can also be a factor. You may have to increase the speed and the time to get them to their destination.
Yes, Mr. Braedon, I can see where those things may be critical to my success. I am going to experiment with those things. I will let you know how it is going.
I appreciate that, sir.
As usual, Mr. Braedon, I will need some time to try these ideas. It may take me several days. Make sure you are able to be by the computer, just in case I need to talk to you. If not you, one of your friends, but I will talk right now only to you.
I understand, sir.

Mr. Braedon, if this works, I just may allow you to see Miss Darmer. I will be sure to tell her just how well you cooperated with me today. She will be pleased. Things will go well for her.

Thank you, sir.

"Michael, do you have any idea what you're talking about?" asked Margo.

"Only some basic physics," said Michael.

"What happens if what you told him doesn't work?" asked Pierre.

"He'll come back to me with an ultimatum to get Edgar to tell him what to do or else he'll take it out on Laura."

Laura sat quietly in her room, looking around. She wondered what Michael did when he was there. What did he think about? She knew her thoughts were mostly of him. She so longed to be back in Paris with Michael, but she knew she must be patient. She knew how Yamani worked…everything in his own time.

When the keys rattled in the lock, Laura sat quietly. She knew it was either the woman or him. Either way, there was nothing she could do about it. As the door opened, Yamani stepped in. Laura looked at him.

"Good day, Miss Darmer," he said.

"Good day, sir."

"I talked to your Mr. Braedon today. He is doing well. I think he is glad to be back at his home."

"Yes, sir."

"I had to contact him, because I had a bit of a problem."

"Was he able to help you, sir?"

"He gave me several solutions to my problem."

"That's good, sir."

"Yes, it is, for my sake, as well as for yours. I told Mr. Braedon I would bring the good news to you personally. I also told him things would go well for you, because of his cooperation. You know, Miss Darmer, I find myself thinking about you often. I can only imagine how much Mr. Braedon thinks of you. After all, I have had you for only a short while and you have made a lasting impression. Perhaps later, if I finish my work early enough, we may enjoy each other's company again."

"Yes, sir."

"Miss Darmer, try to relax, today, everything is alright. I will send the woman with some tea to calm you."

"Edgar, what did the President say was in the buildings in direct line of the missiles?" asked Michael when Edgar walked into the room.

"He didn't say, why?"

"Yamani says they're abandoned. Is that the case?"

"I honestly don't know."

"He's using those for target practice. He intends to destroy them."

"I can see if there's anything that can be done, but I doubt it very much," said Edgar. "Anyway, he hasn't been able to hit anything. He still doesn't know how to control them."

"I know that. That's why he contacted me. He wanted to know if I knew anything about it. I told him to check the angle at which they were coming out of the ground, their speed, and the amount of time they're in the air."

"Mr. Braedon, why would you tell him those things!"

"Because they sound logical. They're elementary physics answers."

"Yes, but why would you try to help him?" asked Edgar raising his voice.

"If I don't, he'll mutilate Laura and I won't allow that to happen," said Michael, his voice showing a touch of anger.

"If he's able to solve this, it'll give him a tremendous amount of power," said Edgar shaking his head.

"Only in certain areas," said Michael.

"Michael, all of this makes my job even more difficult."

"Look, I know him," said Michael. "It's going to take him at least two days to figure out how to get these missiles to do what he wants them to and he will not waste another one until he's practically sure it'll work."

"So what you're telling me is that if those buildings are occupied, the people won't have another chance to evacuate."

"That's what I'm telling you," said Michael. "Unless he really miscalculates, or just can't seem to get control, the next time he fires, he'll hit his target."

Chapter Thirty-Two

Michael sat in front of the computer staring at the screen. It was about the hundredth time he read the letter Laura had written to him. If there ever had been an inkling of doubt about how much she loved him, it was gone now. Every time he read it, he could hear her voice.

He clicked out, leaned his head back against the back of the chair, and took a deep breath and grabbed his ribs. He was so sore it hurt to breathe deeply and he always forgot.

"How are you this morning?" asked Mark standing in the doorway.

"Not bad, if I remember not to breathe deeply," said Michael turning around to face him.

"Hurts, huh,"

"More than you can imagine," said Michael. "Do you think it's wishful thinking that Yamani won't, you know…rape her?"

Mark was quiet for a moment and took a deep breath before he answered. "Michael, I'm not going to lie to you. We all knew if he got his hands on one of the women, he certainly would rape her. That fear nearly consumed us, yet it was one of the things that drove us to find a way to get you back." He looked away and then looked his brother in the eyes. "You know, all the women knew. They all knew before we did. They also knew the best way to get you back was to trade one of them for you. They even proposed exchanging one of them for you as a viable plan to getting you back."

"They would have traded places with me?" asked Michael hardly daring to believe his friends would have done such a thing for him.

"I can't tell you what hearing that idea did to us. It was the first time, I ever heard Pierre really yell."

"Yell? Pierre?"

"Oh, yes. And it wasn't because he was angry it was because he was so frightened at the proposition."

"Is that where Laura got the idea?" asked Michael. "Was it from the others?"

"I think Laura had the idea a long time before that day. I think she was praying the idea would be so logical we'd work towards that end," said Mark and he put his head down and shook it. "We couldn't do it. How could we decide who to send?"

"Mark, Laura would've never put another person in danger," said Michael as he reached and touched his brother's arm. "You know that."

"I know that. We all knew that, but the fear of having one of them taken, or worse yet, handing one of them over was something none of us had ever thought would happen in our lives."

"Mark, I'm not living in a fantasy world. I know what Yamani is like. I can hear his voice in my head; hear his words. I almost know what he's saying to her and there's no escaping him. Hell, I still can't escape."

"Yamani is a master of conditioning. What he's done to you was calculating. He doesn't even have to do anything and he can strike terror into you. He shocked your system, your entire being."

"Every time he mentions Miss Darmer as he calls her, he knows he's evoking a reaction. Every minute he won't allow you to see her he knows your mind is conjuring up all sorts of things he could possibly be doing to her."

"I know that and I'm trying to find something positive about all this," said Michael. "Well, here it is. I do believe this will make our love for each other stronger. There are millions of people out there who wonder every day whether or not their spouse or significant other loves them. I don't have to wonder, I know. I know just how much Laura loves me. She loved me enough to take my place."

Edgar Reinholdt walked into his office at Complex One. It had been some time since he had been there. As he looked around, everything seemed the same. Nothing was out of the ordinary. If he hadn't known his company was the target of information theft, he'd never, to this day, have known it. Now he had the trap set with the bogus contract. He was setting the stage and baiting the spies, the very workers he had placed so much trust in. Only he knew what it was they were developing. Only he knew what it could mean to Yamani and how tempting it would be.

He took a deep breath as he stepped in front of the first door leading into the classified section. He knew how important it was to act as though he knew nothing. He gained access to the corridor that led to the research room. As he walked the corridor, he discretely glanced around to see if the cameras were indeed working as they were supposed to. All was in order. He came upon the second door and gained entrance into the heart of the research facility. As soon as his team saw him, work came to a halt.

"Mr. Reinholdt, it's so good to see you," said Halim getting up and walking over to him. When the other workers heard Halim, they stopped what they were doing and gathered around Edgar.

"When we heard they were after you, we feared for your life," said Dabir.

"Thank you all for your concern," he said. "It's good to be back with you again. I understand you're working on that priority project."

"Yes, sir," said Franz.

"How is it going?"

"At first, very slowly, but now, we seem to have gained some momentum," said Ivan. "We seem to have been successful in isolating some areas that are crucial to the project."

"In what ways?"

"By isolating these areas, we can make it appear that the message came from somewhere else," he said. "If the client needs to operate incognito, they can do so under the guise of some other individual or nation."

"I can see where that could be an advantage, but only if the individual or country knows the other's code," said Edgar.

"This is true and once we have this first part conquered, we'll move on to that area."

"Very good. It's good to know you're able to carry on even in my absence. With that second part, I think we're going to have to be careful how much we give them."

"Mr. Reinholdt, did you ever find out who it was who wanted you?" asked Dabir.

"No. The authorities seem to think it was someone who wanted the company to fall apart in my absence."

"That isn't going to happen," said Franz indignantly.

"When you have a dedicated and self-motivated staff as I have, this company can survive without me."

"What about the man who was taken in your place?" asked Halim

"He's also connected with a large company which was also doing its best to continue without him. Now that he's back, they're dealing with continuing the business, as well as trying to figure out who it is who has taken his place. Now, I think I've disturbed your work enough. I'd like someone to brief me on this project," said Edgar.

It was payday of all things and he was stuck at the station. This was the first time Tom could ever remember there being a healthy balance in his checking account before his paycheck was due to go in. Usually, he cut it close every time. This was an entirely new experience. What he wouldn't give to go out for a pizza and some beer. It was the simple things he missed. He was comfortable enough at the station. He had everything he needed. It could be worse. He knew it. He could be Yamani's guest. The very thought of that proposition made him shiver.

He had never been what you'd call a religious person. As a matter of fact, he couldn't remember the last time he was in a church. Yet, now he found himself praying more than he ever had in his entire life. He never said anything to his colleagues about it. He knew they'd never let him live it down. After all, he was the one who'd make fun of anyone on staff who was a card carrying church goer. He never thought it went with the assumed persona of people who worked at the station.

He was so deep in thought he didn't even hear his door open.

"Don't tell me you're prayin'," said Doug as he walked in and plopped in a chair.

"Praying! Are you crazy?" asked Tom. "What the hell are you still doing here?"

"Dude, we left and came back," said Tony putting two bags on the coffee table.

"Move your feet," yelled Rich carrying in pizza boxes.

Chairs were being wheeled in and carried into his office and soon there were more people in that room than he ever thought it could hold.

"What's all this?" asked Tom.

"We went out for our usual 'Hey it's payday' celebration, but someone was missing again," said Doug. "Then we got the idea to bring it back to you."

Tony reached in a bag and pulled out a six-pack.

"Let the party begin," said Rich.

For the next two hours, there was nothing but the sound of beer cans opening and laughter coming from Tom's office.

"How much longer you gonna be stuck here?" asked Doug grabbing another slice.

"Don't know," said Tom.

"Aren't you tired of livin' in your office?" asked Rich. "Shit, I'd be goin' fuckin' crazy."

"It's not that bad."

"She gonna be alright?" asked Tony tossing his can across the room to the trash.

"Who?"

"The woman," said Doug.

"What woman?"

"That beautiful woman who came to see you twice, I believe," said Tony.

"Oh her," said Tom trying to sound nonchalant. "I haven't talked to her in a while."

"He's got her, doesn't he," said Doug leaning in closer.

"Guys, please," said Tom.

"Dude, we know you can't say nothin', but we just want you to know…we know…you know," said Doug, "and we're not gonna say nothin'."

"I know," said Tom. "I trust you."

"Her fiancé's gotta be goin' fuckin' crazy," said Rich. "I know I'd be."

As Yamani entered the room, he motioned for the guard to leave and the door locked behind him. Laura looked up at him. She knew what'd happen next…knew what he wanted. Laura continually tried to tell herself she had to do what was expected of her because she wanted to return to Michael as a whole person. She kept telling herself what Yamani did to her didn't matter and what he asked her to do to him was of no consequence. Yet, when the reality of the act was in front of her, she knew better. She knew her stomach would churn and she would feel dirty and disgusting when they were finished. She also knew he repulsed her, but she had to keep up the façade that she loved every minute of their time together.

It was only a matter of time before he'd subject Michael to a private showing of just what he did and Laura knew it. She also knew if Michael couldn't produce whatever it was he wanted, Yamani would take their escapades public. As long as it was only the two of them in the room, she knew Michael wouldn't see.

"I thought perhaps you might be a little lonely," said Yamani standing in front of her.

"Yes, sir."

"That is why I am here. I have come to talk to you for a little while and spend some time with you. I know you miss Mr. Braedon and he misses you. We are working very hard on Mr. Braedon's recommendations and if all goes well, I will allow him to see you."

"Thank you, sir."

"I want him to know you are alright."

"That's very kind of you, sir."

"I have told you and Mr. Braedon that I can be a very compassionate man. Please, believe me. I never wanted to cause either you or Mr. Braedon any pain. Mr. Braedon knows what he must do in order to keep you safe." Yamani paused and looked Laura in the eyes. "I know you know what I expect of you in return for your comfort and safety."

"Yes, sir, I do."

Yamani sat down in front of Laura. He reached out and touched her cheek with his hand. His touch felt warm and rough against her skin. She knew his hands were hands that worked in some capacity; she didn't know what. She closed her eyes and breathed deeply. She tried to picture Michael in her mind and feel the touch of his hand against her cheek.

"That is good. Relax. I am not going to hurt you. As long as you are nice to me and do what I ask," said Yamani taking the knife and putting it just out of reach, "I will be nice to you."

Laura nodded. "Yes, sir," she said.

He slowly moved his hands over her body as if memorizing every curve.

"Ah, I excite you," he said, smiling.

He lifted her gown and removed it over her head. He looked longingly at her. Laura opened her eyes and tried to read the expression on his face. He kissed her cheek.

"Just give in to me. Let me pleasure you like you would like Mr. Braedon to."

He paused, looked into her eyes, and waited until he had her attention.

"If you do not allow me, Miss Darmer, I promise you that no one, not even your Mr. Braedon will ever be able to pleasure you. Do you understand me?"

"Yes, sir," she said.

Laura knew all too well what Yamani was referring to. She watched each time as he put his knife just out of arm's reach. She had read the accounts of how he had mutilated women who wouldn't give in to him. She kept the image of Michael in the forefront of her mind and it was his touch she felt.

"You will never forget me, will you, Miss Darmer?" said Yamani gently.

"No, sir, I will never forget you," she said trying to catch her breath.

"I promised you that when we spoke and I intend to keep that promise. You will find, Miss Darmer, I am a man of my word.

"Yes, sir."

"And now, Miss Darmer, I will never forget you…Yamani stopped short of finishing the sentence, but Laura knew exactly what he meant.

D. A. Walters

For Laura, it seemed to be an eternity. She continued to think about Michael and only him. Suddenly she could hear Brigit as though she was sitting next to her.

"I'd think about how much Henri loved me. I'd probably say his name over and over again. I think I'd concentrate on happy times we had. I'd try to put myself somewhere in those times so I couldn't feel what he was doing to me."

Laura kept thinking about Michael until Yamani got up and got dressed.

"I know I will never forget you, Miss Darmer," he said as he touched her cheek, kissed her, and then left the room. Laura took her gown and put it on.

Michael sat looking at a map of Baghdad and the surrounding area. He tried to remember the ride to the meeting place. There was no visual because of the hood. Maybe, he thought, just maybe he might be able to remember what turns they made and even how long it was between those turns. He took a pad and pen, and closed his eyes.

Henri walked into the room and stood quietly for a few minutes. Michael didn't seem to notice him. He kept writing on the paper and looking at his watch. Henri waited for him to finish.

"What are you doing?" asked Henri.

"Trying to figure out where I was," said Michael.

"What do you mean?"

"I have no idea how I got to the place where they kept me, except that I woke up briefly during the ride and the road was bumpy. I was hoping that maybe I could figure out how I got to the drop off point."

"What are you writing?"

"The turns and how long it seemed between them."

"Do you know where the drop off point was?"

"Somewhere near the embassy," said Michael. "I was in such shock about being released, I didn't take much notice."

"Laura would have that in a folder," said Henri, "After you map out the car ride, we may be able to follow it backwards and find where they held you.

"We need a good map of the area showing the streets," said Michael as Henri left the room.

"Laura may have that too," Henri called back.

A little while later, Henri returned to the room with some papers. He handed them to Michael.

"There wasn't anything she left to chance, was there," said Michael looking through the papers.

"Nothing," said Henri sitting back down. "Your life was in danger. She'd never take chances when it came to your life. Now, let's mark out the trip from the airport to the drop off point. Then we'll try to work backwards from what you remember."

"Before we start, let's call Tom to find out if any instructions changed from this set of instructions to the ones he actually used."

Using Michael's directions, the two men worked at trying to mark off the route Yamani had taken when he returned Michael. After about twenty minutes there were several routes marked and each ended in a different place.

"I don't even know why I'm doing this," said Michael running his fingers through his hair. "It's not like we're going to be able to go there and attempt to rescue Laura."

"No, but after she's released, there're going to be a whole lot of people who'll want a piece of him and knowing where he is will enable them to get him once and for all. It's not a waste of time, if that's what you're thinking."

"The waiting makes me feel useless.

"You're anything but useless. You're the key."

"More like the marionette waiting for the puppeteer to pull my strings."

Chapter Thirty-Three

Edgar Reinholdt sat in the leather chair in his office. It felt good to relax at home. He had missed this. He closed his eyes and promised himself just a few minutes rest before he began adding notes about the security meeting to the folders on his computer. When the phone rang, he reached to get it from the desk.

"Hello," said Edgar.

"Mr. Reinholdt, what in the name of hell is going on!" said President Bartram.

"I'm afraid I don't know what you're talking about," said Edgar becoming instantly alert.

"They've hit three isolated targets."

"Where"

"All three outside of Baghdad. One to the north, the east, and the west."

"Were these residential areas?"

"No, all of them were abandoned structures, but that doesn't mean anything, Mr. Reinholdt. I cannot express to you enough how nervous this is making all of us."

"Yes, sir, I understand that. I assure you this situation will be resolved long before they develop the capability to be a formidable threat and adversary."

"Damn it, Mr. Reinholdt, anyone who can control missiles to the extent he can and as quickly as he's been able to do so, may soon become formidable."

"Mr. President, if I may be so bold as to remind you that when your country or any other country, for that matter, was experimenting with missile control, it took you quite a number of years to achieve success. You had an entire nation with the best scientists and engineers at your disposal and they do not. Their only advantage is that they have a modest amount of technology, but nothing in comparison to what you and your counterparts possess."

"Look, Mr. Reinholdt, I know what you're saying is right, logical even. However, the only thing those who scrutinize our administration know is that missiles are being fired and can see nothing more than mass chaos. We react to the outcries of our political adversaries."

"You react to your approval numbers," said Edgar sternly. "Right now, the population is a little nervous. It's not because they know there's a terrorist who's causing this, it's because they think there's a glitch in the system and it seems to be activating itself. This terrorist group merely wants to know it can control the missiles if it needs them. They have no named enemy. When they name one, that's when we begin to worry. Right now, they are like a child with a new toy. They'll soon grow bored with it and move on to something else. Mark my words on this."

"Mr. Reinholdt, we have no choice but to trust you, do we," said President Bartram sarcastically. "You know we can't do anything about this now."

"Exactly, Mr. President, and I know they'll try using the missiles again. When they do, I need to know when and where and as soon as you're made aware."

"Mr. Reinholdt, you have my word."

"I know from a political standpoint how difficult this is for you to handle, but that, Mr. President, is your job. Please understand that this situation is impacting not only on your political arena, but the business of two corporations and the personal lives of many individuals. I know you and the others feel you have a lot riding on this, namely your re-elections. Well for some of us it's our entire existence. When you think about that, Mr. President, you'll understand that I won't jeopardize anything I'm involved in."

Edgar Reinholdt rarely got visibly angry, but the conversation with President Bartram brought him to his personal boiling point. When he called Michael's house in Paris and talked to Pierre, he hadn't yet cooled down to his normal self. All Pierre could do was listen and revel in the assertiveness of the Edgar he had never seen.

"Edgar called," said Pierre when he came back into the room. "Yamani has been able to control the missiles well enough to hit targets north, east, and west of the city. Edgar said he left the President something to think about."

"What was that?" asked Henri.

"He told the President that his and his counterparts' area of concern was in the political arena and their approval ratings and that it was his job to know how to handle it. He also told him that he and the leaders were worried only about re-election whereas the rest of us were not only concerned with the political aspect, but our entire existence depends upon what happens. He told the president and I quote "I won't jeopardize anything I'm involved in.""

"Edgar is such a nice man, but don't push him," said Margo.

"He was still very angry when I talked to him."

"Why not the South?" asked Michael.

"What?" asked Pierre.

"Why wasn't there a target in the South?" asked Michael.

"Because that's where he is," said Gina.

"You know where he is?" asked Michael.

"We're surmising, based on some ancient writings," said Gina.

"Today, Michael and I spent some time trying to trace back the route they took when they released him. Because we didn't know some of the variables, we came up with several possibilities," said Henri.

"May we see the routes you traced?" asked Margo.

"Sure, we were hoping maybe someone could help shed some light on it."

When Henri laid out the maps on the table, the ladies looked at the routes. There were four of them drawn and none ended even in close proximity to another, yet as soon as they saw them they collectively chose one of the routes. Henri and Michael looked at one another.

"That's the one you felt most strongly about wasn't it?" asked Henri.

"Yes, but I don't know why," said Michael.

"It's the place Laura was almost certain you were being held," said Nicole. "Let me get the maps."

Nicole spread the maps on the table. Gwen took Michael's drawings and looked back and forth between the two maps. She put her finger on a spot on the large map overlay.

"What do you think?" she asked.

Monique and Gina looked between the two maps also.

"I'd say that's it," said Monique.

"Yah, that's it," said Gina.

Gwen marked the spot on the overlays with a star.

"Yah, this is it," she said, "close enough to the circle Laura drew to be considered by Yamani as being the Holy Land, while being far enough away to ensure his privacy."

"What is that circle?" asked Michael.

"Babylon," said Angelique. "It's identified in numerous documents."

"Babylon," said Michael looking around at the others, "as in the Hanging Gardens?"

"One and the same," said Angelique.

Gabrielle sat at Edgar's desk, looking at the computer screen. In all the time her husband was in danger, she never once questioned who was after him or why. She was so used to Edgar's work being confidential; she learned a long time ago not to ask. This time, it was different. This time, it was personal. She knew her husband was worried and it wasn't just for himself. She knew it was also for her. Now, she wanted to know why.

She never touched her husband's computer except to answer an email and that was when he was present. Her own computer was set up in a small corner off of the living room where she could access it when the committee was there. But if she was going to understand what was going on, she knew she had to use Edgar's computer. She was sure he put the information there.

She went into his documents and clicked on the folder marked personal. She took her time and scanned through all of the documents.

The one named 'Dear God' captured her attention and she clicked to open it. She looked at the picture of the man in front of her and read the caption for the picture. The name was vaguely familiar, but she couldn't quite place it. She moved down to the second page and began to read.

Edgar,

I think it's important that you know exactly who we are dealing with. I asked Laura to gather some of the information for you. Believe me when I tell you that this is just a very small amount of the information we have. If this is not enough to convince you of the need to diligently keep the security around your wife, I'm certain we can send you things that will impress you. Whatever you do, DO NOT ease up on the security around her.

Pierre

Gabrielle took a deep breath and moved onto the next page. She began reading the excerpts. The world in which she lived was one that was always protected by her husband. He'd never allow anything to harm her in any way. He spent his time making sure she was happy and she knew it. As she read, she realized just what her husband was battling trying to keep her safe and secure. What she was reading was horrific and the words that this was just a small amount of the information kept ringing in her mind. She knew by the tone of the email that this must be some of the lesser treatment. She couldn't fathom how anyone could do these things to someone else, yet she knew the rest must be even worse than this.

When she finished reading, she searched for another file. One after another she opened them and read the contents. Piece by piece, she was beginning to form the picture in her mind. She now knew her husband's business had been compromised and everything that was happening was an effort to gain the information this group wanted. She knew her husband was the only one who could give them what they wanted and therefore that was why she was a target.

She was still sitting at his desk when Edgar arrived home. When he walked in the office, he was surprised to see her sitting there. He walked around the desk and gave his wife a kiss.

"She traded herself for Michael so they wouldn't take me, didn't she," said Gabrielle looking up at her husband.

"Yes, she did," he said taking her hands in his.

"Why would she do that?"

"She knew he would come after a woman and that woman would most likely be you. She also knew that the only other choice would be her."

"What is he doing to her?"

"I don't know."

"Do you think he'd hurt her…do you think he'd do those things to her I read about?"

"I don't know. We're trying to do whatever we can to appease him."

"Are you giving him what he wants?"

"We can't."

"Why not?"

"We can't give him that much power."

"How are you going to get her back?"

"I don't know. Everyone's working on it."

"Edgar, are you in danger?"

"No, sweetheart. They need me to get them what they want."

"And Laura?"

"We'll do everything we can to make sure she stays safe."

Michael stood fixed to his spot where Yamani told him to stop. The guards held him tightly. Before him sat Yamani with Laura beside him. His arm was around her, holding her close to him. Her head was bowed and she looked at the ground.

"Mr. Braedon, I told you I can be a compassionate man," he said. "and you know this to be true, do you not?"

"Yes, sir, I do."

"I brought you here to show you just how compassionately I have been treating your Miss Darmer. I have promised you that no harm would come to her as long as you did what you were asked to do."

"Yes, sir."

"Mr. Braedon, sometimes I think what is happening is happening a little too slowly for me. I may have to become somewhat of an uncompassionate person. I will let you think about it while Miss Darmer and I show you how compassionate I have been."

"Please, sir, not in front of Michael," Laura whispered. "I've done everything you've asked of me."

"Yes, Miss Darmer, I know you have, however, your Mr. Braedon needs a little nudging. A little witnessing of our fun and passion may be what he needs to convince Mr. Reinholdt to give me what I want. You do not want me to have to force you, do you?"

"No, sir."

"All you have to do is pretend it is only the two of us."

"Sir, may I ask a question?" she asked.

"Certainly."

"Why are there cameras?"

"Two will record what we do and one will record Mr. Braedon's reaction."

"Why two to record us?" she asked.

"One so Mr. Braedon can watch it over and over again and the other so I can have one to show publicly if Mr. Braedon does not meet my time limit."

Yamani gave a signal to the men in the room, then he turned his full attention to Laura. As he began his erotic foreplay, Michael became agitated and tried to break the hold the guards had on him. Yamani stopped.

"Mr. Braedon, I advise you to stop right now and watch. Do not make Miss Darmer more nervous than she already is. It will take me some time as it is to calm her. She knows she must give in to me or suffer the same fate as others have. If that is the case, Mr. Braedon, no one, not even you will be able to pleasure her. And I give you my promise, Mr. Braedon, if that happens, you will watch every cut that is made and you will hear every scream…and you will know you caused it."

"Please, Michael, please."

"Laura…Laura! LAURA!"

Michael woke and sat straight up in bed, screaming Laura's name over and over again. The door to his bedroom burst open and Mark came running in.

"Michael, what is it? What happened? You had a dream."

"He's raped her, Mark. That fucking bastard's raped her."

It was another night of sitting around the kitchen table drinking coffee and tea and raiding the refrigerator.

"How long are they going to be in there?" asked Paul taking a bite of a sandwich.

"As long as it takes," said Gina. "When they're finished Mark will be out."

"I think Yamani's raped Laura," said Gwen fidgeting in her chair.

"Where are you getting a notion like that?" asked Jean.

"He's willing to show her to Michael," she said. "He's acting really cocky and he only does that when he has the upper hand."

"He's not going to do anything to physically maim her unless he absolutely has to," said Paul. "He appreciates her beauty."

"He'll use that threat to get Michael to act," said Pierre.

"I'm sure he's raped her," said Gwen. "That'd give him the upper hand. I think Michael knows it."

The group became silent once again. Never in their wildest dreams could they've ever imagined that one of them would be fighting for their life in ways only she could understand.

Mark walked into the kitchen and poured a cup of coffee.

"How is he?" asked Gwen.

"Not good," said Mark. "He's afraid for Laura. He's certain Yamani's raped her. Right now, he's feeling very helpless."

"You know Yamani's counting on that," said Angelique. "He thrives on knowing his opponents are helpless. It puts him even more in control."

"We have to rethink what we're doing," said George. "We know what Yamani's like. People who're like that, people who're so strong in character and set in their ways, never notice when others mimic those ways. We need to get inside his head and learn what he'd do in this situation. Then we have to act."

"You're right," said Jacques. "Laura was inside his head. She knew exactly what would make him give Michael back. She also knew how to go about doing it. She may not have known every step to take, but she knew how to gain his confidence and how to get what she wanted."

Those simple words took Robert back to the day in the office when he questioned her judgment.

D. A. Walters

"All I'm saying is I want you to be sure they can be trusted. You're spending your time reading in there and we're busting our asses coming up with a plan to get Michael back."

"You know what? No matter what it takes I will get Michael back. You can take that to the bank."

Robert took a deep breath.

Monique touched her husband's arm and looked at him concerned. "You alright?" she asked.

"Yah."

"We don't have the advantage of having Laura here," said Gina. "I think she knew this man, while not personally, knew about him from the time she was young. We need to know this man. She not only knew what he would do, she knew why and what would drive him."

"If you're right, that took years," said Jean. "We don't have that kind of time."

"Then I suggest we start," said George.

"If I were a betting person, I'd bet Laura kept every newspaper clipping and magazine article about him," said Gina. "I think she studied him…his patterns, his habits, his preferences. I think, when she was younger, he was a very colorful character to her and someone she could talk about intelligently at the table. That background gave her the edge. She played up to him without ever letting on she knew who he was. She knew how important it was that we kept from him the fact that we knew him."

"I think you're right. I wonder where those clippings are," said Gwen.

"I think they're here," said Mark putting down his cup. "Remember when we came back from the States, we had a box shipped with all our research in it? There was also another package in it that Laura took out. I think she brought her personal clippings."

"It's probably somewhere in the bedroom," said Gwen. "That's where she did her planning. It certainly wasn't out here with us, or we would've guessed what she was up to."

"I do remember her taking the package to the bedroom. Let me see if I can find it," said Mark. "Maybe Michael knows where she would've put it."

Mark walked back into Michael's room. He was still sitting on the bed looking at Laura's picture. His face seemed to be more relaxed.

"How are you doing?" he asked.

"I'd like to say better," said Michael.

"I know you would. I'll settle for about the same."

"That's about it, about the same. Did everyone go back to bed?"

"No, they're putting on more coffee and tea and getting something to eat."

"Why?" asked Michael.

"They're awake and they're going to put the time to good use. Do you know where Laura would've put all her notes on Yamani?" asked Mark.

"I really didn't know she had notes."

"When she was younger, her father used to always like to discuss current affairs at the dinner table."

"I remember Laura telling me about that. She told me she learned all she could about this one man, so that she'd have something intelligent to say," said Michael. Then he stopped and looked at Mark. "Don't tell me…"

Mark nodded his head.

"We think the man was Yamani," said Mark. "She told us a lot of information about him."

"She said she used to cut out everything that was printed about that man," said Michael, "as well as his pictures."

"That's how she was able to recognize him."

"Why do you think she'd have them here?" asked Michael.

"When we went back to the States, Laura, Gwen, and Gina did a lot of research at the library. All of the information they found, we shipped here so we could go through it thoroughly. When we opened the box, Laura took out a package she said was hers. I think it may have all of the things she collected over the years."

Michael got out of bed.

"Let's find it," he said.

"I know she left all that information on the laptop for us, but some of the conclusions she came to didn't follow what was there."

"I've gone through everything and asked myself why about a number of things, but just thought I was too emotional and missed something," said Michael.

"We all did. We missed the fact that Laura had more information," said Mark. "We were so busy looking at what we had found we didn't bother to ask her what was in the package. I thought it was some work she had to do for one of her clients."

"What did it look like? Was it an envelope?"

"No, it was a box, a blue box, sort of wood grained, pretty big."

"It was probably the original box she chose to keep everything in."

Mark and Michael checked the drawers and closets and turned up nothing.

"You're sure it's here," said Michael.

"Yes."

Mark dropped to his knees and looked under the bed.

"Nothing," he said.

Michael got up and walked very slowly holding onto the furniture as he went into the bathroom. He started pulling things out of the linen closet. Mark walked in.

"What are you doing?"

Michael turned around to face him holding the box in his hands.

They returned to the group, box in hand.

"What's that?" asked Paul.

"It's the box that Laura had sent here," said Mark, "the one that was in with all the other information."

"I don't think I ever saw that," said Gwen.

"Laura took it out as soon as the box was opened and put it in her room," said Mark.

"Let's see what's in it," said Raquel.

"I bet it's all the things she's collected over the years about Yamani," said Mark.

"Don't you think we already have it?" asked Gwen.

"Maybe, but then not every article would've been kept. But, since he was her project so to speak, she may've kept things that were obscure," said Mark. "To someone else it may've been nonsense, but to Laura, it was probably another piece of the puzzle."

"Well, let's see what was so important," said Michael. "Let's do it in the dining room where everything else is."

Mark placed the box on the table. Michael opened it and started taking old papers out of it. They were yellow with age and he lifted them carefully out of the box. There in front of them was the man Yamani coming to life before their eyes. Each of the clippings included the date it appeared in the newspaper or magazine. There were also transcripts of news programs that mentioned Yamani or the Ayatollah. Along with all of the printed materials were pictures of Yamani. It was obvious that Laura went to the trouble of asking the newspapers for eight by ten glossies of the pictures that had appeared. No one spoke a word as each item was taken from the box. They busied themselves putting all of the articles and transcripts in time order. On the sideboards they arranged all of the pictures in the order they appeared.

"Wow. I don't think we have any of this," said Robert.

"It reminds me of a collection someone would have for a rock star or a movie star," said Brigit.

Nicole walked out of the room and returned carrying pictures they retrieved from the internet. She placed those at the end of the sequence of pictures.

"No wonder she knew exactly who this was," she said. "Look at his eyes. He may have aged, but there's no mistaking those eyes."

"My God, she never had to even second guess," said Raquel. "She knew."

"Why then, did she make me query about him on the internet?" asked Robert.

"I think she wanted to make sure," said Jean. "Remember when you told us his name?"

"Yah," said Robert, "she told us more information than any normal person would know about any one person."

"She knew all along," said Raquel.

"While we had to spend time getting acquainted with Yamani," said Pierre, "Laura was catching up on what he was doing now."

"Now, what does she know that's going to keep her safe?" asked Monique. "What did she know that we didn't that enabled her to make the connections?"

"It has to be here somewhere," said Brigit.

The conversation continued as they began to look over all of the memorabilia Laura had collected. No one noticed Michael and the envelope in his hand. He sat there staring at his name on the front written by Laura.

"Michael this is unbelievable," said Mark. "This is actually what he was doing, what he was involved in. This is nothing like the other information we had which was more of a collection of studies of Yamani's activities and how they impacted upon society at the time. You need to read some of this…Michael."

Michael kept staring at the envelope. Mark walk over to him.

"Hey, brother, what is it?" he asked.

"I don't know. It was at the bottom of the box. It has my name on it, but why would she hide it?"

"Well, unless you open it, you'll never know. I'll let you have your privacy."

"No…please stay right here."

Michael turned the letter over. It was sealed with a wax seal with Laura's initials.

"She had commented that when we got married, she'd have to get a new impression made. As soon as she said it, I had one made for her. I intend to give it to her the day we marry."

He ran his hands over her initials and then carefully opened the envelope. He took out the papers that were in it and unfolded them.

My Dearest Michael,

If you're reading this letter, it means you've found everything I've collected over the years concerning Yamani. I also know if you've found it, it's because Mark remembered watching me unpack the blue box and take it to our room. Oh, God, Michael, how I miss you. You're everywhere in this room, yet you're nowhere. I hear your voice, hear you calling my name. I feel your pain and want so much to comfort you. I know Yamani will never allow me to have you without strings attached. I also know he won't think twice before killing you. I'm working as quickly and as diligently as possible to get you back. The only thing, my love, is that I have to give him something he'll be able to use. I know this may sound strange to you, but I know him almost better than he knows himself.

I know he's a man of opportunity. He built his reputation by taking advantage of opportunities. It's how he gained so much control while the Ayatollah was in power. His downfall was that he didn't fully see all sides of the situation. He so wanted to be number one, he underestimated those forces that were loyal to the Ayatollah. He won't make the same mistake twice. No matter what I do, I must convince him on every level it's in his best interest to release you. I must make him see you'll be of more use to him free than captive. He must also know I'm acting alone without any other interested parties. That's why, I can't tell anyone. I trust Mark, Gwen and every one of our friends with my life and yours, but I can't jeopardize what I've put into motion. Please tell them I love them and I'm sorry I couldn't tell them. It's so hard doing this alone. Sometimes I just want to walk into the room and tell them what I've done, but I know Mark and the others would stop me. I can't allow that to happen. I don't have the knowledge or the connections to release you any other way. Trading myself for you is all I can do. You, on the other hand, will be able to deal with Yamani on the outside much better than I.

The last page of this letter contains dates of articles and a number after each date. The number refers to the line number where you need to begin reading. They're things I think are most important. They're insights into the way Yamani operates. Maybe you can use them to get him what he wants without jeopardizing innocent people and maybe get me home.

I want to come home, Michael. I promise you I'll hold out as long as I can. I'm telling you honestly that I'll do whatever I have to do to stay alive. I want to come back to you. I love you and I want to spend my life with you. I know what Yamani is going to do to me...I know you know, too. Please forgive me, it's the only way...Oh, God, Michael, I pray you'll still want me when this is all over. I want to be with you again, to feel your arms around me, to kiss you passionately and make love with you. Michael, I want to be your wife.

Michael, I'll understand if you can't love me anymore. That's why I left my ring and locket. I wanted to make it easy for you. If you decide you can't, don't give them back to me. But if you can, and I hope you can with all my heart, I look forward to you putting the ring on my finger again. Michael, I'm scared, but I don't want him to know that. I don't want him to know my weakness. I'm frightened I won't be able to do this. I don't want to let you down. Michael, please hold me close. I will feel you doing so and I know it'll give me strength.

I love you, Michael, with every part of me.

Laura

Michael wiped the tears from his face. It was hard to tell whether his tears or hers had smeared some of the writing. He looked at Mark.

"I want her back...as soon as possible."

Mark gently rubbed his brother's back and wiped tears from his own face.

"Then let's see what these passages are," he said quietly, "and why she thinks they're important."

Yamani quietly closed the door to Laura's room and made his way down to his office. Gehran was sitting on a chair out in the hall. Yamani stopped and addressed him in hushed tones.

"Gehran, what is it that has brought you here at this hour?"

"I have news, sir."

"Wait one minute. Let us go in here," said Yamani unlocking the door to his office. He walked in and put on a light. Gehran followed him and closed the door behind him. Yamani walked behind his desk and sat in the chair. He motioned for Gehran to take a seat.

"Now, Gehran, what is so important."

"I have heard from Dabir. They are working on a new project, one of great importance."

"What will this project do?"

"He said it will allow you to take over more than ten thousand stations at one time."

"That is good news."

"Yes, sir. There is more. He said they are working on being able to hide the identity of the place where the transmission is coming from."

"When will they have the completed project?"

"He did not say, sir, but he said they thought you would like it so they have started collecting the necessary information."

"Excellent, Gehran, excellent. I think I may need to take a short trip."

"Yes, sir. Would you like me to make arrangements?"

"Yes, Gehran and notify Dabir that I will be arriving and wish to have a meeting with all parties."

"Yes, sir."

"And Gehran, find Ahmed and Sadik and ask them to come to see me."

"Yes, sir."

This was indeed good news and he wanted to reward those who worked so hard by visiting them. He needed to make certain that everything here would remain under control. He knew he could trust Sadik to do so. His real worry was the uneasiness he felt as far as Ahmed was concerned, but there still was no basis for those feelings. He also knew the danger if he bypassed one who everyone perceived as important to him.

Within minutes, there was a knock on his door.

"Enter."

"You asked to see us, sir?" asked Ahmed.

"Yes, please come here. I have just received information that is vital to the Cause," said the Chosen One. "I will have to leave for a few days."

"Yes, sir," said Ahmed.

"I am trusting the two of you to make sure no one bothers Miss Darmer. She is the key to everything. The only one permitted to have access to Miss Darmer's room is the woman. Is that clear, Sadik?"

"Yes, sir."

"Ahmed?"

"Yes, sir," said Ahmed quickly, "I will make sure no one bothers Miss Darmer."

"I knew I could count on the two of you. You are truly faithful

Chapter Thirty-Four

Monique sat at the computer typing the passages Laura had indicated in the letter. The others used the time to read the material they had just found. When Monique finished, she printed out copies for everyone. She made certain they were in date order the same way Laura had written them.

"Wait until you read these," Monique said as she handed out the copies. "This man is calculating. He understands the human psyche and knows just how to manipulate people."

"I understand that now," said Michael. "There are things he said to me, things the guard said that play over and over again."

Michael jotted down a few notes on paper so he'd be able to reconstruct what he was thinking. He wanted to keep up with what the group was doing. He was so far behind them that it seemed it'd take forever to catch up on what they already knew. With Laura's life hanging in the balance, he desperately wanted to be at the same level with them.

Michael started thinking about Laura. Out of nowhere he could hear her.

"Maybe it only happens in fiction," Laura said.

"With beautiful women and men who hang on their every word."

"I just think it's about a woman who wasn't about to give up. She became resourceful at staying alive. They all wanted to know what would happen and she led her husband to the point each time where he just couldn't kill her because he needed to know."

"I know I'd hang on your every word."
Laura smiled and kissed him.

For a brief moment there was a smile on Michael's face.

"Something has given you a pleasant thought," said Gwen.

"Scheherazade," he said, nodding his head. "I don't know why. I just thought Scheherazade."

"Something you and Laura had in common?" Paul asked.

"Something that was my love and became special between us. My favorite work of art is a piece by Matisse called "Thousand and One Nights." It's the story of Scheherazade. Laura and I would go to see it every time it was displayed. Then we'd read the stories. We'd talk about how Scheherazade was able to stay alive by telling the tales. I don't understand where the thought came from."

"Yamani kept a number of people around who didn't really seem that important," said Margo. "They were able to give him information and ideas that resulted in gains for him from time to time. He kept them around just in case they might be useful."

"Get Laura's computer," said Gina. "Let's go through those files again. She has to have a journal. Scheherazade is not just an isolated thought, Michael. She sent it to you somehow."

Laura closed her eyes and leaned back. She could almost see the artwork hanging on the wall at the Carnegie. She had always been fascinated by the piece, but when she saw it for the first time with Michael, his passion for the artwork made her love it even more. She became interested in the actual creation of the work; all of the paper that had to be painted first; the shapes, the colors, the green and red hearts that made up the border. She couldn't fathom how Matisse could possibly have used those huge scissors to cut all of those pieces.

They had begun a new tradition. When it was displayed, she and Michael went as often as possible to see it. They would go from there to one of their favorite restaurants and have a quiet dinner. Then they would go home and read the story.

Laura could see the letters, the words that made up the top right border. *'Elle vit apparaitre le matin. Elle se tut discretement.'* She remembered looking them up so she would know what they meant. '*She saw the morning light begin to pierce the night. She discretely grew silent.*'

Wasn't that what she was doing…keeping silent, but for a different reason. Scheherazade grew silent so they would want to hear more. She kept silent so she wouldn't upset or anger Yamani. She kept him wanting more, a different kind of more, one she hated with all her being. Scheherazade kept it up for a thousand and one nights. How long would hers last?

The morning light was beginning to pierce the night, now. She knew he'd soon return. She closed her eyes again and could hear Michael's voice reading to her.

The sun was starting to come up and even though everyone was awake, the house was eerily quiet. They were reading articles, making notes, looking through computer files, reviewing footage, and anything else they thought would be of help. It was by every standard a daunting task. Gaining the release of Laura wasn't going to be quick or easy. They knew this exchange would be for information and not for another person. They knew Yamani had to be dealt with in a certain way and their objective right now was to find how.

Everything was there in front of them. They had every piece of the puzzle now that Laura had. They just had to be able to put it together to get her back.

Chapter Thirty-Five

Laura sat patiently waiting after the woman left. She knew it was only a matter of time before Yamani would make his presence know. It was something she had come to know would happen.

The keys jingled in the door and Yamani walked in with his two guards.

"Good day, Miss Darmer. I trust you are well?"

"Yes, sir. I am."

"Good. I see the woman was here and helped you to get ready for the day."

"Yes, sir"

"She is most kind, is she not?"

"Yes, sir."

"I promised Mr. Braedon if I was successful in using what he told me, I would allow him to see you. Since I was very successful, I am going to keep my promise and allow him to see you. I want him to see that I am treating you well and I want to thank him for the information. That is alright with you is it not?"

"Yes sir."

"Good."

Yamani put his hands on the keyboard and began typing.

Mr. Braedon, are you there?

Yamani's face appeared on the wall. Michael turned on the webcam they added and began typing.

Yes, sir, I am here.

Ah, Mr. Braedon, this is new. I can see you.

I wanted you to know that you were talking to me, sir. Can you hear me?

Thank you, Mr. Braedon. It is almost like we are together again.

Just like Yamani, Michael was adamant about not showing anyone else except him. He didn't want to give Yamani any visuals of the others in the house, especially the women.

First of all, Mr. Braedon, thank you very much for your ideas. They worked very well.

I'm glad for you, sir.

I will have some other questions, but not right now.

I'll be glad to help in any way I can.

Your reward for helping me is being able to see your Miss Darmer. I want you to see that she is well. I have done nothing to harm her. I will make every effort to ensure her comfort and her safety as long as you cooperate. Is that understood?

Yes, sir.

Good. There Mr. Braedon, do you see your Miss Darmer?

Yes, sir. I do.

Yamani watched Michael's expression with great interest as Michael knew he would.

Does she not look well?

Yes, sir, she does.

I know that she misses you, Mr. Braedon, and I have been trying my best to spend time with her so that she is not always alone.

That's very kind of you, sir.

Mr. Braedon, I have several pressing matters that must be taken care of within the next few days. I am afraid during that time, I will not be able to spend time with Miss Darmer, nor will I be able to talk to you. However, when I am finished with these matters, I will return and will contact you immediately so you will not worry. While I am gone, the woman will see to all of Miss Darmer's needs.

You're very kind, sir. Thank you. And please, sir, thank the woman again for taking such good care of me.

I will do that. Oh and Mr. Braedon, Miss Darmer asked for some reading material. So I got them for her. I know how much you want to be together, so I thought I would share the titles with you.

"Muhammad," "The Cat Who Dropped a Bombshell," "How to Win Friends and Influence People," "The Arabian Nights," "Think and Grow Rich," and "How I Write." Quite a diverse set, would you not agree?

Yes, sir.

Look, Mr. Braedon. I have added lamps so Miss Darmer can have light to read and pillows for her comfort.

Thank you, sir. I appreciate it.

Now, Mr. Braedon, can you tell me what color of dress, Miss Darmer was wearing?

Yes, sir. It was blue.

Good. Can you tell me how many lamps I showed you?

Yes sir, two.

Good. Can you tell me the color of the fringe on the lamps?

Yes, sir, it's gold.

Very good, Mr. Braedon. One last look at Miss Darmer and I will say good bye for now. Remember you will not hear from me for several days, so relax.

Yes, sir. Thank you, sir.

With that the screen went blank. Michael turned off the webcam and sat back in his chair.

"Michael, *The Arabian Nights*," said Gwen.

"Why was he questioning you?" asked Mark.

"To make sure I was paying attention to everything," said Michael.

"What is it he has to do that's going to take several days?" asked Margo.

"I don't know," said Michael. "If I would've asked, that would've been prying into something that was none of my business and it wouldn't have gone well for Laura."

"Is it a holy time?" asked Gina.

"No, he would've said so," said Michael. "It could be something with the organization. I have no idea."

"Let's not take time speculating," said Jacques. "That'll waste time and may be his motive in telling us. Did you save everything?"

"Already done," said Robert. "At least this time, there were good shots of Laura. He wasn't in them."

"Even with all she's going through," said Raquel, "she still looks beautiful."

"We can be thankful she'll have a few days of peace without him," said Brigit

Margo put her hands on Michael's shoulders and leaned to speak softly to him. "I'm going to go to the bookstore and get those books."

He looked up at her and smiled.

Chapter Thirty-Six

Tom Richards had been back on the air in Pittsburgh since he returned. He knew Yamani would be monitoring his show somehow. He was ultra-careful not to speak about anything that had transpired between Laura and him. The hostage situation and the release were taboo subjects and his listeners came to respect his wishes. They knew when the time was right he'd tell them all about it. So sure were they and almost everyone else in the market area that his morning show became the number one show.

Tom hadn't left the station since he came back from Paris. Reporters were still waiting for his emergence. All the doors were covered. There were people waiting in the garage where he parked his car and at his home. His friends, who were taking care of his house while he was gone, had to deal with the media every time they arrived.

He yawned and clicked into his email. There was a lot of listener email to go through. It would definitely keep him occupied today. One subject line stuck out...*Yes, Mr. Richards it is me.* He clicked on it.

Mr. Richards,

A thank you seemed to be in order at this time for all you have done. Without you, I would not have the privilege of having Miss Darmer with me. She is much more pleasing than Mr. Braedon and she is able to fill my life with the type of pleasure Mr. Braedon was incapable of giving. Although I have to be away from her for several days, I am looking forward with much anticipation to returning to her. I know she will enjoy the time we will spend together in private. She has shown me just how much she has enjoyed my company numerous times since her arrival. Mr. Richards, I must commend you on your handling of the situation. You are as Miss Darmer told me, "a man of your word," as well as "a man who does not mince words." I understand this situation has caused a great disruption in your life. For that I do apologize. I assure you that with the way things are going and the way Miss Darmer is striving to please me, you will be hearing from me again. As much as I would love to keep Miss Darmer for my own, my own wife would begin to question my love for her. As I have promised, Miss Darmer will be released. The only question is whether it will be without physical damage.

Tom sat back in his chair just staring at the screen. Almost automatically, he copied the email and saved it in the file. Something about it bothered him. It was typical Yamani in every way. Yet there was something there. He read it over again…nothing. He got up from his chair and walked to the kitchen to grab another cup of coffee. When he returned he looked at the email again. Then it hit him. It wasn't Yamani's email address. He sat up in his chair and began typing. He clicked send and decided to get something to eat.

It was several hours before he came back to his computer. He decided clean clothes were in order and he cleaned the kitchen. He also looked for some unusual music for his Monday morning show. There was a new contest starting and he wanted to use really obscure sound bites. He liked making things challenging. He put them on the desk so he could log the titles into the show's outline. He had twenty-three new messages. He clicked to see if anything had come that was important. There was one from Paris. He watched the exchange between Michael and Yamani. Laura looked good, but he could tell she was frightened. He knew he had to send the email from Yamani to them. He scanned over the other new emails and his answer was waiting.

The next time you need something make it a little more challenging. This was easy. This came from a computer at Draven's Copy and Print Center in Frankfurt, Germany. And to answer your next question, it originated there. It wasn't forwarded through there. The man who sent it wanted to know if anyone read the emails that were sent. They told him that would be an invasion of privacy. Since I had all of the information from you and I know people who know people, I was able to get you this nice still shot of the man. Yes, I know...It goes no further and I'm not asking any questions.

Tom clicked on the attachment.

"Shit!"

He immediately sent off an email to Mark.

Mark...call me...It's urgent
Tom

The phone rang. It was almost instantaneous with the clicking of the send button although Tom knew differently.

"Hello?"

"What's so urgent?" asked Mark

"He's in Frankfurt. I'm sending you things."

"I'll call you as soon as we get them and read them."

Mark hung up the phone and looked at the others. His mouth was gaping open.

"What's going on?" asked Jacques.

"That was Tom," said Mark coming back to reality. "Yamani's in Frankfurt."

"What?" exclaimed Pierre.

"Is he sure?" asked Paul.

"He didn't say, I think he's in Frankfurt," said Mark. "He said 'he's in Frankfurt.' He's sure. He's sending things."

"We got it," said Robert putting it through the projector.

This is the email I got this morning from Yamani.

There was absolute silence while they read it.

After I read it something kept bothering me. I kept rereading it. It turned out that it wasn't the content, but where it came from. It wasn't his regular address. I sent the address to a friend to see if he could pinpoint its origination. Here's his answer.

As they read it, heads began to shake.

"Are you ready for the attachment?" asked Robert.

"Yes," said Michael.

Upon the screen before them appeared Yamani dressed in jeans and a sweater.

"Oh my God," said Pierre. "We have to warn Edgar."

"Call Tom and thank him," said Michael.

"Get Edgar quickly," said Mark. "Robert, send those to him."

"Why is he in Frankfurt?" asked Nicole.

"Checking up on his minions?" said Mark. "Remember, he'd never expect us to know he's there."

"Maybe checking out Gabrielle or Edgar," said George.

"What's to keep him from coming to Paris?" asked Raquel.

"Nothing," said Michael. "He knows the company. He can find the address."

"Would he do that?" asked Nicole.

"He just might. We didn't think he'd go to Frankfurt and there he is," said Michael. "There's no way to predict what he's going to do."

Pierre sat in Michael's office. He picked up the phone and called Edgar.

"Hello," said Edgar.

"Edgar, this is Pierre."

"Pierre, what's wrong? When you call on this phone, it can only mean something is urgent."

"Edgar, he's in Frankfurt."

"What!"

"We got word from Tom. We're forwarding you that email," said Pierre. "Trust me, Edgar, there's no doubt."

"What does he want?" asked Edgar, a touch of fear was in his voice.

"We don't know. It may be to meet with the men from your plant. It may be to come to your plant, or it may be to see what you're doing."

"It may be to see my wife!"

"We didn't want to think that."

"We have to think that. I don't know what more to do to keep her safe, short of sending her away somewhere."

"If you do that, you can't control the situation with her and your attention will be divided. At least in Frankfurt, she's well known and so are you. Whatever he'd try to do would take extraordinary preparation."

"Pierre, he tried before."

"Yes, but now you're on your guard as are the rest of us. So is your wife. The thing is to make everyone your wife knows aware. Make it very difficult for him to move."

"I have the email. That store's in the next block from the hotel," said Edgar. There was a moment of silence. "Oh my God. It's him!"

"Yes, Edgar. Thank goodness for Tom."

"Indeed."

"Edgar as much as I'd like to be there, I can't risk it. Be careful. You have an advantage. You know he's there and he doesn't know you know."

"This is true. However, since we don't know what his agenda is, we're going to be looking over our shoulders. At least with him here, he won't be launching any missiles. That'll keep the leaders off my back for a few days."

"Just brace yourself for the next barrage."

Chapter Thirty-Seven

The apartment on the outskirts of Frankfurt was spacious and decorated very simply. All of Yamani's followers were gathered around the large kitchen table, each with notes in front of them. This was a first. All the other meetings between them had taken place just outside of Baghdad. This was different. Any movement of this type anywhere around Baghdad would've aroused suspicion in light of the recent missile firings.

"Which of you possesses the final piece of SecReSAC?" asked Yamani, looking from one to another.

"We do not know that," said Dabir.

"How could you not know?" asked Yamani raising his voice a little.

"Each of us possesses one or more pieces of the puzzle. But we don't know in what order," said Dabir.

"What do you mean by that?"

"Unless we each write down what we know and try to piece it together, we wouldn't know what we have exactly. We may have a complete section and then again, we may have only pieces of every section," said Ghassan.

"Why have you not found this out?"

"With all due respect, sir," said Halim, "when you ordered us not to be seen together, we took that order seriously. Therefore, this is the first time in years we've been all together in one room."

"How long would it take to write down what you know?"

"That would not take all that long," said Dabir.

"Then how long would it take to piece it together?"

"That would take much longer," said Halim.

"How much longer?"

"It could take weeks or months," said Dabir.

"Why so long?"

"Some of the equations are very similar with subtle changes and so are the diagrams," said Dabir. "Those subtle changes can mean all the difference in the world."

"What about the other information you were able to sneak out of the lab?"

"We'd also have to take the time to fit that in too."

"Are you telling me I would be better off taking my chances in getting Mr. Reinholdt to release it rather than to expect an answer from you sooner?"

"Yes. SecReSAC took many months in the lab to develop," said Halim. "Reconstructing may take as long."

"I cannot wait that long," said Yamani shaking his head. "I need to move quickly. Holding hostages is a liability. I need to get this information and release her."

"What do you really want to do?" asked Kardac.

"I want to be able to address the world and I want to have the power to bring the people to their knees if they will not worship as I wish them to."

"The project we are working on now, may give you a partial answer," said Kardac.

"That is what I heard from Gehran. What I want to know from you is what kind of answer?"

"With it, you should be able to command as many as ten thousand stations at a time," said Kardac.

"That would be extremely useful. How soon can it be delivered?"

"We have been making great strides with this," said Dabir. "Much of it was developed with SecReSAC. Now it is just modifying it to what we need."

"How much do you have?"

"Enough to get you started," Halim said as he handed Yamani the envelope.

After Edgar's conversation with Pierre, he knew he must impress upon Gabrielle the seriousness of being safe. The last thing he wanted to do was scare her, but the reality of it all was that he, himself, was frightened beyond telling. He had witnessed Michael's release and Laura's surrender from the center of that very emotional house in Paris. He knew what all of this was doing to Michael and he prayed he'd never have to know what it was like to have his wife in the clutches of that maniac. As he left the complex he spent the time on the drive home trying to find exactly the right words to say to his wife that would make her listen. He wanted to somehow lock her away somewhere safe where no one could get to her.

When he arrived home, Edgar found Gabrielle working on some paperwork at the dining room table. He bent down and kissed her, then took her by the hand.

"Come sit with me," he said quietly. "I need to talk to you for a few minutes."

"What is it, Edgar?" she asked quite concerned. She knew it had to be something serious that would bring her husband home from the office in the middle of the day.

"Gabrielle, the man who took Michael is here in Frankfurt."

"Oh, Edgar, what does he want?" she asked as they sat down on the sofa. She stopped for a second, looked at him, and took both his hands in hers. "He hasn't changed his mind, has he? You're not in danger are you?"

"No, my dear," he said and he reached his hand and touched her cheek. "He still needs me to be free. We think he's checking on his information sources."

"Then he still doesn't have what he wants, does he?"

"No, he doesn't."

"And he still has Laura."

"Yes."

"Are you afraid he's going to try to get me?"

"Yes, I am," he said being totally honest with her for the first time.

"I see," she said calmly. "What do you want me to do?"

"We need to be very careful. We need to be very aware of what's going on around us."

"Edgar, I don't really go anywhere. I can stay here until he leaves. He can't be here long. We have a lot of security watching this place."

"I don't want anything to happen to you. I love you so. I don't know what I'd do if he took you."

"I love you, too, Edgar, with all my heart."

He drew her close to him and leaned back against the back of the sofa. She rested her head against his shoulder. She was so frightened, but she didn't want him to know. Ever since she read everything he had stored on his computer, she thought about it endlessly. She couldn't imagine what it would be like to be in Laura's place right now. She only knew that Laura must be frightened beyond words. She put her arms around her husband and held onto him with all her strength.

Chapter Thirty-Eight

Gabrielle walked into her husband's office as soon as she heard his car pull away. She looked through the papers on his desk until she found what she needed. She sat down in his chair and picked up the phone.

The phone rang several times before anyone answered. Gabrielle was just about to hang up when she heard the voice.

"Hello," said Jacques.

"Hello, this is Gabrielle Reinholdt. May I please speak to either Gwen or Margo, if they're available?

"Certainly, Gabrielle, this is Jacques, I'll have one of them on the phone in a moment."

"Thank you."

Jacques put the phone down on the desk and walked out to the living room.

"Gwen or Margo, Gabrielle's on the phone and wants to talk to one of you."

"Gabrielle?" asked Mark.

"Yes, Gabrielle," said Jacques.

"Let's go," said Gwen picking up the cordless from the coffee table.

Margo picked up the phone in the office and sat in the chair.

"Hi Gabrielle, this is Margo. Gwen's going to be on the cordless so we can both talk to you."

"Good," said Gabrielle.

"What's going on?"

"I need information," said Gabrielle.

"What kind of information?" asked Gwen.

"About the man who has Laura," said Gabrielle.

Gwen and Margo looked at each other. This was the first time Gabrielle had ever let on that she knew anything.

"What do you want to know?" asked Margo.

"I read everything Edgar had on his computer. I know what type of man he is. Laura picked the information to send to Edgar and I understand it didn't tell the whole story," said Gabrielle trying to choose her words wisely.

"Yes," said Gwen, "we wanted him to know that the man was to be taken seriously."

"Now, I understand he's here…in Frankfurt…and I can tell Edgar is terrified," she said trying to sound stoic. "He came home from the office, yesterday, to talk to me. He never does that unless it's vitally important."

"I see," said Margo.

"I think he's afraid I'm going to be taken." Although she said it straight out, it was hard for her to comprehend that she was actually in danger.

"Gabrielle, I know Edgar's doing everything possible to prevent that," said Gwen. "I also know how frightened you must be."

"Do you know about this man?"

"Yes," said Gwen.

"Do you know more than what Edgar had on his computer?"

"Yes," said Margo.

"Margo and Gwen, I need to know more," she said emphatically. "Edgar's always trying to protect me…and yes, I appreciate that, but I need to know. Do you understand?"

"Yes, Gabrielle, we do understand," said Margo. "We understand all too well."

Edgar Reinholdt entered Building One. Even though it was Saturday, it wasn't unusual for him to be there. With this new project, the team was working overtime to try to solve its main connectivity problems.

"Good morning, Erika. How are you this morning?"

"Fine. How are you?"

"Very well, thank you. Have there been any calls?"

"No, but there was a man who came to see you. I told him you'd be in later. He gave me this envelope and asked me to give it to you."

"Did he say who he was?"

"No."

"Thank you. I'll be in my office. Then I want to check on the team's progress."

Edgar opened the envelope as soon as he closed the door. He took out the contents and unfolded the piece of paper.

Mr. Reinholdt,

You have to agree with me that Miss Darmer is a beautiful woman. I know Mr. Braedon would agree with me. I also know we would all love for Miss Darmer to stay beautiful. I know Miss Darmer and Mr. Braedon want this. You can help by making sure you can deliver to me what I need, when I need it. You must make certain, Mr. Reinholdt that you can work within time limits. I love those types of games, don't you? I wanted you to see how beautiful Miss Darmer is, even when she is my guest. Oh, Mr. Reinholdt, your wife is equally beautiful. I should love talking to her also. As you can see I also have her picture. I look at it often.

Edgar sank into his chair. His face was white and his hands trembled as he placed the photos side by side on his desk. He was so wrapped in thought that he didn't hear Erika walk into the office.

"Edgar, are you alright?" she asked. "You're white as a sheet."

He nodded his head.

"Is there something you needed, Erika?"

"They're asking for you in the lab."

"I'll be there directly."

He put the contents back inside the envelope and slipped it in his briefcase. He closed the door to his office and then he made his way down to the lab.

Gabrielle listened intently to what Margo and Gwen were telling her, but she somehow got the feeling that there was much more they weren't saying. Although she wasn't sure she wanted to know it all, something inside her was driving her to have the information.

"Margo, Gwen, I do understand the caliber of this man and I do know his threats aren't to be taken lightly," said Gabrielle.

"Gabrielle, there are literally hundreds of pages about him. There's no way to get all of that to you immediately," said Gwen. "We can send you some of what we're sure Edgar didn't share with you."

"We can send the emails and picture from today and some other pages for you to read, as well as the information we just found out Laura had," said Margo. "If, after you read it, you need more, we'll send more."

"Gabrielle, we need your email address," said Gwen. "We don't want to use Edgar's."

"Thank you," said Gabrielle. "I know Edgar's only trying to protect me, but really, I'm stronger than he thinks."

It was more than an hour before Edgar returned to his office. The problem facing the research and development team was plaguing to say the least. Just as one small mistake caused the birth of SecReSAC, similarly, a simple mistake had caused the current project to be brought to a halt. Once it was discovered and the correction made, the team knew things would go much smoother. They also knew without Edgar, it may have taken them a very long time to find it.

For that hour, Edgar's mind was completely on work and not on the personal ramifications of Yamani's visit. It was important to him that the new project preceded without problems. Now, as he returned to his office, the reality of what Yamani could be up to was hitting him squarely in the face.

"Erika, have there been any calls?"

"No."

"Has anyone else come?"

"No."

"I'll be in my office."

Edgar sat at his desk and reached and took the envelope out of his case. He emptied the contents again and reread the letter. Once again he looked at the pictures. Although he knew Yamani was capable of anything, he was totally unprepared for this. He picked up the phone.

Mark heard the phone ring in the office and hurried to answer it.
"Hello," he said.
"This is Edgar. To whom am I speaking?"
"Edgar, this is Mark."
"Mark, he dropped off a letter at my office."
"When."
"Before I got here. It's very distressing."
"I know it must be. What was in the letter?"
"He was telling me the safety of Miss Darmer and my wife is ultimately up to how quickly I can get the things he wants when he wants them.'
"I'd like to see the letter."
"I'm scanning it in as we speak along with the pictures."
"Pictures? What kind of pictures?"
"Of Miss Darmer," he paused for several seconds, "and my wife. It was taken at the Gala."
"That makes three times that we know he's been to Frankfurt."
"Three!" said Edgar. "What do you mean three?"
"Once to kidnap you, once for the gala, and now."
"I don't need to tell you, Mark, how disconcerted I feel."
"I know, Edgar. He's warning you about what could happen to get you to agree."
"The information's on its way. I just wish this was over. He's feeling very sure of himself."
"Why do you say that?"
"He talked to Michael via the internet, emailed Tom, and brought an envelope to me. He's feeling very much in control. It's almost as though he's waving it in front of our faces."
"But then again, he probably thinks you believe it was delivered by messenger, not by him."
"But he knows the truth and that in itself is making us look very stupid. He's so confident he thinks he's able to move around freely without any fear of being found out."

"Then we need to make his world just a little smaller. And I think I know just how to do it. Edgar, have Erika put a meeting on the calendar between our two companies on Wednesday at nine o'clock. If he comes back, I want him to see evidence that it's business as usual."

"Will you be coming?"

"It'll be Henri and Jean," said Mark making a note on the calendar. "I don't want to risk him seeing us together and I want Henri to get a firsthand look at security."

It wasn't as though there wasn't anything pressing to do, but sometimes they just needed to take a few minutes to do absolutely nothing. Today it seemed as though the phone was destined to keep them from doing all that much. Between calls to and from work, Edgar, and Gabrielle, there was little constructive work being done.

Mark came back into the living room carrying papers.

"What do you have now?" asked Monique.

"An email from Edgar," he said as he passed it around. "Yamani delivered the letter and pictures to his office."

"He's becoming very brazen," said Angelique.

"The good thing about it is he has no idea we know who he is," said Mark. "The bad thing is he can move freely wherever he wants."

"I never thought about that," said Gina.

"That little insight's courtesy of Edgar. The picture of Gabrielle was taken at the Gala. As we figure, he's been in Frankfurt at least three times; first to take Edgar, second to get Gabrielle's picture, and now."

"Edgar talked to Gabrielle," said Margo. "She told us when she called."

"She knows she's a target," said Gwen, "and she wanted to know what he was capable of doing."

"She found Edgar's files," said Margo. "The information you sent him when he was meeting with the leaders."

"She wanted more, so we sent her some other things," said Gwen.

"Well, now, in light of all that," said Mark, "what I told Edgar is even more urgent. We need to make Yamani's world a little smaller."

"How do you plan on accomplishing that?" asked Jean.

"I'll tell you in a minute," said Mark. "First, I had Edgar schedule a meeting between our two companies for Wednesday at nine o'clock. I thought Henri and Jean could go. I figured, fly to Frankfurt in the morning, have the meeting and fly back in time to be here for a late dinner."

"Good, I can take a look at his security." said Henri. "Now, about making Yamani's world smaller."

"I was thinking we could put a little more pressure on Yamani by airing and running a series called "Where Are They Now?" The series will look back on some of the more prominent figures from the late seventies to now, who have disappeared into obscurity. It should create such a stir, especially among those who were directly affected by them."

"You need to make it a magazine that commands attention both in the U.S. and abroad," said Michael. "With their faces everywhere, there'll be nowhere for them to go. What if the article included computer aging?"

"Yamani would be country bound," said Gwen.

"Now, the questions are who and how," said Margo.

"I know Tom would be all too glad to give us some ideas," said Mark. "How long would it take to get something like this together?"

"It depends upon how many people they assign to it," said Gina.

"You're talking a lot of archived material as well as what has come down through the rumor mill," said George.

"We certainly can't give them anything about Yamani. They'll have to do the leg work themselves," said Michael.

"This might just save Gabrielle," said Gina. "Yamani's never going to allow her to be taken without him being directly involved. She would be his trump card. He'd never trust that to anyone else."

"We need to get to Tom," said Mark.

"You said we needed to go to Pittsburgh to touch base every couple weeks," said Pierre. "It's been quite some time since anyone's been there. Take the time now. Why don't Jacques, Nicole, George, and Raquel go and take care of things in Pittsburgh. You can take care of business, shuttle papers, and talk to Tom."

"When do you want us to go?" asked Jacques.

"As soon as possible," said Mark. "We want to tighten his noose."

Gabrielle put down the phone. She had made the last call she needed to make. The information sent by Margo and Gwen troubled her deeply and she found herself looking around her house thinking about all the ways someone could enter and take her. She thought back to the day the note was delivered. When Marie answered the door and no one was there…that would've been an opportune moment. Forcing themselves past her would've been easy.

Gabrielle decided to shore up that aspect herself. She called every one of her committee members and told them from now on, they needed to call when they arrived so she'd know that someone she indeed knew was on the other side of the door. She also made the decision to 'hire' a doorman so she called Mr. Klingman from the security firm and arranged for a security officer to be appropriately attired as one.

Although Edgar had things well in hand, she knew he was concerned not only with her safety and well-being, but also the affairs of his business that were being impacted by this. Her committee members were well aware that Edgar had been a target of an abduction and that there was a threat Gabrielle might be next. She wanted them to know what the man looked like, so she intended to show them the picture Margo and Gwen sent.

By the time Edgar arrived home, everything on her list except for talking to him had been crossed off. She meant what she said to Gwen and Margo about being a strong person and she was determined to impress upon Edgar just how true it was.

"Hello, sweetheart," she said when he came into the living room.

Edgar walked over to her and gave her a kiss. As he did, he looked down at the coffee table and saw the picture of Yamani in the sweater and jeans. He picked it up.

"Where did you get this?" he asked.

"I called and talked to Gwen and Margo. I wanted more information than what was on your computer," she said. "They were kind enough to send this. Edgar, why didn't you tell me these things?"

"I guess I wanted to protect you."

"I appreciate that, sweetheart, but I really need to know," she said quietly. "After I read all this and I know there's a great deal more, I knew more than ever that I also have to take precautions. I have to be responsible for me as well as for my committee members."

"I always thought of myself as your protector," said Edgar holding her hands in his.

"And you are, Edgar, you are," she said smiling at him. "You always have been and always will be my protector."

Chapter Thirty-Nine

Aside from the fact that he was living at the radio station, Tom Richards' life had returned to normal…at least his work life had. He even managed to carve out personal time. He found himself many times thinking about what must be going on in Paris and what Laura must be going through. He wished there was something he could do that would make Yamani give her back, but he didn't have anything to offer him in exchange. When he received the call that Raquel and Nicole would be in Pittsburgh and wanted to talk to him, he was excited. He had finished his morning drive and was finishing paperwork when the receptionist told him they were waiting.

"Hi you two," he said when he came out to the reception area. "Have any trouble getting past the press?"

"Not at all," said Raquel. "They have no idea who we are."

"How're you doing?" asked Nicole.

"I'm fine."

"You have to be tired of being stuck here," said Raquel.

"Sometimes, but there's always something going on. How's Michael?"

"He's hurting, physically and emotionally," said Nicole.

"We can't thank you enough for the information that Yamani was in Frankfurt," said Raquel. "We warned Edgar. We now know he's been in Frankfurt at least three times."

"Three!"

"The picture of Gabrielle was taken at the Gala," said Raquel.

"This man's very mobile for someone who has a hostage."

"That's exactly what Edgar thought," said Nicole, "and we have no idea whether he's been to Paris. We can almost be certain he hasn't been here, because of the distance and the time he'd have to be away."

"We need to clip his wings," said Tom.

"Exactly," said Raquel.

"I wish there was something I could do."

"That's why we're here. Mark told Edgar we needed to make his world get a little smaller."

"How does he propose to do that?" asked Tom.

"Mark took your idea of a documentary and thought of a running a series of articles and shows entitled 'Where Are They Now?' It would highlight those news figures that were prominent from the late seventies until now, who slipped into obscurity," said Nicole handing him a folder. "We came up with some we thought were pretty good."

Tom opened the folder and read the list. There were two columns. The first had a list of those who were most likely forgotten by the majority of people on the planet, while the second column contained the names of those who impacted the world recently.

"Some of these people are probably living nice little existences, plotting their next move," said Tom looking up from reading.

"Exactly," said Raquel. "This would use archived material as well as anything that came from the rumor mill. Michael suggested having the pictures aged using a computer so people would know what they might look like now."

"Do you realize how many people would be looking for them?" asked Tom.

"Yes, Tom. Millions," said Nicole. "They couldn't risk being out in the open."

"That's exactly what we want done," said Raquel. "We want to limit his ability to travel."

"Where do I come in?"

"Contacts," said Raquel. "Obviously we can't bring this to anyone, but we need it to get done."

"I just so happen to know a guy who works for *Newsweek*. This would be perfect for him. Excuse me for a minute."

Tom opened the right drawer of his desk and reached under a pile of papers. He pulled out a folded piece of paper and unfolded it. He picked up the phone.

"Hal, do you have time to meet me?" he asked.

"Sure. You got something?"

"Oh, yah."

He hung up the phone and went to the computer. He entered a chat room with Hal and laid out the idea. Tom made sure that he made it sound as interesting as possible. All he wanted Hal to do was try.

Well, I'll put it out there. Then we'll have to wait to see if they like it.

What do you think?

I like it. It's the kind of piece that'll boost circulation through the roof.

I have a list of ideas I can fax to you.

Great. How quickly can you fax it? We have a meeting starting at ten.

Right now. Use the same fax that's on the paper you gave me?

Yah. I'll let you know when I have an answer.

Tom clicked out of the screen.

"I'll be back in a minute," said Tom picking up the list. "He wants this faxed to him for a meeting."

Tom returned to his office in a few minutes and sat down.

"Did Hal like it?" asked Raquel.

"Oh yah," said Tom. "He has a meeting at ten. He knows it couldn't have come from me."

"Good," said Nicole. "Do you think he has a prayer of getting it done?"

"If anyone can, he can, and the fact that he has the list already is a plus."

The meeting was in full swing when Hal entered the room. Bill Epson, the editor, looked up when he heard the door.

"Nice of you to join us, Hal," he said.

"Sorry, I was making some notes and lost track of time," said Hal taking a seat.

On the board in front of them were all the current stories and those assigned to each. At the bottom of the list was a big question mark.

"Well, now that all that's out of the way," said Bill, "what have you come up with to fill that question mark slot?" Bill looked around at his staff. "So no one has any ideas…no angles on any news event?"

"Hey Bill, I'd like to put something out there," said Hal.

"Alright,' said Bill. "What is it?"

"The world is changing really quickly," he said.

"Wow, that's novel," said Al sarcastically.

The others laughed.

"A lot of people have risen to power and then have disappeared into obscurity. Some of them were so hated that I bet there're people who'd give anything to make them pay. I'm proposing we run a series called 'Where Are They Now?' We can choose someone, dig up archival material, see what rumors are out there and see if someone knows where they are. For those who haven't been heard of since, say, the eighties, we could use computer aging to show what they'd look like today."

"I like it," said Bill. "Who could we do?"

"I took the liberty of making a list and running it off for everyone," said Hal handing a list to Bill and the others.

As soon as they saw the list, the sarcasm was replaced by excitement.

"I forgot about half of these," said Fred. "These are great!"

"What if we do two," said Bill, "one old, one new."

"We can put their pictures on the cover side by side," said Jerry getting up and going to the board. He quickly drew a sample magazine cover to illustrate his thinking.

"Great! Great!" shouted Bill walking to the door. He opened it and yelled, "Karl, Sid, Sally, get in here. Hal has the idea of the century! We need everyone on this."

The three hurried into the room. Karl was the webmaster and could put anything together with little notice. Sid was about the best there was at tracking down any type of rumor on even the most obscure subject. As for Sally, her job was to convince the higher ups at their sister station that this was the most important idea there was in the world…no matter what it was.

Bill handed each of them a list and quickly outlined the idea.

"Let's get readers involved," said Yvette. "How about a website just for sightings and updates?'

"I like it," said Karl. "We can put the link on the main page."

"What about a reward for info and for turn in." said Phil.

"We'll get our media involved," said Bill excitedly. "That's your job Sally."

"This won't even be a hard sell," she said with a smile. "They want market share. This'll give them market share."

"This'll push circulation through the roof! We'll do two a week, right? One old and one new." Bill stopped to look over the list. "I like it. Okay. Hal, this is your baby. We'll start with Afmad Yamani and Bin Laden. Get it organized, I want it for this issue…before someone else jumps on it!"

"Tom, when our mutual acquaintance contacts you, are you going to be able to leave immediately?" asked Nicole.

"My boss already knows I'll have to leave again. He never talks about it. He knows it's too important and the less he knows the better."

"Do you have the money for the flight?" asked Raquel.

"Yes, Laura took care of that. I'm not sure about the flight back from Baghdad."

"We'll take care of whatever you need," said Nicole. "We brought a cashier's check so you can mail it to be deposited in your account. Laura was careful about non-traceable funds. We thought it was best also."

"Thank you."

The three of them talked for more than an hour before the phone rang.

"Hello," said Tom.

"Meet me."

Once again Tom went to the computer.

Well?

It's a go! They loved it!

Great!

D. A. Walters

The list put it over. The more they looked at it the more excited they got.

That's awesome!

They're going to feature two of them each issue with follow-up bulletins. It was like the pairing of the animals on Noah's ark.

That's a good one.

They're also going to run it on their sister station.

Who are the first two?

They want someone old and someone new. They want to start with Yamani and Bin Laden.

Holy God!

I'm doing copy. Sid and his team are doing the archival and rumor mill digging. They're as good as they come. They also liked the computer aging idea. Gotta run. They want it for the next edition. They said they want to jump on it before anyone else can think of it. Tom thanks so much. I owe you.

I'm looking forward to reading it.

"They bought it," said Tom turning away from the computer. "It starts next issue. Plus it'll be a series of reports on their sister station. They wanted one old and one new. The first two…Bin Laden and…Yamani."

They smiled at each other and nodded their heads.

Chapter Forty

Laura was reading when she heard the keys jingling in the lock. She closed her book and sat quietly waiting to see who would enter. The woman came in with tray in hand to tend to Laura's needs.

"How are you today?" she asked as she set the tray down.

"I'm doing well," said Laura. "How are you?"

"I am fine. I see you are reading your books."

"Yes."

"Why did you ask for books?"

"Ever since I was a little girl, I loved to read. I'd borrow books from the library, read them all day, and return them the next day and get new ones."

"Why did you choose these books?"

"They're some of my favorites and a few are new and I didn't have a chance to read them yet. Do you like to read?"

"I love to read the books the Chosen One has written."

"I didn't know the Chosen One was a writer."

"He has written books for anyone who wants to know more about the one true faith. They are full of the words that will help you earn your place in the afterlife."

"I don't know very much about your faith except what I hear the guards talk about. I'd like to know more."

"When the Chosen One returns, I will ask him if you might be permitted to read his books."

"Thank you," said Laura taking the cup of tea from the woman. "You're very close to the Chosen One aren't you?"

"I serve him in this life."

"Are there others who serve him?"

"Oh yes, many others. Everyone who belongs to the faith serves the Chosen One. Everyone has a different job to do."

"I see. And your job is taking care of me."

"Oh yes, as I took care of Mr. Braedon."

"I thank you for that."

"I also take care of the Chosen One, his house, and his personal needs."

"I can tell you love him, just by the way you speak about him."

"I have loved him since the day I met him. He has loved me also."

Laura saw a smile come to the woman's face and she smiled back.

"I must leave you now. I will be back later. The Chosen One has been delayed and will be gone a few more days. I promise I will take very good care of you."

"Thank you."

A few more days. What could be keeping him away? Laura hoped they were getting closer to bringing her home. At least with Yamani gone, she knew she was safe.

Halim sat on a chair in the apartment across from Yamani. He sat quietly for a few minutes before speaking.

"Sir, two people from the consulting company were at the complex today," he said.

"What did they want?" asked Yamani leaning back against the chair. He folded his hands in front of his face.

"They were asking questions about how the workers felt about adding a division that would service the general public."

"What else were they doing?"

"They visited each of the facilities and used all of their time talking to the workers."

"Did Mr. Reinholdt accompany them?"

"No. It was Mr. Paxton who took them around," said Halim.

"Do he and Mr. Reinholdt talk often?" asked Yamani.

"Only if Mr. Paxton has a problem or during scheduled management meetings."

"How long did the people from the consulting company stay?"

"They were there all morning."

"Did you talk to them?"

"Yes."

"What did they ask you?"

"They asked me how I would feel about the company becoming bigger."

"What did you say?"

"I told them the decision was up to Mr. Reinholdt."

What else did they ask?"

"They wanted to know if I liked working there."

"What did you tell them?"

"I told them that I did."

"Anything else?"

"They asked if I thought there was anything that might need changed about how things were run."

"And?"

"I told them I liked the way the company was run."

"Did they ask any questions about Mr. Reinholdt's behavior or say anything about Mr. Braedon?"

"No, sir."

"Good. That means I am only dealing with Mr. Reinholdt and Mr. Braedon. There will be no one else to cloud the decisions."

Edgar looked out the kitchen window as he poured himself something to drink. He watched as the security personnel walked the perimeter of his property and wondered if things would ever return to normal, or whether this would become the norm. Somehow, when this all started, he never envisioned his company where it was today. He thought it would be just a nice little communications company that produced and installed equipment for the average person or small company. Now he was playing in the big leagues. He knew the stakes.

If he did something wrong, gave out too much information, he could cause a disaster that would be worldwide.

He kept going over everything in his mind. Everything had to work perfectly. It helped to have Henri and Jean look everything over and give their approval. It meant he had truly thought of every aspect.

He looked out the window again and saw someone in the hedging. He started to pick up his phone and sat it back down. The figure was familiar and so were the clothes. If he hadn't been certain about the other times, this made him a believer. His heart beat faster and he felt fear grip him. He watched Yamani aim the camera and take pictures. He knew this time they were of him. He glanced at his watch. In a little while, his wife would be entertaining on the patio. He needed to make sure Yamani was gone before then. Edgar watched as he looked at his watch, put his camera down, turned, and walked back through the hedging. Within seconds he saw the security personnel come around the corner. There was nothing he could do about the present situation, but he could take steps to further secure his home.

He walked away from the window and walked into a room at the back of the house. He looked out the window, making sure he was hidden from view. He saw Yamani take position and take pictures. It'd only be a matter of time before he'd have to move somewhere else. Edgar left the room and hurried to his office. From there he had a view of the other side of the house. He grabbed his camera which was sitting on the lamp stand. He knew he could be seen at his desk with the blinds open, so he closed them slightly giving him the advantage. He saw the man walk into position again. Before Yamani was able to raise his camera, Edgar quickly took several shots of him. With the closeness of the hedge to this side of the house, he was sure he had some good ones.

Edgar picked up the phone and contacted security.

"This is Mr. Reinholdt. My wife is expecting guests any minute. Would it be possible for the security team to sweep the area? I thought I saw something."

"Certainly Mr. Reinholdt. I'll have them do it immediately."

"Thank you."

Edgar breathed a sigh of relief and smiled to himself. He had no intentions of catching Yamani. He only wanted him scared off. He could hear the sounds of the men running towards the hedging.

Edgar sat at his desk, opened the drawer, pulled out a legal pad, and began making notes. He knew he needed to step up the security again at his home and made a list of things he wanted to discuss with the security company. He was just about finished when the phone rang.

"Hello"

"Mr. Reinholdt, this is Mr. Klingman from the security company."

"Yes, Mr. Klingman."

"Sir, the men did a sweep of the area and you were absolutely right. There was someone there. They found footprints along the hedging and one of the men saw someone get into a car at the end of the property."

"Thank you Mr. Klingman. I'd like to discuss this further tomorrow. Would it be possible to come to the house around ten?"

"Yes, sir."

Edgar took the camera and plugged it into his computer. He looked at the pictures on the screen. There as big as life was Yamani.

"Oh my dear Yamani, you're getting really careless," said Edgar aloud. "That's going to cost you, but you don't know that. That's my little secret and I'm going to do everything I can to use it against you. I'm not going to let you get anywhere near me or my wife. Now, let me send these off, so the others can enjoy them, too."

"When does that series start?" asked Robert.

"With the next issue," said Brigit. "I believe next week. Why?"

"Because Yamani needs his wings clipped, now. These just came from Edgar. They were taken from his office window at home."

"Yamani's really feeling confident isn't he," said Mark looking at the pictures.

"Yah, confident no one would ever recognize him," said Gwen.

"Edgar's waiting for an email or a package from Yamani with the pictures he took," said Robert. "He told me he thinks Yamani's so confident, he's becoming careless."

"How did Edgar catch him?" asked Gwen.

"He was getting a drink and saw him from the window. He pretended not to notice Yamani taking his picture. He knew he was going to take pictures of the rest of the house, so he went to his office, grabbed his camera, fixed the blinds, and when Yamani got to that side, he took the pictures before Yamani was able to take any. He said, if it wasn't for the fact that he had Laura, he would've emailed them to him."

"Oh God, that would've been so awesome," said Gwen laughing.

"I can just picture the look on his face," said Brigit.

Yamani stood at the table looking over the pictures he took. There they were all laid out in front of him. He smiled as he looked at the pictures of Mr. Reinholdt getting a drink in the kitchen.

"You know, Dabir, he had no idea I was there," said Yamani.

"That is excellent, sir."

"I wish I could see the look on his face when he gets these."

"Sir, that would be amusing."

"Yes, Dabir, it would be," he said. "When will they learn that security does not matter? We get what we want."

"Sir, they think security is the answer to all of the problems."

"Security hasn't stopped you, has it?"

"No, sir. Here is another component in the formula that we need," said Dabir handing some papers to Yamani.

"Good. How close are we to being finished?" asked Yamani.

"Another couple days," said Dabir. "We are working faster than ever so you can implement your plan."

"That is good, Dabir. I must soon get back. I do not trust that everyone back there will do as they should. There are some who may not be quite as faithful as those who are here."

"Surely, sir, that cannot be."

"I am afraid so. For some, the Cause is moving too slowly. Those are the ones who think great wealth and power will be theirs in this life. Those are the ones that need watching."

"I assure you, sir," said Dabir, "we are working as quickly as possible."

"I know that and besides the Divine One, I am the only one you have to please."

"Yes, sir. I know that by pleasing you, we are also pleasing him."

Yamani walked out of his room followed by Dabir. Halim walked through the door and sat on a chair.

"How are you, Halim?" asked Yamani.
"Sir, I am well and you?"
"I am well, also."
"Sir, there is something we have to talk about."
"What is that?"
"You are going to need some hardware for the project. If you would like, I can use my contacts to get what you would need."
"That would be most appreciated. However, how will I be able to get everything into the country?" asked Yamani.
"That, sir, is not an issue. My contacts have connections that will make it very easy."
"How much?" said Yamani.
"Excuse me, sir?" said Halim.
"I said, how much?" said Yamani again.
"I do not know? I will have to ask when I know exactly what we will need," said Halim. "Sir, we cannot put a price on the success of our mission can we?"
"No, we cannot," said Yamani. "However, I will not be taken advantage of."
"Sir, believe me, they would not do such a thing. They are honest, hard-working persons who are determined to further the Cause."
"See to it Halim."

Edgar Reinholdt sat at the desk in his office at home checking his email for the final time that day, a ritual he performed every night just before going to bed. He read through the subject lines deleting anything that wasn't important and saving business emails to his client folder. As he anticipated, the email from Yamani was there. For the first time since this whole thing started, he knew what Yamani was going to do. He chuckled as he opened it.

Mr. Reinholdt,

I hope you are having a pleasant evening. You looked relaxed when I was there earlier. I believe when you look at what I sent you, you will recognize yourself in the window of your kitchen, getting a drink of water. You have a beautiful home and grounds, but your security is lax at best. I had no trouble accessing your property undetected. I just wanted you to be aware of the problem with your security. Perhaps you should consider making some changes. And by the way, Mr. Reinholdt, I will be contacting you concerning some communications problems I am encountering and some expansion work I wish to have done.

I wish you a good night.

Edgar clicked on the attachments and looked at the pictures Yamani sent him. The kitchen was the only shot that had him in it. He had done a great job of pretending not to see Yamani. The other shots of the house showed nothing more than the side he was on. He spent time scrutinizing the picture of the office side to make sure there was no evidence of the camera. To his relief, there was not.

"Well, Yamani, I got you this time."

Edgar forwarded the pictures to the group and to Tom and then went to bed.

Chapter Forty-One

The keys sounded in the door and Laura sat up straight and put the book at her side. The woman had already been there and wouldn't return for several hours. The door opened and a man wearing a guard uniform walked in.

"Miss Darmer," he said as he came to stand directly in front of her.

"Yes."

"I was wondering how you were doing."

"I'm fine."

"I hope you are not lonely."

"Why would I be?"

"With the Chosen One away, I just thought you may need someone."

"I'm fine."

He walked even closer to her towering over her. Then he sat in down front of her.

"You know, I can help make your stay very pleasant."

"No thank you."

He raised his hand and brought it close to her face, in an effort to stroke her cheek. Laura grabbed his hand and pushed it away.

"I said, no thank you," she said forcefully.

"Yes, I heard you. I also know all about American women. When they say no, they really mean yes." He laughed as he brought his face close to hers trying to kiss her. Laura brought both hands up and pushed his face away.

"I'm not like most American women," she said emphatically. "When I say no, I mean it."

The guard continued laughing and edged closer still.

"Playing, what is the expression, hard to get? I like that. It is amusing."

Suddenly his smile gave way to anger. He grabbed Laura's wrists and pushed her back on the pillows.

"Miss Darmer, do not even try to stop me," he said gritting his teeth. "I am not as patient as the Chosen One."

Laura struggled against him. She tried to maneuver her legs in order to kick him, but he held both of her wrists with his one hand very tightly. He reached his other hand back and slapped her across the face. Laura screamed.

"Shut up! I am warning you, Miss Darmer, I will get what I want…one way or another."

He grabbed her dress and ripped it, revealing her naked body. His eyes glazed and he smiled as he looked at her. He licked his lips and breathed deeply.

"No wonder the Chosen One spends so much time with you. It is unfair that he keeps you all to himself. With you there is no sharing, not like the others. But then they were not as beautiful as you. I will enjoy this."

Laura pulled her leg back and kicked him with all her force in his groin. He fell back in pain. She grabbed her dress and tried to cover herself.

"Stay away from me, you son-of-a-bitch!" she screamed. "Stay away!"

He crawled closer to her, stood up, and took his clothes off.

She scrambled to her feet and ran to the door. She raised her fist to pound on the door and Ahmed grabbed her hair and pulled her. Laura fell to her knees and Ahmed dragged her across the floor. He threw her down against the pillows.

"No one is going to help you. Scream all you want. No one is here to hear you. I intend to have you, Miss Darmer. I will enjoy you and no one will ever know."

"He'll know. The Chosen One will know. You'll pay for what you do. He'll see to it."

"He will not believe you. You are nothing to him. You are just another little nobody. I have known him for many years. I am his closest one, the one he trusts more than anyone else. Now you will please me," he said as he put the knife close to her face, "or I will do to you what he has done to the others and no one will come to your rescue. No one will hear your screams but me."

He grabbed her dress, threw it, and came closer to her. Laura began screaming. He pulled back his arm and backhanded her across the face again. Then he reached, grabbed her by the hair, pulled her to her knees, and dragged her to the center of the floor. He jerked her head back and put the knife to her throat. He pressed the tip of the blade into her neck and watched as a drop of blood stained the blade. The very sight of her blood excited him. He thrived on the blood and the screams of the victims and it had been a long time since he was invited to share in such a delight.

"Now what, Miss Darmer," he snarled, "Maybe I should..." He pushed the knife and slowly made a searing bloody trail from the center of her neck to her pubic area. The blood oozed over his fingers and he smiled.

Laura screamed in pain. The door opened and a single shot was fired. The guard fell to the floor directly in front of her and her blood formed a pool at his head.

Laura screamed again and sat back shaking, tears welling in her eyes. Within seconds, two men walked in, their eyes cast down to the ground, and carried the guard out. Sadik, the guard who usually manned the door, came into the room.

"Miss Darmer, I apologize. I felt ill. I asked him to take my place. He usually does for my break. I had no idea. I have sent for the woman. She will be here soon. I do apologize."

"Thank you," said Laura trying to make her voice sound as strong as possible.

She crawled back and sat against the wall, holding a pillow in front of her, fighting back the tears. She realized she wasn't prepared for what had happened. The thought of someone else trying to rape her never crossed her mind. She had prepared herself for Yamani and for no one else. She knew him…knew everything about him, but nothing about the others. She moved the pillow slightly and looked down at the bloody trail. She took a deep breath and felt more pain.

The door opened and the woman came in. She put her tray down.

"You can relax. I can assure you, no one will ever hurt you like that again while you are here," said the woman softly.

"Is he dead?"

"No, but when the Chosen One returns, he will wish he was. Let me help you," she said and when Laura removed the pillow she saw the blood running down her body.

The woman gently took the rag and cleaned off the wound. She applied pressure to try to stop the bleeding. She was not aware of the damage Ahmed had done. She bandaged Laura as well as she could with what she had.

"I have brought you something else to wear," she said "Let me help you."

"Thank you."

As the woman performed her duties, she talked to Laura, calming her. Laura took the opportunity to ask the woman questions about her relationship with the Chosen One. It had become evident to Laura that the woman indeed was his wife. Laura knew she didn't dare ask her how she felt about his activities with her. The woman and the guard on duty were the only ones she knew she could count on…the only ones who would come to her aid.

If that man felt that way how many more felt the same way? How many more would try. She couldn't believe what she was thinking. Was she actually wishing that Yamani would come back soon? He could control them. Even though her fate was in his hands, for some reason she knew she was safe from the rest of them when he was there.

"Your face, he hit you did he not," she said looking at the welts on her face.

"Yes," Laura said quietly, "twice."

"He has left marks," said the woman. "He hit you very hard."

"Yes."

"And your wrists," she said looking at each one. "There are marks as well."

"He was trying to get me to do what he wanted."

"It will not go well for him. I will be back with something for you to eat and some tea to calm you. I will bring something for your face and wrists and more bandages."

Laura sat back against the pillows. She tried to relax. Unscathed, she was trying to return to Michael unscathed. Now, she could feel such fear as she thought about what might happen. Keys sounded in the lock again and she froze. The guard came into the room.

"Please excuse me, Miss Darmer, I mean you no harm," said the guard noticing the look on her face. "There are two women here to clean up the room. Is it alright with you that they come in? I can assure you they will not bother you."

"Yes."

"I will be right outside the door."

"Thank you."

The women entered and went to work cleaning up after Ahmed. They said nothing the entire time they were there and the guard checked on their progress several times. By the time they had finished with the room, the woman was back. She brought lunch for Laura along with ice for her face and the ointment and bandages as promised.

Michael, Mark, and Gwen sat quietly in the living room. They found that Michael would relax if someone was with him.

"I know this is going to sound absurd," said Michael, "but I almost wish Yamani was back with Laura."

"Why would you wish that?" asked Gwen putting down her book.

"I know what he's capable of doing and I know how to somewhat control him and keep him on an even keel. It's the others in his organization I worry about," he said. "There are several who'd like nothing more than to usurp his power."

"Does Yamani know that?" asked Mark.

"He'd have to be stupid not to know there are some in his ranks who'd like to take his place."

"So why does that worry you?" asked Mark.

"If they could get something over on him, they'd try it when he wasn't there," said Michael, "and Laura would be a prime target."

"Why Laura?" asked Mark.

"They know how much he values her and how much she pleases him. I can bet you anything he's not sharing her with them the way he shared the other women he used."

"How do you know he hasn't as you put it shared her?" asked Gwen.

"Just by the way he treats her and talks about her. She's much too beautiful and too valuable."

"If she's too valuable, why would they use her?" asked Gwen.

"Doing something to her would be the ultimate way of getting back at him. She'd never tell. She'd be too afraid of what he'd do to her, if he knew she'd been spoiled by one of them."

Tom Richardson walked out of the studio and into his office. There was a knock on the door.

"Come in," he said.

"Tom, this just came for you by special messenger," said Linda when she walked in. She handed him a package.

"Thanks."

Tom took a look at the return address and smiled when he saw the name. He opened the package and took out all of the packing material. He pulled out an object and unwrapped it. Clipped to the front was a note.

Tom,

Thought you might like a copy before it hits the stands. Enjoy. Let me know how you like it.

Hal

Tom unclipped the paper from the cover. There in front of his face, big as life were Yamani and Bin Laden with the headline...Where Are They Now?

Tom smiled as he looked through the pages. This was so good. He sat down, sent off an email, and waited for the phone to ring.

"What took you so long?" asked Tom when he picked up the phone.

"Hey Tom how'd you know it was me?" asked Mark.

"Let's just say, I had a hunch."

"What's going on?"

"I have a birthday present to get to you."

"I'm busy right now. Can I send Maggie for it?"

"Sure. Just tell her to come to my office."

"Is it bigger than a bread box?"

"I'm not telling you. You'll see it when you get it. Let me know if you like it."

As soon as he hung up the phone, Tom went out to the copy room and copied the cover along with the articles. When he came back to his office he looked around and found a book of appropriate size. He put the pages inside the back of the book. He quickly wrote a note and clipped it inside the front cover, wrapped the book in paper and then put it into a box. He wrapped the box in Christmas paper and made a bow out of the same paper. He took another square of the paper cut to size, folded it in half, and wrote a short note.

Within the hour, Maggie was standing in the reception area waiting for Tom. When he came out, she looked at him and smiled.

"Hi, Maggie," he said.

"Hi, Tom. You have a gift for Mark?"

"It's right here. I'm so glad you were able to come and get it. I want him to have it for his birthday."

"I'll make sure he gets it. Still using Christmas paper, I see."

"You know it. What would a gift from me be without my signature paper?"

"He's going to love it."

"I know he will."

Chapter Forty-Two

Mark closed the front door and walked into the dining room. He turned the package over in his hands and smiled.

"What is that?" asked Michael pointing to the package.

"My birthday gift from Tom," said Mark sitting down at the table.

"It's not your birthday and that's Christmas Paper," said Gwen.

"I know."

Mark put the package on the table, opened the card, and read it aloud.

Dear Mark,

Hope you have a Happy Birthday. I looked all over and finally found this. I know that you've been asking for it. Make sure you read it from cover to cover. Enjoy. Let me know how you like it.

Tom

Mark unwrapped the box and opened it. He took out the other wrapped object and unwrapped it.

"You asked for that book?" asked Gwen.

"No. But there has to be a really good reason to send it," said Mark. He opened the cover and read the attached note.

When this is all over, I'd like to have my book back. The real "gift" is in the back.

Mark closed the book and opened it from the back.

Thought you might like to see this before it hits the stands. It blew me away.

Mark unclipped the paper, smiled, and turned it for everyone to see.

"Oh my God...it's really happening," said Gwen getting up out of her seat.

As Mark laid out the pages one right after the other on the table, the rest of them got up from their seats and came around to that side. There before their eyes unfolded an article complete with pictures...the history of two men. The most striking pages being those that said "Then and Now."

"It's amazing. That's him," said Michael. "That computer generated picture looks as though they took his actual picture."

"There'll be no freedom to move once this hits the stands," said Mark.

There was silence in the room as they read the article. Only after everyone was finished did anyone speak.

"This is unbelievable," said Raquel. "Tom's friend did an absolutely awesome job."   "A website for reporting sightings," said Robert. "Can you believe it? I can't wait to see what they have on it."

"They're planning on giving updates in the subsequent articles," said Gina.

"My favorite thing is that this will also be aired on television," said Monique, "and you know it's going to be all over the internet."

"Talk about creating an international buzz," said Pierre. "Mark, this was a great idea."

"It's everything we asked for and more," said Mark. "I don't know what I expected, but this is way, way better."

"Well, Yamani, let's see what you do when this hits the streets," said Gina.

The woman knelt beside Laura, her face filled with concern. She dipped the rag in the water, wrung it out, and gently placed it on Laura's forehead. She had been there tending to Laura for hours trying to get the fever to break.

"Try to drink a little," she said quietly. She helped Laura lift her head.

Laura took a sip of the tea. Her head was pounding and her skin felt like it was on fire. She felt so weak, so sick.

"Please try to relax," said the woman. "I need to check the wound."

Laura lay back against the pillows. The woman lifted the gown and removed the bandages. She had seen enough wounds to know Laura's was infected. She also knew she needed to take measures immediately to stop it from going further.

The woman got up and went to the door and knocked. The guard let her out and within minutes she was back with another tray. She placed it on the floor and knelt down again. She opened three jars and carefully added some of each to the water. She took a clean rag and wet it.

"I know this is going to hurt," she said quietly, "but it must be done if you are to get well."

Laura nodded and turned her face away from the woman. She closed her eyes and braced herself the best she could. The woman tried to be as gentle as possible and Laura tried her best not to move. Several times she asked the woman to stop just for a few minutes…just so she could catch her breath. The pain was so intense that Laura became nauseated and began vomiting. The woman stopped, rewet the rag from Laura's forehead and put it on the back of her neck.

"I'm so sorry," Laura whispered.

"There is no need to be sorry," said the woman calmly. "This is not easy for you. You are sick and it hurts."

The woman gently washed her face and pulled her hair back. She repositioned the pillows and helped Laura get as comfortable as possible.

"All I am going to do now is dry it. Then I will put on some medicine. I promise it will not burn at all. Then I want to make sure it is well covered. It may feel like it is really thick, but I want to make sure it stays clean. We are going to change those bandages every few hours."

The woman kept her word and during this part of the process, Laura was much more comfortable.

"Would you like more tea?"

"No thank you," said Laura.

"Try to rest now. I will clean up. Maybe you can sleep a little. I promise I will be close by. If you need me, just call for Sadik and he will get me. I will be back in a little while to check on you."

Laura moved slightly getting a little more comfortable and closed her eyes. Before the woman finished cleaning up, Laura was asleep.

Chapter Forty-Three

Tom sat back in his chair looking at the cover of the magazine. He knew it hit the stands today and he wanted to call Hal to tell him what a great job he had done, but there would be time for that later. He knew it was only a matter of time now. He opened the bottom drawer of his desk and carefully removed a folder from under all of the old half-filled moldy coffee cups. It was the perfect spot for anything he wanted to make sure no one would find. He opened the folder and looked at a picture of Laura.

"It won't be long now. Soon, everything will be ready and I'll come to get you as I promised."

He closed the folder and put it back in its place. If this magazine article worked as they hoped, Yamani would have to release her soon.

"Hey Tom, sorry to interrupt," said Tony sticking his head through the door opening.

"Not a problem, Tony, what do you need?"

"Oh, I see you have a copy. I thought it might be a good idea if you used this on your morning drive tomorrow."

"In what way?"

"I don't know. Some sort of contest. Something to actively get the listeners involved. This is big, Tom, big. It's getting play on all the news stations. It's the hottest issue around. Wherever these two guys are, they better stay put, because the entire world's going to be looking for them."

"I know. I wouldn't want to be them."

"You'll do it?"

"Are we going to do it every week?" asked Tom.

"As long as the series runs," said Tony. "Whoever thought of this idea was a genius."

"Let's get the staff together and see what we can come up with. Let's do it throughout the day and get all our listeners involved."

The door to the apartment opened and closed with a bang. A breathless Dabir entered and stood in front of Yamani.

"With all due respect, sir, we have trouble," he said.

"Calm yourself, Dabir," said Yamani and he put his fingers to his lips. Once he could see Dabir had calmed a little, he said, "Now, tell me what this is all about."

"This," he said as he handed a copy of the magazine to Yamani.

Yamani looked at the cover and his expression changed.

"Where did you get this?"

"At the newsstand. I saw it and instantly thought it looked like you. Then I opened it and saw the other pictures and there you were right there in magazine. They are asking people for any information about you. They want to capture you. I passed the electronics store and you are on the television and they're asking for everyone to look for you."

"How did this happen?" asked Yamani.

"I do not know," said Dabir. "It is a series. There will be others."

"I cannot get stuck here. I cannot get caught," said Yamani half to himself. "There is too much at stake. How close are we to having everything?"

"Very close. A few more days."

"I cannot wait. I cannot risk it."

"We will send it to you as soon as we have it," said Dabir. "We must get you out of here."

"Get in touch with our contacts and arrange it," said Yamani.

"Yes, sir."

"And Dabir, you must be very careful. We cannot afford anyone to intercept our messages. No one. Do you understand?"

"Yes, sir."

"Turn on the television."

When Dabir did, the face of Yamani was staring right at them. It was a nightmare coming to life. What was of the utmost importance was getting back to camp and ensuring that Miss Darmer and his wife were safe.

"It's hit the stands!" shouted Jean as he walked in the door waving a copy.

"It's all over the news, too," said Pierre.

"He has to be in a panic to get back," said Gina.

"Let's hope so," said Michael. "He's going to have to move quickly."

"He can't fly," said Pierre. "Even with a fake passport, they're going to recognize him."

"He'll go back through the underground," said Jean. "It'll take him a few days, but he'll make it as long as no one intercepts one of his messengers."

"If I knew exactly where Laura was, I'd pay to have him intercepted right now," said Michael.

"They'll get him, Michael," said Gina. "Someone will see him and turn him in."

"It won't surprise me if it's one of his own who does it," said Michael.

"You really think one of his own would turn him in?" asked Angelique.

"Yes. That's what worries me," said Michael. "I want him to release Laura before someone finds him."

Gwen put her hands on his shoulders. "We're all ready for this, Michael. Everything is in place and ready to go. He's going to be desperate. He has no one else he can deal with. We've made certain of that."

"I know," said Michael reaching back up to touch her hands. "But I also know I won't stop worrying until Laura is back here, safe."

"What if something goes wrong?" asked Gina.

"We've thought out everything very carefully," said Paul. "We've looked at it from every angle."

"Even from the angle that one of his own might turn him in?" asked Gina.

"Perhaps not from that angle," said Mark. "Unfortunately, we can't do anything to get her out of there. We have to trust Yamani with that."

"Can we trust him?" asked Gwen.

"He kept his word with Laura, down to the minutest detail," said Michael. "No matter what he has done, the one thing about Yamani is that when he gives his word, he delivers. Good or bad, he delivers."

Laura sat back against the pillows. She remembered dozing in and out of sleep, but was too tired and weak to stay awake. She had no concept of the amount of time she slept. Now she felt decently rested.

She ran her hands through her hair. It felt stringy. She pulled some in front of her face to smell it and it reeked from vomit. Next she put her hand on her forehead. It felt much cooler and as she moved her hand to check her cheek, she could tell it was still swollen and tender. She moved her hand down and followed the trail of the wound Ahmed made. It was well padded.

Laura heard the key in the lock and froze. The door opened and the woman came in.

"You're finally awake," she said smiling. "How are you feeling?"

"Much better," said Laura smiling back.

"I brought you some tea. You need to drink something."

"Thank you," said Laura as she accepted the cup and took a sip. "Mmm, that's good."

"Would you like something to eat?"

"Yes, I am hungry."

The woman gave Laura a piece of bread. She broke off a piece and tried to chew it, but the pain was excruciating.

"I will make something you will be able to eat," said the woman and she got up and left the room. A short time later she was back with a bowl and a spoon. She handed it to Laura. "This is something my grandmother would give us when we were sick, or had a toothache."

Laura took a spoonful. It was warm, sweet, and delicious. While Laura ate, the woman went to gather everything she needed to bathe her and take care of her wound. By the time she returned, Laura had finished eating and drinking her tea. Sadik helped the woman bring everything in and set it down near Laura.

"I am glad to see you are feeling a little better," he said.

"Thank you," said Laura smiling.

Sadik left the room and locked the door behind him. Then the woman proceeded to help Laura bathe.

"This looks much better," said the woman taking off the bandages. It is going to take a long time for this to heal, so we are going to be extra careful with it." She gently bathed it with the special mixture she made. Then she dried it and bandaged it again and helped Laura into another gown. "If you would like more tea, I can bring you some."

"I'd like some, thank you."

The woman went to the door and knocked and Sadik came in and helped her carry the tray out.

Laura picked up a book, opened it, and began to read.

Chapter Forty-Four

Yamani couldn't believe what he was seeing. It was his whole life playing out before him. Everything he had done coming back like a bad dream. How would he be able to explain all of this to the followers? They had known him all this time as the Chosen One. What would happen if they found out he was Yamani. What if they found out he was the man who was hunted all these years for the torture and killing of all those people. He closed his eyes and leaned back in the chair. He used to do this years ago when things were about to get out of control. Somehow he'd be able to think more clearly and discover a way in which to get out of whatever predicament he found himself in.

This was different. There was no one above him he could blame for the way things were. There was no one directly below him either. He had done this as a safeguard so no one would ever think of usurping his authority…and yet there were those in his ranks who were trying.

Now, it could all crumble away. He thought about the stories he'd told about his rise to being the Chosen One. How would they fit into what was happening? Would he be able to make his followers believe him and not what was being printed and said? There was only one way. He had to address them. No matter what the costs, he had to somehow be able to reach them all. He knew he needed what Dabir and the others were working on. He needed it desperately…not in a few days, but now. He hoped they'd be able to deliver and it'd be everything he needed it to be. If not, he'd need what only Mr. Reinholdt could give him. He knew in order to get it he'd have to promise he'd release Miss Darmer.

for Love and Ransom

After all, Mr. Reinholdt was a businessman and being a businessman would want guarantees. He must be able to think clearly. Everything must once again be calculated down to the minute. He knew he couldn't jeopardize everything he had built by appearing in public. He knew he was going to have to trust those closest to him.

"Dabir," he shouted. "I need paper and a pen."

"Yes, sir." Dabir disappeared into another room and came back carrying paper on a clip board and a pen. "Here you are, sir."

"Thank you. Now, if you would be so kind as to leave me, I need to make some plans and do not wish to be disturbed."

"Yes, sir."

"And Dabir, I will need to see you in an hour. Only you."

"Yes, sir."

Once Dabir had left Yamani got up, closed his door, and locked it. He then logged onto the computer.

Tom Richards worked with the station webmaster, designing a game to go along with the magazine story. They went through numerous ideas, but nothing seemed to be what they wanted. Doug, the late afternoon DJ walked in.

"Tom, your computer's having fits," he said pointing down the hall to Tom's office. "You have an urgent message or something."

"Thanks," said Tom getting up.

"Hey, before you go," said Doug, "do you remember 'Where's Waldo?' I thought we might do Where's Bin Laden."

"Now, that's what I call an idea," said Tom as he hurried out of the room. "I can see the billboards now. Work on that while I'm gone."

Tom sat down at his computer, put in his password and opened the email.

Mr. Richards,
Meet Me. It is Urgent!
Tom logged on.
I'm here.
Good. Mr. Richards, things have changed drastically. I need you to go to Paris immediately.

Is Laura alright?

I give you my word that she is fine. Recent developments are forcing me to move up my timetable. I must know that you are close enough to me to be able to receive Miss Darmer within a short period of time. I made a promise to Miss Darmer that she would be returned alive and I intend to keep that promise.

Yes, sir, I understand that. You're a man of your word. What's happened to make the move imperative?

Let us suffice to say that my enemies would like nothing more than to see me fail and if that happens, if they get that close to me, I will not be able to guarantee Miss Darmer's safety.

Yes, sir.

When will you be able to leave?

I'll have to notify my boss and make arrangements. I can do that immediately. Can you wait?

I will wait. This is very important, Mr. Richards. I cannot stress that enough.

I understand, sir. I'll be back as soon as possible.

Tom turned in his chair. The door opened to his office.

"Tom, Doug said you had an urgent message," said Jim.

"Yes, sir, I have. I need to leave. I don't know how long I'll be gone. He wants me in Paris to be closer."

"When's the next flight?"

"I was just about to check that." Tom pulled up the page for reservations and put in the information. Within seconds he had a list. "The first one leaves in three hours."

"Is there room on the flight?"

"I'm checking that now," said Tom. "Ever notice how slow a computer moves when you're in a hurry?"

"Yes," said Jim. "I swear my computer does it just to aggravate me."

Tom laughed. Finally the screen came up.

"There are several seats left for the flight," he said paging down.

"Book it and let's get you out of here. I'll get security."

"Thank you. I have a few messages to send."

"Do it quickly. You don't want to miss it."

Tom logged on again.

I'm here.

And?

I'll be in Paris in the morning.

Excellent. I will contact you and Mr. Braedon within the next few days. Will you be with him?

Yes, sir, I will.

Until then.

Tom copied all of the conversation and placed it in the folder. He hesitated a few minutes and then decided to put the folder on a flash drive to take with him. He didn't want to be in Paris and need to refer to something and not be able to access it.

He made some quick notes on the Where's Waldo aspect of the show and his morning drive. He knew when things started to get hectic the show would be the last thing on his mind.

He yelled for Doug as he started packing a carry-on bag for the flight. He jammed it with as many essentials as he thought he'd need.

"Hey, what's going on," said Doug as he hurried into the office.

"I have to leave," said Tom. "You doing my show?"

"Who else!" said Doug.

"Here's a few notes," said Tom handing him the paper. "Email me."

"Will do," said Doug. "Be careful. Bring her home safe."

Tom just smiled and sat down at the computer one last time.

George walked into the living room as soon as the email alert popped up from Tom. He had been working in the dining room so he could watch for anything that might come over the internet. Michael was insistent that someone be there all the time.

"Michael," he said, "it's Tom. He wants you to meet him in the chat room,"

Michael got up from the couch and walked as hurriedly as he possibly could into the dining room. He sat at the computer and logged in.

Yes, Tom.

Sorry for the short notice. I've heard from him and I'm leaving for Paris on the next flight. I'll be arriving in the morning.

Is he releasing her?

Not yet, he wants me closer so I can be there within a few hours. He said things have developed and he may need to make plans to move her soon.

I look forward to having you here.
See you soon.

"He's running scared," said Michael turning to face the others. "He knows someone in his ranks might just turn him in. I know it."

"He has every right to be concerned," said Robert. "Every time I check out the website, something new has been added. There's a reward being offered, in fact, two; one for information that leads to the arrest of Bin Laden and Yamani and the other for the actual physical turning over of them. Guess which one is worth more."

"The one where you physically turn him in?" asked George.

"There're a couple of his men who'd do it," said Michael. "There was no love lost between some of them and Yamani. I think he knows it. I can think of at least two who'd do it in an instant, if the reward was high enough."

"Oh, it's getting there. The reward money is growing every time I look," said Robert. "The magazine started by offering a reward of twenty-five thousand dollars for each and individual citizens and businesses are adding to it."

"What are they up to?" asked Gina leaning in closer to get a better view.

"Take a look," said Robert after he pulled up the screen.

"Someone wants Yamani badly," said Gina.

"There were millions of people who have millions of reasons," said Henri.

"He has to get back if he intends to have total control of the situation," said Pierre.

"Even then," said Michael, "he may not have total control. It's going to depend upon how much his followers believe of what's printed."

"At any rate, it has to be a good sign that he sent for Tom," said Gwen.

"I know one thing for sure," said Michael. "I'll feel much better with him here. Please make sure his room's ready. I want him to stay here."

"The situation may have just made Laura more trouble to keep than she's worth," said Jacques.

Yamani was sitting in his chair when Dabir returned. For the past hour, he had been writing down things that needed to be attended to before anyone found out any more about him. All he could hope was that those in his camp hadn't had access to the story. That, he knew, probably wasn't the case. It was important now to think as clearly as possible.

"You wished to speak to me?" said Dabir quietly when he came in.

"Yes, please sit down." Yamani looked calmly at Dabir. "There are those in the organization who have been blinded by greed and power. They want nothing more than to take my place. They will turn me over to anyone who will believe them that I have at one time done wrong things. I believe, Dabir, that you are a faithful follower. Am I right in my belief?"

"Oh yes, sir. I would never betray you. You are the Chosen One. Many make up stories to discredit someone they envy. When I read the magazine, I knew that was what had happened. I knew they had somehow made up an elaborate story to make you look like an evil man. They do not know you as I do. They do not know how kind you are and how intelligent you are. They have no idea why you were chosen. I know the Divine One has smiled on you and knows you are meant to be his Chosen One."

"Thank you Dabir, I knew you were faithful. That is the message I must deliver to my followers and when I do, they will be more passionate than ever. They will be made to see the truth, to see that our enemies are all around us. They will know that everything I have done, I was instructed to do by the Power Greater than All."

"Yes, sir, they will. They will understand. They will know and see and you will triumph even if there is a time of adversity. You have been through adversity before and you know how to persevere and how to be triumphant. I, sir, will always be at your side."

Yamani smiled. He wished he had the confidence of Dabir. He wished all of his followers would see the exposé as something that was contrived to make him look bad, but he knew better. He knew this was the golden opportunity for all those who had ever crossed his path to finally have their revenge. It was coming and he knew it. There were only three paths. The first would lead him to become a stronger force in the world, because his followers would see the enemy as attacking their Chosen One. The second would lead to his immediate death. The third would lead him to conduct a holy war to end all holy wars. While the first would be his preference, he somehow knew it wouldn't be so.

"Dabir, the path may not be an easy one. With everything that is happening, we may have no alternative but to defend our position in order that the message may be spread."

"One would hope there would not be such dissention within the ranks of the followers that it would become necessary to fight such a war, especially among our own."

"Ah, yes, Dabir, one would certainly hope, however, the annals of history are filled with stories of just such events."

"Why would this happen now, sir, when we are on the verge of making such progress? Only a little more time and you will be able to bring the message to everyone."

"Yes, Dabir. We may still have time, however, we will have to work quickly and with great assuredness."

"We should have everything within days."

"Yes, but every day that passes does such damage to the Cause, to the mission, that we may not be able to save everyone. If too much time goes by, we may lose much."

"Sir, let us hope we are able to move quickly."

"If those here are unable to deliver the completed design, I will have no alternative but to make a deal. It is that which I must plan with the utmost of care. Dabir, you must be my eyes and ears here. You must alert me if anything strange happens with the others who are here working on the project. They must not get careless, must not take chances. They must remain unwavering. You must assure them that they are most important.

"Anything you ask, I will do."

Chapter Forty-Five

It was a very weary and worried Yamani that arrived at the camp. The trip from Frankfurt was anything but conventional and the time it took could've been better spent on damage control. If any good could possibly have come out of the inconvenience, it was the extraordinary amount of time he had to think.

Any normal person would've committed choices to paper. Yamani knew something of that nature could spell certain death. If his plans or even his thoughts were intercepted by the enemy, they could spell disaster. He knew even though he might fail in this attempt, he needed to make sure he survived. He was still young enough and healthy enough in his estimation to become the invisible force behind a figure head. He had seen others do it. He knew he could duplicate what they did without the mistakes.

His worry was the present. He needed to control the situation now. It was imperative that he knew who he could count on, who was loyal. He wasn't so naïve to think that everyone in his camp saw things as he did and would sacrifice themselves to save him. He knew there were those who were just waiting to take over. Now wasn't the time to have to fight them. There were so many other formidable people now who'd want to see the end of him as well as the end of his mission.

Yamani sat back on the chair in his office and took a deep breath. He could hear voices in the hallway and knew the beginning of the end was about to start. He longed to talk to his wife and Miss Darmer, but he knew those two pleasures would have to wait. A knock on the door brought him back to reality.

"Come in," he said.

"Sir, if I may," said Sadik humbly. "I would like to talk to you."

"Certainly, Sadik. You know you always have my ear."

"Sir, it is about an incident that happened when you were away."

"What sort of incident?"

"It involved Miss Darmer."

"Miss Darmer? What was it?"

"I was feeling ill and needed to relieve myself and I asked Ahmed if he would mind taking watch for a few minutes. He said he would. I was not gone that long. When I returned, I heard Miss Darmer screaming and immediately sent Qadir for the woman. I hurried down the hall to the room and pushed open the door. He had disrobed and was holding Miss Darmer by her hair. He was holding a bloody knife. She was struggling. I raised my gun and fired at him. He fell to the floor. I did not kill him, only wounded him. Miss Darmer had welts across her face where he hit her and on her wrists from where he had held her. He had ripped her clothes off her and she was cut from her throat to her private area. The woman arrived immediately and cared for her. I had Ahmed removed and taken to a cell. Two other women came and cleaned the room."

"Why did you not kill him?"

"I knew that it was not for me to decide his punishment, but it was for you and you alone to make that decision."

"You are indeed my faithful one."

"Yes, sir, I am."

"When did this happen?"

"The third day you were away, sir."

"I see. How is Miss Darmer, now?"

"Sir, I do not know about her injuries. I know she was ill for some days and the woman has noticed she is very fearful every time the door opens. She relaxes when she sees either me or the woman. I think she is going to feel safer now that you have returned."

"I will make sure I see her soon, but I would like to see the woman and then we will go and pay a visit to Ahmed. He is going to wish you had killed him."

for Love and Ransom

Tom sat in front of the computer checking his emails. Although he had been in Paris three days, there was nothing that had to be answered. The station knew he wasn't to be disturbed. The fan mail would have to wait. There was no way he was going to tie up his computer answering messages that had nothing to do with Laura. Just out of curiosity, he opened an email from one of his loyal listeners who emailed him regularly.

Just hoping you're feeling better. I know how difficult it is to have to have emergency surgery. Even though they have said you'll have to have additional surgeries and may be out for a while, I hope you have a speedy recovery.

Lady Jane

Tom shook his head. He opened a few more and the sentiments were basically the same.

"What's wrong, Tom?" asked Gina.

"The station came up with the reason for my time off the air. It seems I've had emergency surgery and may have to have additional surgeries. I wonder what I have."

"Well, you'll have to find out when you go back," she said laughing. "I do hope you get well."

"Me, too. I doubt when this is over anyone will remember I was sick."

"I think Lady Jane might," said Gina looking at the screen. "Have you ever met her?"

"No. I have no idea who she is," said Tom.

"Don't you even want to know who she is?"

"In radio you meet a lot of crazy people."

For the next hour, Gina listened as Tom told her the stories about some of the listeners he had met. They talked about some of the crazy things people do just to win tickets to see their favorite stars or tickets to a Steelers or Pens game.

He pulled up the station's website to show her the new game they were sponsoring. You could click on either Bin Laden's name or Yamani's name and a screen would come up with hundreds of pictures. If you clicked on the right picture a little animated character would pop up and dance and a new page would appear where you could register to win a prize. All day long the station gave clues about where Bin Laden or Yamani were that day. They would choose a random caller and ask the question: "Where Are They Now!"

"That is so great!" said Gina. "Who came up with the idea?"

"Doug, our late afternoon guy. I love it. Those who are the winners in these contests are going to compete for a cruise the week after the last magazine hits the street."

"What are they going to make them do?"

"They'll have to go all over Pittsburgh trying to collect all of the newsmakers and the one who collects them all and returns to the station first will win."

"That's going to be a lot of fun."

Tom clicked out of the website and pulled up a map of Baghdad. He did this every day. This time, he imagined where Yamani could possibly change the rendezvous point to if something unforeseen happened. He started writing down possibilities and figuring out how to get around the city and out of it with the least number of turns possible.

Several hours passed and the stack of plain paper beside him was filled with notes. He leaned back in his chair and put his hands over his face. *Dear God, what if something goes wrong? How am I going to make sure I can get her out safely? I promised her.*

"You seem to be struggling over something," said Michael as he stood beside Tom.

"I'm trying to think of every route possible and every rendezvous place possible."

"Tom, you're going to drive yourself crazy. You know as well as I do, it's only in Yamani's control."

"If I was sure it was under his control, I wouldn't worry."

"What have you done so far?" asked Michael pulling up a chair.

"I picked places I've already seen and found other places that were near to the original rendezvous points. Then I looked at all the possible ways of getting out of the city from them," he said picking up the stack of papers.

"By the time you find what you're looking for, you may have already passed up your turn. We need to make that workable. That's the map?"

"Yah, from the airport to the city. Then this is the city," said Tom scrolling down the page.

"Okay then, let's get that stuff organized."

Before long, Michael and Tom had all of the directions typed into the computer complete with the appropriate maps. Then they were printed and the route highlighted.

"What we need now is just something to put them in and a way to find them quickly," said Tom.

"I have an idea," said Michael. "Mark, could you get some of those colored tabs that we use at the office? They're in my top right desk drawer."

"Sure."

Mark was back in a few minutes with tabs of every color made.

"Thanks."

When they were finished, the project fit neatly into Tom's passport case.

"You have no idea how much better I feel," said Tom.

"Yes I do. I can see it on your face."

The woman entered Yamani's office and stood inside the door.

"Close the door," he said to the guard. "I do not wish to be disturbed."

"Yes, sir."

The guard closed the door and once the woman was sure that he was away from the door, she addressed Yamani.

"How may I be of assistance to you, sir?"

Yamani came around the desk, walked over to her, and put his arms around her.

"I have missed you."

"I have missed you, also. It has been very lonely without you."

"Things are not good, Maranissa, not good at all."

"What is the problem, my love?"

"They are searching for me. They want to try me for some of my past actions."

"What are we going to do?"

Yamani touched her cheek.

"I am going to have to send you away. I want you to be safe. I do not want anything to happen to you because of the things I have done."

"But I feel safest when I am near you."

"I know that, my love, but I must insist we take more precautions."

"What about Miss Darmer?" asked Maranissa. "What is going to happen to her?"

"She is my key to getting what I need," said Yamani. "Once I have it, I will let her go. I have already taken steps for that."

"She is a very nice woman," said Maranissa with sternness in her voice that one would never use him. "I do not want to see her hurt anymore."

"Maranissa, I give you my word I will do everything possible to make certain she is returned safely."

"You have heard about what happened when you were away."

"I have and I will deal with Ahmed soon. I want to know how Miss Darmer is."

"She is much better. The swelling is going down in her face, even though it is discolored. The welts on her wrists have all but disappeared. The wound is healing slowly, but it is healing now. She was very sick for several days and it was infected, but I worked hard to clear it up. I am doing the very best I can. I think she will breathe a sigh of relief now that you have returned."

"I may not be able to visit her this day. I have much to attend to. Please tell her I have returned and I will see her in the morning." He kissed her gently and stroked her cheek. "I will see you later."

She smiled at him as he walked her to the door. Once she had disappeared through the door at the end of the hall, Yamani called for Sadik.

The door rattled as it opened. Ahmed sat on the floor. He looked up as Yamani entered.

"Stand up when I come into your cell," Yamani commanded.

Ahmed remained on his mat.

"Stand up!" he yelled.

"No!" Ahmed yelled back.

"You refuse the Chosen One?" Yamani said sternly.

Ahmed spat on the ground. Yamani nodded to the guards. They walked over to Ahmed, grabbed him by the arms and pulled him to his feet. He nodded again and the guard hit Ahmed in the ribs with the butt of the gun.

"You are not the Chosen One," said Ahmed gasping. "You are nothing more than a criminal, a wanted man. I have read what was written. I have seen your pictures."

"I am the Chosen One, regardless of what has been written. The Divine One does not care about the past. He cares about the strength of character and the conviction to the Cause. And you, Ahmed, you…the Divine One knows you have not been faithful. You have not heeded my rules. You have hurt Miss Darmer. You have damaged her. I have an agreement with Mr. Braedon and you have jeopardized our agreement. You have jeopardized the Cause." Yamani nodded and the guard struck Ahmed on the backs of the legs.

Ahmed spat on the ground a second time. "I care nothing for your Cause. A Cause by which you get rich and the rest of us stay poor. What is that? Is that the Cause? You will find there are those of us who will no longer take your orders. We have had our eyes opened. We know you are a fraud. You are not the Chosen One. You have lied to us!"

Yamani backhanded him across the face then nodded again and the guard rammed the butt of the gun into Ahmed's stomach.

"No matter what you do to me, I will never believe you," Ahmed gasped.

"Ah Ahmed, you are so closed minded as to not see the ploy of those who want the world rid of us. They will do anything to cause dissention in our ranks. And you…you believe them. You are not the man I thought you were."

"I have had my eyes opened," snarled Ahmed. "I know the truth."

"Ah, that may excuse the manner in which you are speaking to me now, but it does not explain the way you betrayed me when I was gone. You betrayed my trust long before you read any of this. Did you not Ahmed?"

"I do not know what you are saying."

"Ahmed, you went against my orders. You tried to rape Ms. Darmer and you would have succeeded if you had not been stopped. Is that not correct?"

"She's nothing. She deserves everything she gets."

Yamani backhanded Ahmed across the face again. "That was inexcusable. You disobeyed my orders that she be left alone."

"I know what you did with her. You wanted her all to yourself," said Ahmed, blood oozing from the corner of his mouth. "You did not share her like you did the others. She is one of them. She does not deserve special treatment."

"In your eyes no…in mine, she is worth more than you can ever imagine," said Yamani getting close to Ahmed's face. "You have no idea what she will get for us. Miss Darmer is part of a deal that will mean total success for the Cause…a deal that you may well have destroyed by your actions. And for what! For what, Ahmed!" he said pulling away and raising his voice. "For your pleasure! You will never do it again. You will never betray me."

"Betray you!" Ahmed screamed. "You have lied to every one of us. It is you who have betrayed us! And I have not been quiet. I have told everyone and they believe me!"

"Who are they, Ahmed?" said Yamani glaring at him. "Who are those who believe you?"

"I will never tell you. You will have to kill me to stop me," said Ahmed and he paused before he continued, "Yamani." The name came out of his mouth as though it was something distasteful. Ahmed laughed for a moment and then continued. "But, that is what you are good at, is it not? That is what you did all of your life. You killed those who spoke against you; killed those who stood in your way. Then you acted like the coward you are and hid. That is it, Yamani, kill me and then go hide."

Yamani nodded again. The guard rammed the gun butt into Ahmed's stomach. He doubled over, his head hitting the ground.

Yamani grabbed his hair and pulled his head up to look at him. "I am not ready to kill you…yet. You will learn to fear what you made Miss Darmer fear. You will fear every time you hear the keys in the lock. You will never know what will happen to you when you hear them and you will never know when."

Yamani cracked Ahmed's head against the ground, turned and walked out of the cell.

Chapter Forty-Six

Michael sat on the couch looking at the books on the coffee table. He picked them up one by one and looked at the titles. Ever since Yamani shared the news that he had bought Laura the books, he read avidly through the books he had never read before. There had to be a reason why she chose those titles. As he held them again he read the jackets to see if something would spark an idea. He knew *The Arabian Nights* had been a favorite of theirs, but what was the connection with the others. They had never read those or even talked about them. Still, Laura very rarely did something frivolous, especially when the situation was serious and this was about as serious a situation as there was. Her life depended upon this team being able to discover the message she was trying to send. What did he have? How did it all fit together?

"Need some help?" asked Tom as he took a seat in a chair opposite Michael.

"I've been looking at these books and reading them; trying to find a common thread; trying to find out why Laura would have asked for them."

"Do you think they're connected?"

"At first I thought they were connected in some way, but they are so diverse I've been hard pressed to find even one thing that appears in all of them."

"First of all, they are all connected," said Tom. "Laura chose them. That's the connection. It may well be the only connection. Now, look at each one as a piece of a puzzle, you know, one of those children's puzzles with the big pieces that are very simple to put together because they each contain a big piece of the picture."

Tom picked up *The Arabian Nights*. "What is this one about?"

"That one's about the story of how a woman whose husband wanted to kill her, but she stayed alive day after day by telling a story and leaving it unfinished. It's one of our favorites. I think she chose it to feel close to me."

Tom picked up *Muhammad.* "What about this one."

"The author of that book tries to get to Muhammad the man, the prophet. She takes away all of the bias and talks about how he received the word of God in a cave and was told to bring the religion back to the true religion of Abraham, of the prophets."

"Now, that one is Yamani. Think about it. That's how he became the Chosen One. Now this is one I read a long time ago, *How to Win Friends and Influence People*."

"Then you know it's about how to deal with people, no matter who they are," said Michael. "It's the key to getting people to do exactly what you want them to do."

Michael picked up the next book. "Now, this one, *Think and Grow Rich* is about having the right mindset to accomplish anything you want and possess anything you want. It's about thinking positively."

"That's a message for all of us to never give up hope," said Tom. She obviously hasn't." said Tom.

"If nothing else, I enjoyed reading the mystery book, *The Cat Who Dropped a Bombshell*. This was the next to the last in a series, but she chose this one," said Michael. "The key here is bombshell. Is it something unexpected or a launched missile?"

"Or both," said Tom. "It was really unexpected when Yamani took control of the missiles. Maybe he's planning to do it again. Is it possible he would've confided in her?"

"He used to tell me things that were really pertinent at the time because I couldn't tell anyone."

"He could be planning on using the missiles again. Let's face it. It may well be the only way to keep from being captured," said Tom.

"Could he hold an entire area hostage while he does what he wants?"

"That's something only Edgar can answer."

"Then we need to get to Edgar and find out."

"What about the last book, *How I Write*?" asked Tom.

"I think that was just something Laura wanted to read," said Michael offhandedly. He was still contemplating the idea of Yamani with the missiles. "Let's forget about the last book. It was just added in as a decoy of sorts, not for us, but for Yamani."

"Okay," said Tom.

Michael took a piece of paper and drew out a simple square diagram with five pieces, four outside and one in the middle. In each of the four border pieces he put the name of one of the books, *Arabian Nights, Muhammad, Think and Grow Rich, How to Win Friends.* In the center piece he wrote *...Dropped a Bombshell.* The he turned the paper to show Tom.

Tom looked at the paper and then Michael turned it again and under *Arabian Nights* wrote *Michael*, under *Muhammad* wrote *Yamani*, under *Think and Grow Rich,* wrote *has possession*, under *How to Win Friends* wrote *can control*, and under *...Dropped a Bombshell* wrote *missiles*.

"Are the two of you quite finished with the books?" asked Robert as he walked in the room.

"Yes, we are," said Michael. "I think I'd like to talk to Edgar before he hears from Yamani."

"Why?" asked Robert.

"How many missiles do you think are at Yamani's fingertips?" asked Michael putting his hands together in front of his face.

"Hundreds, maybe thousands," said Robert.

"Could he hold a whole area hostage if he wanted to?" asked Michael.

"That, I don't know," said Robert. "It depends upon whether or not he's able to control them."

Michael picked up *The Cat Who Dropped a Bombshell* for Robert to see and then turned and showed him the hand drawn puzzle diagram.

"I think he can."

Edgar sat at his desk leafing through some papers. He jumped when he heard the phone ring. Then he sat back down in his chair and took a deep breath.

"Yes."

"Edgar, Michael Braedon. How are you today?"

"Just a bit jumpy. I was getting ready to run the sequence again."

"Look, Edgar, you know that sequence and can run it in your sleep."

"Now, Michael, I'm sure you didn't call to find out how I'm doing."

"No, I didn't."

Michael reiterated the conversation that he and Tom had concerning the missiles. He asked Edgar about the extensiveness of Yamani's power concerning the missiles under his control. By the time they had finished discussing the problem Michael was more concerned than he had been. His conversation with Edgar did nothing to calm his fears, rather it heightened them.

"Well, were you right?" asked Robert when Michael walked back into the room.

Michael sat down in the chair opposite him. "He said Yamani has access to literally thousands of missiles and not only inside the borders of Iraq. With the knowledge he has acquired, he can command and control them from the comfort of his command center."

"What does that mean exactly?" asked Robert. "Why is that of such concern?"

"He doesn't have to wait for what Edgar gives him to be deadly. He has the capability," said Michael. "What's to stop him from launching missiles before Laura's released. What if the situation becomes so volatile it's out of his control and he can't ensure her safety?"

"I think you're ahead of yourself just a little," said Tom. "He's moving towards releasing her and we've seen no evidence he's going to escalate any activity."

"He never puts all his cards on the table. Every action is thoroughly thought out in his head. Nothing is written down," said Michael. "Even when I spoke to him, he wrote nothing down. He took in everything I said, thought about it, decided whether to do it or not and when he was ready, acted without any warning whatsoever."

"But he hasn't fired any missiles for a long time," said Robert. "That may not even be important to him right now."

"Oh, it's important alright," said Michael, "and the fact that he hasn't fired them lately doesn't matter. He knows how. He spent a great deal of time learning how and perfecting everything. The longer he's inactive, the more time he has had to think."

"Now you know Edgar can control that," said Robert trying to ease the tension. "He has before."

"Edgar is controlling things after the fact," said Michael. "He has no idea what Yamani's going to do next. Even if he did know, he can't take control of everything in Yamani's world. He can't take away a country's right to defend itself, no matter how good the cause may be or how grave the danger."

"That'll change once he delivers SecReSAC," said Tom.

"Providing Yamani only goes through that system," said Michael. "Nothing will change with what he's already able to do. Right now, Yamani acts and Edgar does damage control and that could continue even after he delivers SecReSAC."

"Look, Michael, Edgar says what he's giving them is extremely enticing," said Robert. "From what I've seen, I'd want to use it. It's going to take him from reasonable accuracy to pinpoint accuracy."

"Terrific," said Michael sarcastically, "that makes me feel so much better."

"Yes, but only if Edgar allows it," said Robert.

"And if he doesn't," said Michael, "Yamani can always return to what he knows will work and use that. Now where does that leave us?"

Robert didn't say anything. He knew Michael was right. There was no guarantee that Yamani would use SecReSAC even once he got it. Then again he might use only what he wanted…what was easy. He knew there were those who would bypass something really great just to stay with the familiar.

"You think Laura knew this?" said Robert.

"Oh, yes I do," said Michael. "I think he felt confident in telling her because she had no way of telling us his plan."

"But she did," said Tom.

"And without him being the wiser," said Michael.

Robert shook his head and smiled. "Something as innocent as book titles."

"Along with Tom's idea of a child's puzzle," said Michael looking at the diagram again.

Well, Mr. Reinholdt, it is almost time. I hope you have everything together you need. I know you are an intelligent man and I have no doubt you know what I am interested in gaining from you. You will give it to me, because you know that Miss Darmer's life depends upon your cooperation...as does your own wife's. I am not concerned with your increase in security. You, above all people, should know that I get what I want. I always have and now is not an exception. No amount of security will keep your wife safe in your home if you decide not to heed my instructions implicitly.

Mr. Reinholdt, I could have taken her any time she was in Paris...any time she was with friends. Perhaps you will recognize those times. She photographs very well. Soon I will have a gallery just of your wife. And maybe, Mr. Reinholdt, someday I will get the chance to meet her and enjoy her company as I do Miss Darmer's.

Ah, but back to the very matter. You know what I expect, Mr. Reinholdt, and you know the consequences of disappointing me. Many people will be going to bed at night feeling safe and secure only to have their world shaken before the sun comes up. You will see it Mr. Reinholdt and you will know you caused it.

Edgar clicked on the attachments and saw pictures of his wife at the various meetings she attended in Paris. He sat in front of the computer screen unable to move. He suddenly felt ill. There it was spelled out in front of him, everything he knew and lived with as well as Michael's fears…right there on the screen. Yamani was no fool and anyone who deemed him to be, grossly underestimated the man's ability to make anyone do his bidding. Edgar was confident in SecReSAC, the real one as well as its new and greatly modified version. No one, but he, knew exactly what the real SecReSAC could do, they only knew bits and pieces. What they knew was enough to know it could make any man a formidable adversary against an entire army. The new SecReSAC could do that also, except with one minor twist.

"Listen, Edgar," he said to the reflection in the computer screen. "You know this will work, you've had the answer for weeks. It's a good plan. You've run it so much you can do it in your sleep. Relax and wait. It's going to be fine."

Words did little to convince him.

Chapter Forty-Seven

Yamani sat in front of his computer. It was finally there, the part he needed. He knew he had made the right decisions and taken the right steps by surrounding himself with those who were such experts when it came to technology.

He knew how important all of this was and could envision how great his power would ultimately be. This was the only way to counter all of the media claims that were being used against him. Not doing so would be like fighting a war with spears when your opponent could slaughter you with every modern weapon known to man.

Now if his staff could only understand this new program and quickly get it implemented, he could then address all of them, all of his faithful followers. Somehow he had to convince them that what they were reading was just a plot to make them turn on him.

"Sadik," he yelled.

"Yes, sir," said Sadik coming into the office.

"I need to speak to Qadir, immediately."

"Yes, sir."

Sadik closed the door and Yamani could hear his footsteps fading quickly. He reached and opened the bottom drawer of his desk and took out several sheets of paper. He had written some notes when he was in Frankfurt. He had been able to think clearly then. Once they were written he had committed them to memory and destroyed the papers before he left. He knew how important it was to remember everything, so he reconstructed those notes along with other things he had decided during his trip back.

Several of the issues had already commanded his attention. He had not thought, or rather had not wanted to think, there would've been a traitor in his midst. He wondered how many more would follow Ahmed. How many more believed as he did. It was one thing to have those outside his camp question and distrust him, but for those in his camp to do it was unacceptable. It was important now to address as many people as possible. Qadir must be able to interpret the codes and diagrams and get them to work.

"Come in," said Yamani when he heard the knock.

Qadir entered. "You asked to see me, sir?"

"Yes, please close the door," he said and waited until he had Qadir's full attention before continuing. "I have received the codes and diagrams to the plan from our contacts in Frankfurt. It is extremely important that this plan be put into action immediately. There are those who are trying to put an end to the Cause. T

hey are telling lies about me and about who we are. We cannot allow them to succeed. I must be able to address my followers. I must be able to tell them what the truth is."

"Yes, sir."

"Most of the work is in this envelope. It was completed while I was with them. It is only the last two parts that were missing and they finished those while I was traveling. When I asked them how long it would take to put the plan into action, they told me around four days. I do not have four days, Qadir. With every passing moment, more lies are being told about us. The Cause is in grave danger."

"Sir, without looking at the plan and studying it, I cannot tell you how long it will take, but I promise you that we will work on this twenty-four hours a day until we have it ready."

"I knew I could count on you. You are faithful to me."

Yamani watched as Qadir left and then began writing. Every time he addressed his followers, he always took the time to carefully think out what he wanted to say. He knew from his past how important it was to select just the right words. This was one time caution was in order. Everything from what he had to say to how he said it needed to be orchestrated.

Laura still froze when the keys sounded in the door. There was so much more activity going on than there usually had been. She wondered what was happening. When the woman walked in, Laura smiled.

"Miss Darmer, I have a message from the Chosen One. He has returned and sends his apologies that he is unable to come to see you today. There is much he must take care of."

"I'm glad he has returned."

"I told him you probably would be glad he was back. He has also been told about Ahmed and what he has done. The Chosen One has promised to deal with him."

"Are you glad he's back?"

"Oh, yes, I am. I am very glad. I feel safer with him near."

"There's much more activity today than there has been."

"Now that the Chosen One is back, there is much to do. He must speak to all of his followers. He must remind them to stay true to the Cause, to stay strong no matter what."

"Has something happened?"

"There are those who are spreading lies, trying to discredit him. Some of the followers have even begun to believe the rumors."

"That has to be very disappointing for the Chosen One. From our conversations, it seems the Chosen One only has his followers' best interest at heart. I can't imagine someone wanting to betray him."

"I imagine everyone has their price," said the woman sadly. "Some of them have a thirst for power."

"What about you? How do you feel about those who aren't faithful?"

"I do not understand. They are causing so much trouble. I may have to leave him soon and go somewhere where it is safe."

"Why wouldn't it be safe for you here?"

"Those who want the power might try to get to him through me."

"In all the time we've talked, I've never asked your name. I'd like to know it, if you're allowed to tell me."

The woman smiled at her. "My name is Maranissa."

"That's a beautiful name," said Laura smiling back at her.

"Have you finished your books, yet?"

"I'm almost finished with the last one. I saved the mystery for last. It makes me smile. Would you like to read it?"

"I would have to ask the Chosen One first. He is very particular about what we read."

"I understand. If he says yes, then you're most welcome to read any of the books I have."

"Thank you, Miss Darmer."

"It's Laura."

Yamani kept good on his word to Ahmed. When the keys rattled, Ahmed never knew who was on the other end. That same silence that tortured the other souls that found themselves to be Yamani's prisoners also tortured Ahmed. This time when the door opened it was Yamani who walked into Ahmed's cell. He walked to the center of the cell and towered over him.

There was no doubt in Ahmed's mind that Yamani was going to make an example of him the same way he had done to many others in the past.

"Perhaps if I understood why you did it, Ahmed," said Yamani in a sickening sweet tone, "it would go easier for you."

"Understood! You are incapable of understanding!" said Ahmed with hatred in his voice that Yamani never experienced from him. "You have only one goal in sight and that is what is best for Yamani, is it not?"

"And how are you so sure who I am?" asked Yamani calmly.

"I saw the pictures. They are you, are they not?"

"I saw no pictures that looked like me," said Yamani opening his arms with the palms of his hands facing up. "I only saw what they wanted us to see, but that doesn't matter," he paused and looked down on Ahmed with a questioning look. "Why would you go against me, Ahmed? Why would you go against me by yourself?"

"By myself?" said Ahmed shaking his head. "You really think that I am the only man against you?"

"Well, are you not? I see no one else who is acting out against me."

Ahmed looked into Yamani's eyes and thought carefully before answering.

"They are afraid of you. They will act when everything is together."

Yamani watched Ahmed closely. He was trying to keep as calm as possible while questioning Ahmed. He needed information and he knew how to illicit it.

"Ah, Ahmed, I find that hard to believe," said Yamani turning and taking a few steps to the right. Ahmed's gaze followed him. "I want to hear it from them. Perhaps if you give me their names, I could at least have the chance to answer their concerns."

"Why start now? You never cared before."

"What harm could it do to have those few come here and talk?"

"Few!" Ahmed began to laugh. "Ah Yamani, you are sadly mistaken. There are more against you than there are for you."

"Really, Ahmed, maybe you should enlighten me with the names of those against me."

"It would be easier to name those who are still with you."

"Then name them Ahmed," said Yamani slapping his sword against his left hand. "Name them before I lose my patience."

Edgar Reinholdt's nerves were about as on edge as anyone's could be. He had retreated to his office, his haven. The communication from Yamani concerning his security had him wondering what he could possibly do to ensure his wife's safety while he was away from the house. He knew while she was working with her committee she wasn't thinking about the danger she was in even though she had read more than enough to know what was happening.

He sat watching the computer screen and waiting for the phone to ring with any type of news. When the phone in his office rang, he picked it up expecting to hear Mark's voice on the other end.

"Mr. Reinholdt, this is President Bartram."

"Yes, Mr. President, what can I do for you?"

"You gave us your word that you would take care of the situation with the missiles," said President Bartram with a tone that Edgar knew meant that he was running out of patience.

"I have done so, Mr. President," said Edgar sitting up straight in his chair. "Why do you sound so concerned?"

"Missiles have been fire inside Iraq again!" said President Bartram. "The government is not the perpetrator. I'm beginning to wonder if it's wise to allow this maniac to have the degree of freedom we're giving him.

"Mr. President, I understand your concern," said Edgar trying to calm him. "When did this happen?"

"I just finished talking to their government liaison. The strikes are getting closer to inhabited areas," said President Bartram. "To say they're nervous about this is an understatement."

"Mr. President, he's testing his ability to control the missiles. He's aiming for empty buildings, isn't he?"

"Yes, Mr. Reinholdt, but how can we be sure he won't move on to human targets? The leaders want assurances. They do not want to be blindsided!"

"Mr. President, his targets will change only if he doesn't get his way."

"Mr. Reinholdt, that's our concern exactly. How are you going to know when that time comes? How are we going to be able to prepare if we just sit here on our hands?"

"Mr. President, with all due respect, I'm carefully monitoring him. Remember, I can stop whatever he intends to do. I have no desire for there to be bloodshed at my expense," said Edgar emphatically.

"Mr. Reinholdt, you better be certain," said President Bartram as sternly as possible without crossing the lines of diplomacy. "We cannot afford to make any type of mistake with this. We would hate to take this out of your hands. Do we understand each other?"

Edgar Reinholdt recognized an infusion of Prime Minister Honomito's viewpoint in President Bartram's words. He knew they were waiting for him to admit that he had lost control of the situation so they could charge in and take control regardless of the cost. Edgar had no intention of giving in.

"Explicitly, Mr. President," said Edgar, his tone changing. "You can be assured that I'll be on top of things."

"Mr. Reinholdt, we want this resolved…quickly."

"I understand, Mr. President," said Edgar as cordially as possible. "Please convey my confidence to the other leaders. Tell them they may contact me at any time with their concerns and I'll address them immediately."

Edgar sat up, took the remote in his hand and turned on the television. He watched as they showed the pictures of the demolished buildings, followed by a map that pinpointed the locations of the strikes. To the untrained eye, it would seem the strikes had no rhyme or reason. To him, however, he could tell Yamani was spreading his wings to see just how much he could control and how far he could control them. That meant only one thing and he was ready. All he had to do was wait to be contacted.

Yamani pulled up to a building more than five miles away from his camp. No one would ever notice the pipe coming out of the ground housing wires and cables bringing much needed electricity, telephone, and internet from the city to the building. He got out of the vehicle and walked to the building.

Qadir opened the door to admit him. The room was filled with electronic equipment. This had been a dream and Yamani had seen it to its realization. Everything he could possibly need or want was in this room, accessible only to him and those chosen by him. The time was quickly approaching when everything they had been training for would be put into practice. Soon they'd know if the time spent in Reinholdt's complexes would pay off.

"Everything has arrived from Halim," said Qadir gesturing around the room.

"He is a man of his word," said Yamani. "Does it all work?"

"Oh, yes, sir, everything is set up and operational. Let me show you."

Qadir walked Yamani through a simplistic version of what was actually happening. It was enough for Yamani to understand the sheer enormity of what was about to take place. On the wall, Qadir's team had hung a map of the world. There were arrows drawn radiating from the central point which was the camp. Yamani could see where the arrows continued in seemingly limitless lines, while others seemed to stop dead at random points.

"Why do some of the arrows stop?" asked Yamani pointing to various areas on the map.

"Sir, for one reason or another, terrain, other electronic interference, blocks put into place by countries trying to keep other from accessing their computers. Once we have the other, main program, the arrows will continue," said Qadir reassuring him.

"This is far better than I could have hoped," said Yamani smiling. "Are we able as before to take over all transmissions without being detected?"

"Oh yes, sir. Even if we are detected, there is nothing they can do to stop us and more importantly, there is no way to trace the transmissions back to us," said Qadir.

"Very good, Qadir. How much longer will it be until I am able to use this system?"

"It is ready now, sir. All you have to do is give the command and we will begin."

The two proceeded through a door into another room. On the wall was the insignia that identified every member of the sect. There was a desk and chair as well as other office furnishings. All information regarding the mission and the Cause was within the confines of this building. It was Yamani's way of safeguarding everything from anyone who might want to challenge his authority and bring destruction to what he had built. It was now time to try to undo everything that had been done by the media.

He walked around the desk and sat in the chair. There was no fancy recording equipment, just the basics. For him, the important information was in the message and delivering the message did not require any type of entertainment. They had come to know the Chosen One as a man who could speak about any and all subjects intelligently and without any notes.

"Sir, do not say anything until we give you the signal to begin speaking. We must make sure that we are connected to all of the stations."

"Yes, Qadir."

D. A. Walters

Yamani waited patiently for Qadir's signal. Within minutes all was in order and with the pointing of a finger, Yamani was live to millions of people.

"My faithful ones, those who have been chosen and those who will soon be added to the chosen ones, I have come to assure you that all is well. I have seen what has been printed and what has been televised. As they have admitted in print, they have used the aid of a computer to make a man who disappeared in the 1980's, who was a close advisor of the Ayatollah, look like I do. Why? You ask. Why would they do such a thing? What reason could they have? Ah my faithful ones, there is good reason. Every day, our numbers are growing, not only because of me, but because of you. People are becoming disenchanted with those who wish to rule this world in a manner that does not follow the true teachings. They long for a life where they can feel fulfilled and appreciated."

"Every minute of every day, someone asks about us. Every minute of every day, someone wants to join us. For every person who joins us, another has left them. Soon, our ranks will have more members than any other organization in the world. That is what scares them. There are those who do not want you to be happy. They do not want you to fulfill your destiny. They want you only to be their slaves; to work for their glory, not for the glory of the Divine One. Their god is your money, your time, your sweat, and your blood. They are nothing more than parasites living off of the lifeblood of others. And so they seek to put an end to us, put an end to our Cause, and put an end to me."

"The magazine articles, the stories on the television and the internet, the pictures in the newspapers, the rewards offered are all their doing to discredit the one chosen to lead our Cause. They have made up lies, taken one man's life, made it even more evil than before and have given it to another man. I am not the man they speak of. I could not commit such atrocities and live within the teachings. If they can do this to me, what is to say that they will not begin doing this to others? Anyone who stands in their way will not be safe. They will turn them into someone to be hunted; someone to be feared; someone to be eliminated, annihilated, and disposed of like garbage."

He paused for a moment to let his words sink in. He knew the importance of hitting that emotional chord.

"We cannot let them succeed. We must all work to keep the Cause alive and growing. That is the only way to win against them. You must never turn your back on us and the Cause, for if you do, I cannot be responsible for your immortal souls. Those who refuse to believe will be dealt with in the harshest of manners when the end time comes. For if you do not believe, you will lose your immortal soul. Why should the Divine One, giver of all, bestow upon a non-believer the gift of an immortal soul? For them the end will come amidst much pain and anguish."

"We must be strong during this time of adversity. We must show them that we will not go away, in fact, we will grow in numbers because of their attacks. Do not fall for their vicious lies and empty promises. Carry the message of the Cause to all people. They will soon see they have no other choice than the true way."

Yamani signaled Qadir that he was finished. He waited patiently for Qadir's signal that they were off the air.

"Now, we get busy," said Yamani.

With that, he left the studio and walked to his vehicle. Qadir was close behind. Yamani turned to him.

"Keep trying to expand our coverage. It's time for me to acquire the final piece. I'll see you back at camp later."

Chapter Forty-Eight

Laura knew by the manner in which the keys turned in the door that Yamani was on the other side. Her heart started beating faster when he entered the room. He stopped just inside the door and waited for Sadik to close it. Once they were alone he came to stand just over her.

"I want to apologize for the actions of Ahmed. Please know he was not acting on my orders. I have spoken to him at length about his actions."

"Thank you, sir."

"So, Miss Darmer, I trust that aside from that incident, you were well taken care of in my absence?"

"Yes, sir, very well taken care of. Thank you for your concern."

"Miss Darmer, I have told you and Mr. Braedon that I have no intention of harming you unless someone does not live up to their end of the agreement."

"Yes, sir."

"The end is quickly approaching, Miss Darmer. This is a most critical time. Everything must work within the confines of a very limited time frame. If they do not do as I say, I will have no other choice…" he paused and changed his focus. "What do you think the chances are of Mr. Braedon convincing Mr. Reinholdt to give me what I want?"

"I believe that Mr. Braedon will convince Mr. Reinholdt to give you what you ask for. I worry, sir, about the time constraints."

"Why is that Miss Darmer?"

"I know that when I have to do something and I'm being timed, I sometimes make mistakes out of nervousness and sometimes just can't seem to get everything done on time and am a few minutes late."

"What does that have to do with the situation?"

"I was just thinking about Mr. Reinholdt. Whatever you want must be very important and if it's that important, then it must be in an area of maximum security. That means Mr. Reinholdt probably has to go through multiple security checkpoints both in and out. They may involve specific codes, all different. That combined with the nervousness of the situation may cause him to be late. All I'm asking is that the time be reasonable."

"Miss Darmer, I am a reasonable man. I will not ask someone else to do something that I would not be able to do myself. I am not doing this to try to make them fail. I want what he has. I am putting on the time constraints so that they do not delay in getting me what I so desperately need. Others are putting the real constraints on me."

"I'm not sure I understand."

"Let us just say that there are those individuals who would like to see me disappear. They want to see all of my work and efforts fail," Yamani was ready to expound on that thought, but stopped. "But enough of all this," he said gently. "I did not come to upset you. I came to reassure you that no one will harm you because I am back. I want you to relax. We may not have the luxury of being able to spend very much time together. So right now, I want you to put all of your worries aside and I will do the same and we will enjoy each other's company."

Yamani moved closer to her and lifted her gown over her head. He gently removed the bandages that covered the wound and studied carefully the handiwork of Ahmed. He traced it with his fingers from beginning to end. Then he gently lowered her and her hair swept up and fanned out on the pillow. She watched him as he took everything off. She was becoming a master of being able to replace him with Michael without his knowledge.

"Relax," Yamani whispered. "Relax and enjoy. This is a night you will never forget."

Laura knew it was useless to fight the feelings. She knew the consequences all too well. Each time he came wanting her, she watched him put his knife just outside his reach. It was the constant reminder of what would happen if she disappointed him in any way. She had those visions emblazoned in her mind.

Today was no different. She listened intently to every direction she was given and never once gave him cause to believe that she was not enjoying their time together. When he was finished, Laura made no effort to move. She stayed in position and waited for him to speak.

It seemed like an eternity before he moved or said a word. Laura stayed motionless, afraid any movement might set him off in the wrong way. She knew all too well the dire importance of cooperation, of doing exactly what he wanted or expected. She could almost read his mind, almost tell what he wanted. She knew she had done it tonight. She hoped he'd remember all she had done for him. She needed every edge she could get so he'd ease the constraints for the exchange. So far, she'd managed to stay alive, had managed not to insight his wrath. She knew the end was coming quickly, but this was the most crucial time. If something didn't go the way it should, she knew Yamani would come back to her and not only would she suffer, but all those who loved her would suffer also. She was his pawn, his trump card. He was counting on Michael's love for her to get him what he wanted.

Yamani reached to gently kiss her and then got up and dressed.

"Miss Darmer, you have done well tonight," he said with a smile on his face.

"Thank you, sir," she said politely. "May I get dressed?"

"Yes, Miss Darmer, I want you to be comfortable. I know you will not forget this evening and all we did together. You will never forget how much you enjoyed being with me. I could see it in your face. I will be sure to tell Mr. Braedon how much you have done for me, in detail if need be. I am positive he will want you home as quickly as possible. I hope, for your sake, no one needs any persuasion to get for me all I need and desire. Although I am a very patient man, my patience wears when I have much to attend to. As much as I would love to spend more time with you, I am afraid it may not be possible. I will send the woman to you until it becomes too dangerous for her to do so."

"Why would it be dangerous for her? I don't understand."

"Those who want me may decide to take her in order to get to me," said Yamani quietly, stopping to make his voice sound as strong as possible, "and I could not stand to think of anyone hurting her in any way."

"I understand that," said Laura, her voice showing a compassion for his situation. "I know what it feels like to watch someone you love hurting."

"I know you do."

"What are you going to do with her?"

"Send her away with someone I know I can trust."

"What if she's recognized?"

"I have to hope and pray she is not."

Laura thought for a moment before she spoke.

"Sir, if I may offer an observation. People know her because of the way she looks when she's dressed the way she always is. I know this would possibly be against your teachings, but for the sake of her safety, couldn't you permit a disguise of sorts?"

"Explain."

"What if she was to dress in a more modern way, hair styled and uncovered or covered lightly with a scarf and make-up? You know, so she'll blend in with the rest of the people."

"Miss Darmer," he said shaking his head. "I will really have to think about that."

"I understand. Remember, the only other person who will know will be the one you've trusted to escort her into hiding."

"I will have to think about it."

"It's a good idea," she said trying to convince him. The last thing she wanted was for anything to happen to Maranissa.

"I promise Miss Darmer, I will consider it," he said kissing her on the cheek. "Now, I will leave you. I have more to attend to."

Yamani yelled for the guard and the door opened.

Michael sat in his dining room at the table. His mind was definitely not on the conversation taking place. Instead, he could see it all so clearly...all that was happening to Laura. He knew beyond a doubt Yamani had violated her again. He knew she had gone along with him and in his heart knew why. It was just so hard for him to think of another man touching her, of someone else being able to give her pleasure. His solace rested in the thought that she constantly thought about him, about them, during those times. He hoped he was right; prayed she wasn't falling for Yamani. He had read numerous accounts of victims who had grown to love their captors. Surely Yamani wouldn't have had enough time to do that. He knew Laura; knew she'd resist that with her whole being.

Then why did he have these feelings? Could it be she was pretending so well to like and respect him, she had almost crossed that line? One thing was for sure. This couldn't go on. She was frightened and he knew it. No matter how she looked on the outside, he knew she was terrified inside. That's why the feelings were there. They were an extension of hers.

"A penny for your thoughts," Gwen whispered as she put her hands on his shoulders.

"Not now," said Michael quietly, shaking his head and looking down. "Not now."

"Why not now?" she asked as she sat facing him.

"I'm just not sure," he said and paused for a moment. "I don't like what I'm thinking."

"Now, I know that there are only two people who cause you to think that hard, one's Laura and the other's Yamani. Which was it, or was it both?"

"Both."

"I see. And what do you think is happening."

"I don't know."

"Yes, you do," she said gently, "and it frightens you, doesn't it?"

"Oh, yes."

"You do have faith that Laura loves you."

"I don't doubt that for an instant," he said and then stopped. "I'm afraid he may make her start loving him."

"Oh, Michael," she said taking his hand, "that's never going to happen. Laura knows him, knows his tactics. She knows how to play him so he believes whatever she tells him or does."

"Yamani has ways of making you give him what he wants."

"I know that and I wouldn't be a good sister-in-law if I led you to believe otherwise. Your fears probably have basis in truth, but as far as Laura's love for you, that's unquestionable. Look where you are right now and then think about where you'd be right this minute without her love. She didn't do this to betray you. She did this to save you."

"I know that, Gwen."

"Michael, the mind can play horrible tricks on us. It can make us question everything we know to be true. It can also help us to figure out what we can do not to feel so helpless."

"Like what?"

"Well, you know now it's only a matter of time before Yamani contacts Edgar. Then there'll be a time limit to deliver and a specific amount of time when he'll try out the new program. When he is convinced that it works, he'll make the plans to release Laura. When you think about it, it's not that long a time. Have you thought about what you're going to do when you see her again?"

"Thousands of times."

"Anything special?"

"Oh yes. Everything has to be just right."

"And do you have everything?"

"No. I'm afraid of getting my hopes up."

"Alright it's time to stop that way of thinking and get ready for Laura's return. She's coming back and I wouldn't be surprised if she was here sometime during this next week. So you see Michael, you don't have much time to make everything perfect."

Gwen got up and walked to the other side of the table, took a piece of paper and a pen, and then put them in front of Michael.

"Make your list. I'll be back in a few minutes and we'll see what we can do with it."

She bent down and kissed him on the cheek.

Yamani knew that even though he had the power to make Edgar give him what he wanted, he needed to make certain that Michael exerted enough pressure on him to make him do so. He wanted to make certain that Michael made Edgar know with what urgency his request should be met. He knew exactly how to do it. He sat down at the computer in his office, got everything out of the drawer he needed, and began typing.

Michael looked up at the wall and saw the message from Yamani appear.

Mr. Braedon, meet me.

Michael logged onto the private site that Yamani had set up. He saw Yamani appear before his eyes.

"I trust everything is alright, sir," said Michael assuming the tone he always used when he spoke with the Chosen One. It was so easy for him to slip into that complacent manner that he did so without thinking.

"Everything is fine, Mr. Braedon," said Yamani. "I just wanted to tell you about the enjoyable time I had with Miss Darmer earlier this evening. Are you alone?"

"Yes, sir, I am," said Michael. That was a question that Yamani never asked before.

"Good, because I am not sure you would want everyone else knowing the details of our encounter."

"Thank you, sir, for being so considerate."

"Mr. Braedon, you and Miss Darmer are among the few who really know how compassionate and considerate I am."

"Yes, sir, but that's because we have personally witnessed your compassion and consideration."

"Yes, Mr. Braedon, you have; have you not," Yamani said rather contemplatively. "I promised Miss Darmer I was going to tell you how well she did tonight and how much she pleased me. It may well be the last time I will be able to enjoy Miss Darmer's company at length."

"Why is that, sir?"

"There have been some developments that may occupy my time more than I would like. But enough of that, Mr. Braedon. You know that I am enjoying Ms. Darmer's company so much more than I enjoyed yours."

"Really, sir."

"Oh, yes, Mr. Braedon," said Yamani with a smile on his face. "I am enjoying her so much more. She is a very beautiful woman, Mr. Braedon. You are a very lucky man."

"Yes, sir."

"Now, relax, Mr. Braedon, while I tell you my story."

Yamani began his story and repeated in detail everything that had gone on between him and Laura. With every detail, Michael's stomach churned. He wanted to lash out at Yamani, but knew he couldn't.

"So you see, Mr. Braedon, Miss Darmer will go to any lengths to please me."

"Yes, sir," said Michael trying to keep his voice at a level tone.

"Mr. Braedon, I want you to know that I shared her with no one. She is not like the others. I knew you would want to be certain that she was treated with respect and so I am the only one who has had her."

"Thank you, sir," said Michael. He could feel the anger growing inside him. He wanted this to be over. He knew he couldn't show Yamani how angry he was, nor could he speak against what Yamani had done.

"She enjoys being with me. As a matter of fact, she couldn't wait until I returned from my journey. Even the woman noticed that she relaxed once she found out I had returned, but enough of that, Mr. Braedon. Let me continue."

The story seemed to go on for hours and when Yamani finally finished, Michael searched for the right words and mustered all of the control he could find within himself.

"Sir, I want to thank you for taking care of her. My one fear was that she would spend so much time alone. I know how busy you are and it's such a comfort that you've been able to spend time with her."

Even though Michael's voice never cracked and his face showed no indication of his true feelings, Yamani knew he had made the impression he needed to make. He had thought about just how he would've felt if someone had his wife and what would make him respond and he did it to Michael.

"Well, Mr. Braedon, we are almost at the end of this ordeal. I am sure you are glad to know that. Once Mr. Reinholdt delivers what I am asking for and I find out it is the real thing, then I will make arrangements for Miss Darmer's release." Yamani paused to give greater emphasis to the next sentence. "If, however, anything should not be as I want it, Miss Darmer will suffer greatly and so will you, because you will watch. I will see to it."

"I understand, sir. I have great confidence all will go the way you want it," said Michael trying to reassure himself as well as Yamani.

"I am counting on you, Mr. Braedon to impress upon Mr. Reinholdt and all involved just how important it is to follow my orders explicitly. Any deviation at all will result in extreme pain for Miss Darmer. Do I make myself clear?"

"Yes, sir, abundantly clear."

Gwen returned to find Michael looking straight at the wall, fists clenched, tear stains on his face. She knew better than to say anything. She could tell that whatever had happened was something he'd never discuss with her. She quietly slipped out of the room and walked out to the patio.

"I'm sorry to interrupt you," she said.

"You need something?" asked Mark.

"Something's happened, I don't know what, but Michael's sitting in the dining room staring at the wall with his fists clenched and tear stains on his face. I left him alone to make a list of things he needed to get before Laura returned. I know this isn't because he was thinking about her. Something happened and I know by the look on his face he's not going to talk to me about it."

Mark got up from his chair, put his arms around his wife and kissed her. "You're the best, you know that?"

"You keep telling me that," she said smiling at him. "Now go see your brother."

Michael was in the exact position that Gwen had described. Mark sat in a chair facing him.

"Michael, what's going on?" asked Mark quietly. "What's happened? Talk to me."

For the first time since he talked to Yamani, Michael looked away from the wall. He looked at Mark. "Yamani raped her. That bastard raped her!" he yelled. "He told me. He gave me every little detail of what they did."

Mark suddenly felt nauseated. It was one thing to surmise what was going on and quite another to hear it.

"I don't need to ask you how you feel about that. It's written all over your face. What did he tell you? Talk to me."

Michael shook his head. "Mark, I've never told anyone the details of making love to Laura…just as you have never told anyone what goes on in your bedroom." He stopped to gain some control. "He told me everything. That fucking bastard! I can't repeat it."

"Michael, you know this is his way of making sure he can cause you as much pain as possible. He wanted to see your reaction."

"I gave him none," said Michael angrily through clenched teeth. He hit the table with his fist. "Oh, I wanted to. I was so angry, but I knew he wanted that."

"I bet he made it sound as though Laura enjoyed every moment of their being together."

"Oh, yah."

"You know that's not true. You know she'll do whatever she has to do to come back to you."

"I know that. I know he's threatened her. I know how he does it." Michael leaned forward towards his brother. His voice got really quiet and he spoke exactly. "He starts so subtly that it really sticks in your head and you just keep hearing him tell you what he's going to do and you'd do anything to keep him from torturing you. Then you hear him tell you how compassionate he can be provided you do what he wants."

"You know he's doing the same thing with her and she has done what she had to do. Just like you did," said Mark quietly. "You'd tell him whatever he needed to know in order not to be tortured by him. He never had to torture her once, because she already knew what he was capable of doing. Now she's doing anything to stay alive."

"I hate him, Mark. With all my being I hate him! I wish someday someone would do to him just a fraction of what he's done to others…and you have no idea how I really wish that person could be me."

"I think I do," said Mark. "You're not the only one of us who wants a piece of him."

Michael got up from his chair. He started walking around the room. He stopped when he got to the wall where Yamani appeared and turned and faced his brother again.

"What he's done to her is inhuman. It was calculating and aimed to destroy her emotionally. I mean look at me, Mark," he said as lifted his shirt. "You know what I looked like when I came home. My wounds are healing and when I look at myself in a little while, there won't be anything there to remind me. Hers are different. They're never going to go away."

"You're right, the physical will heal, but what you endured will always stay with you. What you choose to do with it is what makes the difference. The same will be true with Laura. She's tough, Michael. Don't count that out."

"I know she's tough, Mark," said Michael sitting back down. "No matter how tough she is, all I want to do is protect her."

"I know that...and you are. Everything you're doing here you're doing to protect her. Every time you talk to him," said Mark gesturing to the wall, "and give him the information he needs and the respect he demands, you're protecting her."

Michael looked down, picked up the pen and started playing with it. Mark quietly sat waiting for his brother to say something.

"He warned me," said Michael without looking up. "He said if we don't do everything he wants exactly as he tells us, Laura will suffer greatly and so will I because I'll be made to watch." He looked at his brother. "He said he'd make sure of it."

"Michael, every one of us knows what's expected. We've impressed upon Edgar that he's to do everything he's told to do within the time limits given. He's ready for that. Tom knows what has to be done. He's been through this before. No one's going to jeopardize her life or her well-being. We're nearing the end of this. The end is really in sight. All we have to do is be patient a little while longer and have trust in those who have to actually deal with Yamani."

"I want to call Edgar. I need to make sure. I need to tell him he has to do whatever Yamani wants," said Michael as he grabbed his brother's arm. He looked directly into Mark's eyes. "I need to do this. I can't take the chance, not with Laura's life."

Chapter Forty-Nine

After the conversation with Mark and Michael, Edgar sat with his head in his hands. He knew beyond a doubt it was now all up to him. He knew if Yamani went to the trouble of contacting Michael and telling him everything he and Laura did, it was only a matter of hours at most before he contacted him. As much as he needed to get a cup of coffee, he didn't dare leave his desk.

Edgar watched as the email from Yamani appeared.

Mr. Reinholdt,

I know you have been patiently waiting. Now is the time. You will deliver SecReSAC to me. If you do not, I cannot be responsible for the condition of Miss Darmer when she is returned. You will have a time schedule you must follow. You will have no time to contact anyone. I have my people watching you. If you deviate in the slightest, it will not go well for her. I advise you to keep your mind on what you have to do. You are to first click on the link below. There you will find detailed instructions waiting to be printed. Print one copy and only one copy. I spent a great deal of time going through everything and timing it. I have not guessed at anything except the amount of time it will take to get through the security section. As a favor to Miss Darmer, I added several minutes to the time in that area to make sure even someone who is nervous should be able to succeed. Remember, you must stay within the limits. For every minute you are late, Miss Darmer will suffer...greatly.

Just imagine if it was your lovely wife. Your time begins when you click the link. I will be in touch once I have SecReSAC in my hands.

Edgar took a deep breath and clicked the link on the bottom of the page. As soon as the new page appeared, he printed the copy as he read the screen. He knew Yamani wasn't lying about watching him. He knew how to get onto the property without being detected. As soon as the copy had printed, he left the house, not even taking the time to tell Gabrielle anything. The first few steps were straight forward. He knew how to drive to his complex and knew how long it would take to retrieve the information. As soon as he turned left out of his drive, he looked in his rear view mirror. It was obvious he was being followed. It was Yamani's way of letting him know that he was to do only what was on that page.

As he reached the access road to the complex, the car pulled to the side of the road. Edgar drove down the road and past the security guard at the gate. He parked the car and walked into building Number One. Erika was at her desk when he walked through the door.

"Good morning, Mr. Reinholdt. How are you this morning?"

"I'm fine. How are you?"

"Just wonderful. There are already messages for you to answer."

"I'll get to those when I return. Right now, I have some urgent business to attend to. Tell everyone I'll return their calls before the end of the day."

He continued walking down the corridor to the security section. He stopped only long enough to put in his code. Once the door opened, he walked through and hit the button to close it. At the end of the corridor, he turned right to go down another small hallway. There were doors on either side where high level security work was being done. As he passed several of the windows, he could see faces looking out at him. He knew at once that Yamani's contacts on the inside knew the plan. He kept his eyes straight ahead looking at the door and running the next sequence of numbers through his mind. He keyed them in and the door opened. Only four more to go before he was at his goal. The next four went easily. He knew all the practice had paid off. When he reached the room, he opened the safe where the files were kept. He put his case on the file cabinet and opened it. Then he opened the drawer and took out the folder marked SecReSAC, put it in his case and closed and locked the case. He closed the file drawer and reset the lock, walked out of the safe and continued through the course again resetting the codes as he went.

When he reached Erika's desk, he stopped momentarily.

"I'll be gone for a few hours. I'll take care of everything when I return."

"Yes, sir."

Edgar left the building and got into his car. He placed the case on the seat beside him and then drove up the access road. He turned left out of the road and the car at the top began following him again. He grabbed the directions from the visor and looked at the next steps. They seemed simple enough and he'd be able to keep on time provided there was no traffic. He was unsure why there were so many steps to this, but whatever the reason, Yamani's orders must be followed to the letter. He pulled up to the printing shop Yamani had used before. He walked in and went to the counter.

"May I help you, sir?"

"I need to scan three pages into a computer and email them."

"Certainly sir, you can use the equipment in the first office."

"What's the smallest block of time you can buy?"

"An hour."

"Alright I'll pay for an hour," said Edgar and handed the man his credit card.

"Thank you."

As soon as he got into the office, he closed and locked the door. He unlocked the briefcase and scanned the first, fifteenth, and last pages. Then he returned them immediately to his case and locked it. Next he proceeded to send off an email to Yamani. He loaded the files on his flash drive, deleted everything from the computer, and left. When he got into his car, he checked the time. He was ahead of schedule. His next stop was an office supply store to pick up a special envelope. He parked the car and locked it, went into the store and found the envelope. The lines at the check-out were long. He looked around and saw that no one was at the copy desk. He took out his wallet and made a copy of his license. Then he walked up to the copy desk and checked out.

When he came out of the store he looked over the parking lot and found the familiar car waiting a few spaces away from him. The driver had a good view of him. After he got into the car, he locked the doors, opened the case, took out the folder and blatantly put it into the envelope so that the driver could see what he was doing. He wanted there to be no mistake he was following the directions explicitly. He sealed the envelope as directed and put it back in the case and locked it once again. Then he looked at the time and the paper to find the next stop.

At the airport, as instructed, he parked in the short term lot and walked to the terminal. Once inside, he found the area where the customer information center was located. He looked up, read the signage, walked towards the right, and stood off to the side. Within minutes a tall dark haired man with a mustache walked up to him. He was dressed in a dark suit with a blue tie, just as the paper said he would. Edgar immediately recognized him as the man from the lobby in the hotel the day he and Michael checked in as well as the man who got the keycard.

"Mr. Reinholdt?"

"Yes, I'm Mr. Reinholdt."

"Sir, I am Mr. Wassum. I am the special courier in charge of transporting the documents."

"Yes, Mr. Wassum, may I please see some identification?"

"Of course, sir." Mr. Wassum took out his license and a card that was unmistakably from Yamani. As he did, Edgar saw the tattoo on his hand as well as the matching insignia on the card.

"Thank you. I wanted to make certain you were indeed the person."

"I totally understand, sir. I am so glad you could meet me here. It will help me a great deal. I will be able to take the next flight."

"It was no problem at all. Your company is such a good client. I hope this helps. Please let me know if there's anything else I can do for you," he said as he handed over the envelope to Mr. Wassum.

Mr. Wassum put the envelope in his own case and extended his hand to Edgar. "Thank you, sir. It was nice meeting you."

"It was nice meeting you also. I hope you have a good flight."

"Thank you."

Mr. Wassum turned and walked towards the gates and Edgar watched him for a minute or two. Then he walked back to his car. Even though he had delivered the package, the car still followed him back to his complex. Once he parked and walked to building Number One he turned and looked up the hill before he entered the building. The car was no longer visible. Edgar took a deep breath and went in with a smile on his face.

"Erika when you have everything together, I'll be ready to do whatever I have to."

"Yes, sir. There's quite a bit to take care of. I'll have everything together in about five minutes."

"That's fine. I'll be in my office when you're ready."

Once in his office, he logged on to his computer. As expected there was a message from Yamani.

Mr. Reinholdt,

My men tell me you have done a perfect job in getting the documents to the courier. I thank you for that and so does Miss Darmer. As promised, Miss Darmer will not be harmed. My courier tells me you delivered the item with time to spare. Congratulations. I'll be in touch once I check out the file.

Edgar sat at his desk. Automatically he saved the correspondence. Then he sent an email to Paris to let them know delivery had been made. Greatly relieved, he picked up the phone and called his wife.

The news that Edgar had delivered the SecReSAC plans was one more step in getting Laura back. The group was on an emotional roller coaster, but no one was experiencing the heights and depths as much as Michael. At times he did nothing more than pace the floor.

"Michael, Yamani made it clear he was going to check out what Edgar gave him," said Mark. "Then he'll be in touch with him once he checks out the file. He must be convinced he has the real thing."

"Is it good enough to pass?"

"Oh yes," said Henri. "He shared some of it with us. Yamani will be impressed. There are things Edgar put in the early stages that'll enable Yamani to do things he'd never be able to do without it. It depends upon how much he has to be impressed."

"Enough to make him feel powerful and safe," said Michael.

"Keeping safe may be a problem," said Tom as he entered the room.

"Now what?" asked Gwen.

"Someone's traced Yamani to Baghdad."

"How?" asked Margo.

"Someone claims to have seen him and took a nice picture of him. It's all over the internet," he said as he put the picture on the table.

"Quite a good shot of him," said Mark. "He's being careless."

"If people believe this picture is real and that Yamani might be in Baghdad, there'll be a number of those who consider themselves international bounty hunters who'll descend upon Baghdad to get him and collect the reward money," said Tom. "That's going to make things a little more difficult when it comes to getting Laura out. If they're able to track him from Baghdad to his camp before he's able to release Laura, we may have to find the camp in order to get her."

"That'd mean hiring someone to get in there and get her out," said Jacques. "It's a given none of us have the skills to do it."

"Do you really think Yamani will allow it to get to that point?" asked Nicole.

"Hire someone," said Michael taking a deep breath. "I wouldn't even know where to look."

for Love and Ransom

Chapter Fifty

Yamani sat at the table with his experts. They had been reading through the file that was sent. Qadir put the disk into the computer. Logistics appeared on the screen. He looked at what appeared and began working diligently.

"What are you doing, Qadir?" asked Yamani.

"With this, you will be able to command as many stations as you want. You will not need to have their addresses this program will get them for you. This is what you have wanted," said Qadir turning and smiling at Yamani. "It is a good thing we were able to get everything before. This will make it go smoother."

"How long will it take you?"

"We will be ready to test it later today. Finally, you will be able to reach everyone," said Qadir with a smile.

"That is great news," said Yamani. "What else can this do?"

"You will be able to command anything controlled by any satellite in orbit. That means virtually everything will be at your command once we are able to put this together. The only thing standing between you and all the power the world has to offer is time."

"Explain."

"You will have the power as soon as we are able to apply this and make our computer interface with theirs. There are so many applications it may take quite some time, but the wait will be worth it."

"Right now, concentrate on the communication end. We might have to wait for the other things," said Yamani.

"Yes, sir."

Yamani left the building. Keeping control was essential. With the news that Ahmed had delivered, he was unsure of how many he could trust. He knew beyond a doubt that there were those who were totally loyal to him and the Cause. The others were somewhat debatable. He couldn't allow anything to go wrong…not at this point. He had to protect both his wife and Miss Darmer from anyone who might try to usurp his authority. He knew beyond a shadow of a doubt they'd go after those two first. Another meeting with Ahmed was definitely in order. He was close to talking and Yamani knew exactly what it would take to make it happen.

Tom sat in front of the computer. He knew there had been an article about international bounty hunters that had appeared in one of the news publications. He remembered the station using it as a basis for a game. What he needed now was the information in the article.

He found the pictures on the website in the gallery, but nowhere was there any mention of the article. He knew it would have to be recorded somewhere.

He got up from the chair and walked into the kitchen. Michael, Nicole, Jacques, and Monique were sitting at the table eating.

"Michael, could I call the station?" asked Tom.

"Sure," said Michael. "Do you want to find out how you're feeling today?"

Tom looked at him and laughed.

"So you heard?"

"Oh, yah. Gina told me all about it."

Tom shook his head.

"I think I'm recovering slowly. I want to talk to someone to see if they can find an article we used about international bounty hunters."

"This has to be good," said Nicole sitting back in her chair ready to listen.

"Let me make the call first and then I'll tell you all about it."

"Can't wait," said Monique.

Within a few hours, Yamani was back at the command center and his experts were ready to try out Mr. Reinholdt's "gift." Emails had been sent to operatives in various countries around the world. It was important to Yamani to know whether he indeed was reaching everyone. Each was instructed to send emails as soon as they saw the broadcast.

Yamani sat in front of the camera for the second time and delivered the same speech he had delivered before. As he did the rest of his men took emails off the computer. Once the speech was finished and they were back at the table, they presented Yamani with the greatest news he had thus far. It was a complete victory. Every operative emailed they were watching his broadcast and they never believed anything other than the fact that he was the Chosen One.

Yamani was obviously pleased with the success of the experiment.
"I will be able to do this from anywhere, is that correct?" he asked.
"As long as we have a telephone line," said Qadir
"Then, this should work almost anywhere, except where we cannot get service.
"Exactly. Everything we need to duplicate what we just did is on this computer. As long as we have it, we are fine," said Qadir. "I will make copies of the disk so that if something happens to either the computer or the original disk, we can always recreate what we have done."
"Excellent, then we must not let this out of our sight."
"Yes, sir."
"Now, there are things I must do. If you would excuse me, I will be in my office."

Yamani sat down at his computer. Two emails had to be sent immediately. Within minutes he had sent one to Edgar and the other to Michael. When he finished, he sat back and smiled.

Mr. Reinholdt,

To say that I am pleased is an understatement. So far, SecReSAC is everything you claimed it to be. With all the preliminary work already accomplished, my experts were able to put the communications aspect into practice. You have kept Miss Darmer safe once again by your honesty. I am sure that she and Mr. Braedon will be forever grateful.

As Edgar read the email, he smiled. As he had planned in the modified file, every command Yamani gave to a satellite first had to go through his computer. From there, he gave the real command to the satellite to allow the communications to go forward. Unless all the commands were right, it would never reached his computer and therefore never reach the satellite. Instead an error message would appear seemingly generated from the satellite's main computer.

He knew with this success, Yamani would celebrate and contemplate his next move. Whatever it was, he'd be ready. It didn't matter where he was, he'd be able to answer and allow or disallow any and all command requests.

At last, he was in control. He was ahead of Yamani. He could keep Laura safe as well as his wife. He was certain of it from his end.

The broadcast was viewed by the group at the house in Paris. They knew once it was over, an email would be coming. They hoped it would be the one announcing the release of Laura.

Mr. Braedon

I trust you are well and you were able to watch my broadcast. You see, Mr. Reinholdt has kept his end of the bargain. I knew you would be able to convince him that it was in everyone's best interest. I sent him a note telling him how grateful you and Miss Darmer were that he had followed all of the instructions and delivered the real file. It will not be long now, Mr. Braedon, only a few more tests to make. You will hear from me soon. I will be seeing Miss Darmer. I will be sure to tell her we talked and everything is going well. She will be pleased.

"God only knows what he's going to tell her," said Michael. "I know he'll probably twist things somehow."

"That's what he does best isn't it?" asked Gwen.

"Oh yes it is," said Michael. "The only time he's straight forward is when it comes to something that's important to him."

"Even then, he uses coercion to get what he needs. Obviously, he still needs something else or he'd be releasing Laura," said Tom.

"He wants power," said Pierre. "He wants to be able to control those missiles and the missiles of any country. I can bet that's what he's waiting for."

"Is Edgar even giving him that power?" asked Jacques.

"I don't know. I'm not even going to ask, because I don't want to know," said Pierre.

Yamani walked out of the Ahmed's cell. Ahmed's screams were still ringing in his ears. He was certain that everyone within the confines of the camp heard and knew just how intolerant he was of traitors.

All in all, Yamani would call the proceeding successful. He had in his knowledge the list of those who were faithful. Throughout it all Ahmed continued to call them stupid and blind when he referred to them. It only confirmed what Yamani already knew. He had chosen well those who were to continue with him in this endeavor. They'd be the ones through which the Cause would continue.

Yamani walked down the hall to his office. He sat at his desk, leaned back, and took a deep breath. How fortunate it was for him to have found out about Ahmed and the others before it became critical. He knew he needed to start listening to his instincts. Reaching into the bottom desk drawer he removed a folder from under a pile of books. He set it on the desk and opened it. He looked down the list of names, the names of all those who called this camp home. He carefully went through and copied down all the names that Ahmed didn't tell him. Those were the ones he wanted to meet with, the ones he wanted answers from. Some of them he knew beyond a doubt were in league with Ahmed. Others he'd stake his life on were not. Those were the ones who'd listen most attentively to whoever had the biggest voice at the time. Those were worth saving. They'd be good followers.

He compiled three lists. One contained all those who were indeed faithful, no matter what. Those were the ones he'd make provisions for…those he'd keep safe. The second list contained the ones who could be easily swayed. Those he'd make certain were safe and knew that they were under his compassionate care. The others would be dealt with in time.

"Ahmed," Yamani said quietly looking at his name on the list, "you were once thought to be indispensable. Now you are nothing more than a problem to be disposed of. After today, I would hardly find you formidable."

Chapter Fifty-One

Yamani sent for Maranissa. The time was coming when he had to see to her safety. He kept going over everything in his mind. It was a war between what he believed, tradition, and common sense. It all came down to how much he loved her. He knew the answer to that. She was the woman who gave him perspective. She was the one who loved him unconditionally, no matter how much he hurt her. It was time for her to know how much he loved her.

When Maranissa entered the office, the guard closed the door. Yamani walked to her, took her in his arms and kissed her.

"I love you, Maranissa. I know sometimes I do not show it, but I love you."

"I know you do," she said. "I have never doubted it for a moment."

"Maranissa, it is only a matter of time before someone finds me. I must send you away now while we still have time."

"Where are you sending me?"

"Somewhere safe. I will join you in just a little while, as soon as I have finished here and Miss Darmer is safely back."

"You will be careful."

"I promise I will be careful. However, we must get you out of the country. We must disguise you. Miss Darmer has offered to help. I am going to allow her to do it."

"Whatever you say."

"But first, we need to spend this night alone, together. I want to memorize you."

Long before the first signs of daylight, Laura heard the keys in the lock. Both Yamani and Maranissa came in. Laura looked at the two of them.

"Miss Darmer, please pardon us for disturbing you," said Yamani closing the shutters on the windows in the room. As he closed the second one, Laura turned on the lamp. "I have decided to accept your offer to help Maranissa. It would please me greatly if you would prepare her for her journey. I think you will find all that you need in here." He placed a case on the table. "I will be back to check on you in a little while."

Once he left, Laura asked Maranissa to change into the new undergarments and the dressing robe.

"Are you going to cut my hair?" asked Maranissa.

"No, it's too beautiful to cut, we'll work with it."

Laura tried several different styles before she decided upon the right one. Then she took care of her eyebrows and gave her the best manicure she could with what she had. As her nails were drying, she put on make-up. After everything was done, Maranissa disappeared behind the screen and put on the clothes that Yamani had bought for her. When she came from behind the screen, Laura smiled at her.

"Wow, you are beautiful," said Laura.

"Really?"

"Really."

Yamani came in the door at the same time. He stopped when he saw Maranissa turn to him.

"Oh Maranissa, you are breathtaking. Miss Darmer, you have done magnificently."

"Thank you. It pleases you?" asked Laura.

"Yes, Miss Darmer, it pleases me."

He walked over to his wife and put his hands on her arms. "I do not want to send you anywhere," he said to her. "Maranissa, where you are going, you will dress like this. I have bought several other pieces for you to take with you. Then when you get there, you will be able to shop for other things."

"Miss Darmer, thank you," she said. "I will miss you."

"Maranissa, I'll never forget you."

"Miss Darmer, I must get her out of here now. There is a car waiting. Her plane leaves in a matter of hours."

"Someday, Maranissa, our paths may cross once again. I look forward to that day."

With his wife safely on her way, Yamani could once more turn his attention to the matter at hand. He drove out to the command center, parked and went inside.

"There have been people asking about you in the city," said Qadir as soon as he walked through the door.

"What are they asking?"

"They have a picture that was taken in the city when you came back from Frankfurt."

"What do they want?" asked Yamani.

"They're trying to find out information about you and anyone you are seen with. They want to know if anyone knows where you live. Someone said that one of them was hiring a guide to search the outskirts of town."

"Then it is true. The bounty hunters are here," said Yamani. "We need to move before they get here."

"I am afraid some of our own may try to sell you out for a share of the reward," said Qadir. "It would be quite a lot of money. More than they could ever have."

"I know you are right, Qadir. There are very few I can trust. What we discuss here goes no further. Is that clear?"

"Yes, sir," said Qadir. "I would never tell anyone anything."

"What else have you found in this folder that might be of immediate interest?"

"This," he said as he walked over to the computer. "Look. Let us say I want to take down a building on my property that is old and dilapidated. I can search the map and find the area. Then I can find the sector it is in and finally, the actual building. Using that, I can fire and hit that building exactly."

"Can you do that anywhere?" asked Yamani.

"Anywhere," said Qadir. "I have been trying different places ever since I discovered it."

"Has anything been blocked?"

"Nothing so far."

"How do you know you will hit it?"

"See, I isolate the building. Then I access the missile from the closest site to it. Now I type in projected trajectory. And there it is. It shows exactly where the missile will come from and where it will go. How is that!" said Qadir smiling.

"That makes it all worthwhile. No more guessing. No more trial and error, just accurate hits every time."

"Yes, sir."

"This makes it totally foolproof."

"Yes, sir. There is no mistake unless you isolate the wrong building."

"I do not intend to do that," said Yamani.

He looked around the building for a few minutes. Then he turned to Qadir once again.

"I want everything packed to be moved. I want you to be ready at a moment's notice to move to the location we discussed."

Today, Laura's thoughts were torn between her thoughts of Michael and thoughts of Maranissa. She truly hoped she had gotten away safely. In all the time Maranissa had taken care of her, she never realized how beautiful she was. Laura doubted that Yamani realized it either. It wasn't until he saw her that he was really spellbound. She smiled when she thought about it.

Laura was reading one of the books Maranissa had let her borrow when Yamani walked in. She put it down on the table so she could give him her undivided attention.

"Did Maranissa get away safely?" she asked quietly as soon as the door was closed.

"Yes, she is safe. I owe you a great deal of thanks."

"I know you can't tell me where she is, but I'd appreciate if you would thank her again when you see her. She took such good care of me and of Michael and I do so appreciate that."

"I will definitely tell her. Now, Miss Darmer, we are going to have to get you out of here. If you have any doubt you are loved and cared about, all you have to do is look at all that these people have done and gone through to bring you home."

"Yes, sir."

"When I was shopping for Maranissa, I bought something for you so no one who may have seen you before would recognize you because of your clothing. Mr. Richards will know where you will be. He will not have to guess whether or not it is you."

"When will we leave?"

"As soon as everything is in order. I need you to be ready for anything. We may have to leave quickly. I will do the best I can to make sure you are safe."

"Thank you, sir."

"I will miss you, Miss Darmer. I will be back. Do not go with anyone except for me or Sadik. Is that understood?"

"Yes, sir."

Laura watched him walk out the door. She looked around the room that had been her home for more than two months. She thought about what it looked like when Michael had been in it and what it looked like now. The difference was drastic. The more she thought about it, the more she realized it was Maranissa's touch more so than Yamani's that decorated the room. She opened the bag Yamani had given her. Inside she found a skirt, blouse, scarf, a pair of sandals and a large handbag. Her passport was already inside and the clothing she had worn to Baghdad had been washed, folded and put in the bag also. She knew she was really going home. She took the undergarments out of the bag and put them with the new clothing. She gathered the books he had given her and put them in the bag along with the notebooks and pens.

She disappeared behind the screen to dress. It felt so good to be in real clothes, to know that soon she'd be going home. All of the toiletries she had, she also put into the bag. She knew all she had to do was wait.

Chapter Fifty-Two

For days Tom kept vigil in front of the computer. He was afraid he'd miss Yamani's signal if he didn't. When he had to get up and leave the room, someone would always take his place. After listening to the latest reports and looking at the website, he knew that Yamani's world was closing in on him fast. He could only imagine what was going on. There was a ding from the computer.

Mr. Richards, Meet Me.

Tom stared at the screen.

"This is it," he yelled as he logged into the private chat room.

The others came running from various parts of the house.

"What's going on?" asked Mark.

"This is it. He asked me to meet him."

Mr. Richards are you there?

Yes, sir.

Mr. Richards, you are to take the first plane out of Paris in the morning. The same flight you and Miss Darmer took when you came the first time. Do you remember?

Yes, sir, I do.

We are going to use the same meeting place as before, the place where you found Mr. Braedon.

Yes, sir.

Mr. Richards there are people here who want to take me into their custody. If they should see me, we may have to change the meeting place. I am sending you several different places. You must be careful to make certain no one is following you. I will have my people watching, but I cannot guarantee this will be incident free.

I understand, sir. All we can do is our best. I have every faith we'll be able to avoid your opponents. I'll make certain I'm not followed.

I think there may be a leak in my camp who may have told these men I am here. I have not given anyone any details concerning Miss Darmer. We will be gone before they wake in the morning. I will keep her safely hidden until it is time to meet you. Once again, you are to be booked on the return flight.

Yes, sir.

It is important to get you out of the country. Then I will do what I have to do.

Yes, sir. I'll see you tomorrow.

If anything changes. I will let you know before you leave there.

Yes, sir.

There was no other conversation from Yamani. Tom opened the email and printed it. The directions were exactly the same as they were the first time. There were several other rendezvous points listed with directions from one to the other.

"Well, this is it. Tomorrow, she'll be home," he said. Then he looked at Michael. "I promise I'll bring her home safely."

"I know you will," said Michael.

"The way I figure it, I'll get back here with Laura while my show is on the air," said Tom. "I'd like to break the news of her return then, if that's alright with you."

"Tom, with all you've done for us, putting your life on hold, putting yourself in danger, it's the least we can do for you," said Michael.

"Now the only thing that could be better is having the scoop on Yamani, too."

"I need to call Edgar," said Mark. "I promised him I'd let him know when Laura was to be released. He needs to be on top of Yamani especially then."

The remainder of the evening was spent in cleaning up everything associated with the last several months. There were boxes of papers that were labeled, sealed and put away in storage. Robert took Laura's computer and transferred all of the pertinent files to external storage drives and DVDs. He took care of all of the other information that was collected and transferred all of it to external storage drives and DVDs also. One set was packed and put into storage and the other placed in the office where it was accessible.

All of the pictures that were taken of the house, the office, and the team during this time were being printed and placed in photo albums. The ladies created labels describing the activity that was going on. When they finished, there were still pages left…enough for homecoming pictures.

Michael walked into the room with a smile on his face.

"Everything ready?" asked Gwen.

"Everything except for Laura being here," he said.

Yamani opened the door to his office and looked down the hall. Sadik was positioned in front of Laura's room guarding her door. He motioned for Sadik to come.

"I need to have a special meeting with everyone on this list," said Yamani quietly.

"Yes, sir."

"Please get Gehran and Khali. I need them to do this for me."

"Yes, sir."

Yamani stood at the door while Sadik went to find the other two. Although Ahmed was no longer a threat, there were still others who might try to get to Laura.

Gehran and Khali came into the building with Sadik. Sadik took his position by the door once again while Yamani took the other two into his office. They sat in the seats in front of his desk.

"I need to have a meeting with all those who are on this list, Gehran," he said handing him the list. "I have a very special assignment for them and need to give them the information personally without any of the others around. The time for the meeting is on the paper. Please tell them they are to tell no one about it."

"Yes, sir."

"Khali, those who are on this list are to be told that they are not to come to camp today under any circumstances. I will have a special message for them much later in the day. Please impress upon them that they are to stay at home and wait for that message."

"Yes, sir."

"When you are finished, I will see you there."

Neither asked where there was. They knew. They were the ones who were greatly trusted.

Yamani watched them leave and then closed his eyes to pray.

Chapter Fifty-Three

It was still dark when the keys sounded in the lock. Laura woke and saw Yamani coming through the door.

"Miss Darmer," he whispered. "I am sorry to wake you, but I need to move you to a safer place."

"Yes sir," she whispered back. "I'm ready."

"Quickly, we must hurry before anyone wakes."

Laura grabbed her bag and walked quickly to Yamani. He took her by the hand and they walked out of the back door. He led her away from the camp quite a distance to where Sadik was waiting in the vehicle. He helped Laura in and climbed in himself. Then the car sped away. Yamani kept checking for anyone who might be following.

Qadir was already waiting at the alternate location. It had been prepared by Yamani and kept a secret from everyone for just such a purpose. Only the essential equipment was set up. Gehran had everything up and running.

"I am glad to see you were able to find it," said Yamani.

"Yes, sir. This is quite hidden," said Qadir.

"For good reason. I do not want those who would betray us to find us and then turn us over. Gehran did you deliver the message?"

"Yes, sir, they have assured me that they will all be there waiting for you."

"Good," said Yamani. "Now, is everything operational from here?"

"Yes, sir. I just ran through a check," said Gehran.

"We need to keep this running for just a little while longer. Once Miss Darmer has been delivered, then we will put the rest of the plan into action. Right now, make very certain that all can be accomplished."

"Yes sir,' said Qadir. "Did you get away undetected?"

"Yes, Qadir, quite undetected. They were all asleep as they should be."

"When is Miss Darmer's rendezvous?"

"The same time we had for Mr. Braedon."

He handed Qadir, Sadik, Gehran, and the others who were there envelopes.

"Inside you will find your orders and your destination, plus the means to get there. Each of you will be brought back to me at different times and by different routes. Do not let these out of your sight. You are all vital to the Cause and it is for your safety this is being done."

"Yes, sir. We understand."

"Where is Khali?" asked Yamani.

"He had a few more messages to deliver to those who lived further away."

"Very well. Can we give the satellite a delay command?"

"I have not tried that. I have however created a remote where you can store whatever commands you want and use it to access the satellite via your cell phone. Once you have decided exactly what you want to do, I will program the remote and all you will have to do is put in a code you decide on."

"Have you tried it?"

"Oh yes, sir, I have and I am pleased to say that it works perfectly," said Qadir smiling.

Laura sat where Yamani told her to and didn't say a word. She busied herself reading a book and trying to listen to the conversation. Although it sounded simplistic enough, Laura knew it was indeed complex. She wondered what it was that Yamani intended to do. Why were so few of his men with him now? She knew his intention was to run, to hide, and then to resurface again as another entity. She wondered just how long he would stay in seclusion this time. Would there ever be a time he wouldn't be a wanted man?

For Laura, it was strange to be in the company of a man she had used as her pet project growing up. Never did she dream she'd ever meet the man, let alone be his hostage. There was something that would be unresolved when this all ended. She knew who he was, had known from the beginning and had done a remarkable job of keeping that information a secret. He'd never know at least from her that she had known him and researched him from the beginning of his career and that's how she was able to use him to her own end. Only hours remained until she would be safely on her way home. She prayed all would go without incident.

The door of the building opened and one of Yamani's faithful came in visibly out of breath.

"Khali, what is it?" asked Yamani.

"I have just seen Marid. He was with one of the bounty hunters. They were talking about you. Marid told him for a price, he could take them to your camp."

"What did the other man say?"

"He wanted proof Marid knew you before he would agree to anything."

"What did Marid give to him as proof?"

"He handed him a photo of you at your desk in the camp."

"Was anyone else in the picture?"

"No, sir."

"Did he say anything about Miss Darmer?"

"No, sir."

"What did the man say to that?"

"He said he would pay Marid half of what he was asking to take him to the camp and the other half if there was proof there that you had been there. He also said that if Marid helped him to capture you and take you into custody, he'd give Marid ten percent of the reward money."

"What did Marid say?"

"He said yes."

"I see. Did they start out?"

"No sir, they are waiting until after daylight. The man insists he needs provisions to make the journey," said Khali.

"Good. By that time, we will be getting ready to meet Mr. Richards at the rendezvous point. If all goes well, we should be passing them on the way. There will be no way they will recognize us. Thanks to you, Miss Darmer, I have taken precautions so we might also be disguised."

"I don't quite understand," said Laura speaking for the first time.

"You will see."

Laura watched each of the men go into the next room and come out a little while later looking only slightly like themselves. They had shaven, trimmed their hair, and changed clothing. Looking at them now, one would assume they were influential business men and not members of a religious faction.

"I'm very impressed," said Laura. "I'd never know who you were if I hadn't seen you change. She paused and then looked at Yamani. "Sir, just one thing."

"Yes, Miss Darmer," he said.

"If you're going out of the country, your passports are going to show the old you and not the new one. Something like that could detain you until you were able to prove your identity with certainty."

"You see how invaluable she is?" They took out their passports and looked at the old pictures on them. "It is a problem, Ms. Darmer. One we need to solve immediately."

"Hand me your passports," said Gehran. "I will take care of this."

Gehran collected the passports and began taking the photo page out of them carefully. He placed them on the table. Then he took his bag and took out a camera. One by one he took the pictures, put them on the computer, edited them and printed them out. He placed the new picture overtop of the old one, scanned the page, printed it out making sure that both sides lined up and then cut them perfectly to fit. He then creased them and placed them back into the passports.

As Laura watched everything that was happening, she couldn't help but think that Gehran was their Robert. Give him anything and he could use that computer to work his magic.

"Gehran, now this is impressive," said Yamani smiling at the document before him.

"These look and feel real," said Sadik.

"They are," said Yamani looking around at each of them. "Remember that."

Gehran destroyed the other sheets as well as the paper that they were made from. He erased everything he needed to from the computer.

"Now it is all good," said Yamani. "Thank you, Miss Darmer."

"You're welcome."

Yamani looked at the time.

D. A. Walters
"Pack everything. It is time to go."

Chapter Fifty-Four

Tom Richards landed at Baghdad's airport according to plan. He went to the rental car agency and picked up the car. Then he took the prescribed route into the city. There was evidence of activity off in the distance as he looked across the open spaces. One never knew what to expect when coming into this city. He heard the bounty hunters had descended and according to his sources were on Yamani's trail. He didn't care what happened to the man after he turned Laura over to him. That would be for another story, one he hoped he could write the words "The End" to soon.

He kept his concentration on what was happening. There was no way to contact Yamani. All he had was a list of alternate points in case one wasn't good.

He was nearing the first rendezvous point. Swarms of people ran in the streets. Gun shots rang out and the noise of the crowd became a deafening roar. Smoke rose from a building off to his right. Tom knew there was no way he'd be able to get through them to make the first point. What were they shooting at? Why was all hell breaking loose? He turned the car around in a side alley and headed off the other way. He heard an explosion and behind him a cloud of smoke and dust and debris with people and body parts flew through the air. He stepped on the gas and made a left turn at the next street. By the time he came to the middle of the block, he was beginning to recognize shops.

"This was where I left Laura standing. It was on that street corner," he said aloud looking from side to side.

A black car drove quickly through the intersection. Right behind it gun shots riveted the street. Tom recognized the car. He knew it was Yamani's.

"Shit! The second point's not good either."

People were running in front of him, pushing through others and knocking them to the ground. Tom looked in his mirror, put the car in reverse, gunned it, and turned around in the street. How was he to get to the next stop?

"Think Tom think! It's not that hard! Ignore the gunshots and just drive!" he said loudly.

He turned down a small side street and came out over a curb on the other side. His car bounced and swerved just ahead of the black car. In front of him, men ran towards his car with guns drawn. There was nowhere to go.

"Fuck this!" he yelled trying to think of what to do next.

He stepped on the gas and gave it all it had and drove straight for the crowd. Several of them ran to the side while the others who were hit by the car rolled over the top and to the ground behind him. The black car followed very closely behind. Tom knew they had to clear this section.

"Where the hell is the last point!"

He couldn't remember, but the way he figured it, someone must have known every one, because they were waiting for them. He drove to the end of the street, past the mosque and made a left turn. He knew this would bring them to the American Embassy. If nothing else, he and Laura could find haven there. He pulled into the left lane and slowed a bit hoping the driver of the black car would understand.

Sadik was at the wheel of the black car trying desperately to dodge whatever was coming their way. Even in the midst of the confusion, Yamani recognized the car as it dropped from the curb and pulled right in front of them.

"Get close to him Sadik and follow him. That is our Mr. Richards. Stay down Miss Darmer. It seems someone in my ranks has sold us out."

The car rocked as people banged into it and Sadik kept driving. He followed Tom as closely as possible.

"Where is he going?" asked Sadik. "The next stop is not that way."

"Maybe he realizes that someone must have leaked the information," said Laura.

"I think you are right," said Yamani.

"What is he doing?" asked Sadik, as he watched Tom move the car to the left.

"Drive to the right of him," Yamani commanded. "The embassy is right in the next block. Stop outside it. Miss Darmer, you will very quickly change cars through the door to your left. Understand?"

"Yes," she said. "I've seen it done many times…in movies that is."

"This is not a movie," he warned. "Those are real bullets they are shooting."

The noise was growing behind them. Gun shots were once again ringing out. Tom stopped the car in front of the Embassy Gates. He leaned across the passenger seat and opened the door of the car as Laura opened hers. Laura stooped low as she exited the black car and quickly stepped into Tom's. Without waiting for her to close the door, Tom stepped on the gas and sped through the streets. The door bounced on its hinges several times before banging shut.

"Get down and stay down," Tom yelled. "No matter what happens, we're not stopping until we get to the airport."

"Are we on the right road?" she asked.

"One more turn," he said as the car made the turn on two wheels.

Yamani glanced back and saw the savage crowd gaining on them. From every side street more people and more cars entered the chase. He picked up the remote control beside him.

"Qadir, let us get rid of these people." With a minimum of time, Yamani sent a signal to the satellite.

"Step on it Sadik!" yelled Yamani. "Get us out of here!"

"Yes, sir."

Sadik stepped on the accelerator and the car took off. Yamani looked back behind him again. He could hear the unmistakable whistle and felt the ground shake on impact. The car shook, but Sadik held steady to the wheel.

"That should slow things a bit and buy us time," said Yamani looking at the shocked face of Qadir. "Keep driving. We are not safe yet. Make sure to make the turn I told you to make, Sadik."

"Yes, sir," said Sadik, his eyes riveted on the road ahead of him.

Yamani watched as the car carrying Laura and Tom sped on its way towards the airport. He marveled at how well things had gone to this point. No one could've ever expected he would rise again to such a power. Only Maranissa knew some of what he had done in the past and she still loved him. He knew he had to take care of things to make certain he'd be able to fulfill his dream as the Chosen One. Only those with him in the camp, those attached to Ahmed stood in his way. Whoever sold him out today had to have been with him when the exchange was made. He knew without doubt who it was. He made it his business long ago to know those who were close to him. He could size up a person in just a matter of minutes.

Ever since those days with the Ayatollah, he knew how valuable it was to know those who had turned to become your enemy. He also knew how vital it was to make certain they never found out you knew. Even with all he had been through, even though he had survived betrayal before, it still was hurtful to know that those whom he held so vital to the Cause would be the very ones to sell him to the bounty hunters.

Sadik made the turn right outside the city and set on the course that would take them out of the country over unmapped roads. When he had gone some distance so there was no way to be seen from the main road, Sadik stopped the car. Qadir got out of the car and went around the back. He reached behind the license plate and started to peel away the cover. He held it away from his face, lit it on fire and watched it burn until it almost reached his fingers. As the wind picked up, the charred fragments were carried away with it. Within minutes he got back in the car.

"Good," said Yamani, "Now when they try to find the car with those numbers, it will have vanished."

They were on their way once again and Sadik made another turn. Once he did, Yamani ordered him to stop. Sadik brought the car to a stop. Yamani looked off into the distance and then at his watch.

"Ah, the meeting I called is just about to start," said Yamani sarcastically. "Everyone should be there by now...including our bounty hunter and his guide."

He keyed in a code and waited. Then he watched as the smoke rose from what used to be his camp. Qadir and the others stared at him and Yamani looked directly at Qadir.

"Traitors must be dealt with, Qadir, or we will never be safe," said Yamani.

"Yes, sir."

"Now while the government i+s trying to explain away once again how they did not fire missiles, let us get out of here."

"What was that?" asked Laura as the first missile hit.

"That was Yamani taking care of business," said Tom looking back at the carnage that was behind them, "and buying us time to get away."

"What?" asked Laura.

"He can control the missiles now with great accuracy. He needs to get away, too, you know. Everyone's looking for him."

"I knew he had them and could control them, but not like that!"

Tom continued driving, not bothering to explain anything else and Laura really didn't need to know all the details at that moment. There would be plenty of time for that once they were back in Paris.

"Why does it seem to be taking so damn long to get to the airport?" asked Laura.

"Because we really want to get the hell out of here."

Although they were getting closer and the sounds of the mayhem were far behind them, Tom didn't slow down at all. The speed limit meant nothing. He knew the police and the military would be busy trying to restore order in a city totally out of control. He had a promise to keep and the sooner he could get Laura to safety the better.

It wouldn't be long now. He had to return the car and get her to the plane. Once they were in the air, it'd be alright.

"What the hell was that?" he asked as he looked into the distance following the sound of the second explosion.

"That's Yamani taking care of the traitors in his camp, or what used to be his camp," said Laura.

Tom looked over at Laura with a look of shock.

"How much longer?" she asked.

"Not much. Just relax. The action's back there. They're not looking for you. They don't know that the two of you are connected. Thank God."

Edgar Reinholdt had been up for the most part since he turned over SecReSAC. He dozed very sporadically over the last days. This was his idea to give them what they desired, but to monitor what they were trying to do. He had modified the program so he had the ultimate control not Yamani.

It was a struggle with his conscience to allow Yamani to detonate the last two missiles, but given the timetable, he knew something had to have happened that was endangering the exchange. The first one in the city was the most difficult to allow and now he sat and watched the reports of the casualties from it. The second was so far out of the city limits no one even cared what happened there. He could only surmise that Yamani had blown up his camp so as not to leave any trace of his existence.

Yamani words rang through his mind and he couldn't shake them. *"Many people will be going to bed at night feeling safe and secure only to have their world shaken before the sun comes up. You will see it Mr. Reinholdt and you will know you caused it."*

Although he knew that statement was Yamani's way of instilling guilt in his victim, it was true to an extent. He was allowing it, but he hoped the Lord would know he did so for very just reasons.

Gabrielle came into the room carrying a tray. She put it on the desk and looked at Edgar.

"Edgar, you must get some sleep. You're going to make yourself ill," she said touching his cheek.

"I promise, sweetheart, I'll get some sleep as soon as Laura is safely home," he said turning his head and kissing her hand.

"How close do you think she is now?"

Edgar looked at the clock on the desk. "Hopefully she's in the air. They're going to call as soon as she's safe."

"I brought you a little something to eat."

"Thank you."

She bent down and kissed him on the cheek.

"I miss you, Edgar. I know sometimes I'm consumed by my work, but I never forget you."

"I know, sweetheart. I never forget you either. When everything's back to normal, I'd like to take a few days and go away…just the two of us."

"Oh Edgar, I'd love that."

"I'll need enough time to press charges against those who are stealing from me and make sure the leaders are alright with what's happened. That shouldn't take more than a few days. In the meantime, decide where you'd like to go and we'll make reservations."

"I'll give the ladies things they can do on their own while I'm gone," she said and paused. Then she looked Edgar in the eyes. "I know where I want to go."

"Where's that?"

"To the island. To that wonderful beach. It's so quiet," she said as she reached to kiss him again. "Remember the last time?"

"How could I forget," he said as he pulled her down on his lap and kissed her.

"Oh, Edgar."

Chapter Fifty-Five

The ride from the airport was a quiet one. Neither of the occupants wanted anyone to know who they were and what had happened. Laura kept looking out the window at the scenery. She could feel all the emotions rising in her as she thought about all that happened since she left. She took a deep breath and tried to control herself one more time.

When the car came to a stop outside the house, Tom opened the door and helped Laura out. He took the bag from her; put his arm around her waist, and the two of them walked up the walkway to the front door. Tom reached to knock and the door opened. He let Laura go first. Pierre stood in front of her and hugged her.

"Welcome home."

"Thank you," she said her voice trembling.

She made her way from one to the other. There were so many things she wanted to say to them. All of that would have to wait. She had waited so long for this moment and now she stood there in front of Michael. There were tears in his eyes and hers. He opened his arms and she fell into them, clutching onto him tightly. Michael closed his arms around her. He kissed her hair and they stood there in each other's embrace.

There were smiles amid the tears of everyone in the house and they stood for a minute watching the two. One by one they made their way to the kitchen and sat at the table with Tom.

"How are you?" asked Gwen.

"Much better now," he said taking a drink from his cup, "much, much better. I didn't think we were going to get out of there. The bounty hunters had stirred the people into frenzy."

"They were showing some things on CNN about a bomb going off in a crowd."

"I couldn't get to the first rendezvous point. There were, I'd have to assume homemade bombs going off everywhere. Someone must have tipped the hunters off to the fact that Yamani was going to be there this morning. I turned around and went to the second point, but that was just as bad. At the third site, I finally got in front of him. I knew where the fourth site was, but by that time I realized someone had snitched. So I made a turn and headed for the Embassy. I hoped Yamani would follow. I pulled the car into the left lane when I got near the embassy gate and he pulled his car to the right. When we got right next to one another, we opened the doors and made the switch. I didn't even wait for her to close the door. I floored it and didn't stop until we got to the airport. It was a little after we made the switch that the first explosion happened. Then a while after that, the second."

"What happened to Yamani?" asked Pierre.

"At one point he was following me. I looked back when the first missile exploded and he was still there. Then he disappeared. I have no idea where he went."

"Then it's possible he got away," said Mark.

"Possible. I don't know where he'd go. It's not like he can freely walk around," said Tom.

"I wouldn't underestimate him. He could be anywhere," said Angelique. "Whatever mistakes he made in this project at first, he learned very quickly how to regroup. I'm sure he had a plan for his disappearance."

"Did anyone call Edgar to tell him she's safe?" asked Gina.

"I'll call him," said Mark picking up the phone. "I know he'll be grateful it's over…at least this part is."

Time seemed to be suspended as Laura and Michael stood in the foyer. Now there was safety where once both of their lives hung in peril and neither wanted to let that feeling go. It was quite some time before either of them spoke.

"How are you, baby?" Michael asked lifting her chin and looking in her eyes. He smoothed her hair back and kissed her.

"I'm alright," she said. "How are you?"

"A lot better now that you're here," he said breathing a sigh of relief.

"It's still hard for me to believe that I'm here…I really am here. The last few days were just so crazy and now being here…"

"It was like that for me when I walked in this house. I was so grateful to be here, but so unprepared," said Michael. "I honestly thought I'd be dead before I'd ever be back here and when I did walk through that door, it took a long time to get used to it."

"I'm feeling it," said Laura touching his face. "I can feel you and I know you're real, but I still feel like someone is going to wake me and I'm going to be right back in that room."

"Never," said Michael shaking his head, "never again."

She smiled up at him.

"Would you like to sit and talk," he asked. He couldn't believe how nervous he was. It was like being on a first date all over again.

"Not right now," she said and paused a moment. "I know this sounds crazy, but what I really want is to get a shower and get into some of my own clothes."

"Whose clothes are these?"

"Yamani bought them for me, just in case someone would find out what I had on when I got there. I want to get out of these and get rid of them. I'd like to burn them…watch them go up in flames."

"I certainly can understand that. Let's go, get you a nice shower and then we can talk, alright?"

Laura walked into the bedroom and stopped and looked around. The room was beautiful. Michael had transformed it. There were flowers and candles everywhere. He even had new curtains hung and a matching comforter.

"Oh, Michael, it's beautiful."

"I'm glad you like it," he said giving her a kiss. "I wanted it to be special."

"It is. It really is."

Michael reached down and kissed her again and then walked into the bathroom and started to run the water. Laura walked over to the bed and ran her hands over the comforter. He had done all this for her. There were tears in her eyes and they started running down her face. She wiped them away and walked over to the dresser. She bent down and smelled the flowers. It was a smell she had missed. Michael knew how much she loved flowers and how happy they made her. He always tried to have flowers throughout the house. She reached down, opened the drawers, and picked out something comfortable to wear.

For the first time since she left this room, Laura looked in the mirror. There looking back at her was someone she hardly recognized. She lifted her head, pulled down on the scarf, and looked at the trail that Ahmed had made. She wondered if Michael knew about it or if Yamani had kept it to himself.

"Laura," she said quietly to her reflection, "you look terrible. You definitely need some rest. No, you need a lot of rest and a complete makeover."

Being in this room made her realize how little sleep she actually did get when she was prisoner. She felt so tired and she knew it'd take time for her energy level to return.

"Patience, Laura, you need to have patience."

She looked around the dresser for her ring and locket, but they were gone. She hoped Michael would find it in his heart to give them back. She knew she couldn't ask.

Michael walked back into the room and stood by the nightstand.

"Your shower's ready," he said.

"Thank you," she said looking at him.

"I'll be right here, if you need anything."

Laura nodded and walked into the bathroom. She shut the door but didn't close it all the way. She had enough locked doors to last a lifetime. She got into the shower and felt the warm water wash over her. It was so soothing, just the way she dreamed it would be all those times after she had done Yamani's bidding. She shuddered at the thought.

His words, his voice rang over and over again through her mind. Those seeds of doubt he planted that Michael would never want her again. She could feel it all…all the confusion, all the fear. The more water that washed over her the harder she cried. Soon she was sobbing and scrubbing her skin harder and harder.

This was not the way she envisioned her homecoming. She had dreamed about Michael taking her in his arms, taking her to their room, and making love with her. He was her knight on a white horse who came to rescue her…but now she knew Yamani still stood in the way. Even though he wasn't there, he was so very present. She wanted…she needed to get rid of him forever.

"I just want to wash you off me," she sobbed over and over again. "I want you out of my life for good!"

Michael reached in his pocket and pulled out the ring and the locket. He wanted so very much to put them where they belonged. He wanted so desperately to tell her that none of this mattered…that whatever Yamani made her do could never change his love for her.

The sound of Laura's sobs called him back to the present. Michael put the ring and locket in his top drawer and walked into the bathroom. He knew what was happening, he had been there. His mind went to the day he came back to the house and how he just wanted to make himself clean again; to wash every trace of Yamani away. He took his clothes off, stepped into the shower, took her into his arms and held her as she sobbed against him.

"I want to wash him away. I can't get the feeling of him off of me."

"Oh baby," he said. "Even with all the water in the world, we can't wash him away. It's going to take time, but the memories will fade. We have to be patient and be there for each other. The more we talk about it, the easier it'll become to put this behind us."

"Michael I can't do that," she said shaking her head. "I just can't talk about it. Not right now."

"I understand. I'll be here whenever you're ready," he said looking into her eyes. "I'll listen whenever you want to talk. We'll do this together. You're not alone. I'm with you and I love you, Laura. I love you." He kissed her hair gently and held her quietly.

He closed his eyes so thankful she was back with him again. He wanted nothing more than to take away the hurt she felt, but he knew it was something that would be there for a long time.

Even though it was warm in the shower, Laura began shivering. Michael turned off the water, reached past the curtain and grabbed a towel. He wrapped it around her and helped her out.

for Love and Ransom

She looked at Michael when she finished drying off and fastened the towel around her. He looked at the red trail that started at her neck and continued downward. His heart ached. What had Yamani done…or was it someone else. He wanted to know, but didn't want to upset her any more.

"I don't know why, I can't seem to stop crying."

"It's something you need to do. Think about all the times you felt like crying when you were there…did you cry then?" he asked as he fastened a towel around his waist.

"No, I couldn't."

"Why not?"

"I'd never show them any weakness," she said with clenched teeth. "I'd never give them that satisfaction."

"What about now?"

"I just want someone to take care of me," she said, her voice softening. "I'm so tired of being strong."

"Oh baby, you don't have to be strong anymore," he said as he wiped her tears. "I'll take care of you. I promise."

He put his arm around her and held her tightly as they walked into the bedroom. Together they stood by the bed. He took her face gently in his hands, looked into her eyes and kissed her. He knew what he needed and it was Laura, totally and completely. He had waited a long time for this and it seemed like an eternity. Her arms went around him and she could feel the desire for him burning inside her. Her hand moved to touch his cheek and he turned his head to kiss her hand when he felt it.

"Michael," she whispered, "Oh God, Michael. I want you…I need you."

He kissed her harder and more passionately. He held her so closely she gasped. Her hands followed his body down his sides. He pulled away slightly and looked at her face, drinking in her beauty. He loosened her towel letting it fall off her. He lovingly kissed her neck and then took her hands in his and brought them up to his lips.

"I love you, so much."

He picked her up and laid her on the bed. She smiled and looked into his eyes. Everything was right, she knew it.

For a time, no one existed for each of them except the other. The closeness each had missed, the softness of the touch and the undying love they felt were the first steps in the healing they would need.

Tom's detailed description of what had happened during his time in Baghdad was only made more real when they watched the reports on television. It was amazing to everyone that there was someone there recording everything.

They actually were able to watch as Yamani's car was shot at and the bombs went off in various parts of the crowd.

"That's my car!" Tom exclaimed as he watched the car drop from the curb and get in front of Yamani.

"Oh my God!" said Angelique. "They were really shooting at you!"

Tom watched as he gunned the car and headed for the group coming at him. He cowered a little and shook his head as he watched the people roll over his car and fall to the street behind him.

"There wasn't anything else I could do," he said apologetically.

"How did you even drive through that?" asked George. "Is that Yamani behind you?"

"Yah, he must have told his driver to get close, because all of a sudden he was right on my ass."

They watched as Tom made the left turn, the black car followed and then both disappeared. There were several seconds before the cameraman had them back in view. It was obvious he had to run to get to the corner to get more footage. Several blocks ahead, they could see the two cars side by side with the doors open and Laura go from one to the other. Then they watched as Tom's car took off with the door bouncing and Yamani close behind.

Everyone was on the edge of their seats and then without further warning the whole area exploded and the cameraman turned his attention on the carnage and destruction brought on by the explosion.

Tom was white and frozen in his place.

"Tom, are you alright?" asked Paul.

"Yah, you know it's one thing to live through it," said Tom, "and quite another to see just how bad it really was."

"We should have recorded that," said Gina.

for Love and Ransom

"Way ahead of you," said Robert.

"I love you, Laura," he said as he kissed her. "I always have and always will."
"I love you, too."
Michael kissed her again.
"Are you alright?" he asked.
"Oh, yes. Are you?"
"I am now," he said. "You're just what I needed."
He kissed her, got out of bed, and helped her up. Laura walked to the dresser and took the clothes she picked out and got dressed. Once Michael was dressed, he looked at Laura and there were tears on her face again.

Michael put his hands on her face and wiped the tears away. He kissed her gently.
"I love you," he said quietly. "I always will."
"I love you, too."
"Sweetheart, there's something I have to do before we say or do another thing." He reached in his pocket and took Laura's left hand in his. He slipped the engagement ring onto her finger. "Now, it's where it belongs."
"Oh, Michael," she cried watching the diamond glisten in the light.
"And now this." He took the locket and put it around her neck. "I mean every word that is on this locket. I will love you forever."
"I love you, Michael. I love you," she said quietly. "I feel so needy. I just want your arms around me. I want you to hold me and never let go."

Michael held her tightly and she rested her head against him. She was finally home. She could feel his heart beating and his arms around her holding her. She knew he loved her and she could finally feel herself relaxing.

Michael could feel the difference in her body minute after minute. He could feel the sense of calm with her against him. He closed his eyes and thanked God she was finally here with him. He promised to have patience and to love her no matter what she told him. He also promised not to press her for answers to the questions he was dying to ask. She pulled away slightly and looked at him.

"A penny for your thoughts," she said.

"There's so much I want to say…want to do," he said stroking her cheek, "but there are people in this house who need to talk to you, if you feel like it, that is."

"I need to talk to them and thank them for doing everything. Without them, I wouldn't be here. I know that."

"We both have much to be thankful for and they've been so very faithful. I'll agree to share you with them for a little while, but then I want to spend time together, just the two of us." He smoothed her hair gently and looked in her eyes.

"I'd really like that."

"There's no way I'll ever let you go. I love you so much and I can't wait to show you just how much."

"You already have."

Chapter Fifty-Six

When Michael and Laura walked into the kitchen, everyone stopped talking. They walked over to take their usual place at the table. There were smiles on the faces of all those present.

"I apologize that it took so long to join you, but I needed a shower and I sort of had a little meltdown." Laura said reaching to take Michael's hand. "I first want to thank you for everything you did to bring me home. I know that without you and all you did, I wouldn't be sitting here. I thought of you often and I'm so sorry I didn't tell you what I was doing, but I felt you would've stopped me."

"You're damn right!" said Pierre. "We would've done everything in our power to keep you housebound."

"I know," said Laura smiling at him. "That's why I just couldn't tell you. It was one of the hardest things I ever did. Making the decision to do whatever I had to do to save Michael was easy. Keeping it from you was the difficult part."

"You gave us so many clues," said Gwen, "but we just didn't get it until you were gone."

"For that, I'm really thankful," said Laura smiling. She looked at Robert. "Have you gone to the bank?"

Robert's face was beet red. "You have no idea how many times I heard your voice and my own stupidity. Would it help to say I'm sorry?"

"Already forgiven. You had no way of knowing."

"It all became clear when Tom walked in the door with Michael," said Robert shaking his head.

"What are you talking about?" asked Gina. "I've been here the whole time I must have missed something."

"After I told Tom the leader's identity, he was able to get a lot more information. When I needed to have it sent, Robert wanted to know what it was and how I got it. I told him a friend did it as a favor and that I'd never jeopardize anything concerning Michael and he should know that."

"I told her that I was just making sure," said Robert, "and then she leaned over the table and got really close to my face and I'll never, ever, as long as I live forget what she said. 'You know what? No matter what it takes I will get Michael back. You can take that to the bank.' Then she turned on her heels and walked out."

Gina smiled at Laura. "Guess you told him."

"I know you have questions for me. Please bear with me. There are some things I just can't talk about yet. There are things I can't even think about without getting emotional," said Laura her eyes welling up.

Gina got up, walked to the counter, and picked up the box of tissues. She placed it on the table in front of Laura.

"Thank you," said Laura taking a tissue and dabbing her eyes.

"Honey, we understand. You take your time. No one's going to pressure you into doing anything you're not ready to do. What we want you to know is we're here for you…all of us," said Angelique gesturing around the table. "We're good listeners."

"I know you are," said Laura brushing away a tear.

"Tom," said Michael, "how did the announcement on your show go?"

"I didn't want to do it unless both you and Laura agreed," said Tom.

"I don't have a problem with it," Laura said. "You've been so instrumental in all of this. Without you, I wouldn't have been able to have gained Michael's release or my own. The only thing I ask is that I don't have to say anything. I just can't right now."

"I wouldn't ask that of you. Perhaps when you're ready to tell your story, you'll let me be part of it, along with Hal. After all he did on the series, I think he'll love to seeing how it's all linked together."

"I think you should ask him," said Michael, "but let's take care of your announcement first."

for Love and Ransom

It was business as usual at WXDX in Pittsburgh. Everyone was wrapped up in the new contest and the DJs were enjoying all of the interaction with the listeners. Although other stations were running promotions, none were as successful as the take-off of 'Where's Waldo.' No one was more excited than Jim Prescott, who saw his market share rise steadily.

He was all too glad to take Tom's call and was excited to have the opportunity to break the story on the morning show. He put Tom on hold and walked into the studio where Doug was.

"Doug, Tom's on the phone. He's brought her back and wants to break the news on the show."

"Awesome. How about right after this song?"

"Do one more, but between, tell the listeners there's going to be a world exclusive breaking news story right after it that they won't want to miss."

"Got it."

Doug set the stage for the announcement and then got on the phone with Tom to go over a few questions he wanted to ask. As soon as the song finished, Doug gave the lead in and then began his interview.

"Tom, how're things in Paris?" asked Doug.

"Much better now. I called because I wanted our listeners to be the first to know I've received the hostage this morning in Baghdad and returned her safely back to Paris. If you remember several months ago, Michael Braedon was taken hostage by a fanatic religious group and I was chosen to accept him when he was released. I made the announcement about his release from a television station in Baghdad. What was never broadcast were the terms of his release."

"Just what were those terms, Tom?" asked Doug.

"His freedom was actually gained by his fiancée, Laura Darmer. She offered herself as a surrogate hostage in place of Mr. Braedon. The terms were accepted and Ms. Darmer became the hostage and Mr. Braedon a free man."

"How did it happen that Ms. Darmer was released?"

"Quickly speaking, Mr. Braedon, his family, their partners, and friends worked non-stop using every resource at their disposal and some very creative avenues to gain Ms. Darmer's release."

"Where do you come into all of this?"

"I was approached by Ms. Darmer when she was thinking about making the exchange. I was the one the captors agreed upon as an intermediary."

"How did you feel about turning her over?"

"That was so very hard for me to do, but they threatened that if it wasn't done, all of us would be killed. There was no real choice."

"When did you know she was going to be released?"

"Last evening I received all the details and she was released this morning."

"When will we be able to speak with Ms. Darmer and Mr. Braedon?"

"Ms. Darmer and Mr. Braedon have asked for a little patience. They've promised me an exclusive interview and I'll be bringing that to you in the next few days, as soon as Ms. Darmer is able to rest a little."

"Well, Tom, we look forward to hearing from you again. Please give Mr. Braedon and Ms. Darmer our best."

"I'll do that."

Tom pressed the end-call button and sat smiling at the group.

"Now," said Pierre, "what about the interview with Hal?"

"I'd like to set that up for as soon as possible. I think it's important to get the real story out instead of the story the media will conjure."

"Do you think Hal will have any problem with coming here for the interview?" asked Mark.

"Let's find out," Tom said while he placed the call to Hal. "Hal, this is Tom Richards, pick up the phone."

"Hey Tom, what's happening?"

"Listen, I just brought Laura Darmer back to Paris from Baghdad. She was the one who traded herself for Michael Braedon. Interested in the story?"

"Hell, yah. You know I'm interested. When?"

"Depends upon when you can get here."

"Where's here?"

"Paris."

"Consider me there. I'll call you later with my arrival details."

"Hey Hal, this is so big, your boss is going to be thanking you for weeks. The sooner the better buddy."

Breakfast, real breakfast was something that Laura hadn't had since she left. Everything smelled wonderful and every time she tried to get up to help, she was politely told 'thanks, but no thanks.' She ate a little so she wouldn't hurt anyone's feelings, but with as emotional as she was, her stomach wouldn't allow much. As they were eating, the phone rang and Mark picked it up.

"Hello."

"Tom?"

"Just a minute. Tom, it's for you."

"Hey Tom, I'm on my way. It pays to have connections and a boss who wants this for this week's edition."

"Call as soon as you touch down. We'll send a driver to get you."

"He's on his way," said Tom handing the phone back to Mark. "He said it pays to have connections and a boss who wants it for this week's edition."

"That's cutting it really close isn't it?" said Brigit. "That doesn't give him much time at all."

"Yah, but I've seen Hal under pressure," said Tom, "and believe me that's when he's at his best."

"I believe you," said Michael. "Look what he did with that Yamani and Bin Laden piece."

"I feel like I'm out of the loop," said Laura. "What piece are you talking about?"

"You have to see it," said Jean getting up. "I'll get it for you."

Laura looked through the pages of the magazine and read every article. It amazed her that they were able to do this in such a short time. No wonder there was such activity when Yamani returned. This explained everything.

"Whose idea was this?" she asked.

"Mark's," said Angelique.

"To be fair, I got the idea from the entry in your journal," he said. "The one where Tom told his friend he needed the information for a documentary."

"Michael came up with the idea of computer aging the photos," said Angelique.

"This is amazing," said Laura.

While they were telling Laura all about the process, the phone rang again and Mark answered.

"Hello."

"Mark, this is Edgar."

"Hey, Edgar, are you relaxing, yet?"

"I'm starting to do so now. I just finished taking away everything I've given Yamani. I called my attorneys and told them information had been stolen and I had the names of the perpetrators as well as the evidence to convict them. I also called the leaders and told them the situation had been resolved."

"Did you tell them who it was?"

"I told them I'd give them that information after the men in my facilities had been arrested."

"That's a good move. Right now we're waiting for Hal to get here to do an interview. We promised Tom and him they'd have exclusive rights. I'd like for this to hit the newsstands before anyone else finds out. I don't want them scooped."

"Not a problem. By the time the paperwork is completed and the men are arrested, the issue should be out."

"How's Gabrielle?"

"She's so glad this is over and Laura's home. This hasn't been easy for her. I promised her we'd get away, just the two of us. As soon as I meet with the attorneys, I intend to make those reservations."

"That's a wonderful idea. We may just have to do something like that, especially after this story hits."

"I think I'd like to tell the leaders that day."

"That shouldn't be a problem. We can get the exact date and time for that matter from Hal."

Michael motioned to Mark that he wanted to talk to Edgar.

"Hey, hold on a minute, Michael wants to talk to you."

"Edgar, I can't begin to find the words to thank you for everything you've done. I owe you my life and Laura's."

"Michael, I'm just so glad the two of you are free and home."

"I'd like to invite you and Gabrielle to come back to Paris. This time we could really relax and enjoy ourselves."

"I'd like that and I know Gabrielle would, too. I'll call you as soon as we get back from our trip."

"Talk to you soon."

Even though everything was over except for tying up the loose ends, the security officers were still present at the Reinholdt residence. Edgar looked out the window and saw an officer walking the perimeter. He had made the decision. The cost of the security was small compared to the price of peace of mind.

He walked into the living room. Gabrielle was sitting on the love seat making some notes. Edgar sat down beside her.

"How's everything going?" asked Edgar.

"It's going well," said Gabrielle putting the notebook on the lamp table beside her. "I'm getting everything ready for the committee so they'll have something to do while we're gone." She looked at Edgar. "We are still going aren't we?

"Of course, sweetheart. I've already taken care of some things and it should only take another couple days."

"Did you make the reservations?"

"I just have to wait for the police to get the warrants issued for the arrests of the men at my facility. Then I'll make them."

"Edgar," said Gabrielle with a serious tone, "I need to do some shopping. I just can't wear those same old things again."

Edgar looked at her and smiled. "Shopping it is. I think I need a few things, too."

"Oh, Edgar, this is going to be fun. Let me get changed."

"Gabrielle, Michael wants us to come to Paris sometime after we get back from our trip. Do you think you'll be up for it?"

"Yes, yes! Now I really have to shop. I certainly can't go to Paris in the same old things."

D. A. Walters

Edgar smiled and shook his head as he watched his wife hurry out of the room. It was so good to see the smile on her face again.

Chapter Fifty-Seven

There was calmness in the house as everyone sat and relaxed for the first time in months. It had been agreed that any work could wait until another day. For them it was a holiday. This was cause for celebration. Nothing was as pressing as spending time together with family and friends. Pierre had called the offices telling the secretaries to reschedule all appointments and give all employees the rest of the week off.

Flashes of Maranissa and Yamani raced through Laura's mind. None of the memories were in any semblance of order, just bits and pieces. Voices and faces and then Ahmed, she could see him, see the knife, feel the pain. She shuddered.

"You alright?" asked Michael.

Laura looked at him with a forced smile and wiped a tear from her cheek. Michael pulled her closer. She rested her head against his shoulder and he kissed her hair. The tears just seemed to come from nowhere and she couldn't stop them.

It was hard for the others to imagine what was going on in Laura's mind. All they could do was try to put themselves in her position, but no one really knew the hell she was living. Freedom was such a wonderful, vital gift and to give up that freedom would be devastating. Getting it back could be overwhelming.

"Maybe some soup," Raquel said finally breaking the silence. "That's nice and light…not to mention quick and easy."

"And some breadsticks?" asked Henri.

"Sure, I can use your help in the kitchen, Henri," said Raquel. "You take care of the breadsticks and I'll start the soup."

"Maybe just a tiny dessert, too."

He followed her into the kitchen and in less than an hour they were sitting down eating.

Hal was true to his word. Connections were an understatement. What everyone thought was nothing more than being able to somehow get on a commercial flight without jumping through all the hoops turned out to be a private jet placed solely at Hal's disposal. Not only was it for his convenience, but a reminder of the time constraints of getting the article ready for the next issue.

Hal and his photographer, Don settled in and began the interview. He was a master at interviewing and it showed in the questions he asked. It was evident he had put the flight time to good use. Even though he was obviously leading the interview into a particular direction, nothing prepared him for Laura's answer to the next question.

"You've explained how you came to the conclusion that you were dealing with an entirely different group of kidnappers, but did you know who they were and if so how?"

"When I saw his picture, I recognized him as someone I had read quite a lot about growing up. My father liked to talk about current events and I knew I couldn't keep up with everything, so I chose one man who, at the time, was very influential. Little did I know that he and Michael's captor would be one and the same. I was almost one hundred percent sure it was him, but I wanted to know for certain. Robert emailed the captor's picture to some of those who were very knowledgeable about terrorists. I got the answer I was looking for. It was the confirmation I needed."

"And who was this person?"

"His name is Afmad Yamani."

Hal stopped the recorder and looked stunned at Laura and then at Tom.

"I told you your editor was going to be thanking you for weeks," said Tom smiling.

"Did you know this when you suggested the 'Where are they now?' series?" asked Hal.

"Yes, but I didn't dare ask you to do the story on him first, because we couldn't risk the questions. When the decision was made, we were ecstatic."

Hal started the recorder again.

"Why did you pick him?"

"I liked the sound of his name and there was something in the news about him almost every evening. My father would ask questions about him…what I thought…If I were him, what I'd do next…and other sorts of questions."

"When did you realize it was him?"

"When I saw him and heard his voice as he interrogated Michael the first time. Then when I saw the pictures of the Chosen One that Professor Laban sent me, I was certain."

"Do you still have any of that information?" asked Hal turning off the recorder again.

"We packed it and put it in the garage," said Pierre

"Is there any way I could see it?"

"Sure," said Gwen. "We cleaned up because we wanted everything put away when Laura came home."

"We also took a lot of pictures all throughout and kept a running log of what we did," said Angelique.

"Could you set it up the way it was?" asked Hal.

"Anything you want," said Mark.

It was back and forth to and from the garage multiple times getting all of the boxes. Everyone worked to set up the scene the same as it was. When everything was out, Hal and Don started to look through it. Robert took the pictures of Yamani from the time Laura first came to be interested in him to the present and laid them out in date order and the man aged before their eyes.

"This is absolutely amazing," Hal said as he arranged some of the old clippings for shots.   Don, get shots of all of this."

Don took pictures of everything. He and Hal looked through the album that chronicled the events. They chose specific pictures and asked for copies. Robert marked them all and then set to work finding them and burning them to a disc.

All the while they were looking at everything, Hal continued the interview. Towards the end, he once again addressed Laura.

"Did you ever tell your captor you knew who he was?"

"No, I felt he valued his anonymity. All through this he had no idea. I was afraid if he found out I knew, he'd become violent."

"Was there any change in him once the story was released?"

"I knew something had happened. I wasn't sure what. Prior to that, he gave no indication that I'd be released any time soon. When he came back from being away, he began talking about releasing me. I assume now it coincided with the release of the article. He only told me there were people who wanted to see him dead and I needed to be ready to go any time."

"Was he the one who turned you over?" asked Hal.

"Yes," said Laura.

"Tom, was he the one who contacted you?"

"Yes, he was," said Tom.

"When did he do that?"

"It was the day the story hit. He told me to get to Paris and wait for further instructions. I left on the next flight."

"What do you think made him move so quickly to release her?"

"We had received word that the bounty hunters were in Baghdad acting on a tip that Yamani had been spotted there. He knew he couldn't move about freely with a hostage, so he needed to get rid of her," said Tom.

"What was it like when you got there?"

Tom gave Hal a graphic description of the release of Laura in Baghdad.

"Do you think Yamani got away?"

"I have no idea. He was following our car until we got outside the city. Then he was gone. After that, there was an explosion off in the distance beyond the city. Whether he got away or not, I can't say."

"You know, this is a great story," said Hal. "I'd like to call my editor. I only wish I could be there to see his face."

Hal looked at his watch and figured out what time it was back in the States. He knew it was late, but he also knew Bill Epson, his editor, would be working overtime. Since this new series started, it wasn't very often that he couldn't be found in his office.

"Mr. Epson's office," said a sweet voice when the phone answered.

"Hi, there, Loretta, this is Hal. Is Bill in?

"Yes, he's been waiting for your call. Hang on a sec and I'll put you through."

"Hal, so what do you have for me?" asked Bill without so much as a hello.

"Just this, the name of Michael Braedon and Laura Darmer's captor."

"Is it good?"

"Oh yah. Real good."

"Who the hell is it? Don't keep me in suspense."

"Afmad Yamani."

"What!" Bill screamed. It was so loud that Hal had to move the phone away from his ear.

"You heard me. Their captor was Afmad Yamani. Listen, we have pictures, memorabilia, you name it."

"Loretta!" he yelled.

"Yes, Bill," she said walking quickly into the office.

"Get me Karl, Sid, and Sally, now. I don't care where they are. I want them in my office immediately. This is big...really big."

"Yes, Bill."

"Hal, this is what we're gonna do. The 'Where Are They Now?' issue will stay the same. That's already well underway. We can put that to bed by morning. This we'll make a special edition. We need corresponding articles."

"I can think of a few just off the top of my head."

"Good! I'll give you a call when those three get here. Talk to you then."

Hal hung up the phone and turned to the others. "Well, now," said Hal. "Ecstatic is not the word to ever describe my editor, but it certainly fits this time."

"I told you," said Tom. "I knew he'd love it."

"So, is he going to give you space in this issue?" asked Brigit.

"No," said Hal. "He's giving this its own special edition."

"What!" exclaimed Pierre.

"Yah. Can you believe it? He wants corresponding articles."

"Well, there's certainly enough information here to do a few," said Gwen. "Not to mention Tom's side of the story."

"I have one," said Robert. "What about Edgar. You could interview him about the new face of terrorism."

"That's good," said Henri, "and would reach a whole other group of people."

"Whoa," said Hal, "One at a time. I have to get these things down."

for Love and Ransom

Epilogue

It was amazing what nearly a week of normalcy could do for anyone. Even with all the events of the past months, there was a calm that had not been present for so long. Rest, good food, and tender loving care were the prescription that made all the difference.

When the courier brought the package from the office, Michael immediately called everyone. They were anxious to see how this issue turned out. With each issue of the special series, there was increased interest and increased circulation and they knew that this special edition would be no different. They knew they had to brace themselves for the deluge of well-wishes and sentiments that would follow as well as the requests for interviews and appearances.

Once everyone arrived at the house, Michael opened the package. He took out the copies and handed them out. He sat back on the couch with Laura. Page after page they relived the drama only they could fully understand.

"This is unbelievable," said Michael breaking the silence.

"The pictures are great," said Robert. "Look at the detail. You can read some of the articles."

"I can't wait for the reactions from their readers," said Gwen.

"Hell, I can't wait for the reaction from the government," said Mark.

"That should be good," said Jean.

"Well, this time tomorrow, the governing bodies of all those countries will know exactly what was at stake," said Pierre. "Then we'll probably really see a barrage of negative publicity concerning how the leaders handled it."

"Then someone may just have to set the record straight," said Laura. "Anyone hungry?"

"Starved," said Henri.

"Good, dinner's ready and all it needs is to be served," said Laura.

Robert walked over to the dining room table. "I'm going to put this computer away so we can have dinner on this table for a change," he said.

"What a novel idea," said Brigit.

"Before you do," said Michael, "I want to send an email to Hal and Tom."

He sat down in front of the computer and went into his email. There was the familiar new mail alert. Michael clicked it.

"Oh God," he said.

The rest of them looked at the screen.

Mr. Braedon,
Meet me.